Bet Your Rocks Off

Bet Your
Rocks Off

PETER BURDEN

First published 2005 by Hoof Print
Hereford HR1 3NP

Copyright © Peter Burden 2006

Hoof Print is an imprint of Hay Press Ltd

A CIP catalogue record for this book is available from
the British Library.

ISBN 0-9550050-3-5 / 978-0-9550050-3-9

Cover Design & Typeset by Tim Watkins, Hereford

Printed in Great Britain by Antony Rowe Ltd., Chippenham, Wiltshire

The core plot for *Bet Your Rocks Off* was brought to the author by a friend who wishes to remain anonymous but to whom the author is none the less deeply grateful.

CHAPTER ONE

I'd always thought five in the morning a fucking awful time for any plane to arrive; bad if you were on it; worse if you were meeting it.

But this was a very special flight – a 707 chartered from Orlando, Florida and modified to transport racehorses, or any other livestock considered valuable enough to airfreight across the world. It was carrying twenty-eight top quality thoroughbreds belonging to the Sheikha Madame Jeanne al Hassan and her son, Abdel.

Some were being brought to England to race; the others – eleven yearlings and three four year olds – would be travelling on by lorry to Madame al Hassan's stud in France. The yearlings were going simply to give their owner some young-stock to look at in the broad, beautiful pastures around her house. The older horses we had identified as suspected ring-worm cases; before coming back to England, they were going to a quarantine yard we had specially created from an isolated set of buildings on the Normandy estate.

But the plain truth was that twenty seven of the horses on the plane weren't important; they were mere window dressing, walk-on parts in the drama I was staging. One was the star - a colt that meant more to me than any other horse I'd ever seen, backed, ridden, trained or owned; Private Mountain was a young horse of commanding presence, flawless conformation, and an identical blood-line to Private State, winner of a great *Prix de l'Arc de Triomphe* ten years before.

What was more, and what really mattered, was that this special colt was the safest bet to win an English Derby since Levi Goodman won it in 1844 with a four year old called 'Running Rein'.

Even safer than that.

It was a matter of historical record that the unfortunate Mr Goodman had his collar felt before he ever saw any winnings or prize money. But we were staging our coup rather more skilfully than he. If we won, we would keep the prize money; we would collect - by the sackfull - from the bookies; and we would still have a stallion worth around ten million pounds.

What we were planning was, simply and without hyperbole, the coup of all racing coups.

It would be utterly undetectable after the event, and only four people in the world would ever know that it had happened: Annie Tenbury, who trained the colt; Abdel al Hassan, who had paid for it; ex-Corporal of Horse Harding - my tried and trusted gofer – and me.
I'd come to meet the plane and its cargo at this ghastly hour despite the loss of a good night's sleep, although I'd undeniably reached that stage in life when sleep becomes important.

It was at least ten years since I'd had the stamina to go out in an evening, swallow a few cocktails, drink a bottle of wine with dinner, move on to a night club, sink half a pint of Kummel, and end up busy in bed with some luscious girl until four in the morning before jumping into my car, driving from London to Lambourn to ride out for a trainer - all without a minute's kip - and still go soldiering for the rest of the day with no serious disruption to my health or senses.

Now, for this sparrow-fart landing, I'd cut my usual bottle of wine to a miserable half with last night's dinner and put myself to bed early. But I was bright-eyed as a canary on coke as I drove into Luton Airport at four forty on the mild morning of Saturday the First of May.

I followed the chain of confusing signs which direct anyone determined enough to persevere to the freight section where the horses were due to be off-loaded. I parked my old black Bentley twenty yards from the horse boxes that were already waiting for the plane, and stepped out into a crisp, quiet morning where I hungrily inhaled a full lung of sweet, dawn air, as yet untainted by the tang of aviation fuel.

I stood for a moment and gazed into the pale magenta sky where a lark drifted up, trilling over the flat grassland beyond the perimeter fence. There is a lot to be said for early summer mornings, not least that they don't have to be shared with thousands of jostling, sweaty punters. I was going to see a lot of early dawns over the next five weeks and I was looking forward to it.

Parked beside the five large white boxes I had ordered from Lambourn was our own smaller, blue box. Between them, a group of a dozen or so men made up the reception party. The Lambourn drivers clustered around ex-Corporal Harding who was pretending he was still a soldier, busily brewing up on his camp stove.

I regarded Harding with practical affection. He had the build and temperament of a wire-haired, short-legged terrier, as well as the charm and resourcefulness. He also knew from long, sometimes hard experience exactly how to please his master.

Three of our new Irish lads, uncertain of what to expect, lingered nearby with the al Hassan's farm manager, Dick Hill. Dick was there despite his clearly expressed view just a year before that horses were a bloody nuisance that got in the way of his running a serious agricultural operation. But during the previous season, I'd encouraged him to have £20 on Private Mountain at 10-1 in his first race as a two-year-old. The colt had won and Dick had reinvested the proceeds on it at 33-1 to win the next Derby. As a novice punter, he wasn't interested in each way bets, even at that price, and stood to earn £7,500. Now committed, he'd become a lot easier to handle; he'd even volunteered to leave before me at three in the morning to drive the lads up to Luton in the Land Rover towing a trailer to carry back the tack boxes.

Corporal Harding saw me climb out of the R-type. He walked over. 'Morning, Sir H. Would you like a mug of tea?'

I nodded and wandered back with him to the group to say hello to all the lads and drivers.

Harding fished a bottle from a webbing bag and pulled the cork out. 'Good old 'A' squadron custom, eh?' he grinned. 'Dash of rum in it, Major Sir Hugo?'

4

Bet Your Rocks Off

Like a lot of the mess staff in cavalry regiments, he could be absurdly snobbish and had adopted the habit, in public, of addressing officers complete with their title, if they had one.

'Why not,' I muttered, aware that poor old Harding had never been near any action in an armoured vehicle in his life. During his service as an officers' groom in the Royal Palace Horseguards, he had never been required to get up at three thirty to do any real soldiering; he had probably even considered it an affront to his dignity to be ordered up at five in the morning for early rehearsals of Trooping the Colour.

Twenty minutes later, as light seeped over the flat horizon, we saw our plane appear through the dark blue sky in the west. While I was dreamily watching the dot burgeon into an aircraft, my reverie was interrupted by a sour-faced vet from the Department for Environment Food & Rural Affairs who had arrived, manifestly resentful of the unsociable hours of his calling. I hoped he wouldn't try to give some purpose to his life by refusing entry to any of our horses. He joined us and seemed temporarily mollified by the large slug of rum which Corporal Harding handed him.

Henry Teacher, the agent who'd arranged the flight, drove in, half-late, as always and in a panic. I walked back with him to the lorries where the drivers were still gathered in a cloud of cigarette smoke, laughing and joking in hoarse, early-morning voices over the growing whine of the four massive Rolls Royce jet engines.

While we exchanged a little racing gossip, I had a good look around. As far as I could see, none of the racing press had thought it worth coming - if they'd picked up the event at all. That was a relief and a minor hurdle cleared. With luck, and the Two Thousand Guineas being run that afternoon, the arrival of the al Hassan horses from Florida wouldn't even get a mention in *The Sporting Post*.

As the plane touched down five minutes before it was due – not bad after a ten hour flight – I couldn't suppress a shudder of excitement at the thought of what the horses' arrival would trigger.

As the jumbo jet lumbered across the airport from the end of the runway, a mobile phone trilled in one of the pockets of my Barbour. Stifling the irritation that the instrument still caused me, I pulled it out.

'Hello?' I grunted.

'Good morning, Hugo.' It was Abdel. 'Did the plane arrive?'

'It's just landed.'

'You haven't seen the horses yet?'

'No.'

'Call me when you have; let me know that everything is in order.'

'Yah, sure,' I said, bridling at Abdel's habitual superciliousness, though, God knows, I ought to have been used to it by then. I clicked the phone off - but not before Abdel had.

I had no right to resent Abdel al Hassan.

It was his money - the thick end of fifteen million quid so far - that had bankrolled this venture.

Bet Your Rocks Off

More to the point, it was his idea, grown from a seed of mine, watered with a little of my knowledge, and liberally fertilised with money from his own apparently limitless funds.

****

It was six years earlier, in the summer of '98, that Abdel al Hassan had first given me a hint of what he had in mind. We were talking in a suite in the Amstel Hotel in Amsterdam.

Although I'd known him since I was thirteen and a new boy at Harrow, I had no idea why he'd invited me to join him there for breakfast. When I was shown into his suite, he was standing at the window, looking out at the morning sun glinting off the canal ten floors below. He was dressed like an Anglophile Harvard don, in a pale yellow lambswool v-neck sweater and burnt umber cords. He looked as immaculately groomed as he always had. He was one of those men that you knew from twenty paces was going to smell deliciously clean - rather like the Harrods parfumerie. Strange, for a boffin, but then, he'd never conformed to any of the stereotypes of the research scientist.

He was four years older than I and, though the years had been unjustly lenient with me at forty two, as I then was, I'm not sure that he didn't look younger.

Of course, he'd never been interested in women or fatherhood, with all the concomitant stress these indulgences demanded. Being half Arab, teetotal and rich beyond sanity had also probably helped to protect his fine, café-latte features from the ravages of a normal life.

'Hugo, how kind of you to come,' he greeted me. 'Until I saw you on that plane the other day, I don't believe we'd met since '73 – at the International Sportsman's Club, but, of course, I often hear about you from my dear mother.'

Although he said he never ate breakfast himself, he'd made the gesture of ordering a full monty English version of the meal for me. While I ploughed into the OJ and Corn Flakes, we chatted trivially about mutual friends. Once I'd started chewing my way through some surprisingly good kippers, I was telling him about the winnings I'd salvaged from the disqualification of his mother's horse, Adare, after it had passed the post first in the Strand Trophy at Royal Ascot three days before.

'I suppose when you heard I was coming over for the race, you guessed we expected to win?' Abdel said.

I nodded.

'Hugo, you can't imagine the humiliation my mother felt when our horse was led away in disgrace, depriving her of the chance to receive a trophy from the Queen herself.'

'I have some idea.'

He looked at me and sighed. 'Perhaps you do. I'm delighted at least that one of our friends was able to show a modest profit from it all,' he said, and I believed him, though, in my current circumstances, the five thousand pounds I'd made, despite being far short of the two hundred thousand I should have won, was a far from modest sum.

Bet Your Rocks Off

Abdel paced the room, wrinkling his narrow nostrils at my kippers. 'As I indicated to you on the plane, I thought you might be able to advise me.' He pierced me with his laser-beam eyes to emphasise what he was saying. 'I want my mother's dignity restored; and I don't care what it costs.'

His words made me suddenly more attentive.

'Tell me, Hugo, if you were to have another bet, comparable to the one you had on Adare, what would be the surest way of winning?'

Abdel spoke flawless, upper crust English, if you overlooked a slight American inflection that must have crept in over the twenty years he'd lived in the States. But there was always a slight ambiguity, an enigmatic undertone to his quiet delivery, so that one never knew quite what he was asking.

'The surest way? That's difficult to say. It would depend what your ground rules were. But in principle, the surest way to win is to cheat.'

'Do you mean with the assistance of drugs?'

'Good lord, no! I wouldn't consider that. And besides, the chances of getting caught are about ninety nine point nine percent - unless you came up with some new, undetectable stuff?' I added, glancing at Abdel, wondering if this was what he had in mind.

'How then would you be sure to win in a true run race, without recourse to drugs, either as a stimulant, or a stopper of the opposition?'

'I would use the same method as the late Ringer Barry; I'd run a three year old in a two year-old race.'

'What do you mean?' Abdel's dark eyes flickered with interest. 'Who was Ringer Barry?'

I grinned. I always enjoyed talking about racing villainy. 'Ringer Barry was an amateur rider and professional crook who used to change horses' names and gamble like hell, just after the First War. One of his biggest coups was to buy a half useful three year old and run it in a selling race for two year olds at Thirsk. He took the equivalent of a quarter of a million pounds from the bookies.'

'Because he knew in those circumstances, the horse was bound to win?'

'Of course; it would be like running an athletic fifteen year old boy against an equally athletic twelve year old - no contest.'

'What if one ran a four year old in a three year old race?'

'As long as everyone thought the four year old was only three, there'd be a similar ratio to their performances.'

'If one ran a four year old in the Derby, would he win?'

'If he was a Derby class horse, he'd be as close to a certainty as you could get. The race is open to three year olds, all carrying nine stone. By the handicappers' weight for age table, a four year old would normally carry an extra twelve pounds. So you can see the advantage would be incontestable. But, of course,' I made a face at the unfairness of it, 'as soon as they blood-tested him after the race, they'd see at once he was the wrong horse; you'd lose the race and probably end up doing a few years' stir as HM's guest.'

'Yes,' Abdel said thoughtfully. 'I thought that might be what would happen. I must say, as I'd expected, you seem a very useful source of information - at least as far as racing is concerned. I would like us to meet again soon, and talk about it some more..... If you wouldn't mind,' he added, with a sudden, uncharacteristic show of deference.

Abdel's royal summons to Florida arrived soon after that, and when I saw him again in the Jacksonville Inn, I was burning with curiosity about his thoughts since our meeting in Amsterdam. I was more than intrigued when, at the start, he insisted on absolute secrecy.

'When we met in the Amstel,' Abdel said once the formalities were over, 'you recommended that I read some books - 'Great Racing Gambles and Frauds'. I bought all four volumes and found them fascinating, especially the Running Rein affair. You told me, if you recall, that if one were to run a four year old in the Derby nowadays and it was of that class, it would win?'

'Yes, of course he'd be a good thing, but, as I also told you, it's just not possible.'

'Tell me why, again.'

'There are dozens of reasons, Abdel. For a start, a horse can't just appear from nowhere and win the Derby. It would have to have run in races beforehand and people would know it; they'd know what it looked like. Besides, every horse has its own passport and no two horses are the same.'

Abdel lifted one hand, gently, as if he were about to stroke an invisible fluffy cat with his long brown fingers. 'Not necessarily. If one could produce two horses which looked exactly the same, and were exactly the same, one a three year old and one a four year old, would it then be possible to win the race with the four year old.'

'Abdel, like I said, there'd be no problem winning the race with a four year old if you could get it to the post with people thinking it was a three year old, but you and I know that no two horses look <u>exactly</u> the same; they don't have the same DNA or whatever it is. You must know all about that - that's your field, isn't it?'

Abdel inclined his head slightly in confirmation. 'I've been working in genetics for over twenty years.'

I began, at last, to see the connection with our conversation. 'So you know all about identical twins, and matching DNA and so on?'

'Yes, I do.'

'Do you think,' I said excitedly, suddenly inspired, 'there might be a way of changing the older horse's blood, to match the right one, before a race, so it showed up correct in the post-race test?'

'That would be far too lengthy a process, and besides, any bodily matter can be used for a DNA test - saliva, blood, urine, hair, skin, hoof clippings, even.'

'God! What a pity,' I said, deflated.

An impatient grimace flickered across Abdel's face. 'It doesn't matter,' he said. 'My speciality is cloning.' He allowed that to sink in. 'Mammals,' he added.

'Good God! I didn't know that had been done yet.'

'There is a laboratory in Britain very close to it, I think, but we have already achieved it here.'

At that stage my understanding of cloning was hazy. 'Isn't that incredibly complex? What exactly does it involve?'

'The science isn't very complicated, but the microsurgery to achieve it requires fantastic precision. The nucleus is extracted from a body cell of an existing individual; this is transplanted into an egg cell - that's to say, an ovum, whose nucleus has already been removed. The ovum is then induced to develop without fertilisation; the resulting embryo is composed entirely of cells derived from the single implanted nucleus, and a creature is born genetically identical to the individual from whose cell the original nucleus was taken. The potential benefits to livestock rearing are obviously enormous but, frankly, the US Administration is so fearful of public reaction to possible human applications, they've suppressed all reports of it.'

'But how can they do that, if you want to publish papers?'

'That's obvious,' Abdel shrugged. 'This research is all government funded; they control the uses of the results, and the release of information.'

'What mammals have you cloned, then?' I asked, hardly daring to listen to the answer.

'Rats, rabbits, goats,' he paused, 'and horses.'

'Holy shit!' I whispered. 'Do you mean you can reproduce an existing horse, absolutely identically?'

Abdel nodded. 'I could take any piece of genetically coded material from a previous Derby winner, and grow an exact replica by uterine implant in the laboratory. So far, it's only been done with small sturdy Icelandic ponies, but, theoretically, there's no reason why it shouldn't be done with a thoroughbred horse.'

'That is fantastic!' I gasped. 'Though in a way, it'll be an absolute disaster for racing. But provided you were the first in there....! Well, you could pull off the coup of a lifetime!'

'That's what I thought,' Abdel said, though he was keeping much calmer than me - after all, he'd had time to get used to the idea. 'But tell me Hugo, if we did run a four year old in the Derby and won, what precisely would happen?'

'First of all, could you produce **two** replicas, a year apart in age?'

'Certainly.'

'Well, then, if we ran our four year old, we'd have to have his three year old identical twin brother available for the Jockey Club to come and look at after the race if for some reason they'd smelled a rat. Do you remember the famous remark in the Running Rein case where the judge says, 'Produce the horse'? Unless we could produce a three year old which the authorities would accept as the horse that had won the Derby and whose blood matched the winner's sample, the horse would be disqualified and we'd all go to prison.'

'I see. The Jockey Club wouldn't just disqualify us without evidence, then, even if they were as convinced as they could be that we'd pulled off a coup, as you say, but didn't know exactly how?'

'No, Abdel, they wouldn't; they wouldn't be allowed to. The Jockey Club is a quasi-legal body and the normal rules of evidence apply. They can be 'convinced' of what they fucking well like, but they've got to **prove** it, too.' I was riding one of my favourite hobby-horses now. 'I can give you a good example - a horse called Hill House. He belonged to a particularly bent owner called Len Colville whose trainer had been supplied with some magic liquor by a retired ICI chemist. I don't know what the hell it was, but apparently if they gave a horse a jab of the stuff it would find an extra ten or fifteen lengths. They decided to give Hill House a double dose of this stuff, for the most valuable handicap hurdle race of the season - the Schweppes, at Newbury. By the end of the day, everyone on the course knew the horse had been sorted out because Colville's trainer couldn't stop boasting about it. You've never seen anything like it. The horse had often refused to start and even when he did get going, he tended to sulk and hang about the back of the field for the first mile. But that day, he was like a bloody tiger.

'As the tapes went up, he went off flat out and his jockey had a hell of a job holding him. He won as he liked with the crowd booing. The Jockey Club Stewards and their minions knew perfectly well the horse had been sent on, and of course they went demented. They ordered a test, but not surprisingly, the dope had been masked with a massive dose of cortisone which, you probably know better than me, we all have in our bodies anyway. I should think there was more cortisone than blood in Hill House's veins. From what I heard, it was a pantomime. The press screamed, the horse was taken off to Newmarket for more tests, and there were pictures of it on the front pages of every paper in the country. But in those days, the scientists couldn't pin anything on the trainer and he kept his licence.' I looked hard at Abdel, trying to gauge how serious he was. 'It'd be the same if we ran a four year old ringer. Of course, we'd have to have trained him right, but if we could produce a three year old that matched and the Jockey Club couldn't find the four year old, we'd be home and dry. And we'd make a bloody fortune!'

'As far as that goes,' Abdel said calmly, 'I already have a bloody fortune - several of them in fact. What I want to do - and you must appreciate that I want to do it expressly for my mother - is to run a horse in her name in the Epsom Derby. And I want to be absolutely certain that it will win.'

****

What a fantasy I'd thought it all was at the time. It had seemed absurd that it might ever be possible actually to pull off a coup on such a monumental scale.

But Abdel with quiet but awesome determination had listened to all the advice I'd given him over the next few years, until two identical horses had been 'born' from their surrogate dam a year apart.

They were exactly what I had ordered - two cloned replicas of an ideal European horse, Private State, an Arc winner and easily good enough to have won the Derby, had he run in it as a three year old. More than good enough, if he'd run as a four year old.

Abdel had provided all the funds I needed to set up two private training establishments, one in Florida and one in England, in addition to Madame al Hassan's existing stud in Normandy.

And he had agreed with me that Annie Tenbury was the ideal choice of private trainer.

After I'd finished talking to Abdel from Luton Airport on that summer's dawn, I stuffed my phone back into my pocket and tried to quell the churning in my guts that had started when the 747 from Florida had landed. While we were waiting for it to taxi to the freight compound, I walked back to my car with Corporal Harding.

'Everything seems in good order and ready to go, sir,' he reported.

'Let's just hope we'll be in good order on June 5th.' I looked at my father's battered old Aspreys' chronometer. 'At this moment on Derby Day, I'll be getting ready to take the horse up to Epsom and you'll be setting off from France with the spare horse.' I looked at him and nodded with a grunt. 'Eh? In thirty-five days and twelve hours we'll know if we've made a million or two.'

'It's just like the old days, sir; chips down and all to play for, as you used to say.'

'It's a bit more serious than the old days. We were playing for peanuts when we were at it in Germany and France. This time, if we get caught even trying to run a ringer in the Derby, we won't just get a slap on the wrists; we'll be looking at a good stretch - Ford Open for me, I expect; somewhere less salubrious for you.' I gave Harding a flash of manic mince pies to drive home what I was saying. 'But if we go out and actually <u>win</u> the Derby, and <u>then</u> they find out, they'll throw away the key.'

Harding looked disdainful. 'How would they find out, sir?'

'Corporal Harding, we have to be very careful. If the Jockey Club get the faintest whiff of what we're doing, they can get any information they want, whether it's strictly legal or not. Let me tell you something,' I said, mounting a favourite hobby horse, 'since that wall in Berlin came down, MI5 and MI6 have been fumbling about looking for some excuse to survive. They've stopped worrying about commies and they've become the covert surveillance arm of the police instead.' I was well in my stride now. 'D'you know, I wouldn't be surprised if all the phone calls in this country were being monitored and taped at GCHQ in Cheltenham so the police can listen to them unofficially whenever they feel like it. And I'm certain the Jockey Club can get at those tapes, too.'

'Really, sir. I think that's a bit OTT.'

'Well, Corporal Harding, I don't. And I want to tell you this again. When you're over in France and you need to say anything about our Derby horse, you never do it over the phone when I'm in my office. If you have to talk about him, drop the word 'cider' into the conversation as naturally as you can and I'll ring you, eight o'clock sharp that evening in the bar in Le Mesnil. I've already got the number. And if I need to talk to you about the colt, I'll do the same and ring you in the bar later. I'll always be speaking from a different call-box. And in any of the conversations we have on the phone you never, ever refer to the colt by name, or use the words 'Sir Hugo, or even 'Major'.'

'Are you sure this is all necessary, sir.'

'Those are your orders, Corporal.'

It was all very well for Harding to think I was over-reacting but, for me, more than chips were down. I was punting everything bar my bollocks, and I'd probably have staked them if I'd found a taker.

I already had twenty-two grand on the star horse in the chartered jet to win the Derby. I'd had five grand placed each way at 66-1, off-shore and tax-free through the professional I used for that sort of thing, before the colt had even run his first race the previous August, and I'd carried on getting money on ever since at an average of 45-1 to win, and some for a place, widely and in such a way that the multiple book-makers would never identify informed stable money.

If the horse went in at Epsom on June 5th, I already stood to win one point one million. If he came second, third or fourth, I'd still be two hundred thousand up.

Provided there were no accidents in the stables or on the gallops, the colt didn't contract the virus and he turned up at Epsom ninety-five percent fit, I planned to have another fifteen grand on with the bookies, just before the off, at around twenty-five to one I hoped, and another ten with the Tote, on the reasonable chance that it would return better than SP. So, if he won - and I was as certain as I'd ever been that he would - I should walk away with around a million and a half quid.

On top of these winnings, if we pulled it off, there was my bonus from Abdel - a share in the stallion itself.

I wasn't a compulsive gambler, but I was an habitual one, especially when I had the advantage of inside knowledge. I was used to the tension, the sense of danger - like the troopers in my old regiment had become used to the dangers of patrolling the streets of West Belfast. When you'd been exposed to it long enough, it became a way of life.

I'd been putting the chips down since I was at Harrow and riding in my first point-to-points, and I'd realised very early that the whole raison d'etre of greyhounds and racehorses is gambling.

I'd never forgotten the words of my first guv'nor, Jim Gervaise. 'Now, boy, I'm not telling you to bet, but if you do, always get value for money. And above all, **bet with your balls**.'

Over the years since, gambling on horses had paid for all my sport and most of my living expenses. But now I planned to extract what was - for me, not being Jimmy Goldsmith - a very serious dividend from the bookies; though you couldn't really call many of the multiples 'bookies', when they were patently no more than a gang of grey accountants who happened to operate betting shops, and hated real gamblers.

Of course, if all went well on Derby Day, then they'd really have something to scream about - and they would. So, I didn't doubt, would Emma, my ex-wife if the press ever got hold of how much I'd won and chose to tease her with it.

CHAPTER TWO

I held my breath as the ramps were run up to the front of the chubby fuselage and we waited for the first animals to be led down. But before a horse or a groom had appeared, my eyes were dragged ineluctably upwards, to the passenger door from which Annie had just appeared.

Some stairs had been rolled into place by the airport staff who'd suddenly materialised. She walked down them looking as if she'd just stepped off a page in Vogue, flawless in a Karl Lagerfeld suit with a Louis Vuitton brief-case to carry all the boring paperwork - horse passports, vaccination certificates and so-on. I shook my head and smiled.

I hadn't seen her for over a month; I'd been in France with Corporal Harding, setting up the isolation unit at the al Hassan stud, the <u>Haras du Mesnil</u>, and in Wiltshire, preparing our racing yard, while Annie had stayed in Florida to supervise the crucial training schedule she'd worked out for our Derby horse.

As I walked towards her, she looked to me as beautiful as she'd ever been and I allowed myself a faint tingle of desire that went back over seventeen years.

Peter Burden

It was that long since I'd seen her body in anything less than a bikini, but it was obvious that at the age of thirty-eight, she would still have got the thumbs up from any hardened old glamour snapper. Her hair may or may not have been naturally the colour of ripe corn, but her skin had a genuine, healthy tan and hadn't yet turned to leather. And her famous, fuck-me eyes still glinted a wicked, knowing turquoise.

Facially, she'd scarcely changed since she'd turned up from the States eighteen years ago, trailing one of the better looking junior officers in my regiment - the Hon Alexander Thistleton, elder son of the Earl of Tenbury; six months later, she'd seriously rocked the regiment by marrying him. Three months later his father had died and Alexander had inherited the Earldom.

Annie reached the bottom of the steps and strode towards me. On her face was a big smile; she knew exactly what effect she was having on the early morning libidos of all the men gathered round.

As she reached me, the plane's screaming engines were finally turned off. In the quiet that followed she leaned towards me and kissed me on the cheek. 'Hi, Hugo. Haven't you been to bed yet?'

'Of course I have,' I huffed indignantly.

She took a step back and looked at me thoughtfully. 'But you haven't shaved, have you? And I think,' she said in her softened and civilised American accent, 'if I were asked to describe the colour of your face, I'd say eau-de-nil.'

'Better than eau-de-Mississippi,' I countered, refusing to rise, much. 'And of course I've bloody well shaved. You know I always shave as soon as I get up.'

That's the way it was with Annie - always a challenge to keep you on your toes, and God help you if she saw you weaken. But she could more than carry it off. She had the wit, the strength and the looks. And I knew, since we'd become friends again, what a hell of a lot of good it did me - especially as we hadn't become lovers this time.

Annie reached out and stroked my cheek with the back of her warm hand. 'Relax, Huggy. You're looking wild and gorgeous as ever.'

Wild and gorgeous, for God's sake!

I shook my head impatiently. 'Please don't call me Huggy – it's hardly appropriate. Anyway – how are the horses?' I asked. 'How did they travel?'

'No real problems - one of the two-year-olds was acting a bit dumb and a couple of the yearlings kicked themselves,' Annie said.

'And the Derby horse?'

She laughed, nodding. 'Could <u>not</u> be better,' she said emphatically. 'You'll see when we take him off.'

Behind her, in the bowels of the aircraft, the travelling grooms had already started to dismantle the inside of the plane, and eleven yearlings destined to summer at Madame al Hassan's stud in Normandy came off first. The couple which had knocked themselves about on the flight were inspected closely by the ministry vet and Corporal Harding dressed their grazes with anti-biotic powder before they were led away and put into the first of the white boxes.

23

The three older horses which we'd identified as having ring-worm were loaded separately into Corporal Harding's blue box and would follow the yearlings over to France to be housed in the new isolation yard.

As the rest of them were led down, I told the lads which horses were travelling in which boxes down to Beckhampton. Our Derby colt, entered to run in the classic under the name of Private Mountain, was led down last. I couldn't stop myself from walking up to greet him.

After a quick glance around to make sure no one was watching, I told the groom to whip off his travelling rug. Annie was right; he looked magnificent; his coat of rich, dark bay gleamed, pointed up by a pair of long white socks on his hind legs. He was palpably fitter and more muscled than the last time I'd seen him, a month before. I was very relieved that the newspapers and the bookies had not sent spies to spot this new arrival.

Within an hour and quarter, all the boxes were loaded, the tedious formalities with the import agent and the ministry vet had been completed and I was saying goodbye to the travelling grooms with a fifty pound note for each.

The sun was up and activity around the airport had increased. The lorry engines were fired into life and driven slowly off the apron. Two of the Lambourns and Cpl Harding's box were heading off for the small round hills of Normandy; the other three, with the remaining fourteen horses headed for the rolling Marlborough Downs.

Bet Your Rocks Off

Annie dropped gratefully beside me into the well-worn leather seat of the '54 Bentley. I aimed the grand old car at the M1 and put my foot down on an empty, Saturday morning motorway.

The R-type was forty-five years old and still happy to cruise at eighty mph. It sucked up juice at ten to the gallon, but I loved driving the handsome dinosaur.

'This jalopy seems to shake some tail,' Annie said, pretending she wasn't impressed. 'I can't believe it's the same old heap you bought in the States.'

'It spent a good while at the restorers after it got back here,' I admitted.

'It looks a whole lot better than the pile of junk you sent from Florida. How long did it take?'

'I finally got her back about a fortnight ago. This is her first long trip. Let's hope she keeps going.'

'Don't expect me to push if she doesn't,' Annie said.

'Well, I'm certainly not going to,' I replied indignantly.

Annie laughed. 'Maybe you'll be able to afford a new one soon.'

'Maybe, but that's not the point. We're not in your homeland now; new isn't always best, you know.'

'I didn't say you <u>were</u> going to buy a new Bentley, I just said maybe you could afford to, if you wanted. I mean, at least we're over the first hurdle, and both colts are in Europe.'

I nodded. 'That was a smart move of yours to pull the four year old's mane and trim his tail, otherwise I don't think I'd have told them apart.'

'But I didn't,' Annie gasped. 'I trimmed the three year old.'

I turned and stared at her for a few seconds. Luckily we were on a straight, empty stretch of motorway. 'Holy shit!' I hissed.

Annie giggled. 'It's okay; don't stress yourself; only kidding.'

'Don't make bloody jokes like that; it's just too serious and you've got me worried. Check and see if you've got the right papers.'

Annie opened her flimsy briefcase and pulled out a stack of passports. 'It's fine. We have the four year old Green Mountain following us back there on the freeway, and I have papers saying he's three year old Private Mountain. And your Corporal Harding is taking Private Mountain to France with Green Mountain's papers. No problem.'

'I hope not,' I said. 'There's the remote chance that a French ministry vet might see something funny in his teeth, but that's a thousand to one shot.'

'Longer than that,' Annie said dismissively, and shook her head with a laugh. 'This scam is so fantastic!' She looked at me and her voice became serious. 'Listen, I'll do my bit; I'll get our boy to the Derby leaping out of his skin; just you be sure and get that three year old back and ready to swap as soon as the race is over.'

'I will, don't you worry. God, I'm glad we're into the last few furlongs now. I expect even you're beginning to feel a bit of a tingle.'

'Sure,' Annie said. 'But I won't really get excited till the day - when I get my share of the bucks. What d'you reckon that'll be?'

'Your cut should come to around half a million quid,' I said. 'If we win the race and sell the three year old for stud. And you'll get it all in cash, tax free in Switzerland. Of course, as you trained it, you'll automatically be paid out 4% of the first prize - about fifty thousand dollars, but you'll have to pay some US tax on that.'

'I'll live with that. But when do I get the big money?'

'Basically, when the horse is sold. Even if we get caught after winning the race, the way I've put most of the money on, I'll still collect the bulk of my winnings before the shit hits the fan. Provided the police can't prove they were my bets or find the money, I'll keep it even if the whole enterprise goes belly-up. In which case, I'm guaranteeing you a quarter of that in compensation. Of course, if the horse runs but doesn't even get placed... ' I lifted my shoulders with a noisy raspberry.

'But we <u>are</u> going to pull it off!' Annie laughed, all gung-ho.

'We could still have a bit of heat for a week or two after the race.'

'We've survived a little heat before,' she said dismissively. 'Remember Deauville?'

'I certainly do,' I grinned at her, and applauded myself on my choice of partner for this coup of coups.

'It's all a bit of a blur to me now,' Annie said. 'I was so goddam young! How the hell did it all happen?'

'You were young,' I chuckled and stole a quick glance at her. 'And almost as lovely as you are now. God you caused a rumpus in the mess!'

'Don't remind me. But tell me how we ended up in Deauville.'

'The Regiment went on block leave for the whole of August and one of the other officers had been asked by a rich Frenchman to go to Deauville to play in his polo team. This frog lent him a super flat overlooking the boardwalk. It was too good not to use it, so I went and stayed with him and brought four horses from Germany with me. One of those was Annapurna. Remember him?'

'Oh yes,' Annie grinned.

'You probably didn't notice at the time, but they water Deauville heavily and as soon as I got Annapurna on to soft gallops he started to work really well. I soon realised he'd win a good race and I'd clocked that on the last two Sundays in August there were a couple of amateur riders' races over a mile and three quarters - the first was for gentlemen riders and the second for ladies - but worth twice as much; it was on the last weekend of the season, when they always up the ante. I guessed that a mile and three quarters on soft would have been Annapurna's perfect distance as a four year old,' I grinned at the pleasant memory of having got it all so right. 'I sat down and tried to work out the best way to play it. As it happened, one of the other horses I'd brought - a five year old gelding called Crossbow – only went on the rock hard and wouldn't get a yard more than a mile and a quarter.'

'Mmm? Annie nodded.

'However,' I went on, 'he'd won his last four races in Germany - including a couple of Class Four handicaps with a proper jockey. So, I rode Crossbow in the first amateur race in the second to last Sunday.'

'I think I was there but I can't even remember what happened to you. You didn't come anywhere did you?'

'I took the lead after a mile and he ran out of puff in the soft ground at exactly a mile and a quarter and finished last by a hundred yards.' I couldn't help smiling at my recollection of the scene. 'The next weekend the French racing paper made a snide joke about how would Annapurna fare when the gallant English officer's horse finished last the previous weekend, having won four races in Germany, and he now ran a horse which had been unplaced twice in Germany that year, ridden by an unknown Milady Tenbury who was claiming seven pounds as a novice!'

'My God,' Annie groaned. 'They never did find out Lady Tenbury was born Annie Kapinska, on the wrong side of the tracks in Mingo Junction, Ohio!'

'No,' I agreed. 'You're right, and other people hadn't put two and two together. The press certainly never twigged you were a serious rider. Do you remember, it was the first time you'd ridden under the name of Tenbury and I think you were still claiming seven pounds because you'd only ridden fourteen winners. But there was another thing - both amateur races had peculiar old fashioned conditions - three year old maidens didn't get an allowance but maidens of four and upwards did, and what's more all winners got a penalty! As it happens there were eleven runners and Annapurna was set to carry bottom weight - even less than the three year olds who were all winners. It was a good class field, actually - a lot of the Paris trainers often used to have runners ridden by their daughters. In fact, Maurice Milbar's was ridden by his mistress!'

Annie laughed. 'I remember, those French jockettes were taking a very superior attitude in the changing-room so I told them I'd probably never be able to hold Annapurna and I'd have to go a full gallop for the first mile.'

'It worked like a dream, didn't it,' I nodded. 'You went off at a good gallop - but not too silly - and after a mile and a quarter I should think you were about thirty lengths up!'

'Yeah, but then I gave Annapurna a breather and the pack got to within three lengths as I reached the straight - then I kicked on again,' Annie grinned at me.

I nodded. 'He was going away again. He won by five lengths. The crowd couldn't believe it. And the stewards didn't even hold an enquiry!'

Annie shook her head, grinning at the memory of it all. 'Oh, Hugo; that was so great! Just talking about it has brought it all back. God that was a wild time!'

The rest of the drive back to the yard passed in similar pleasant reminiscences, strengthening the bond between us, though somehow pushing away the possibility of our relationship returning to the intimacy of those times. The last leg of the journey took us along the old Bath Road through Marlborough. We passed the singular lump of Silbury Hill and were soon at the Beckhampton roundabout where we turned north. Two and a quarter hours after leaving Luton, we took the first left before Avebury, into a small lane which led past Square Barrow, a big rectangular Neolithic burial mound which had given our yard its name.

I drew up outside a small, pretty brick and flint cottage which had been built a hundred and twenty years before. The head dairyman whom it had probably once housed would have been perplexed by the recently ragged, dragged and stippled walls and furniture which Annie had commissioned from a wrinkly, coke-sniffing Chelsea decoratrix and paid for with part of the bonus she'd earned from Abdel the previous year to help create the air of permanency we wanted.

Annie laughed as I staggered up the neat gravel path with the two massive suitcases she'd had dumped in the boot of my car at Luton.

I put them down, unlocked the front door and handed her the keys. 'Welcome back to Dairyman's Cottage,' I said, and unceremoniously heaved the cases into the small hall.

Annie squeezed past me and swept around the ground floor rooms, crowing with delight, then dashed upstairs to look at the bedrooms.

'I've got to hand it to her,' she called from the landing. 'Susie Monro's done a fantastic job. These bedrooms are incredible!'

'Are you pleased, then?' I asked doubtfully.

'I'm thrilled to bits!' Annie said, coming back down the stairs

'Well, I'm glad to hear it,' I said soberly. 'Do you want me to take all these cases upstairs?'

'Huggy Bear, please; no more gallantry.' She put an affectionate hand lightly on my arm. 'I don't think I can take it, and I don't want to upset our lovely relationship by putting unfamiliar strains on it. Besides, from the sound of all that huffing, I'd say I'm better equipped to carry them.'

'Suits me,' I shrugged. 'And I must insist,' I added more haughtily, 'that you don't call me Huggy Bear – especially within hearing of any of the staff; I'd lose all authority.'

'Of course, Hugo, I understand how important your dignity is to you.'

I ignored the jibe. 'By the way, I gave Mrs Brockett a few essentials to put in the fridge for you.'

Annie walked through to a pale honey and ochre room which had been converted from a perfectly serviceable kitchen into a combination of ship's galley and Andalusian parlour, like a picture from some ghastly life-style glossy. She opened the fridge and found milk, eggs, bread and bacon, which Dotty Brockett, our shared daily had got in from Waitrose in Marlborough, along with a couple of bottles of champagne and a tin of foie gras which I'd bought in Normandy the week before.

'As you say,' Annie gave one of her throaty, American laughs, '... essentials. At least I won't die of thirst or starve.' Holding up one of the bottles of champagne she said, 'Not exactly Dom Perignon. Where did you get this?'

32

'When I was over in France last week checking that Corporal Harding had everything ready, I asked Madame al Hassan's butler, Mario to get me some foie gras and champagne. He's Italian so he's got a much more intuitive understanding of English taste than any Frenchman would, and that's what he got me. I'd never heard of it, but he says it's as good as any of the grandes marques, and half the price,' I told her with some satisfaction. I prided myself on my uncanny skill in achieving the highest quality for the lowest cost.

'Good old Hugo,' Annie said approvingly, looking around her transformed kitchen. 'You really have done a fantastic job.'

'Good God, you don't think I had anything to do with it, do you? I didn't think there was anything wrong with the place before; you were happy enough with it for the last couple of years after I'd had it all freshly done. Frankly, I think it was a complete waste of your money re-doing it all - and I couldn't have stood another five minutes with that growling old fag-hag friend of yours. I think she wears Napalm for scent.'

'I don't think she cares a whole lot for you, either,' Annie said with a grin, re-arranging the flowers I'd asked Mrs Brockett to put in a vase.

'I couldn't give a toss,' I said, 'as long as I never have to see the fat old cow again or listen to her coughing down the phone.'

'Now, Hugo, you know I don't like that barrack-room language.'

'That's not language, that's description....'

'That'll do. You know darn well we agreed it would look much more like we had real long term plans here if I'd obviously spent money on the place.' As she talked, Annie peeled the foil and wire from the neck of the bottle. She aimed the cork at me and popped it, catching the frothy spume with a glass which she filled. 'There you are, partner, and here's to Private Mountain.' She filled another glass and took an appreciative gulp.

I laughed at her infectious confidence. 'I suppose if we get a result on June 5th, you can just see yourself in *Hello*. "....the lovely Anne, Countess of Tenbury, in her charming, Susan Monro designed home at the famous Square Barrow yard where she trained....."'

'Com'on, Huggy. *Time* magazine, maybe; *Hello*, no thanks.'

Half an hour after we had walked into the yard at Square Barrow, the lorries started to arrive. Each had one of our lads in it. We unloaded the horses, took off their protective bandages and gave them all a small bucket of water with a sachet of electrolyte to replace any minerals they might have lost sweating on the plane.

When the lads had them all in their stables, we gave them a small feed. Annie insisted on closely overseeing this. Corporal Harding had acted as our head lad in England since we'd set up the yard two seasons before but as he was now on his way to France, ostensibly to look after the quarantined horses, Annie mixed the horses' rations herself as the lads came up to the feed boxes.

Bet Your Rocks Off

When the feed was done, Annie sent the lads back to their hostel, which I'd had converted from an old stone barn, and told them to come back at four-thirty. As the last of them left the yard, she turned to me. 'That's good,' she said. 'You picked a better bunch than last year.'

We started walking back towards the box where our substitute Private Mountain was settling in.

'They're all Paddys again; every one of them from Cork,' I said.

'Will any of them guess the colt's older than he's supposed to be?'

We were standing outside his box now, looking in and admiring him.

'No,' I said confidently and opened the door to let us in. 'And he looks great! You've done a grand job. What a clever little woman you are.'

She lunged at my groin with a pair of shears she was carrying; I side-stepped smartly.

'Watch it, piggy,' she said, 'or I'll set the vet on you. He'll know how to quieten you down.'

I laughed. 'Seriously, I'm impressed.'

Once the colt was settled, we left his stable. Annie nodded and yawned. 'It's going to be a pile of work with no head lad, and I'm bushed as a dog; I haven't slept in thirty-six hours. I'm going to bed.' She took a last look in each box. Satisfied that all the horses were happy, she set towards her cottage fifty yards away.

I wandered back to my own house and let myself in. Upstairs in the small cubicle that was my bathroom, I slid under the shower. I'd been on the go for over ten hours myself and needed to freshen up. When I'd stood beneath the jet for ten minutes, I stepped out and padded through to my bedroom. I'd become rather fond of this room. All the furniture, including an absurd, oversized Edwardian mahogany bed, had come out of the old family drum and I could almost pretend I was still back there in a second-floor kid's room within easy shouting distance of Nanny.

This room had views to the south and west, with a big stand of beeches fifty yards away from where a chorus of birdsong roused me gently from my slumber each morning.

I shed my towelling robe and looked at myself in a large dressing mirror. Forty-eight next month, five foot eleven, and still tipping the scales at under twelve stone.

I glanced at a photograph in a frame on the tallboy - my father at my age, just after the war when he was still in the regiment - Colonel Sir Ralph Tarrington of Her Majesty's Royal Palace Horseguards.

I'd never really known him. When I was two, he'd died of a heart attack in the royal tennis courts at Lords, the day before the Queen's coronation, at which he'd been due to command the Sovereign's Escort.

Everyone had always said how like him I looked, especially in uniform. If they meant it, it was a compliment. He had a lean, well-proportioned face, fine, light brown hair and piercing blue eyes. He had been a notoriously handsome man and, as far as I could gather had rogered his way through half the debs who came out between nineteen twenty-five and nineteen thirty-five.

He'd married my mother in the middle of the war when she was a twenty year old WRAC driver who had apparently felt it was one of her duties to comfort a gallant soldier. In return, she'd once told me, he'd been a faithful husband to her, or, she'd added wryly, he had been very adept at covering his tracks.

Thinking of the shy but beautiful and self-possessed young woman who had born me, I looked at the photo beside my father's. It was a studio portrait, taken before my mother was married. She looked to me far too innocent and gentle to become my father's wife, and she had never lost that gentleness, even in her bitter struggle against the cancer that had killed her in her early fifties.

But she had been capable nonetheless of forming and stating firm opinions. She had, for instance, never liked Emma, which wasn't surprising, in that my ex-wife was one of the most insufferably patronising, supercilious women most people had ever met. It was when she overheard Emma trying to subject me to a ritual humiliation over my reluctance to book us the biggest suite at the Cipriani on our honeymoon that my mother expressed the view that, in marrying her, I had already committed the biggest mistake of my life.

Feeling a lot better for my shower and a change of clothes I went down into the small office which was squeezed between the kitchen and the sitting-room. From Monday to Friday, the office was the nerve centre of the operation, manned with almost tiresome efficiency by a stout, cuddly woman of around forty, built along the lines of a hot air balloon and called Pat, who had been our secretary in England since Day One. I had chosen her because all her references said she was unfailingly cheerful through any crises, was competent, but not overbright, and was clearly so honest that it would never occur to her to suspect other people's aspirations.

I checked a few messages, poured a glass of wine and went into the kitchen where I cut myself a slice of ham and settled down to watch the Newmarket Guineas meeting on television for a couple of hours.

At four thirty, the lads reappeared for evening stables. I phoned Annie to wake her, knowing she'd hate to miss the first evening session.   She came out quickly, anxious to check her charges again after their long day. Some thoroughbred horses could be serious hypochondriacs and needed little excuse to ail, so we had them all out and trotted them up before giving them ten minutes in the horse walker to calm them and stretch their legs.

It was such a beautiful afternoon, Annie hitched a rope to our Derby horse and led him out on to the square of lush turf in the middle of the yard to let him pick grass there for a quarter of an hour.

When we'd finished that first evening, I controlled any desire I might have had to do more, I gave Annie a kiss on the cheek.

'Goodnight, Hugo,' she said firmly.

With a slight sense of disappointment, I watched her go back to her cottage before I walked across the yard to my place.

Bet Your Rocks Off

In Florida, I'd found that Annie and I would go for days without seeing each other, even though we were on the same estate. It helped, of course, that her bungalow there overlooked the training barns while mine was in the middle of the stud farm, half a mile away.

Here, though, we would be living much closer and I knew it might get a little tricky as the tension built up. And there were good, practical reasons why it seemed wiser not to dine with each other as long as we were working together.

For one thing, I found dinner without wine wasn't worth eating, and I didn't measure my intake by the glass - as far as I was concerned, a unit of alcohol was a bottle - added to which, I'd always suffered from a complaint that was the very antithesis of brewer's droop, and we'd agreed, with some reluctance on my part, that fornication was strictly off the agenda.

CHAPTER THREE

Unlike most of the women I knew, Annie had always been an early riser, and she'd needed no persuading to take charge of the first feed. By six-thirty on Sunday morning, I knew she would be in the yard to give each horse a single scoop of nuts and oats, and to check that nothing had happened to them during the night.

Like me, she believed horses were happiest with a regular routine and, not being Roman Catholics, Sundays were the same as any other day for them. They would, though, do a little less work because we planned to make do with fewer work-riders, who naturally charged more for getting out of bed early on a Sunday.

Annie told me later that she'd already reached the last couple of horses when the first of the Irish lads walked into the yard just before seven. On her way back to her cottage she'd asked one of them to throw a handful of gravel up at my bedroom window.

The rattle woke me at once, but I lay for a few minutes thinking about the days ahead. It was going to be a hard five weeks. Between now and Derby Day, Annie and I had to use every ounce of knowledge we possessed to get our horse fit enough to win. At the same time, we'd have to organise our public relations in such a way that his victory didn't come as a total shock and cause an uproar.

Ten minutes after I'd woken, I was shaved and dressed. I walked straight out to the yard, where Annie and I spent a quarter of an hour talking through the needs of each of our fourteen horses.

Pleased that things looked nice and normal, I went back to the house, where I put kippers under the grill and coffee in a pot.

Over breakfast Annie and I carried on the discussion about horses that would dominate our conversation for the next five weeks. We'd just about finished when we saw our three work riders arrive for their first day.

'I told them to come in at eight today,' I said, 'but seven from tomorrow on, if that suits you.'

Annie nodded, and we went out to meet them.

I gave each of them a friendly greeting, confident that I'd made the right choices.

'Right, this is Lady Tenbury who will be your guv'nor from now on. This is Ray Manning, who was stable jockey for a German yard for three years, and Ulrike who rode work for the same yard. And this is Liam Brennan who's done his apprenticeship in Newmarket since he left Clonmel four years ago. I think you saw him ride a couple of times?'

'Yes. I remember. Welcome to Square Barrow. I'm looking forward to working with you for the rest of the season, and as long as you do what I say, when I say it, and do it brilliantly, you'll find me an easy boss.'

The three work riders grinned. They didn't know yet that she wasn't joking.

Annie and I both went out with the first lot to get a good look at our riders. We had instructed the lads to get the three year olds ready first, including, of course, the four year old Green Mountain - known to them and the rest of the world as the three year old Private Mountain. To avoid any confusion or potentially disastrous slips of the tongue, Annie and I had agreed always to refer to the colt simply as "Mountain"; partly, too, I felt, to convince ourselves of the mighty lie we were telling the world.

As there were only four three-year-olds to exercise, I rode on the hack while Annie herself got up on our star. When the horses had done enough to show us that our new work riders were up to the job, I rode back beside Annie. It was a perfect May morning, and I was as happy as a pig in shit to be up on a horse again, and to have this lovely, clever woman beside me as we prepared the most challenging race-track coup ever staged.

With the others ten yards ahead of us, we rode silently for a few minutes, listening to the rising larks and the sporadic bleating of late lambs looking for their mothers. I took a deep, satisfied breath and turned to Annie.

'I dare say you'll be glad to have a proper English Sunday lunch today.'

'Hugo, do you enjoy any physical pleasures besides eating?'

I grinned at her. 'You know perfectly well I do, but as eating is the only one you and I can share, I like to do it well. Ferret the fishmonger dropped in a nice fresh Devon crab yesterday with my Sunday kippers so I'll make a proper crab cocktail to start, then a roast leg of small Welsh lamb and mint sauce, plucked and chopped with my own fair hands.'

Annie nodded. 'Mmm. Sounds perfect.'

When Annie had gone off to shower and change, I poured myself some more coffee and opened up *The Sporting Post* which had appeared for the Sunday racing at Newmarket.

After a lazy half-hour with the papers, I went back into the kitchen which overlooked the yard and began to mess about with the crab, getting great pleasure from plucking out large, unbroken hunks of the crustacean's muscles from its spiky shell. Tannhauser blasted uncompromisingly from the wireless, and a bottle of my bargain champagne was poised ready in an ice bucket on the table.

'Hugo!' Annie's voice sounded faintly over the mighty chords. I switched off the wireless and turned to find her standing in the room.

'Mornin', guv'nor,' I grunted in stable English. 'What would you like - Bloody Mary or champagne.'

'What are you drinking?'

'It's only five to one; I haven't started yet.'

'Martyr! But as I can see a bottle poking out of that bucket, I'd love a glass of champagne. What are we celebrating?'

'We're not - but I've got an awful lot of this stuff and at six quid a bottle, it's practically cheaper than Malvern water.'

As I poured a couple of glasses, the phone rang.

'Be an angel and answer that,' I asked Annie.

She made a face at the angel reference, but picked up the phone. 'Hello - Square Barrow Yard.' She listened and put her hand over the receiver. 'Hugo, it sounds like some real old guy who says he's 'The Scotsman' and wants to talk to you.'

I took the phone from her. 'Hello, Jimmy - how are you?'
A voice which age and a rural Scottish upbringing made hard to interpret crackled down the line.

'Fine. I'm down staying wi' a grand-daughter who's just moved to Hungerford. It'd be good to see you again. And I hear you've one of the Mountain family for Madame al Hassan in with a chance for the Derby - you'll tell me if I should have a bet on him?'

'How long are you down?'

'Going over to Newmarket Wednesday for a few days, then I'll be back for a week or two.'

'I can't see you tomorrow; there's a point-to-point, but I could meet you on Tuesday, at quarter past one in the betting office by the railway bridge. I'll take you out to lunch if you like; we can catch up on the news then.'

'That'll be fine.'

I put the phone down.

'Who's 'The Scotsman'?' Annie asked.

'Haven't you ever heard me talking about Jimmy Collins? He was the lad who looked after me when I did my 'Two' in the school holidays at Newmarket in Jim Gervaise's yard. Back in the fifties and sixties he looked after the al Hassan's flying grey filly, Grey Mountain. He must be well over seventy now.'

'I hope you'll be nice to him.'

'Of course I will. I always send him a Christmas card - that's how he knew where to find me. Old Jimmy's a wise old bugger; he knows everything about bloodstock pedigrees too. He taught me a lot more than any of the masters at Harrow and I've always been grateful to him.'

'That's not something you often own up to. And what's this about a point-to-point tomorrow?'

'It's a Bank Holiday. The Avon Downs point-to-point is just up the road at Barbury Castle - I thought we'd go and have lunch and watch the first two or three races.'

'I suppose you mean gate-crash that poor Peter Vickers' lunch party like you did last year - it was so cringe-making! Has he invited you?'

'Of course not - one doesn't send out invitations to picnics at point-to-points and he must expect plenty of people like us if he's such a bloody fool as to take gull's eggs and Fortnum's Lobster and Salmon Pie and wonderful burgundy, instead of cold sausages and beer like everyone else.'

'I don't think I really want to go.'

'Who's going to drive me back after all that lovely wine if you don't?'

Annie sighed. 'Okay, I'll come but you must promise not to eat all the gulls eggs - you must have eaten the lot last year!'

'Balls! I'd have been constipated for a week. And think of it from Peter's point of view. He probably thinks it's very nice to have a baronet like me and a countess like you attend his picnic - bloody fool.' I addressed myself to my culinary achievements. 'Now, let's start - this crab looks outrageously good!'

Monday dawned grey. The downs were draped with low cloud and there was a distinct moistness to the atmosphere in our low-lying yard. Not a good day for anything much, but at least it wasn't raining. The point-to-point would still be on but before that, we had a serious morning's work to do.

Annie was a demanding perfectionist in everything she did, and by the end of our first proper session with the star colt, she was tense with frustration.

She'd ridden the animal up the gallop unimpressively behind our top lead horse. When they reached the end, Annie trotted over to me, slowed to a walk and gave me her verdict.

'It's not there yet,' she said irritably.

'It'd be pretty miraculous if it were,' I said with genuine optimism. 'I mean, the poor bugger hasn't worked on grass for nearly two years.'

'I know that,' Annie shook her head. 'But I tell you, we'll have to keep at him some.'

'He looks bloody well,' I said to encourage her.

'Handsome is as handsome does,' she muttered moodily and turned her horse for home.

Bet Your Rocks Off

On the whole, though, apart from Mountain's lacklustre performance, our horses had worked well that morning. Although it was only the Derby colt that really mattered, it was important from a public relations point of view that we were seen as a fully operational yard with a full string in serious training.

Besides, Annie was a resilient creature, as I well knew, and she was back to her normal fizzy self by the time she climbed into the Land Rover to come with me to the races at Barbury Castle.

We drove into the races to find the usual mix of rustic sportsmen, faux squires and aspiring wide boys. A dry day and good going had produced a respectable turnout of runners and punters; I was looking forward to the afternoon. Living as I did most of the time in America, I still savoured English point-to-point races for their earthy, amateurishness.

We parked as close to the course as we could, in case we wanted to do some serious watching. But our immediate goal was a kind of makeshift stockade of gleaming new Range Rovers that enclosed the Peter Vickers party.

It said a little for Peter's growing sensitivity to the mores of the rural gentleman that he hadn't come in his Bentley Mulsanne, but my heart sank when I saw the quality of the other guests. It revived, though, when I spied the quality of the Burgundy, and the quantity of gulls' eggs. On balance, I reckoned for the sake of the food and wine, I could tolerate an hour or so of banter with a gang of suburban nouveaus talking loudly about property prices and their children's private schools. I wasn't so sure about Annie, though, and in fairness to her, I suggested a sortie to the paddock where we could have a chuckle over some of the runners and riders for the first race.

On the way back, passing the bookies, I put a hundred quid on a horse which in my view was at least a stone better than anything else in the parade ring and ridden by a girl who knew what she was doing.

The bookie was an old adversary. He took my money but, as I walked away, I noticed that he immediately cut his price for the horse from two-to-one to evens. While this was flattering to one's judgement, it reminded me just how careful I was going to have to be when I briefed my betting team on Derby Day.

I caught up with Annie who turned to me with a grin.

'There's a little treat waiting for you back at the corral.'

'Oh?' I asked cautiously, detecting a hint of wasp in Annie's voice.

'One of your little fillies-in-training.'

'Narrow the field a bit,' I asked.

'*He* should give you a hint.' Annie nodded towards our lunch party.

Word of Peter Vickers' picnic must have got about. The group hanging around the boot of his car sopping up the freebies seemed to have doubled in size. Standing out from the other newcomers was a tall, white-haired, aristocratic looking man whose handsome frame and hand-me-down charm disguised, I knew, a small, dim and greedy mind. Sir Toby Allerthorpe, KBE, was Member of Parliament for a neighbouring and unshakeably Tory constituency.

The seat was a sinecure, and though Sir Toby seldom opened his mouth to justify the faith of the thirty-odd thousand voters who returned him to Parliament at every election, he was still popular in the district. He never said anything rude - at least, not to people's faces or in public. He always accepted invitations - at least, from any of the grander houses in the area, and he always agreed with every political idea any of his constituents proposed.

His copy-book had been only faintly blotted when his first wife, Margaret had divorced him on the grounds of uncomplicated adultery. Margaret's father had funded Toby's first election campaign, and had been angry at being cheated out of an MP for a son-in-law, but no-one else had minded much; they understood that Margaret had served her purpose in Toby's life and they had rallied round.

Nevertheless, none of Laura Buckton's contemporaries could understand why, in her mid-twenties and full bloom, she had decided to become the pompous old fart's second wife.

I'd first come across Laura in the mid-eighties. Her father, Tom Buckton was dead now, but then he'd been one of a dwindling band of old-Etonian jumping trainers, and the smartest of them since the death of the great Peter Cazelet.

Tom had trained on an estate just north of Bath and his tall, lanky frame made him a distinguished figure at all the big National Hunt meetings at Kempton, Sandown, Cheltenham and Aintree.

Peter Burden

That year, Peter Baring, an ex-officer of my regiment had asked me to ride a horse he owned in the Grand Military Meeting at Sandown. Tom Buckton was its trainer.

I was stationed at Windsor at the time, occupied with teaching a few manners to the young black horses we used on ceremonial occasions. Two weeks before the race, Tom had rung me.

'I hear you're to ride Rass Na Mhor for Peter Baring. You'd better come down and school him a couple of times. He's not the easiest of rides,' he added ominously.

I arranged to go down a few days later to stay with him at Nethercote, the handsome, historic manor house where he lived more like a nineteenth century squire than a professional race-horse trainer.

But there was nothing old-fashioned about Laura, a nubile, skinny-legged eighteen year old who was his seriously spoilt, only child. Her short dark hair was aggressively spiky; she wore tatty old jeans, with patches of smooth brown flesh showing through the holes at the top of her thighs. There was a look of permanent detachment in her dark blue eyes, and faint disapproval on lips which, like her breasts, were big and soft.

As it turned out, I didn't meet her until I'd come down to dinner, and I was immediately conscious that Tom had failed to mention her existence before then. I wondered if he found her an embarrassment - or me.

At the age of thirty-three, I was riding regularly, in good physical shape and still unmarried. A number of run-ins with the

Bet Your Rocks Off

Grub Street gossip-peddlers had given me a reputation that made people react to me either with hypocritical snottiness, or eager curiosity.

Laura didn't react at all.

As soon as I saw her, I sensed that she could be tricky. I didn't usually find this an attractive trait in a woman, but when they were as outrageously horny-looking as this one, it was utterly tantalising.

During the hour it took to eat dinner, Laura barely addressed a dozen words to me, and ignored my few conversational sallies, but there was also a niece of Tom's, Alice Constable at dinner. She was staying in the house, as far as I could gather to help in the yard, probably as an unpaid lad. She was a perfectly presentable, well-built sort of Sloane in her mid-twenties - the sort that used to hang around the Guards Polo Club all the time with their sun-glasses pushed up on the tops of their heads, wearing shirts from Harvie & Hudson and yacking about people they knew in Scotland. And always game for a no-holds-barred, commitment-free shag after a few hard chukkas.

I didn't concentrate too hard on her, but made it subtly clear that a later coupling was an option. She seemed to lap it up and was almost salivating with expectation by the end of dinner.

Later, when I'd already been in bed for half an hour, trying to deal with repetitious fantasies involving my host's daughter wearing no clothes, my door was gently opened. I guessed it was Alice, come with a bag of oats for a hungry horse.

I rolled over in the single bed to accommodate my visitor, who walked across the room and stood beside it.

'Hello, Alice,' I breathed. 'How lovely to see you.'

'You obviously <u>can't</u> see me,' said a voice in the dark that definitely wasn't Alice's.

'Laura? What the fuck are you doing here?'

'Can I get in?'

She didn't wait for an answer and I felt her warm, silky skin slide against my legs until her thighs came in to contact with one of the swiftest erections I'd ever produced.

The four hours that followed turned out to be what could be called a truly seminal experience.

I'd never known a girl quite like Laura. She seemed to have the sexual appetite of a ravenous wolf, and the imagination of Salvador Dali. She demonstrated a luscious desperateness to explore every possible source of sensation she could find and went at my hard, healthy body like a terrier with a bone.

By the end of it, I felt like an empty sponge - a very contented limp, empty sponge.

And - the greatest satisfaction of all - she went away with half a grin on her sulky lips.

Looking back on it when we met again, after a gap of fourteen years, I supposed that I must have presented a rather unusual figure and a challenge to an eighteen year-old girl used to getting it all her own way with the unsubtle and predictable hunting bloods of the Beaufort country.

Bet Your Rocks Off

I say 'supposed', rather than 'knew', because she never specifically told me why she'd turned up in my room that first time I'd stayed in her father's house. And she had never told afterwards, on the couple of dozen occasions on which we'd met in the months that followed.

The morning of that first night, though, feeling fulfilled but deprived of sleep, I went down at seven o'clock and rode out a horse for Tom in his first lot.

I came in for breakfast later to find not any modern nonsense about eating in the kitchen, but a proper breakfast, with entree dishes filled by Tom's butler on a hot-plate in the dining room.

Laura didn't appear for this feast, but if Tom Buckton had any inkling of what his daughter had been up to in my bed the previous night, he gave no sign, while I kept finding myself in a hot flush every time I thought about it.

After breakfast we went out to the stables, where I finally met Rass Na Mhor. The horse had unquestionably good form and he'd won his last three novice chases, two at Worcester and one at Doncaster. He didn't seem an unpromising prospect. But Tom was a proper toff, and he had nothing to lose by telling me the less attractive truth about the horse.

'I have to say I told Baring I didn't think the undulations at Sandown would be ideal for this horse; he likes to go left-handed and he carries his head high; he'd be much better suited to a flatter course.'

Peter Burden

To say Rass Na Mhor was not my type of horse would be an understatement. He stood over seventeen hands, more like a heavyweight hunter than a racehorse. I was a light-weight amateur and I preferred finer, flat-bred horses.

Generally, I didn't like riding over fences anyway; I wasn't particularly afraid of them, but the type of horse I liked was more suited to the flat or hurdles.

I rode out Baring's brute feeling like the flea on a dog's back and managed to hang on for a few sorties over a run of three schooling fences. It was a terrifying experience. As soon as Rass Na Mhor saw them, he flew at the fences at full pelt, with his head high in the air and slightly to the left. I felt more like a sack of spuds than a jockey, but I was still on him at the end of each run.

The next week I went down and repeated the performance with Baring's horse, and Tom's daughter.

The daughter rode like a bucking bronco; the horse was hell. I spoke to Tom afterwards about Rass Na Mhor.

'I wonder if that horse is really suitable for an amateur like me.' I didn't dare tell him I just didn't want to ride the horrible brute, or the rumour would soon have got round that I was yellow - though 'scared shitless' would have been closer. I reckoned odds of evens against our jumping safely over Sandown's three unevenly spaced railway fences down the back straight.

But there was no getting out of it, and the day of the race was a corner of hell I never wish to revisit. Rass Na Mhor was being offered at even money, favourite in a field of eight; a few of the tipsters had even napped him. On the right course, in the right hands, he would have been a sound bet at evens, but with me in the saddle and at Sandown, I thought it was 10-1 on that we wouldn't even finish.

I needn't have worried about the railway fences. Disaster struck long before we got to them. We jumped the first two safely enough, though perhaps not with great style, and galloped up past the stands to turn right-handed down the hill.

When we reached the corner, the fucking animal cocked his jaw to the left and it was only with a huge tug on the reins and a crack with my whip down his left shoulder that I got him round the bend. As soon as we reached the falling ground, he stuck his nose even higher in the air. I don't think he saw the third fence at all, though he must have felt it; he hit it like a steam train. We turned a couple of somersaults a deux before we parted company, and I carried on with a few more of my own.

Luckily, my guardian angel - an overworked spirit in a thankless job - had reported for duty that afternoon and I walked away at the end of my roll, bent, bruised, terrified; and determined never to ride over English fences again.

I never saw Rass Na Mhor after that. He broke his own leg and his jockey's collar bone next time out. At least, I thought, my terror had been justified.

I did, however, see Tom Buckton's daughter.

I called in from time to time when I knew her parents would be away racing, usually without warning, and when she was there, we always ended up in her bed, usually with the same wild intensity of the first time, and, like the first time, we hardly ever spoke; there didn't seem any need.

Nor did we say much to each other when we met and made love over the next few months, until, quite by chance, I heard that she had gone to Florence, to learn about the history of art, and - I guessed - to be vigorously serviced by oily Spags with bodies like Donatello's St George and breath like St George's dragon.

It didn't matter much to me; not seeing her, and not screwing her. It was like being denied oysters in one's diet - regrettable, but by no means catastrophic, as long as there were other treats on the menu. After that, I thought of her only occasionally, when my new wife was being uncooperative or unadventurous.

But when I heard Laura was marrying the turgid old bore, Toby Allerthorpe, I did wonder what on earth she was doing. I knew Toby was all puff and image in his public life, and I strongly suspected his sex life was the same. But like a lot of dim, greedy men, Toby had become obsessed and efficient about accumulating wealth for himself. In his years in parliament, he had single-mindedly applied all his animal guile and social talents to securing as many paying jobs of influence as he could find. He now sat on the boards of innumerable companies as non-executive director and was vice-chairman of a small merchant bank. He had also been at the winning end of a few heavy take-overs in the City, gaining six and seven figure lumps at each throw.

Bet Your Rocks Off

He had capped this by becoming Minister of State for Arms Procurement under the previous Tory government, which provided him with a group of rich, powerful friends who always had a use for a presentable Tory MP of traditional views. For Toby, this important role was helped by having an attractive, younger wife who offered discretion, sex - when he needed it - and a fine house, with stables, in the heart of Beaufort country, which old Tom Buckton had left her when he had died - though, regrettably, not the funds to keep the place up. In return, Toby supplied this upkeep, comfort and status for Laura, five grand a month pocket money, access to more or less anyone she felt like meeting, and complete non-interference with her personal freedom.

CHAPTER FOUR

Peter Vickers, who was the most ostentatious of the big City money-makers in the district, lived near Devizes in an over-decorated Victorian mansion of the type that estate agents liked to call 'imposing' - a euphemism for 'huge, ugly and would make a good loony-bin'.

The year before our Derby challenge, Vickers had decided to host a heavily subsidised charity event - a Russian 'Dinner a la Romanov' in aid of the Countryside Alliance -reckoning this might open up a quick route to the place in the local squirearchy that he so desperately sought. The hundred and twenty-five quid that each guest had to pay to the charity didn't even cover the cost of all the caviar, champagne and vodka that Vickers had bought.

I'd been happy to cough up for a pair of tickets, and took Annie with me. I even wrote out another cheque for a thousand pounds in support of fox-hunting, for if our new masters at Westminster banned it, point-to-pointing would go, and the life source of National Hunt racing would be cut off. Besides, as far as I could see, it was just a matter of different perceptions of personal morality, not a matter for government. After all, I thought buggery was immoral, but I didn't feel it was the government's job to ban it.

At the Russian bash there was a tremendous crowd of the type that becomes likeable and humorous only as the level of alcohol in the blood increases. Annie was soon buried in a group of her own admirers, and I left her to it. After a sensational dinner and a cabaret performed by a gang of moustaches singing incomprehensible songs to their untuned balalaikas, I drifted outside into Peter Vickers' extravagantly tended gardens to smoke a Monte Cristo No 2 which someone had been generous enough to stuff into my fist, while still enjoying the effects of the various exotic vodkas I had drunk.

It was a beautifully warm evening and I was sitting on a stone bench beside a formal pool lit by naked flares, gazing with distaste at the oversized carp gliding among the lily pads, when a woman wandered across the terrace and sat down beside me.

I looked at her. In the warm, yellow glow of the flares, she looked very arousing and faintly familiar.

'Hello, Hugo.'

I tried to sharpen my focus with narrowed eyes.

'It's no good squinting at me like a pissed frog,' she laughed. 'You don't remember me, do you?'

'No, but you're very lovely, whoever you are. Do I really know you?'

'Oh yes. You've known me, biblically, quite a few times.'

'You mean I've fucked you?'

'Yes.'

59

'I never understood all that 'biblical' crap,' I said, scouring my memory for a fix on her identity. 'And I still haven't got a clue who you are,' I admitted.

'Do you remember coming down to ride Rass Na Mhor?'

'Of course!' I laughed. 'Laura! I've done everything I can to forget that fucking horse, but I'm sure I can remember every thrust of that first night you crept into my room. Though I have to say, you look even more beautiful now.'

'Thank you.'

'Are you better in bed, as well?'

'I think you should judge for yourself, don't you?'

I gazed at her, no doubt with flagrant lust burning in my eyes, which did nothing to put her off.

Remarkably, despite ten years of marriage to Toby, she really did seem scarcely to have aged since she'd first slid into my bed in her parents' house. Her big eyes still moved with the same lazy knowingness. She didn't appear to have added an inch to her waist, and her dark chocolate hair, cut short in defiance of prevailing crimpers' propaganda, emphasised her persistent youthfulness.

Like the old days, we didn't find it necessary or even, perhaps, desirable to engage in long conversation; but like a pair of randy students at a May Ball, we soon discovered that the animal attraction had not diminished with the years. In an old-fashioned, al fresco grope behind the rhododendrons, I slipped my hands inside her scanty lace drawers, over the silky hair of her vagina, where I inserted a busy middle finger into the moist warmth to tickle up her eager clitoris.

The time and place put coitus out of the question, but she was just undoing my flies for a postprandial Oval Office job when we heard her flatulent old husband bellowing with studied good humour from the terrace outside the marquee.

'Laura! We've got to go. Lady Buckingham wants to go to bed.'

'Shit,' Laura whispered to me. 'The Fuckinghams are staying with us. They lend us their place in Barbados; we'll have to take them home.'

She gave my pulsating cock an apologetic squeeze and helped me stuff it back into the confines of my barathea trousers while we held one of our longer conversations.

'Can you come over to Nethercote next Thursday, lunchtime?' she asked.

'Yes.'

'See you then. Don't be late. Toby's agent's dreary wife is coming to tea - fuck her!'

We walked back from behind the rhodies, chatting innocently and whistling for one of Vickers' Labradors who was shuffling about in the undergrowth behind us somewhere.

'Hello, Toby,' I called to the MP as we reached him, although I hadn't seen him for years. 'I hope you're well. Wonderful party, eh?' The second statement, at least, was true.

'Not bad for a common little shit like Vickers,' the MP said. 'Good to see you, Hugo. And don't forget to let me know if you've got any nice coups coming up.' He gave an asinine laugh, intended to convey what a man of the world he was.

'I charge for inside information, Toby, same as you do.'

Toby's chuckle was less certain this time, and Laura gave me a lovely little pout as I walked back into the marquee.

After that, 'lunch' with Laura became a regular vice for the rest of that summer. When I left for Florida again at the end of September, I made no commitment to ring, write or see her ever again; but I'd known that when it suited us both, I would.

As soon as I saw Laura at the Barbury Castle races, I knew that she'd come because she thought I'd be there. Toby, of course would have come anyway, to show his support for the pro-hunting lobby. But point-to-pointing would normally have been far too low-powered to hold much interest for Laura.

Although I admitted to myself a slight quickening of the pulse, I was conscious of Annie's critical eye on me. I turned to her.

'Annie, darling, it's none of your business - is it?'

'No, it's not,' Annie said lightly, 'But it's still a little sad.'

I didn't rise. I didn't care enough about Laura to defend her. But I had suddenly found I was in urgent need of one of her 'lunches'. Not that I let it show when Annie and I rejoined Peter Vickers' motley gang of wannabe gents and their bitchy wives.

'Hello, Hugo,' Toby boomed, evidently relieved to see a bona fide toff. 'Any tips for this one?'

I wouldn't trouble the moths in your wallet over this one, Toby.' I was buggered if I was going to see him win on my advice. Then it occurred to me it might be helpful to get rid of him for a few minutes. 'But you could try Walnut Whip.' The early favourite, since replaced by my selection.

Annie, to her credit, wandered over to look at a tack stall, though, God knows, we didn't need any more down at Square Barrow.

Laura seemed to materialise beside me. 'Hello, Hugo.'

'Laura, how lovely to see you!' I dropped my voice in deference to Toby. 'Lunch, sometime?'

Laura made a face - wicked, sexy, spoilt - which produced an agreeable hot flush in my groin. 'Mmm. But Toby's 'working' down here for the next fortnight. I'm going to London - to the flat.'

'Next Tuesday, then. You could come to the Club.'

When I woke the following day, a dawn erection prompted brief thoughts of Laura, before I heaved myself out of bed to get on with life in earnest.

I was happy that the yard seemed already to be settling into a routine. It was beginning to feel kosher, with the lads barracking each other and all the horses displaying their individual temperaments. But Annie came in to breakfast still grumbling about Mountain's lack of sparkle and, while I applauded her dedication, I had to pull her up sharply for gross pessimism.

At midday, though, satisfied that in general we'd got off to a good start, I took the Bentley from the garage and drove it to

Hungerford. I parked it behind the public library and walked down to Stan James, the bookies just below the arch of the bridge over the High Street.

It was in a sixteenth century building and the betting shop itself was a low-ceilinged room, clean and tidy - not full of smoke, half empty plastic coffee cups, discarded betting slips and overflowing ashtrays like most of them. As soon as I walked in, I saw Jimmy sitting on one of the tall stools, wearing an old cap and a tweed jacket I seemed to remember from thirty years ago. He was crouched over his paper, chewing a stunted bookie's pencil.

'Morning, Jimmy.'

He turned round sharply, looking a lot older than last time I'd seen him but as bright-eyed as ever.

'Hello, boss,' he nodded with a grin.

'Let's go and have a few bevvies at the Three Swans.'

Jimmy perked up like a dog that's heard its bowl rattle and followed me out of the betting shop.

I commandeered a table in the bow window of the oak-panelled bar and waved Jimmy into a chair.

'I assume your habits haven't changed - a half of bitter and a large malt chaser?'

'Aye,' Jimmy growled.

I ordered his drinks and a pint for myself and   we sat down with them by the window.

'I must say, Jimmy, you're looking very well.'

'You don't look so bad yourself, Sir Hugo.' He stressed the 'Sir' in a way which didn't convey much respect. 'But then, you always were a handsome bastard. All them ladies...' Jimmy's eyes were lighting up at the thought of it but I soon saw that he was also determined not to miss the chance of a bit of inside information, as I had hoped.

After all, besides the genuine pleasure of seeing Jimmy, my prime motive for meeting him was to push along my PR campaign. I was going to use every means I could subtly to disseminate information into the river of gossip that watered the plains of inside knowledge.

'This horse you've got for the Derby,' old Jimmy probed. 'I'm glad he's not a grey.'

'No, he's a good dark bay with two white socks....'

'Thank God for that, eh? None of the greys or chestnuts from the Grey Sovereign-Grey Mountain line stay, in my opinion. But you've got a chance with a bay from that family.' His bright little Celtic eyes sparkled at me. 'But will he win?'

'I fucking well hope so!'

'Who's this Lady Tenbury who's training him, and is she any good?'

'She's an American. She came over as a nanny to Penny Waugh and married her brother who was in my regiment. She grew up on a farm in Hicksville, Ohio, and she was a bloody good rider in her day.'

'Hah, I thought so,' Jimmy cackled triumphantly. 'She was the girl you got into trouble with in France.' He chuckled and wheezed. 'I remember the papers - "Scandal in Horseguards - Baronet runs off with Earl's wife". She was married to another officer and you ended up in bed with her when he was away on active service. Am I right?'

'I've often found friends' wives the easiest to get into bed and they always keep their mouths shut - at least, with their husbands.'

'Age doesna seem to have improved you. D'ye know what Jim Gervaise once said to me? "Your friend Sir Hugo will end up either leading in a Derby winner or being led into the dock of the Number One Court at the Old Bailey".'

I couldn't help a short laugh. 'Perhaps I'm in for the double, as Sir Jim would have said.'

'Keep to the point - tell me about this Lady Tenbury and France - you know I looked after Annapurna before you had him.'

'Okay, do you remember when Mme al Hassan gave me Annapurna after he'd knocked a fetlock joint at Newbury —must have been in the early '80s? I had him gelded and pin-fired and took him to Germany the following spring as a four year old but I didn't get him fit to run until July. By then the training grounds were hard as hell and he really needed good or soft ground and at least a mile and a half.'

Jimmy nodded silently.

'I rode him in a couple of Class B amateur races over a mile and didn't get in the first six.'

'You bastard! That was a bloody good horse. When he was at Sir Jim's, we thought he might win the Queen's Vase at Royal Ascot or even the St Leger, before that accident at Newbury.' Jimmy shook his head in disapproval. 'Hugo, you must have pulled his fuckin' back teeth to stop him - not winning a Class B with him was impossible! He'd have won a little race like that by a hundred yards on three legs!'

'Now, now, Jimmy. That's not very kind. Let's just say I was worried about his joints.' I noticed that both Jimmy's glasses were empty. 'Same again old friend?'

'Aye, I think I'm going to need one to listen to this.'

I stood up and walked to the bar where I bought another round. I sat down by the window again. We both took long, thoughtful drinks.

'Let me tell you how I worked things at Deauville.'

I leaned back in my chair and described to Jimmy how I had set up the coup, nearly twenty years before, when Annie had won the last race of the Deauville season, and he loved it, almost drooling over the details.

I took another drink, enjoying the luxury of spinning out the tale to such an appreciative audience. 'Nobody would know it to look at her now,' I said, 'but Lady Tenbury is very street-wise and game as a grouse.'

'I bet!'

'Be quiet, you dirty old man!'

'Ah. I remember the name now - Annie Kapinska - a tough little jockey.' Jimmy nodded. 'So, she was your Lady Tenbury! You wicked, evil, scheming bastard!' Jimmy cackled and choked on a mouthful of beer.

'No more than your old guv'nor,' I said, thinking how Jim Gervaise would have loved it.

'By God!' Jimmy gave the table a thump with a gnarled fist. 'You must have had a hell of a party that night!'

'We did!' I laughed at the memory of it. 'Madame al Hassan was there of course; she always spends the summer at her place in Normandy. She was thrilled to bits and threw a monster dinner party for us.'

'That story,' Jimmy said, shaking his head in approval, 'the way you planned it and all - that would ha' done credit to Sir Jim at his best. You know what he used to say?'

'Oh, yes, I'll never forget his three golden rules for betting. One – Get them ready and back them first time out. Two – Only back them if you can get value for money, and three – if you bet – Bet like a man!'

'Aye. If y'ginnae bet - Bet y' rocks off!' Jimmy nodded. 'But what happened when you got back to Germany.'

'That picture in the paper of Annie wrapped round me in the night club at The Normandie after the al Hassan party didn't help. Feathers were ruffled.'

'What the hell did her husband do?'

'He was such a complete BF he believed her when she told him we weren't lovers! It was only after the Divisional General sent for him and told him to control his wife as she was making a public exhibition of him that he started wondering.'

'What happened to her? Is she still married?' Jimmy asked, enjoying the salacious detail.

'Good God, no! Tenbury left the Army a few months later to run his ancestral pile up in Cumbria. Annie tried it, couldn't stick it and went - didn't even ask for redundancy pay - which was more than Tenbury deserved.'

'Why didn't you marry her, then?'

'Because my life doesn't run rigidly down the tram-lines of love as laid down by Messrs Mills and Boon - love, marriage; horse, carriage - balls! Besides, she's far too independent to be married to someone like me.'

'You mean she's got a brain,' Jimmy said sardonically. 'But all that matters now is, can she train?'

'She's had a good crop of winners in the States. Her horses always look well, run well and she's brilliant with the staff especially the Hispanics we use back in Florida.'

'Do those bull-fighting fellows really know how to look after a horse?'

I laughed. Jimmy had never had much time for foreigners, though he'd always tolerated Irishmen - up to a point.

'They weren't much use over here,' I said. 'They didn't like the cold and they soon got homesick, but they know horses all right. I wouldn't have anything else back in Florida.'

'What have you got here, then?'

'Paddies from the south of Ireland, where they know how to make them. I've a friend in Cork City - master of a pack of harriers who sorts me out a few from the point-to-point yards.'

Jimmy nodded. 'I suppose you know what you're doing. When do you first run Private Mountain?'

'On June 5th.'

'In the Derby?' Jimmy opened his bright eyes wider. 'That's some task - to win a Classic first time out in the season. Sir Jim did it a couple of times in the Guineas but never even tried it in the Derby.'

'We have to do it this way. I don't like bringing horses to this country from the warm Florida climate before early May.'

'The Guineas over a mile isn't so bad first time out,' Jimmy said, 'but the Derby over a mile and a half? That's a different matter - especially for a horse trained by a girl.'

'Some of those girls, as you call them, are bloody good trainers - Jenny Pitman.....'

'Och, you couldna call her a 'girl'!'

'All right, Jimmy, if you wish to be pedantic - a woman. But Mrs Pitman won two Nationals and a Gold Cup.'

'Hah - she was a great trainer of jumpers but winning the Derby, Hugo, is a different thing from winning jump races.'

'You're right, of course, Jimmy. And so you should be at your great age. Thanks for the warning.' I gulped down the last of my pint and looked at my watch. 'God, I must dash! But remember to get a bit of wedge on the Mountain. And if you still believe in God, keep bothering him about it till the horse is past the post.'

'I will, Hugo, I will.'

CHAPTER FIVE

Ray Manning, the best of our work-riders, was a taciturn West Country man, with a small head, a slightly pushed-in face and no discernible compensating charisma. Ulrike, by contrast, was one of the prettiest young creatures I'd ever seen in a racing yard. Despite this, they always came in together each morning. Although Ulrike had come from Germany with Ray, and I'd taken her on at his suggestion, I didn't know exactly what their relationship was, and I didn't much care, but it did mean that when Ray's car broke down, as it did on Wednesday morning, he rang to say they'd both be late.

That sort of thing always made me grumpy; I hated people screwing up carefully laid plans. But Annie calmly said that she'd give the two year olds a day off, while I drove five miles east up the A4 to collect Ray and Ulrike.

When we got back to the yard, I jumped out of the Land Rover still more irritated than the mere lateness of the riders justified. But so much hung on the right use of our thirty-five days' preparation before the Derby that I was frustrated by the possible waste of a single day.

Annie recognised it at once.

'For God's sake, Hugo, don't get so stressed out about it. It's no big deal. We'll get the older horses out on time.'

'But I haven't had any breakfast yet,' I blustered, trying to get the anger under control.

'You haven't done any work yet, either.'

'All right, all right,' I tried to laugh at myself. 'What are the horses going to do?'

'I'm giving them four furlongs at half speed up the long grass gallop, and the last three all out.'

I nodded.

Mountain, High Sierra, who was our five year old lead horse, a winning four year old miler called Rocky Spa and my hack were already tacked up. Five minutes later they were walking out of the yard, up on their toes and snorting; they'd sensed they were going to do a bit of work.

One of the reasons for my wanting Annie to train for us had been specifically so that Mountain would be ridden exclusively by her - because she was herself a very able work rider, and because the less anyone outside had to do with the animal the less chance there was of them coming to any dangerous conclusions. She got up onto him again that morning, still looking sceptical after his efforts over the last couple of days.

But that morning's work looked very promising to me, especially beside a lead horse with High Sierra's form - a Group Two winner over ten furlongs, fifth in the Derby, and second in the Eclipse as a four year old.

Bet Your Rocks Off

Hacking back to the stables beside her, I asked Annie what she thought.

To my great relief, she gave her faint, enigmatic smile. 'Either those lead horses are total donkeys or this animal is something else.'

Before the next lot, she came over to my house for breakfast. I bunged a handful of coffee beans into a grinder and once we'd both had a good caffeine hit, sitting at the kitchen table from where Annie could still keep half an eye on what was happening in the yard, I picked up the pile of mail that our postman had thrown grudgingly through the yard gates.

I opened the first envelope. 'Helen Johnson says they'll be here tomorrow, around six thirty. They're coming for Badminton Horse Trials. They want to take us out to dinner somewhere on Saturday.' I looked up at Annie, knowing that she had strong views about this sort of thing. 'Where shall we go - the Hare and Hounds up at Lambourn Woodlands?'

'You can go where you like; I'm not coming. You know darn well they were good friends of Alex's and they just think I'm a whore.'

'Don't be ridiculous. They don't think anything of the sort and they're looking forward to seeing you! I don't suppose they give a monkey's about what happened between you and Alex. That was all water under the bridge years ago. After the Deauville coup, Joe Johnson told me to my face he thought I'd behaved like a complete shit over you and ought to be thrown out of the Regiment!'

'What did you do about that?'

'I had a bloody good laugh at him and managed to avoid speaking to him in the mess for the next six months.'

'So why are you friends now?'

I laughed. 'That's no mystery. I had a couple of horses running at Hanover the following April - you and Alex had left Germany by then - but Joe was still around. He came and asked me if I was going to have a winner. I reminded him that I was a complete shit, and of course I knew exactly how my horses would run - but he could wait and find out for himself.' I gave a cynical nod. 'I don't have to tell you, greed overcomes better judgement every time; he apologised on the spot for poking his nose into my love-life.'

'Did your horses win?'

'No; I knew they wouldn't before they started. They weren't meant to; I was only there to handicap a couple of new four year olds I had brought out from England. I told him so, but I also gave him the winner of another race.'

'Are you sure they're not still mad at me for leaving Alex?'

'Absolutely'

Annie seemed prepared to believe that her ex-husband's friends no longer bore her a grudge, and I think she was quite intrigued to see some other people from what must have been a bizarre period in the life of a farm girl from the backwoods of Ohio.

At half past seven the following morning, Kevin Prendergast, the jockey we'd retained for the season, drove his heavily sponsored Saab into the yard. I appreciated that he must have had to start very early to get from his cottage in East Sussex.

On the whole, I didn't like jockeys hanging about the place too much; it was bad for discipline. But although it was unlikely we'd have anything to race for another ten days or so, Annie thought he should get a feel of what we were running this year as soon as possible.

Kevin had been champion apprentice at Newmarket, but when he'd seen a lot of the talented riders stay south, where the pickings looked richer, he'd headed for Yorkshire and a few very good seasons with the Malton and Middelham yards before he'd come back - to marry a girl who wouldn't move north, and to ride for trainers in Sussex and Epsom.

Neither of us particularly liked Kevin - there was an unattractive grumpiness about him - but he was undoubtedly a good jockey and probably among the top ten riding that year. He was still only twenty-six and canny enough to have made very good use of his experience. He'd never won a Derby only because he'd never had the horse to do it on. But he'd ridden Private Mountain to his one victory the previous season and had come back very impressed, begging Annie to let him ride the colt in the next running of the classic.

But he wasn't only able and keen, he was also left-handed and rode consistently to orders, both of which were qualities important to our strategy.

Annie announced that she wanted to see if any of the two year olds showed signs of talent on grass. She put Kevin up on the best of them and asked me to lead off the first lot on the stable hack, Barnaby River.

Barnaby River didn't look well and I was a little doubtful that he was up to the job - even to leading a gang of two year olds. As we lurched out of the yard, I speculated on his future, which was lying somewhere between a Frenchman's lunch and a dog's dinner - until I was struck by an altogether more constructive potential use for his future.

Before Annie went up in the Land Rover, she told the work riders to watch out. 'These horses will be excited - maybe panic a little when they feel the turf under their feet at speed, so hang on to their neck-straps and be ready for them to act like jumping beans. Just three furlongs on the grass at half speed, then pull up.'

The horses lined up and Annie drove on up to the top of the gallop, from where she had a ring-side view of the fiasco that followed. The men thought they knew enough to ignore her instructions. Ulrike was too obedient, and Kevin too experienced to get caught, but as soon as they jumped off behind me, the adolescent horses bucked and plunged exactly as Annie had predicted. Two of them managed to dump Liam and Ray before galloping past me up the track as if the hounds of hell were after them. It took me twenty minutes of patient cajoling to catch them and lead them back to the bottom of the gallop and their riders. And even then, Annie behaved as if it had all been my fault.

But it was unusual for things always to run smoothly in a yard of fit, over-bred racehorses and I'd have been surprised if we'd gone much longer without a few dramas. I left Annie to deal with Ray and Liam and took myself off home for a quiet afternoon and a nap.

When the Johnsons arrived a little before seven, I was glad of the distraction. Joe was a tall, thin man with black curly hair, ears which stuck out and a permanently bemused expression on his face, as if someone were trying to explain quantum physics to him while he had a hangover. He wasn't the brightest of sparks but I'd known him at school and in the regiment, and he'd become part of my own personal history.

Helen, his wife looked like a nervous pug. She and Jo had two sons, currently absorbing more money than they possessed on Harrow fees alone. While she didn't overtly blame Joe for their circumstances, I had the impression that she felt vaguely short-changed by her marriage to him.

The pile of cases in the back of their battered old Mercedes estate worried me a little but I did my best to be a good, willing host as I showed them to the only spare bedroom, with loo and shower attached.

'If you want a bath, you can borrow mine.'

'That'll be fine. It looks lovely here,' Helen gushed. 'Where's Annie?'

'She's down in her cottage by the gate. She promised she'd be up around now to help cook dinner,' I said, wondering if she would come.

Joe and I started back down the narrow stairs. 'I thought you lived together,' he said, sounding cheated.

'No. We work together but that's all,' I said firmly, walking into the dining-room and opening the French doors onto the terrace. 'As Apollo is being so obliging, shall we drink outside?'

The reference was lost on Joe. 'Yes, great,' he said bluffly. 'I'll stay down here while Helen unpacks; there's not enough room up there for both of us!'

'I'm so glad political correctness has yet to taint you, Joe. What shall I get you, Helen,' I called upstairs. 'G&T, whisky or Pimm's?'

Once Helen had unpacked enough kit to fill a small dress shop, she came down and joined Joe and me on the terrace, where we had a fine view of the sun blazing obliquely through the stringy clouds above the downs to the west.

Helen put in a bid for a refill of her Pimm's glass and sat down with a pair of sunglasses resting on the tip of her nose - a la Jane Fonda, c'67. 'Nice place,' she cooed.

'Yes, lovely - especially as I'm only here from May to September.'

'Where are you for the rest of the year?'

'The States, mostly - Florida.'

'Florida?' Helen asked. 'Isn't that all blue rinse and Disneyworld?'

'A bit of racing, too,' I said

'I don't follow racing much - especially since the Lloyd's fiasco,' Joe remarked gloomily. 'Are any of the horses in your yard here special enough to be worth a bet some time?'

I pointed to the box where Green Mountain was resting contentedly. 'Private Mountain, the horse in there, is still about 30-1 for the Derby.' I knew Joe would never put on enough to rock the odds. 'I backed him ante-post for this year's Derby before he ran at Ascot in July last year; I got sixty-six to one!'

'What?' Helen looked doubtful. 'You backed a horse to win this year's Derby in July last year? Wasn't that a hell of a risk?'

I wondered for a moment if I could be bothered to explain. 'We bred him to win the Derby, by Private State.' The name of the great horse obviously meant nothing to Helen. 'Private State was trained in France and only ran twice in England when he was four and won both times - the Coronation Cup and the Eclipse. And he won six of his seven races in France. And Mountain's dam was a very useful mare, too. From his performance on the gallops last year, we knew he could go a bit - so I backed him before he ran.'

'Ought I to have a bit on him now?' Joe asked.

'No,' I said. 'But give me a ring a couple of days before the race and I'll tell you how he is. We're not running him before the Derby, so he'll be at least twenty to one on the day.'

Annie walked into view across the yard. I thought she still looked distinctly moody about the morning's fracas. We all stood up to greet her. To my relief, Joe put on an exemplary display of the kind of charm Annie always said she wished I had.

'Annie! Come here and give us a kiss. It's lovely to see you again after all these years - Hugo has been telling us about your exciting Derby horse. I do so hope you win!'

Women of any age can be as unpredictable as two year old fillies and Annie seemed surprisingly susceptible to Joe's unsubtle flannel. She gave him and his wife hugs and kisses, and I guessed that a tricky evening had been averted.

'Hugo,' she ordered, as if I were one of her Irish lads, 'fill up Helen's glass.'

As the air was still warm, we decided to eat outside. Joe and I began to get drunk and earned a bollocking from Annie and Helen. But neither of them could contest my logic. 'If one can't get drunk with one's old friends once in a while, on a nice May evening,' I argued succinctly, 'then when the fuck can one get drunk?'

Annie knew when she was wasting her time. Giving in with good grace, after dinner she took Helen off to show her all the frightful things Mrs Monro had done to her cottage.

As they walked out of the yard, Joe took a long slug of my best Armagnac. 'How did Lloyd's work out for you?' he asked tentatively.

'Okay,' I said, on my guard out of habit. 'I did five years there after the Army, before I started working with al Hassan.'

'You weren't a member?'

'No.'

'Christ! You're lucky - those fucking city slickers virtually wiped me out. They're a bunch of out-and-out villains. Do you realise, they stole - and I mean 'stole' - £750 million from the investing public and not one of them has ended up in prison, while any poor sod on the dole gets banged up for pinching a pair of Marks and Sparks knickers. As far as I'm concerned, what's gone on at Lloyds is the greatest outrage in the history of the City. How the hell did you avoid being a member?'

'I **was** bloody lucky. You know I left Emma a year or so before I left the Army - stayed on to do my sixteen years so I got a lump sum when I left and a small pension.'

'Yah, I wish I'd stayed on, too. I did twelve years and got no pension at all - it'd be useful now, I can tell you. But how did you escape getting caught up in the Lloyds net?'

'You're quite right, of course. They are a gang of crooks,' I said. 'When they saw all that shitty, long-tailed asbestosis type of business lurking a few years up the line and stinking like a can of garbage, they rustled up the sales boys, all the oafish C-stream thickos who wouldn't realise what they were selling, and deliberately set out to trap twenty thousand or so new punters who they could dump all the rubbish on. Not that I'm saying I realised all that at the time, and frankly if Emma hadn't been trying to stitch me up for every penny I had, I'd probably have gone for it.'

'There you are,' Joe said. 'And you'd have thought a hardened old gambler like you would have smelt a rat.'

'It did occur to me that if it was such a bloody good wheeze, why on earth did they suddenly want twenty thousand other lucky sods to come in and share it with them? Luckily for me, I had fuck all

81

to invest. After I'd been out of the army for a year, Emma wanted a divorce, and did her best to screw for all the money she could. We had a nice little house in Kensington worth three hundred and fifty grand after the mortgage, and I still had four cottages on what was left of the family estate in Hampshire. They were all let on peppercorns to old family retainers. But they were nice places, worth a hundred and fifty grand a piece if they'd been empty. Emma got them valued with the sitting tenants at four hundred thousand, and after years of haggling, they've just been sold, and she gets the proceeds in final settlement.'

'What a cow! Her father's worth a few hundred mill isn't he?'

I shrugged. I was inured to the injustice of it by now.

'But you're not too badly off?' Joe asked.

'Let's say I don't want for anything that really matters to me.'

'Do you have to work quite hard at this game?' Joe waved a hand at the yard.

'Oh yes. I'll be up at sparrow-fart tomorrow, and riding out by seven-thirty. And in the afternoon, the vet's coming round to chop the balls off High Goaler, one of our naughtier two year olds.'

'My God!' Joe laughed. 'Poor sod.'

'He'll be okay - I should think he's done it dozens of times.'

'I didn't mean the vet- I meant the horse.'

'Oh, he'll be all right. A bit sore for a few days, and then he'll forget he ever had them. And think of all the hassle and expense he'll save, not needing to get his leg over.'

'But all these horses,' Joe said, not really understanding the point of anyone keeping so many. 'Who did you say they belong to?'

Bet Your Rocks Off

'The al Hassans. Do you remember Madame Jeanne al Hassan - used to appear in Tatler and Queen the whole time? She's a French woman who married a much older Saudi man - a wheeler-dealer with royal connections and staggering amount of wonga. After he died, the press were always trying to second guess her sex life. They never got it right, though; she was far to clever for that, but she's over seventy now and they've rather lost interest.'

'But how come she's got all these horses with you?'

'And Annie,' I added, 'she's the trainer. I've known Madame al Hassan for years. Her son, Abdel – you must remember him – was at Harrow with us. I got to know her when I was Abdel's fag.'

'My God! I do remember him. Wasn't he rather a bugger?'

'Not with me,' I said. 'His mother made sure of that.'

'All right, Hugo,' Annie's voice floated through the velvety darkness of the yard. 'We don't want any more of your sexual reminiscences. And we've got a lot to do tomorrow.' She stepped into the pool of light around my outdoor dinner table, with Helen behind her. 'You guys have had enough. They can probably hear you blaspheming and shouting down at the pub in Avebury. Beddy-byes for you, Hugo.'

'And you, Joe,' Helen said, not to be outdone.

As the sounds of the women clearing up faded and my guests were safely installed in their room, I could start thinking about sleep and found my mind wandering back over thirty-five years to my first meeting with Colette al Hassan - not that I ever thought of her as

Colette or dreamed of addressing her as Colette - she had always been *Madame* al Hassan.

I had arrived at the Headmaster's House at Harrow in the September after my thirteenth birthday. The House was in the centre of the school, overlooking the High Street and I'd been put in a triple study with another new boy and Simon Ponsonby, who'd already been there for a term.

Simon was supposed to teach us how to survive during our first two or three weeks. We had to learn the initials of all fifteen or so House Masters and their house names, colours of all the houses, where they were and so-on, before being put to work as fags for the house monitors.

There were two types of fags, 'general boys' who had to wait on the monitors' table at breakfast and answer 'boy' calls. The other type of fag was a 'special', who acted as valet for one monitor, but in return was exempted general fag duties. The special had to make his fag-master's bed and put the bed up - rooms were used as studies and bedrooms, each boy having a bed which folded up against a wall. He also had to clean his master's shoes, tidy his room, collect his laundry and, worst of all, clean his corps equipment.

Abdel al Hassan was on my landing in my first term and none of the fags who weren't new boys wanted to be his special. He had a reputation as a martinet, and a bugger into the bargain.

In the end, for want of volunteers, the most junior boy in the house was selected. My name, together with that of the other five new boys in the House had been added to the School role in alphabetical order; and since all the other new boys had surnames that started with letters in the alphabet before Tarrington, I drew the short straw and became Abdel al Hassan's special fag.

I started my duties on the third Saturday of the Winter term - and the following day, around four in the afternoon, Abdel put his head out of his study door - all of six yards away on the same corridor - and bellowed, 'Boy'.

At the time I was only five feet one inch tall and acutely conscious of my size. On Sundays, until I reached five feet four inches or had been at Harrow for three years, I had to wear the dreaded bumfreezer - an Eton jacket and a large round stiff collar, like a five year old from a Victorian Pears Soap advertisement - rather than the tails worn by the taller boys.

'Tarrington, I need a clean pair of shoes.'

I guessed Abdel was showing off to someone in his private study; there was nothing wrong with the shoes he was wearing. But, dutifully, I scuttled off to collect another pair from my room and brought them back while Abdel waited in the doorway.

When I came back, I realised he must have been trying to impress the lovely looking woman I could see now, sitting in the back of his room. His mother, I assumed, had come to take him out to tea.

I handed the shoes to Abdel and was on the point of buzzing off when the woman spoke.

'Come here little fellow, and tell me your name.' She had a warm, soft French accent.

I must have looked ten or eleven, not nearly fourteen. Obediently, I walked into the room.

'My name is Tarrington.'

'No, dear; what is you Christian name?'

'Hugo.'

'That is a very nice name. Abdel says you are a new boy this term. I hope you are not too unhappy Hugo; you look so young.'

'Mother,' Abdel said testily, 'his name is Tarrington.'

'Abdel, do not interrupt me when I am talking. I shall call the dear boy what I like,' this wonderful woman told her son before turning back to me. 'Do you know who I am?'

With hindsight, I guess she meant, did I know she was Abdel's mother. But I couldn't disguise my priorities, even then.

'Yes,' I said. 'You are Madame al Hassan and you own the wonderful filly, Grey Mountain trained by Jim Gervaise - I saw her win her tenth race at Newmarket in August.'

'Hugo, you like racing! That is nice.'

'Yes,' I nodded eagerly. 'I love it and when I grow up I want to be a jockey.'

'Do you have a horse?'

'No, but I've got a super pony called Toast, and when I'm older, I hope to get a proper horse.'

'Do you love Toast?'

'Yes, he's super. We go to Pony Club Camps sometimes, and hunting and have great fun.'

'How lovely! I am certain we will be great friends Hugo, and when you are older perhaps you can ride one of my horses in a race - at Deauville, where I live in August.'

Abdel was becoming impatient, fiddling with his tie and making irritable faces. 'Mother, we must go,' he said.

'Do not 'Mother' me. And you are not to be nasty to my young friend Hugo and what is more if you touch him in any way, I will see you are very seriously punished - I know your preferences.'

This remark went right over my head at the time, though it obviously annoyed Abdel who glared at his mother surlily.

'Do you understand me?' she pressed him. 'Answer me - clearly, Abdel?'

'Quite clearly, Mother. I understand what you say and will respect your wishes.'

'Yes, you must.' Turning to me she said, 'Now run along Hugo, and do not be afraid of Abdel. If he is nasty or frightens you in any way - you are to tell me when I come here again.' She reached out a hand and lightly touched my cheek. 'Now, tell me, what is your favourite cake?'

'Fuller's Walnut,' I answered promptly.

A few weeks later, Madame al Hassan came to Harrow again. With her she brought for me a Fuller's Walnut cake and a book, the Badminton Library of Flat Racing, with a picture of Grey Mountain pasted in the front.

Over the next two terms, before Abdel left Harrow for University, Madame al Hassan and I became good friends and later, after Abdel had left, she always came down to the school before or after Royal Ascot to take me out to tea. I only discovered later that she had always written to my mother beforehand to ask her permission.

In the time I knew him at school, Abdel remained a frightening figure - a school monitor, head of the CCF - with a reputation for being a brilliant scientist and the cleverest boy in the school. But although I never became close to Abdel, or at all friendly with him, after his mother's intervention, he always treated me half decently and never made any kind of homosexual pass at me; while all the presents which Madame al Hassan gave me made most of my other co-fags extremely jealous.

I left school when I was eighteen at the end of the summer term. From Harrow, I went straight up to Trinity College, Dublin, having spent the last two summer holidays doing my 'two' with Madame's trainer, Jim Gervaise at Newmarket.

Madame al Hassan was by then an important influence in my life. Not only had she regularly taken me out to tea in summer when I was at school, she had always sent me a long letter at Christmas about her horses, written in French because, she said, it was good for me to be bilingual. With the letter would be the year's best racing book from Joe Allen's famous bookshop in Buckingham Palace Road.

She told people that I was her honorary godson and it was through her that I kept abreast of my old fagmaster's career after Harrow.

Abdel had gone up to Cambridge where he scored a double first in Chemistry and Biology. After that, he'd qualified as a doctor in Heidelberg, learning to speak fluent German in a mere three months. In Germany he'd been showered with more academic prizes and from there he went on to do research at Harvard in the US. I gathered from Madame al Hassan that work had become his driving passion.

She spoke about it once when we were having lunch at Claridge's. 'You know, I cannot understand Abdel - he works twelve hours a day, seven days a week. Perhaps this is a product of hybrid vigour or something like that; the Arabs are not known for devotion to work and certainly my own family have always tried to put pleasure first.'

'Maybe he's trying to prove something,' I suggested, being the amateur psychologist.

'I have no doubt,' Madame al Hassan said. 'I only hope he doesn't succeed.'

It suited Madame al Hassan's circumstances to pay tax in Switzerland, where her main house was in Geneva, rather than in France, where she owned the *Haras du Mesnil*, a manor house and stud farm in Normandy. This sadly limited her to spending a maximum of ninety nights a year in France so she chose always to open up the house near Deauville for the months of July and August.

However, like many rich, sophisticated woman, she also wanted to spend as much time as she could in London; she'd acquired the habit when her son was being educated in England, always basing herself at Claridge's.

I learned very early on that Madame al Hassan made an unbending point of keeping her word. When she took me out to tea after Royal Ascot in my last summer at Harrow and told me that next year she would take me to the meeting on the Thursday and, what was more, she would get me a voucher for the Royal Enclosure, I was delighted, but not surprised when she did just as she'd promised. My belief that she must have had some serious pull in the right circles was confirmed when I realised she also had a special pass to the Royal Household car park. And when we went and had a bottle of champagne after the Gold Cup in the Blue Stand Bar there was always a table reserved for her in the corner.

The second year I went with her, I gallantly tried to pay for our champagne. She gave a faintly disapproving shake of her head. 'No, Hugo. It will be dealt with by the hall porter at Claridge's.'

After that, if I was in England for Royal Ascot, I always went with her in her chauffeur-driven Daimler on the Thursday. The hotel sent us with a marvellous picnic lunch and we always split a bottle of vintage Bollinger with it.

It was entirely through her, I reflected, and her invitations to Royal Ascot that I had made many of my early contacts with smart owners. These had become invaluable years later when I became a broker specialising in bloodstock insurance at Lloyd's, from which I had made a useful amount of money - unlike my poor guest, Joe Johnson.

CHAPTER SIX

On Friday morning, with the help of some well-earned guilt and a withering look from Annie, I successfully fought off a serious hangover.

Usually I favoured a good dawn shag to see off the results of alcoholic excesses, but that day, I had to make do with half a pot of strong coffee and seven sharp furlongs.

By the time we'd finished three lots, the Johnsons had disappeared to Badminton. Which was just as well, because the vet arrived early, before lunch, to perform his delicate operation on the fractious two year old, High Goaler, and I didn't think Joe could have stood the pain.

The Johnsons didn't reappear until I was halfway through the late feed. On the way back, they'd stopped to have dinner with some other friends of mine, Alfie and Birgitta Templeton who lived only five miles from us. I'd turned down an invitation to join them; as in horseracing, so in the great race called human existence, pacing is all, and I didn't want to hit the bottle three nights in a row.

Bet Your Rocks Off

By Saturday morning, Apollo the Sun God had abandoned us; the balmy, Wodehousean weather that had wrapped England in a cloth of gold for the last week had vanished.

As soon as I saw the sky in the morning, I thought we'd be very lucky to get through the morning without feeling some serious moisture. But this would not deter us from our schedule.

It was the horses' eighth day in England, and they were due to start some serious fast work.

The Johnsons arranged to meet us that evening at the Hare and Hounds, a dining pub between the M4 and Lambourn. They went off early to spend the day at Badminton, leaving us alone to get on with our job.

The threatened rain arrived while the third lot were out. By the time they were hacking back, it was tipping down. The horses arrived in the yard hot and steamy and we took a long time to dry them off. The lads had to stay back late to walk them round, which cost me a can of cold beer for each of them.

Annie said she had something to do over lunch, and left me in charge for the rest of the day. I was very curious to know where she was going, but I pretended I had no interest and restrained myself from asking.

When she reappeared, she said nothing. I knew she was trying to get me to probe her, but I liked playing that game too.

I was no wiser after evening stables, when Annie and I had both changed into what's commonly called smart casual - for me , the racing man's uniform of yellow lambswool V-neck sweater, well pressed dark cotton trousers and discreet suede loafers. We talked only about horses as I drove her and one of our lads over to The Fox & Feasant to meet the Johnsons for dinner.

It was only on the way that Annie chose to tell me where she'd been.

'Some friends of mine have moved into Stanton Park,' she said lightly. 'I went over to see them.' She knew I'd be impressed, or at least interested; I'd often said I thought Stanton was by far the most beautiful house in the area - a truly classic late Jacobean manor, which still had all its original paintings and furniture.

The most recent incumbent had died a few months before, apparently heirless.

'Oh,' I said, wondering how Annie might have known this obscure inheritor. 'Who's that?'

'She's a very old friend of mine. You know her too, apparently.'

Something in the way she said it put me on my guard.

'And I'm sure you'll like him. In fact, I invited them to join us for a drink in the pub, after we've finished dinner. I didn't think I could take two hours of the dreary old Johnsons undiluted.'

'You might have told me,' I expostulated.

'I just have, Hugo,' she said impatiently.

'Who are they then?'

'The Jackson Carter-Rices.'

'The big American banker, friend of George Bush?'

'That's him. He's running the European end of the bank for a while and they decided to rent a nice big country place, so's they could do a bit of entertaining. I guess we might get over there a bit.'

'Who's his current wife?'

'They haven't been married long.' She paused. 'Remember Calista?'

I tried to disguise the gulp that leaped down my throat. 'Calista? Yes,' I said vaguely. 'Rings a bell. American?'

'Yes, Hugo. That's the one.'

Did I remember Calista?

I certainly did, and, in theory there was no reason for me to regret my one and only encounter with her. It had been a couple of years before, in New York. I'd been at a party; we'd been introduced. She'd come back with me to the Pierre, where I'd been staying on Abdel's account, and we'd had one of those crazily sexy nights that seem to go on and on for ever, where our only object was to satisfy a shared hunger for more and greater erotic sensations.

The encounter had left even me feeling a little hedonistic after I'd tried a few things which I'd never done before and which I felt I could only do again with a total stranger.

For no reason that I could quite identify, I fervently hoped that Calista and Annie hadn't exchanged notes.

'Oh yes,' I croaked. 'I remember - good-looking, about mid-thirties now? I didn't know she was married actually.'

'She wasn't when you met her, so don't worry.'

'Worry? Why should I worry?'

I looked at her, and with a surge of relief I could see from her face that she was fishing; she didn't know what Calista and I had done.

'Hugo, I know you, remember. And I don't think you'd have let Calista by without making a play.'

'I don't succeed every time, you know. I'm not quite the streamlined Adonis I once was. Anyway, what's Jackson Carter-Rice like?'

'About sixty and looks at Cal the whole time like a puppy looking at a bone.'

'That sounds very unpleasant.'

'Matter of fact, he's a nice guy. I think You'll like him.'

We arrived in the car park at the same time as the Johnsons, and we all went in together.

I turned to Bertie, the ginger-haired lad who'd come with us. 'I won't ask you in for a drink. You're not to stop at any pubs or anywhere else on the way home.' I pulled a tenner from my wallet and waved it at him. 'But you can spend all of this in the Waggon and Horses as soon as you're back.' I watched him back the Bentley in the car park, and I hoped I wouldn't regret my decision.

Inside the pub, Joan, the barmaid greeted us busily. 'Hi, Hugo, Annie. Your friend, Mrs Carter-Rice, she just phoned. She's afraid they won't make it tonight, but she'll call you tomorrow.'

I tried not to let my relief show.

Annie made a face. 'That's too bad,' she said, and gave the Johnsons a quick, irritated glance, as if it were their fault.

'Right. What would you all like to drink?' I blustered heartily, to cover up.

When I'd organised the drinks, I looked at the menu. 'What shall we have? It's all delicious.'

The landlord of the pub appeared behind the bar and greeted Annie. 'Hello, darling. I suppose you're getting all excited about the Derby - the first woman to train the winner?'

'Takes a lot to get me excited....'

'No it doesn't!' I protested indignantly.

She ignored me. 'And there's still a month to go, but I guess it'll get to me nearer the day.'

'It must be about time a woman won the Derby,' Helen said.

'Anyway,' the landlord said. 'Best of luck if I don't see you before.'

We ordered dinner and took our drinks to sit at a table in a agreeably dark corner of the pub, Joe had evidently decided he couldn't leave after having spent three days on a yard which was going to produce that year's Derby winner without picking up a few details to impress his friends.

'Tell me, Hugo, what's the story at Square Barrow? The country you were riding over this morning looked pretty flat to me.'

'It's quite high, about four hundred feet above sea level, but between Avebury and Calne to the west the land is very flat for downland. If you can remember from your geoggers at school, it's what's called a peneplain.'

Joe laughed. 'I know you got a BA from a real university, but I always thought you wanted hills for training racehorses, like around here.'

'I think hills are absolutely fine for training jumpers and hurdlers, but I like more level land for young flat race horses. Not dead horizontal gallops, but just a few nice ups and downs. Basically, that's what Newmarket is - heathland as opposed to downland. I suppose you could call Square Barrow a heathland training establishment set on downs.

'Do you run the estate, too?' Joe asked enviously.

'Good God, no!' I said. 'It's run by a firm of smart London agents. In fact, I don't even know who owns it - something like the al Hassan Farming Co. (Caymans) Ltd.'

'But what on earth led to a family of Franco-Arab billionaires retaining you to run their racing operation here in England?' Joe asked.

'I manage their racehorses in France and the States, too, you know,' I said pedantically.

'Okay, but how did you land the job?'

'To tell you the truth, I never went fishing for it. It all happened through the strangest concatenation of circumstances.'

Joe frowned. 'Concatter what?'

'I'll tell you what happened,' I said.

Annie's eyes shot up. 'Do you think we have time for this?'

Bet Your Rocks Off

'If Joe and Helen want to hear....'

'Oh, just get on with it, Hugo,' Annie muttered through clenched teeth.

'Nine years ago', I said, leaning back in my chair, confident of an attentive audience, 'Madame al Hassan had had a brilliant season.

Her three year old filly, Miss Kilimanjaro won an Oaks Trial at Haydock and went on to come third in the Oaks itself at Epsom - the first time Madame ever had a horse placed in an English Classic.

But on Gold Cup Day at Ascot, Madame told me she thought Miss K's two year old half brother, Adare was better - the very best out of their dam. Sir Jim Gervaise, who'd just been knighted, fancied him for the big two year old races that autumn. He even thought the colt could win a Classic as a three year old.

So Adare first ran at the big September meeting at Ascot, and I made sure I bumped into Sir Jim before the race.

As if I was still working for him, I asked him if he thought Adare would do the business that day, and whether I should have a penny or two on him for a Classic the following year.

He looked doubtful and said the little bastard had turned randy. He told me to watch how he behaved in the parade ring before putting any money on him, and not to worry too much about the Classics.

This was an ominous warning, and accurate. As soon as Adare came into the ring, he started to snort and holler and wave his cock around. Then he went out on the course and ran sixth of eight.

Sir Jim wasn't in the habit of having horses finish at the back; I guessed there must be some serious problem with this one.

In her Christmas letter to me, Madame threw some light on to it.

Sir Jim says Adare has plenty of ability but thinks too much of girls. He will run him in the Craven Stakes at Newmarket and see how he goes. He is still in the Two Thousand Guineas and the Derby but do not back him until after the Craven.

I went to the Craven meeting and once again saw Adare make an exhibition of himself in the paddock. He ran poorly, beaten by twenty lengths. Obviously he wasn't going to run in the Classics, let alone win one.

I didn't give the colt a lot of thought until Madame talked about him over our usual picnic on Gold Cup Day at Royal Ascot. She said that Sir Jim had persuaded her to let Adare be gelded and at the moment the poor animal was contemplating life as a eunuch on her stud farm in Normandy. He was due back in Newmarket the following week.

Apparently Sir Jim was planning to give Adare two or three quiet runs that autumn, in the hope that he might make a very good horse the next season.

I pricked up my ears. Sir Jim talking about a four year old maiden being good suggested strongly that he was going to use him for one of his legendary touches in a handicap.

Madame thought he might win at the next Royal Ascot, and as he couldn't go for a classic, she most wanted him to run in the Strand

Trophy. The Queen presented the prize and Madame would have loved to receive a Cup from Her Majesty's own hands.

Interesting, I thought. The Strand Trophy was a top class handicap over a mile. Since the war, it had become the biggest betting race run on the Flat, after the Derby. It was what is always described as a cavalry charge of thirty or forty horses down the straight Mile, limited to four and five year olds. Sir Jim had won it at least twice, with horses at 16-1 and at 30-1.

I have to tell you that Sir Jim's handling of Adare from then on was an object lesson in handicapping and deception. First time that autumn he ran him in a good maiden over six furlongs at Newmarket; Adare didn't finish in the first eight of the twenty-four runners. He ran next in a similar, smaller race at Leicester, where he was a fast finishing fourth.'

I looked around at my audience to see how much of the information I was spewing forth was actually sinking in. Somewhat unusually, Annie hadn't heard the story and seemed to be taking a professional interest. Joe and Helen were still obviously intrigued by these inside revelations of racing's mystique.

'I'm not boring you, am I, Helen?' I asked politely.

'Oh, no, Hugo! It's fascinating.'

I took this as a compliment and carried on.

'The following year,' I said, 'Jim didn't bring Adare out until mid-April when he ran in a six-furlong maiden apprentice event at Nottingham, again finishing fast and beaten by only half a length into second place. Over the Whitsun Bank Holiday weekend, Sir Jim ran him at Kempton in another apprentice maiden over seven furlongs; he got boxed in turning into the straight and only finished third. I'm pretty sure Jim gave the kid riding him instructions which meant he'd have been unlikely to win. I can imagine it now.

Tuck in on the rails; then remember, keep to the rails, four or five lengths off the leaders, and start to improve your position with two furlongs to go. Take up the running in the last hundred yards if you can.

Old Jim would have known it was almost certain that an inexperienced apprentice would get boxed in round the tight last turn at Kempton, and wouldn't be able to follow these instructions.

A week after that third at Kempton, I had a letter from Madame with the disappointing news that she wouldn't be able to take me to Royal Ascot on the Thursday as she usually did. Apparently Sir Jim was hopeful that Adare would run well in the Strand Trophy that day and Abdel was coming over from America to watch. I concluded that Jim had told Madame that the horse would win, which was why Abdel was making his first appearance at Ascot since he'd gone to live in the States.

I could not ignore the runes. It was time for a real man's bet.

I decided to have £2,500 each way, ante-post, for starters. But I was worried that if I moved the betting market downwards by conspicuous punting, Sir Jim would decide not to run him at all, or worse, have a gamble on another horse instead, so I knew I had to spread the money around. I planned to get it all on over three weekends and I called in ex-Sgt-Major Ron Rawlings from my old regiment to help. He was working as a waiter, which is what they call those chaps in red uniforms at Lloyds, and I'd used him several times before for the same purpose. He recruited three other ex-sergeants from the regiment to help him and I devised a simple set of rules for their operation:

1. Bet only on Friday and Saturday afternoons when the betting shops are busy.

2. Stake no more than £10 each way in any one shop.

3. Place only one bet each per weekend with the national chains like Corals, Hills and Ladbrokes, and not more than two bets altogether with local chains.

My system was helped by the sergeants' geographical spread. One of them worked in Lloyds with Ron and lived in Essex; Ron himself lived in Windsor; a third lived in Liverpool, and the last in Newcastle, so, using this method, the odds hardly moved, and I remained confident that Sir Jim was going for a touch. I'd ended up getting my money on at an average of 32-1, and if the horse won, I'd collect a little over a hundred thousand – twenty grand if he was placed, which would be better than a kick up the arse.

The Tuesday after I'd finished my antepost operation, the price did start to move and by the weekend before Royal Ascot, Adare was quoted at most of the big bookies at 20s, almost certainly a result of money from Sir Jim and the rest of the stable going on.

'Hang on, Hugo,' Helen's tiresomely excited voice interrupted me. 'I can't see why you said it was such an object lesson in deception or whatever, or why the trainer was so sure Adare would win at Royal Ascot. Even I know everyone *wants* to win there, like the Cheltenham festival.'

'It's fairly obvious,' Joe grunted at her.

'But let me explain to Helen anyway, or she might feel left out of the conversation.' I tried not too sound patronising, though it was hard.

'Conversation?' Annie snorted. 'This isn't a conversation, it's a monologue.'

'Fine.' I held up both hands in submission. 'I'll stop at once.'

'Oh, no, Hugo,' Helen pleaded. 'I'm sure Annie didn't mean it.'

'All right,' I said to Helen with what I hoped was a winning smile. 'If you really think she didn't...'

'Just get on with it, Huggy,' Annie muttered across the table.

'Okay, Helen. This was an object lesson in deception because as a two year old and in the spring of his three year-old campaign Adare was considered a good horse. He'd been running in Group races - championship races where horses of the same age normally carry the same weight. Now he'd run badly in his first three races - two as a two year old and one at three - because he was a randy little sod. So they had his knackers off. I'm sure I don't have to explain what that means, do I Helen? So Sir Jim wanted to win handicaps with him as he had no stallion value and he'd have known by the time he was four that

Adare needed at least eight or ten furlongs. So, he carried on running him over slightly shorter distances. That way he wouldn't show his best and the handicapper would give him a reasonable weight.'

'But what a cheat!' Helen gasped.

'Not really,' I said. 'It's perfectly sensible to run an immature horse over short distances, then increase them. But Jim also ran him in apprentice races, with inexperienced jockeys. Some punters would have astutely – though, in this case, incorrectly – guessed he didn't think much of the horse. Anyway, as Jim had planned, the public and the bookies thought Adare was a very average sort of animal. They forgot that only a year before, he'd run in one of the classic trials. So, when Jim Gervaise entered him for the Strand Trophy as a four year-old, the punters didn't fancy him at all, which was how I got my first money on at over 30s.

But where old Jim showed his true guile was in being completely prepared for the aftermath. If he won, and the Stewards sat up and asked why the hell the horse had suddenly improved so much, he'd have had two indisputable answers ready:

It's obvious from today's running that he's a better horse over a mile than over six or seven furlongs, and he needs a stronger ride than an apprentice can give him.

Although the stewards would have had a pretty good idea he was at least half cheating, they'd have had to accept his explanation.

He was a clever old bastard, Sir Jim, and he always made sure he got his PR right, too. No one could object to a horse winning the Strand Trophy when his form was 4,2,3 - admittedly in crappy little races, but at least it looked as if he'd always been trying - which of course he had, but basically over distances too short for him.

Helen Johnson was looking at me, shaking her head with a worried expression. 'I'm sorry Hugo, but I still think it's cheating.'

I stifled the withering look that was stealing over my face.

'Don't worry about it, Helen,' I reassured her. 'Racing is still full of honourable men, I promise. Anyway,' I went on, 'I was pretty sure that was Jim's strategy, cheating or not, and I was bloody glad I'd managed to get my money on. And as the odds were still looking good, I thought it would be crazy not to try and get more on. The trouble was, I'd run out of readies by now, and £2,000 of the £5,500 I'd already laid out in the antepost market was Emma's alimony for May and June, and that had already produced a fusillade of threatening letters from Pilthers and Co, her solicitors.

But fortunately, at some point during the richer years, I'd accepted the kind offer of a couple of gold credit cards which I'd seldom used. Fortunately - inexplicably, really - both had massively high limits.

I'd arranged for Ron and a couple of his colleagues to come to Ascot and for each of them to put on a grand with the bookies on the course. I told them to place ten bets of £50 each way and try to complete the job before the price came in. I'd reckoned that a £50 bet in a strong market at Royal Ascot just wouldn't be noticed by a busy bookmaker, whereas a £100 bet probably would. While the three sergeants got busy, I had another grand each way on the Tote; a thousand pounds in a Royal Ascot pool makes very small waves.

Bet Your Rocks Off

The Strand Trophy was the fourth race, so I arranged to meet Ron Rawlings and his two companions after the sixth, by the horse exit to the paddock.

The race went like a dream.

Adare was drawn towards the centre, in stall 12. Almost as soon as they broke, the field split into three groups, one of eleven horses on the far side, a larger group of around twenty-five in the middle of the course and a third small bunch on the stands side.

For the first six furlongs, Adare was tucked in three or four lengths behind the leaders on the right of the middle group. I could see his jockey asking him to quicken and by the time they got to the seven furlong marker he was disputing the lead. His pilot gave him a couple of slaps with the whip and he quickened again and went by the winning post three lengths ahead.

Adare's number went up in the frame immediately, with a 'P' for the placed horses, while the judge scrutinised the photo-finish machine for second and third.

I'd watched the race from the top tier of the Members' stand. As soon as the horses had flashed past the post, I shoved my way through the throng of brasses and jumped-up jack-the-lads who were clogging up the stands and ran down the back stairs to the ground floor. As I reached the bottom, the loud-speakers blared the good tidings, to a few isolated cheers:

Here is the full result of the fourth race: First, No.22; second, No.9; third, No.11, and fourth, No.28. Tote pays, win No.22, £39.60; place, £15.10.......

That was all I needed to know.

My £1,000 each way on the Tote had made me over £53,000, to add to my £100,000 win from the antepost and perhaps another £40,000 to come from my cash bets in Tatts. Nearly £200,000, for an outlay of £10,500.

With my heart pounding from a massive surge of adrenaline, I found a good position on the balcony overlooking the unsaddling enclosure. A few minutes later I was rewarded by the sight of Adare being led in to an appreciative cheer by Madame al Hassan with Abdel beside her.

Madame looked flawless in a what could only have been a couture Chanel suit. Just above her left breast she was wearing a spectacular lump of tom - a diamond brooch I recalled from previous Ascots; the four biggest stones were light yellow and weighed over ten carats apiece. She had told me, years before in an unusual display of frankness, that it was worth well over a million quid and only left Asprey's strongroom once a year for the Royal meeting.

I hadn't seen Abdel in the flesh for nearly twenty-five years and he struck me as having changed considerably in that time, not through ageing, though; he looked like a fit, health-conscious, well-tanned American - even in a top hat and tails - and markedly less Arab than he'd appeared to me as a schoolboy. I guessed Madame had wanted him by her side for this moment of crowning glory for her, and I was as delighted for her as I was for myself at the outcome of the race.'

'Was it a popular win?' Joe interrupted my narrative flow.

'Yes,' I nodded. 'Though not so many in the crowd had backed the horse, he'd won with authority; the knowledgeable racing public knew Madame had been running good horses for over forty years and Sir Jim was a popular old trainer getting towards the end of his career. When he walked slowly from the weighing-room with the aid of two sticks to greet his horse and Madame al Hassan, the crowd gave another great cheer.

But just as the group gathered around the winner's slot, another announcement came over the loudspeakers:

Stewards Enquiry, Stewards Enquiry. The public are advised to retain all betting tickets.

I ignored it. As far as I could see, Adare had won well and with no scrimmaging. He'd come in cleanly on the outside of the middle group. The enquiry, I was sure, must involve the placed horses.

From where I stood, not more than fifteen yards away, the al Hassans, Sir Jim and the jockey looked completely at ease while they had their photographs taken.

Sir Jim went back into the weighing-room with the jockey, leaving the al Hassans chatting to his assistant and travelling head lad. Madame looked around contentedly at the crowd and waved at one or two friends. I caught her eye, and she blew me a kiss, nudging Abdel and pointing me out to him. He gave me a nod and an uninterested wave.

Five minutes after Sir Jim had disappeared, Her Majesty arrived in the unsaddling enclosure to present the Trophy. No follow-up announcement had been made but any moment I expected to hear: *The enquiry does not affect the winner.*

The travelling head lad took Adare off to give samples for the winner's mandatory dope test before returning him to the stables. Another five minutes passed, feeling a lot longer. The Royal party was becoming edgy; the al Hassans and Sir Jim's assistant were beginning to look apprehensive.

Abruptly, the loudspeakers boomed into life:

As a result of the Stewards' Enquiry, the winner is disqualified. Details of the enquiry will be posted on the Public Notice-boards. The amended result is as follows: First, No.9; second No.11; third, No.28; fourth, No.15. Revised Tote payments: Winner, No.9, £9.90......'

A great groan went up from the crowd around the ring. There was outright booing from the rougher punters in Tatts and the Silver Ring. Everyone seemed agreed; it was an incomprehensible decision.

The al Hassans and Sir Jim walked swiftly and, in Madame's case, with dignity from the winners' enclosure. I was instantly plunged into a state of deep shock. I watched while an old couple just below me rooted frantically through a waste bin down between the course and the paddock, looking for the ticket they'd chucked away. I remember feeling totally detached, as if I was miles away.'

'But Hugo, what the hell happened to your monster bet?' Joe asked in a low voice, evidently appalled at the scale of my loss.

I tried to laugh at the memory of it. 'After the sixth race, still in shock, and unable to find Madame or her trainer, I made my way to meet the three sergeants, as arranged, to give them all a drink in commiseration.

To my amazement, I found them all grinning and in fine form. When I asked them why the hell they were so happy, they said it could have been worse and they'd managed to salvage something from the wreckage. I thought maybe they were going to tell me they hadn't managed to get all the money on, but it wasn't that. I hadn't really registered, but it had taken so long to announce the enquiry and the result, and the horse had been such a clear winner, the bookies had just started paying out. Even after the Enquiry was announced they had carried on - they didn't think it had anything to do with him. The sergeants had got eleven of our thirty bets paid before the announcement was made that Adare had been disqualified.

Sergeant Rawling's patted a bulge in his jacket and grinned as he told me they'd got somewhere between eighteen and nineteen grand in readies. He tried to straighten his face and asked me if I thought we ought to give it back.

I told them, not fucking likely! Loads of people would have torn up their tickets on the winner and wouldn't be collecting. It was a case of swings and roundabouts - and we'd had a bit of the swings that day.

I invited them all back to the Number One car-park, where I had a couple of bottles of Champagne in a coolbox in the boot of my car.

I passed the bottles to Ron who opened them while I handed round my Locks hat-box, which soon filled up with cash from the NCOs' pockets.

When they all had glasses in their hands and had swallowed the first mouthful of champagne, I was regaled by a barrage of questions, with them all wanting to know what the hell had happened.

I had to tell them, I had no fucking idea. I'd watched the race really closely through my glasses and I had them on Adare the whole way. I was sure he'd done nothing wrong and it would be bloody interesting to see what the papers had to say about it next day.

When we'd finished our drinks, I went round and sat in the front seat of my car and counted out a bundle of notes for each of my team. I said I hoped this would more than cover their losses and expenses, and thanked them very much for their help.

As they were leaving, I told Ron I was off to Amsterdam on business next morning, and asked him to call in at the office the following Tuesday, when I'd have something for him to pass on to our friends who hadn't made it that day.

As I watched him go, I sat on in the car for a while and took a few deep breaths. It had been a miraculous escape from the jaws of disaster. The five grand or so I'd made would help cover my living expenses for a month or two and I'd be able to pay off the arrears on Emma's alimony.'

'But what about Madame?' Helen asked. 'She must have been furious.'

Bet Your Rocks Off

'Fury isn't an emotion in which Madame indulges, but I know she was very upset and I felt very sorry indeed for her. For the first time, her age had shown on her crumpled face as she'd been led from the unsaddling enclosure by Sir Jim, who was also visibly shaken.

I didn't sleep a lot that night and went out early to get the papers; I thought they might have a cathartic effect on my ravaged senses. Naturally, Adare's disqualification was front page material for the racing press and it knocked a surprise defeat for Manchester United off the back pages of the tabloids. It even made a major headline in the broadsheets.

The official reason for the disqualification was reported as being *'the crossing and taking of the second horse's ground in the final furlong'*.

The press were unanimous in their condemnation of the judgement.

Most unfair decision at Ascot in living memory!

Ascot stewards go blind then mad!

Worst decision since 1913 Derby.

Grande dame of racing robbed by Ascot stewards......

All that sort of thing. Not one of them had the guts to suggest it might just be a simple bit of old-fashioned racial prejudice, which I still think it was.'

'But do you really think it could have been that?' Joe asked.

I raised a shoulder in a gesture of ignorance and uncertainty. 'I don't know, but Madame and Abdel were utterly convinced of it, and I half believe them. Even quite sophisticated people – if you can call a gang of Jockey Club Stewards sophisticated – can behave in very odd ways. And I suppose Madame with her half French, half Arab background was more vulnerable than most. Anyway, as soon as I thought it decent, I rang Claridge's, who told me that Madame al Hassan had already left. I wasn't surprised but I was disappointed at not being able to see her in person. I immediately sent a postcard to her house in Geneva, inscribed simply, 'Love, Hugo'. I couldn't think what else to say.

And I guessed that, sadly, after such a public humiliation, she'd never come racing in England again.'

CHAPTER SEVEN

I was returned brusquely to the present, and to the familiar surroundings of The Fox & Feasant by a waitress who whisked a plate with half my pudding still on it from under my nose.

'Hang on,' I protested. 'I haven't finished it.'

'Oh yes, you have,' Annie said. 'And I've told them to bring the check.' She turned to Joe Johnson, 'I hope you don't mind, but Hugo's got to get back and do the late feed. And you know what he's like - give him his head with a story, and he'll carry on till the bloody birds wake up.'

'Well, yes, all right,' Joe agreed reluctantly. 'But I'd like to know what happened after Adare's race was taken away.'

'And I have no doubt you're going to hear it. But only when you've paid the bill and Hugo's done his tasks.'

An hour later, after I'd given all my charges their last bucket of scoff for the night, I found myself sitting up over the whisky with Joe Johnson for the second time that week. On this occasion, I was grateful that Annie and Helen stayed up with us.

'So,' Joe asked doggedly, once he'd got a full glass of Glenmorangie firmly in his grasp, 'when the Stewards took away their horse's win, the al Hassans were all hurt and huffy about it, but here you are, six years later, with dozens of their nags winning races and entered for the Derby. How on earth did you swing it?'

'I told you, it didn't happen through any initiative of mine,' I resumed happily. 'By what I thought was the merest coincidence, a few hours after I'd bunged off a card of condolence to Madame, I bumped into Abdel. I had to go to Amsterdam that day, and I'd just boarded a midday flight from Heathrow. Despite my reprieve from complete disaster - thanks to Ron Rawlings' quick work - I was feeling pretty gloomy. After all, morally, I should have been a couple of hundred grand to the good that morning and on top of that, I really did feel desperately sorry for Madame.

I plonked myself down in a seat in business class and looked at the papers again. I was extracting a little consolation from the pundits' total outrage at the stewards' decision when I heard a vaguely familiar voice saying, 'Good morning, Little Tarrington.'

I looked up and, to my astonishment, found Abdel al Hassan standing in the aisle beside me. Without thinking, I asked him what the hell he was doing there.

He said he was going to Amsterdam, like me, and my office had told him I was on that flight. He had plans for the trip anyway, and wanted to talk to someone about what happened the day before. He'd heard from his mother had told him that she usually took me on Ladies' Day and he apologised for depriving me of her company.

I waved aside his concern over that but expressed my view that she must have been devastated, as I thought she'd been really looking forward to being given a trophy by the Queen.

Bleakly, Abdel agreed she had been very hurt indeed. He wanted somehow to make it up for her, preferably without her knowing. He added that she had often spoken to him about my knowledge and understanding of racing and bloodstock.

I demurred, naturally, but he asked me how long I would be staying in Amsterdam and the name of my hotel.

Still rather surprised by his sudden appearance, I gave him one of my business cards and scribbled the address of the small place where I always stayed, and watched him glide back to his seat.

I had a lot of work to do as soon as I reached Amsterdam, and not a lot of time to think about Abdel al Hassan. It wasn't until next morning as I sat in the breakfast lounge of my hotel that I thought anything might follow our brief, though not, apparently, coincidental meeting on the plane.

A smart young messenger in uniform arrived from the Amstel Hotel with an envelope for me.

Inside, beneath the Amstel's heading, was a short letter.

June 18th

Sir Hugo,

Sheikh Abdel al Hassan has asked me if you would kindly come for breakfast with him on Sunday, at 9.45 am. If so, we will send a car to collect you at 9.30.

Peter Burden

Please ring the above number on receipt of this letter and let me or my assistant know if this is convenient.

Yours sincerely,

P. Hines, General Manager.

It sounded like a Royal Command. I told the messenger I'd be coming, and went to my room to ring Mr Hines to confirm.

The next morning, on the dot of 9.30, I left my hotel and was limoed round to the Amstel Hotel. On the way there, with some misgivings, I pondered Abdel's reasons for being in Amsterdam.

His mother had hinted to me several times that her son was a confirmed homosexual. More than once she had complained that Abdel would never get married because he didn't like women and thus, sadly, she would never have any grandchildren. She'd also said on another occasion that when Abdel came to Europe, he liked to go to Amsterdam as, she'd heard, there was greater sexual tolerance there.

I started to give the Johnsons an account – without any reference whatsoever to cloning or Abdel's field of expertise – of that momentous meeting with him in the Amstel Hotel, in which he'd first revealed his fervent desire to see Madame's honour restored at any cost, when a commotion out in the yard at Square Barrow diverted our attention for a moment. It sounded like one of the regular scraps between the stable terrier and some of the cats.

Bet Your Rocks Off

One of the young horses, startled out of his sleep, whinnied and clattered his hoofs.

Joe took the opportunity of a break in my narrative to fill up our glasses. While he was doing it, Annie flashed me a warning glance. I thought for a moment about what I was saying, and I decided that it would be wiser, given Joe's less than perfect record for discretion, to skip most of my conversation with Abdel that sunny morning in Amsterdam six years before.

But Joe and Helen were still on the edge of their seats. I was pleased with myself. It wasn't often one could tell a tale so engaging without recourse to untruth or embellishment.

'Well,' I resumed, 'we chatted around possibilities and chances, the strategies and costs of winning the Derby until that particular meeting ended, as far as I could tell at the time, very satisfactorily. Once I'd finished my breakfast, Abdel stood up and made it clear in the grandest possible way that he'd had enough of my company.

He thanked me and said he would like to discuss the idea with me at more length, on a professional basis. He suggested that I might come and see him the following month in Florida where he now lived. I asked him what exactly he wanted to discuss, but he would only say that I'd sown the seeds of some fascinating ideas for the expansion of his family's racing interests. He also asked me not to tell his mother about our meeting or conversation.

I went back to London to get on with my comfortable but somewhat static career, and consider what this offer from Abdel really held for me. Although over the years I had inevitably grown somewhat cynical about Greeks - or Arabs - bearing gifts, I couldn't force out of my head the unspeakably succulent prospect of being asked to organise a racing operation for a man of Abdel's colossal wealth, with 'money no object'.

If, on that basis, he wanted a Derby winner, I'd have a bloody good crack at delivering one, and undoubtedly earn a hefty bonus for myself into the bargain.

When I woke one Saturday, two weeks later, I found a message from Abdel on my fax machine:

Further to our last meeting, I can confirm that I am considering expanding the family's racing interests and would appreciate your advice here in Jacksonville.

If you are willing to come as soon as possible I will reimburse you £1,500 for your air fare and accommodation other than in Jacksonville and pay you a fee of £3,000. When you are in Jacksonville I will provide accommodation at the Jacksonville Inn. Mr Pierre Tari in the al Hassan City office has instructions to advance you funds in whatever manner you may require.

Please let me know within forty-eight hours if you will be able to comply with these arrangements.

A a H.

I read the fax and calculated there was at least £4,000 profit in it, for less than a week's work. Properly handled, I was fairly certain I could persuade my firm to pay for me to go out to Florida on business and they wouldn't need to know about a short trip to Jacksonville. An extra £4,000 would help to make up for the disappointment over Adare.

The next day, I faxed Abdel to say I'd be there the first week in August.

I made arrangements to fly out to Miami on August 1st and booked myself into The Breakers - a tad flashy but in my opinion, one of the great hotels of the world - certainly provider of the greatest breakfast.

After a day's useful R&R, and a couple of quasi-business trips out to the Polo Club, on Friday I set of for Jacksonville in my rented car.

It was an easy drive, three hundred and fifty miles up the Atlantic coast of Florida. I took my time, stopped for an awesome plate of seafood near Daytona Beach, and thought about my conversations with Abdel back in Amsterdam.

When I arrived at the Jacksonville Inn, I found a note from Abdel to tell me he'd see me at five.

At least, I thought, one always knew where one stood with Abdel. Perhaps it was his scientific mind, but even when I had fagged for him at Harrow he'd been excessively pedantic.

It came as no surprise when, at exactly 5pm, there was a knock on my door and Abdel walked in. He shook me warmly by the hand and invited me to help myself to a drink from the bar. I was mixing myself a much-needed vodkatini........ '

'Hugo!'

From the semi-darkness on the edge of my terrace, Annie's firm, warning voice cut across my narrative. 'We all know you have an amazing capacity for total recall, especially about your drinking habits, but it's after midnight.' She glanced apologetically at Joe Johnson. 'It may be Sunday tomorrow, but we've still got a full day's work. And I have to be up at six.'

Joe swigged down the last of his whisky. 'I'm sorry, Annie, it's our fault, encouraging him. But Hugo just tell us quickly what happened.'

'I'm not much good at précis, I'm afraid, but to cut a long and fascinating story short, Abdel told me he was absolutely determined to see Madame's honour and reputation restored. More recently, he's been hinting that she's not as well as she always used to be and that's made him even more eager to please her. But the point was, although Madame already had a small but highly successful private stud, and several horses in training here, Abdel wanted to set up a much larger, completely vertical breeding, training and racing operation with the sole aim of winning the English Derby for his mother. He said he was prepared to commit whatever it took and he wanted me to be overall manager of the whole operation - on a whacking great salary, exes and bonuses. When I told him that to achieve what he wanted, he might be looking at anything - as much as twenty-five million - he said that was fine, as long as he got good value.'

'Good Lord!' Joe exclaimed. 'Twenty-five million! It seems an absolutely crazy sum to spend!'

'Maybe, but there it is. Like a lot of gay men, Abdel adores his mother more than anything else. The most important thing in the world to him, besides his work, is to see her happy and proud again.' I grinned. 'I have to say, it's suited me very well and, you never know, it might even show a profit.'

As I watched the Johnsons going up to bed, I felt confident that my PR initiative was working, and the version I'd given Joe of my relationship with the al Hassans would circulate effectively and soon become common currency in the racing world. And, of course, although most of what I had said was perfectly true, it was only the extraordinary things which I hadn't said that really mattered.

If it could be avoided, I didn't like giving horses fast work on a Sunday; it made them sweaty and a lot of extra work for the lads cleaning them down.

But we had other priorities the morning after our dinner at The Fox & Feasant. We needed to know more about the true strength of Mountain's quality in order to set the right amount of work for him over the next four weeks.

After breakfast, we went out to work him against Rocky Spa over the first eight furlongs of the long grass gallop.

Annie mounted up and put Ulrike on the four year old miler. She told her to go a good gallop to the five furlong marker, then kick on.

They started off up the gallop looking comfortable and balanced. Rocky Spa was a proven star over a mile and no slouch over shorter distances. He came up the gallop a good lick, with Annie just cantering behind him.

But by the time they hit the sixth furlong pole, Annie was beside them. A hundred yards on she was three lengths clear, and she hadn't moved on him.

I was throbbing with glee as I started up to them. Our Derby horse had beaten a colt which had won five times at seven and eight furlongs, and by the time I'd cantered to the end of the gallop, Mountain was hardly blowing and almost dry.

I was thrilled to see how well he had coped with the ground. I'd still been harbouring faint worries that he might only go on the top. Annie told me he'd never been going more than three-quarter speed.

But we would really see what he was made off when we galloped him against High Sierra the following week. If he could beat High Sierra the way he'd just beaten Rocky Spa, he would go on to win the Derby by a dozen lengths!

Annie thanked Ulrike for her part in the highly successful work session and sent her on ahead to the yard.

She and I rode back more slowly and talked, both trying to control our excitement.

'That went a hell of a lot better than I thought it would,' she said.

'It's looking good,' I agreed. 'But even with all the advantages we have, we can't afford for him to go out at anything less than his peak.'

'We've got nearly a month,' She nodded, confident now. 'I don't see why we shouldn't have him dead right on the day.'

'You're doing a grand job,' I said, evidently too patronising.

'Why, thank you, Sir Hugo,' she said with pantomime grovelling.

'Piss off, Lady Tenbury.'

CHAPTER EIGHT

When all the lads had knocked off for the morning, and Annie had gone back to her cottage to shower and change, I lingered in the yard. I couldn't stop myself going back to have another look at our star who had worked so well that morning.

I let myself into his box. He looked round from the hay-rack where he was picking at his lunch. 'Hello, Boy,' I murmured. His ears, eyes and nose confirmed that he'd recognised me and he carried on eating unperturbed, displaying a valuable calmness he had inherited from both his parents.

Even after four years, I found it remarkable that he had developed like any other thoroughbred colt - that the very singular manner of his conception had not in any palpable way affected his growth or - just as important - his psychological development.

He was, in fact, a surprisingly quiet colt, and didn't object at all when I lifted the sweat rug draped across his back and felt his flanks. They were completely dry. I whipped off the string rug to reveal his dark bay coat gleaming with health.

Standing back, watching him, admiring him, I marvelled at how much thought, energy, commitment and cash, as well as scientific skill had gone into producing this animal and his identical, younger twin in France.

The sound of a thrush confidently tootling his territorial air in the absence of the lads and their clatter heightened my sense of being here alone with the outrageous, ambitious plans and hopes which Annie, Abdel and I had so meticulously conceived and nursed over the past five years.

I could vividly recall the bizarre, implausible conversations I'd held with Abdel over the few weeks following Adare's humiliation after he'd won at Royal Ascot seven years before, as well as our surreal breakfast meeting that Sunday morning in the Amstel Hotel, when he'd first hinted at getting his own, sweet revenge on the English racing establishment who, he considered, had insulted his mother beyond forgiveness.

Sitting in the stable at Square Barrow, I was looking at the real, living result of the crazy, theoretical conversations Abdel and I had held over those three days at Jacksonville - a perfect four year old clone of Private State, who himself had been one of the best horses in Europe in the 1980s.

Inside my house which was feeling mercifully less full since the departure of the Johnsons early that morning, I opened a bottle of my bargain champagne and called Annie up to celebrate our four year old's brilliant gallop. I even offered to cook a supreme small rib of Hereford for us.

In return, Annie agreed to do evening stables, so that I could treat myself to a bottle of claret and a lazy afternoon in front of the television.

I was nodding off after lunch when a tap on the window startled me back to life.

I looked up and saw a face – a big, doe-eyed, model sort of face, surrounded by a mass of shiny blonde hair and a naive, less subtle version of Annie – gazing at me through the glass. I felt that the face was familiar, but it was only when I'd got up and opened my front door that I realised I was looking at Calista Carter-Rice.

Instinctively, I found myself glancing down at Dairyman's Cottage.

'It's okay, Hugo, Annie's not in. I just tried. I think she must be out walking the dog or something.' Calista spoke with a soft, easy California accent which I'd always found rather sexy in the same uncomplicated way as miniskirts and false eyelashes.

I tried to look puzzled. 'I don't mind if Annie's in or out.'

'Can I come in and wait, till she gets back, then?'

'Of course,' I said blithely, and opened the door wider.

Once I'd settled her in my drawing-room with a glass of champagne, I found it hard to strike a balance between the habit of a lifetime that demanded I treat all good-looking women as possible sexual partners - especially if they already had been - and the certainty that, somehow, any repetition of our last encounter would create problems.

'It's real good to see you again,' she said. 'When Jack and I came to England, I was sure we'd run into each other, specially when I heard you and Annie were working together. It's so great!'

'She only told me a couple of days ago that you'd moved near here. I gather you've taken Stanton Park?'

'That's right. It was Annie's idea, and it's so beautiful. Jack's real happy, like a little boy, messing around with the armour and stuff.'

'We must see more of you,' I suggested.

'But no so much as last time?' Her eyes glittered wickedly.

'Not with a husband so close.' I shook my head.

'Listen, Hugo. What we had that time in The Pierre, that was fantastic - a real great one-nighter, but I wouldn't do it again; Annie's my greatest friend.'

'But Annie and I aren't an item,' I heard myself say.

'I don't know about that, but I do know she'd be real sore if she knew I'd been with you.'

I shrugged doubtfully, suddenly finding myself in unfamiliar territory, and steered the conversation to trivial gossip while I wondered why Annie would be 'real sore'. Perhaps Calista, though a friend, was also one of her few rivals; perhaps that was why she was a friend; I'd always found women's relationships with one another rather confusing. But, whatever the score, I made very sure to avoid any obvious flirting with Calista and although it had been a pleasure to see her, at six o'clock I excused myself with a few non-existent chores and watched her drive away, still puzzled by what she'd said about Annie.

With the excitement of Sunday's gallop, as well as anticipation of my date with Laura at the Club Rooms on Tuesday, oddly spiced by Calista's visit, the next day dragged horribly.

We worked most of the fit horses in the morning, and in the afternoon I went into Marlborough to stock up on drink, the Johnsons having made a serious dent in my stock of good stuff. When I got back, Annie was standing in the yard waiting for me, obviously uneasy.

I stopped the Land Rover next to her and turned off its rattling motor.

'What's the matter with you?'

'We just had a call,' she said enigmatically, and seemed reluctant to expand.

'One of the drawbacks of being connected to the telephone network,' I prompted.

'Shut up, Hugo. I'll tell you about it inside.' She nodded at one of the lads who'd sauntered back into the yard when he shouldn't have been there. 'What do you want, Sean?'

'I... I'm sure I left a cigarette somewhere.'

'Still alight?' I thundered.

The Irish lad winced. 'Y...Yes, Sir Hugo.'

'There's a half-smoked fag behind your left ear.'

'Jesus!' The lad made a grab for it, inspected it, and evidently decided it must be his missing smoke.

'And if I ever see you lighting another one in this yard,' I growled. 'I'll kick you so fucking hard across the Irish sea, your toes won't even get wet!'

'Jesus, I'm sorry, Sir H.'

I nodded at him and watched him slink away, shaking my head. The last thing I wanted was our precious colt to be cooked before he'd won the Derby for us.

'Right,' I turned to Annie. 'Let's retire to Tarrington Towers and you can tell me what's troubling your pretty little head.'

'So, help me! Hugo, if you give me any more of that crap, I'll sneak in one night when you're lying in bed snoring off one of your drunken stupors and cut off your *cojones*.'

I opened the door to my temporary home and ushered her in. 'All right, all right. Stop fussing. What's the trouble?'

'This guy called, from the Department for Environment and Rural stuff. He says he's coming to blood test some of the horses, Wednesday, at eleven - if that's okay - he said.'

'Which horses, and why?'

'God, I don't know! I didn't ask...'

'No, I don't suppose you did, being a woman...'

'My God, Hugo! When I come to cut off your balls, I'm going to do it with dagging shears.'

'What the hell are dagging shears,' I asked, intrigued.

131

'They're for cutting the shitty bits of wool off a sheep's backside,' Annie said through gritted teeth.

'Make sure you wash them first, then,' I answered primly, picking up the phone. As it happened, I didn't like the sound of the promised visit either, but I tried to make light of it. 'Don't worry about the Defra geezer; I'm sure it's a just routine thing.'

'I don't think it's routine at all. What are you doing?'

'Finding out what's going on.'

I got through to the office of our transport agent, Henry Teacher. His secretary Lucy answered and said he wasn't there; I guessed he was out getting drunk, or screwing one of his travelling girl grooms, but when I told Lucy about the Defra man, she dismissed it with a laugh. 'They normally come after importation and test the colts for ASI. Don't worry about them; they shouldn't give you any problems. I'll ring them to find out which ones they're doing and fax you tomorrow, okay?'

When I put the phone down, I turned to Annie with a grin. 'False alarm. The girl in Henry's office says they often test a few colts from a batch that's just come in. She'll let us know which ones. Then we can make whatever arrangements we need.'

When we'd finished morning stables the next day, I went back into my house and stood under the shower for ten minutes to calm myself. When I was confident that every trace of horse shit had been washed off my person, I donned a dodgy-looking Italian suit which Annie had made me buy and which, Privately, I fancied broadened my appeal.

Bet Your Rocks Off

I took out the small Mercedes we'd hired for the season and drove up the M4 to London.

I was heading for my club - the most absurdly elite club in Britain - known for the last couple of centuries as the Club Rooms, or now, just the Club.

It was a miracle of survival that would have startled Darwin that this unique and anachronistic institution had lasted into the late twentieth century. Its ethos and purpose were so politically incorrect, it was almost incredible that it hadn't been torn apart, brick by brick, by Women's Lib, Gay Lib and the Commissioners for Racial Equality.

It had been founded over two hundred years ago by a maverick third Marquess of Dover.

The third marquess was rich enough to hold any outrageously eccentric or self-indulgent views he chose. He particularly disliked seeing any of his younger brothers, of whom he had six, and all of whom were members of the smart clubs of the time - Boodles, Bucks, Whites and the Bachelors'.

He believed in the divine right of kings and the aristocracy to rule, so, naturally, he regarded members of the House of Commons as rabble-rousers.

The Marquess had lived in a large house overlooking Birdcage Walk, five minutes walk from the Lords, Buckingham Palace, Carlton House and Downing Street. He found going to the clubs in St James's irritating as he invariably ran into one of his brothers or some other MP who had upset him, so he solved the problem simply by turning his own London house into a club.

Peter Burden

It was founded with the minimum of discussion, and an almost non-existent rule-book, which was still its greatest attraction.

And because there were so few rules, no-one ever abused them.

When he died, the Lord Dover left his huge fortune in trust to support the Club, to the fury of his next eldest brother and heir, who had been left with a cavernous country house and not enough capital to run it.

By excluding guests from the two main rooms - on the ground floor was a splendid library, on the first a magnificent dining room, both with sweeping views over Green Park - the number of people actually going there was limited and even during the mad rush for scandal by the tabloids in the latter end of the twentieth century, it had managed to attract little attention from them. In the years before, it been helped by the fact that all the press barons - Northcliffe, Beaverbrook, Rothermere and Astor - were members themselves.

The floors over the two main rooms were divided into sets of chambers for members who wanted to stay there. Each comprised a small sitting room overlooking the park, a bedroom and a private bathroom. Even now, the charge for one of these chambers was still a risible £3 a night.

Despite having run at a loss for over two centuries, the club was still immensely rich as most of the past presidents had been reasonably astute investors of its endowment fund and two had been positive financial geniuses. It therefore paid its staff extravagantly, and served some of the best food in London.

Bet Your Rocks Off

I liked the place for several reasons - the unquestioning archaic arrogance reflected in its founding struck a rare chord within me, but one of its chief advantages, apart from economics, was a discretion which allowed guests to visit members in the private chambers - though they had to use the Garden entrance.

This had once been known as the Tradesman's entrance, but that had caused some well-bred female eyebrows to arch, and a past president had arranged to hide the rubbish bins behind a screen, hang up some baskets of flowers and put a pair of bay trees in pots by the steps. Conveniently, the path which led to the Garden entrance also led to a number of perfectly respectable other buildings, which meant that a lady could be seen going towards it by her less adventurous acquaintances without fear of gossip, and over the years a great many women had come and gone through the Garden Door.

I drove up to the front entrance of the Club Rooms at half-past four and a steward leaped down and took the Mercedes round to a car-park. I went into the library and ordered tea.

The chief steward found me. 'My Lord, Sir Hugo, will you be dining in the Upper Room or in your chambers?'

All the club servants addressed every member as 'My Lord', followed by his title, whether he was a Duke or a mere baronet like me.

'I'll be dining in my room tonight,' I told the steward. 'And there'll be two of us.'

'Very good, m'lord, Sir Hugo. Can I recommend the gulls' eggs? Or the chef has made a very nice grouse terrine, and afterwards you could have a cold lobster salad, hot steak and claret pie or grilled calves' liver.'

I didn't want the Club servants, discreet as they were, dashing in and out of my rooms while I was busy with Lady Allerthorpe. 'I think we'll have gulls' eggs, lobster and some cheese.'

The chief steward took his cue. 'Very good, m'lord, Sir Hugo, and wine?'

'We'll have a bottle of champagne to start - a Bollinger RD '82. Can you recommend a Chablis with the gulls' eggs?'

'I always think most Chablis are a little sharp for gulls' eggs. Perhaps a white Rioja, the Marques de Meriota 1987....?'

'Yes, let's have a bottle of that; and what about the lobster and the cheese, Mr Steward?'

'May I suggest a Pouilly-Fuisse? We have a fine Daniel Barraud '95 which members find cuts into the richness of the lobster.'

'Very well, I'll leave that with you.'

'Yes, m'lord Sir Hugo, and what time would you like the food and drink to be ready in your chambers?'

'About eight fifteen, thank you.'

'It's a pleasure, m'lord.'

'It will be, Mr Steward; it will be.'

'I'm sure it will. Your lordship's always had very good taste in these things.'

Bet Your Rocks Off

I spent the rest of the afternoon reading the papers in the sauna bath which an enlightened management had recently installed, and came out refreshed and fighting fit for the evening's encounter.

At half past eight, Laura walked into the sitting room of my temporary chambers.

'Hello,' I said eyeing her with approval. 'You're looking expensive.'

'Feeling it, too. Is that a bottle of champagne poking its little knob from that bucket?'

'Have a glass.' I poured one for her and topped up my own.

'I like this place,' Laura said with unusual enthusiasm. 'Tradesman's entrance, back stairs, champagne - I feel like a nineteenth century harlot.'

'Well, you'd pass as a very high class twentieth century call girl from Madame Claude's.'

'Madame Claude?'

'One of the great French Madames - going strong from the fifties to the eighties.'

'I suppose you were a client.'

'God, no! Far too expensive for me; anyway, I never had to pay when there were always enthusiastic amateurs like you about. Why are you all tarted up like that?'

'I went shopping in Beauchamp Place - bought this from Jennifer James - I thought it would do for Epsom or Ascot.'

'Jennifer?' I laughed. 'She was around when I was at TCD; she was one of the enthusiastic amateurs, I can tell you! I read in some gossip column that she'd moved in a crimper twenty years younger then her.'

'A bender, I expect.'

'He might be a touch camp, but I can assure you, with Jennifer he won't be a poof and he'd need a largish cock to keep her happy.'

'I know how she feels,' Laura said, taking off her jacket to reveal pert breasts in a skimpy silk bra. 'I went to Janet Reger as well - got some new undies - what do you think?'

'Come here and I'll test them for accessibility.'

'I knew my tits half falling out of a bra would get you frothing.'

I reached an arm round her waist and drew her to me.

'Hang on, Sir Hugo.'

'Oh, come, Lady Allerthorpe.' I unbuttoned my fly. 'The May pole beckons.'

'You can wave that thing around as much as you like,' Laura said, delivering a gentle smack on my rigid cock. 'I'll think of something to do with it later, but right now I'm starving. I was far too busy spending Toby's money to stop for lunch. Give me some more champagne and let's have dinner.'

Reluctantly, I tucked away my disappointed member. 'This is new - spending loads of money and staying the night away from home.'

'Yeah, good, isn't it. Things have got better since Toby stopped being a minister and got back into the City.'

'Yes,' I nodded. 'I hear he's rowed himself into the thick end of half a mill a year. But doesn't he mind who you sleep with?'

'I don't know; I've never asked. He gets it when he needs it, which isn't often. He'd never want a divorce; he's very fond of Nethercote and he likes people to think he's old money and although he went to Eton, his father was a grammar school boy from Sheffield who made a pile in the war. Toby's so pathetic, he's still embarrassed about it.'

We sat at the small, intimate table and started to make short work of the gulls' eggs and lobster.

'Did your father leave you all the furniture and everything at Nethercote, then?'

Laura nodded. 'He certainly did.'

'No wonder Toby puts up with you; but why do you put up with him? I mean - I never understood why you ever married the dreary old bastard.'

'There was fuck all in the bank when Dad died. I had to flog half the pictures on the wall just to pay death duties.'

'And Toby came up with the money?'

'Yeah,' she nodded. 'He's no trouble, and he looks the part, you must admit. Besides, he's the front bench spokesman on Agriculture and if the Tories get back in the next six or seven years, he'll be in the Cabinet. I think I'd like being the wife of a Cabinet minister - that'd turn you boys on.'

'You don't need anything else to turn us boys on.'

'Maybe not now,' Laura said with a practical approach to her sexual needs, which I had to admire. 'But there's no harm in planning for the future.'

'But what on earth made you marry Toby in the first place? He must be twenty years older than you.'

Laura shrugged. 'I didn't fancy marrying some young tit of a cavalry officer, like my father wanted. When Toby came on the scene, I was feeling vulnerable; he was a friend of my uncle's, making a pile of money in the City and I fancied being the trophy wife of a rich MP.'

'Didn't your parents mind?'

'They were both dead by then.'

'What happened to you mother?'

'When I was twenty-five, living in Florence and pretending to work as an art restorer, she was driving out to see me and got killed in a horrible pile-up on the AutoRoute in France. I thought of selling everything and moving to Italy for good. I'd had a few good lovers there. But I was back in England, sorting things out when Toby came on the scene. I suppose he was the father figure I needed at the time and for the first three or four years of our marriage he was a passable screw.'

'But what are you going to do for sex now?'

Laura helped herself to another hunk of lobster and grinned. 'Well, this has been an interesting conversation. It must be the first time we've ever talked about anything since I raped you when I was eighteen - not that you minded! What am I going to do about sex? I'm certainly not going without! I thought I could rely on you and your old totem pole - at least until you go back to the States.'

I tried not to nod too vigorously.

'As long,' she went, 'as you let me in on any of those little gambles I think you've got coming up.'

'You're proposing that you let me fuck you, and in return I let you know when I'm going to let a horse off, like we did at York last year?'

'Mm,' she nodded. 'That seems fair to me.'

'My God! What's happened to romance? Where?' I added, practically.

'I can come over to Avebury.'

'Oh no you can't. I don't flaunt women in front of Annie, and she doesn't flaunt her men in front of me.'

'I don't think she likes me.'

'That's because she's never fucked you. Anyway, why should she like you? You're not very nice. But she understands. She saw you at Barbury point-to-point, in fact she pointed you out and said 'Lady Allerthorpe's just arrived. You'd better get round there and get stuck in; she'll keep you quiet for the rest of the summer.''

'I think she still fancies you.'

'Can you blame her?'

Laura laughed, in a nice way, and put her hand on my thigh. 'I do believe this lobster's made me feel rather horny.'

Later, we were lying back in the fine Georgian bed with which the room was furnished.

Laura had lost none of her enthusiasm, though her approach was a little less slap-dash than it had been as a teenager. And the fact that I still didn't like her particularly as a person, didn't at all affect her qualities as a fucking partner.

I was thinking how wise and pragmatic I was about these things when she interrupted my thoughts.

'Should I have a bet on your Derby horse yet?'

I laughed. 'No, he's only about 25-1; you'll probably get that on the day and a lot could go wrong before then.'

'Why do you think his price won't shorten?'

'For a lot of reasons. For one, he's not having a race before the Derby; for another, Annie's a virtually unknown trainer, and no woman has ever trained a Derby winner. But you'll come to Epsom, won't you, and put a big bet on the Tote for me, like you did at York?'

'Just try and keep me away.'

CHAPTER NINE

The next day, I left the Club at seven and drove back to Wiltshire. I asked the stewards not to go near my rooms until after ten, by when Laura said she would have left - not that she cared if anyone saw her.

It was another of those iron-grey mornings whose existence I'd forgotten while I'd been working in the States. In Florida, either the sun was shining brilliantly, or Hurricane Percy was blowing up your arse all day; but we never got any of these miserable, dour relentlessly grey days that England can produce even in summer.

I arrived at Square Barrow after breakfast to be greeted by a tight-lipped Annie.

'I thought we'd agreed,' she said through gritted teeth like a contralto John Wayne, 'you were going to stay off the booze, and start in early every day. I've already done first lot.'

'And I bet it went better without me,' I said breezily.

'Yeah, it did; and I hope it hurts.'

'You hope what hurts,' I asked, wide-eyed and innocent.

'Whichever of your organs you've been abusing.'

'My liver's okay.'

'I don't want to hear about it. If you want to watch this lot, you'd better get up on Barnaby.'

'What are you going to do?'

'I'm riding Mountain and Ray's taking High Sierra.'

To back them up, Liam was on Iceland Hawk, a good four year old who had won a Group Three sprint and Ulrike was on Spanish Partridge, who'd shown promise as a handicap sprinter the previous season.

Barnaby River's lad produced him, while I slipped on some chaps and creakily heaved my leg over, trying not wince at the undeniable soreness in my overworked groin.

But when our Derby colt worked well over five furlongs of the all-weather track, making a very creditable showing against the sprinters, I felt it had all been worthwhile.

After the last lot, I was glad to get inside and have a decent cup of coffee.

I was just nodding off in front of the Racing Channel replays from the day before when I was jerked back into life by a hideous clamouring of the electric bell at the door.

A man in a nasty, cheap tweed jacket was standing at the door, holding a black plastic brief-case.

'Good morning. Mr Tarrington?'

'I'm Hugo Tarrington,' I nodded, aware that some people had difficulties with titles.

Bet Your Rocks Off

He pulled a card from his wallet and handed it to me. This informed me that he was Kenneth Walters, BSc, from the *Department for Environment, Food and Rural Affairs.*

'I've come to take blood samples from some of the horses that have been imported to these stables.'

An hour later, the Defra man had just finished and was standing in the office when the phone rang. As he was talking to Annie, I picked it up.

'Square Barrow.'

'Hugo?'

I'd have known the husky French vowels anywhere. 'Hello, Madame,' I answered, pleasantly surprised. She had never rung me at the yard before; one somehow couldn't imagine her leafing through a book for the number. 'Where are you?'

'In Geneva. But Hugo, I am going to Le Mesnil to see the yearlings. I shall be there tomorrow evening.'

Abdel and I had decided that it would not be a good idea if his mother became too familiar with either of our versions of Private Mountain. She was not in any way party to the scheme, and would have been profoundly disapproving of anything that smacked of cheating. 'I'll come over and meet you there,' I said quickly.

'That would be very charming of you, Hugo, as always.'

I guessed she was the only woman in the world who thought me charming, but I'd always found it easy and naturally to behave properly with her. 'I look forward to it,' I said. Besides, I wasn't sure I could rely on Harding to handle any problems that might arise.

We chatted a little before she rang off. As soon as I'd put the phone down, I picked it up again to dial the office at the stud, on the edge of a small village near Pont l'Eveque.

"Allo?' Corporal Harding answered in an attempt at a French accent.

'Hello, Harding,' I said.

'Morning, Sir Hugo.'

'All well?'

'Fine and Dandy, Sir H, apart from the beer's terrible round here.'

'Maybe you should try the cider sometime,' I said, glad of the cue he'd unwittingly fed me.

'I will, Sir H. Was there anything in particular you needed to know.'

'No,' I said breezily. 'Just checking.'

While I'd been speaking to Harding, Annie had finished her discussion with the Defra man and was already walking across the yard with him to his car.

I could see through the window, even at fifty yards, that she had the man eating out of her hand. When he had driven off with a shy, somewhat overawed wave, Annie came back to my house.

'What did he say?' I asked.

'No problems,' she shrugged simply. 'You were right,' she added almost accusingly.

'Sorry,' I laughed. 'Let's hope they don't bother us again.'

'Who were you talking to?'

'Madame and Corporal Harding. I'm going to have to go to France for a few days while she's there, to deal with any suspicions she might develop.'

'But can't your Corporal Harding deal with it?'

'No, not if it gets awkward. That's not part of his job.'

'I guess you're right. I'll just have to manage without you for a couple of days. How are you getting there?'

'I'll get a private plane from Bristol to Deauville. I'm sure Abdel will understand.'

'If you're still here tomorrow morning, I want you to watch our boy work again and tell me what you think.'

I nodded, glad that she still, apparently, valued my opinion. 'I'll fix to leave about midday. Madame won't be there until the evening anyway.'

I rang the bar in Le Mesnil at seven that evening, and asked for the Englishman.

'Hallo,' he said.

'Madame's coming to look at the yearlings. I don't want her to inspect your special pupil too closely.'

'It shouldn't be hard to put her off, should it, Sir...' He stopped himself, just in time, from using my name. 'Not if you point out he's got a very contagious disease.'

'No,' I agreed. 'I'll see you tomorrow.' I put the phone down before he could say anything else to identify us. Whatever he thought, I was still convinced that someone, somewhere was listening to every word I said over the phone.

Annie had particularly asked me to watch the gallops next morning because Mountain was going to work properly for the first time over a mile.

At this stage in his training, there could still be disappointments.

It wasn't a bad morning, and I tacked up Barnaby River myself with a profound sense of excitement.

Annie put Ulrike on a maiden four year old called Dome Climb and Liam on Rocky Spa. As usual, she rode Mountain herself while and Ray got up on High Sierra. When they were all at the bottom of the gallop, Mountain and High Sierra jumped off seven lengths behind the other two. For the first six furlongs they held their position.

But by the time they reached me where I was standing at the seven furlong pole, I had the thrill of seeing them all flash past me together in a cluster. Breathing a contented sigh, I watched the horses pull up and trot back towards me with their riders standing in the stirrups.

'How did he look?' Annie called breathlessly as she trotted up.

I smiled. 'As if you didn't know. But we mustn't get complacent,' I added.

'He felt fantastic,' Annie said, facing me now. 'This was the first time I've felt a real surge of power from him - you know - that awesome acceleration you get only once in a while.'

'Yeah, I know,' I nodded happily. I still could hardly believe this magnificent horse with his massive hidden advantage was truly here in our yard. 'Make sure you look after the bugger while I'm away.'

She ignored that, which I deserved. 'What did you think of Dome Climb?'

I'd hardly given the other horses a thought. 'He looked pretty good.'

'I told you he was useful,' Annie crowed. 'Did you see? He lay up the whole way with Rocky Spa and he's a good horse; he's sure as hell going to win a few races for us this season.'

'Oh yeah?' I said, still doubtful. 'What distance do you think he wants?'

'On today's work, a mile; and he'll be ready to run next week. He's a light-winded animal and all he'll need is four or five sharp furlongs a couple of days before he runs. So, when shall we run him?'

'If you really think he's within 21lbs of Rocky Spa, I'll find a little handicap for him. At least he'll be way down the ratings and we could have a little gamble.'

'No, no we won't have a little gamble; he deserves a <u>proper</u> bet!'

'Don't make me laugh, Annie. Only an idiot would back that wishy-washy chestnut. What are you going to do, have a tenner each way on the Tote?'

Ulrike, the only other female on the team, evidently felt she had to chip in to show solidarity. 'I think Annie's right. He's a fantastic little horse - easy as good as Rocky Spa.'

'Listen, Hugo,' Annie said, 'I'm not talking about tenners on the Tote. I'm talking about a proper bet with the bookies. He'll definitely win if you find the right race.'

'Fine,' I said, giving in to the combined passion of the two women. 'I'll find him a Grade E handicap somewhere next week, over a mile. I suppose at that level he must have half a chance and start at tens or twenties. Personally, I don't think he'll win - he isn't good enough. But I don't think he's bad enough to not be in the first three, either.'

'That's very big of you,' Annie said.

I laughed. 'Okay, I've said I believe you. Now while I think of it, how do you think High Sierra's going?'

Annie didn't answer at once, she reined in and let the others get further in front and beyond hearing. 'He'd have done better with a more co-operative rider.'

'What are you talking about? Ray's a bloody good rider.'

She shrugged a doubtful shoulder. 'D'you know, there's something about that guy; he just gives no more than he has to, and then he acts like he's doing you a favour.'

'Well, I'm not surprised. He was a pretty good apprentice once; rode plenty of winners and did well in Germany for a year or two. Now he's just riding work; obviously it's a bit of a come-down.'

'Sure,' Annie agreed. 'But <u>why</u> did he come down? I mean - what went wrong for him?'

'I don't know; it just went sour, I suppose, and I imagine he got fed up with living in Germany. Perhaps he thought he could do better back here.'

A couple of hours later, sitting about in Bristol Airport while I waited to be driven out to the private plane I'd booked, I found a couple of suitable races for Dome Climb the following week. There was a Class E, all age handicap at Bath on Tuesday 20th and an exactly similar race the following day at Leicester, both over a mile. I rang Annie and asked her where she would prefer him to run.

'Let's take him to Bath; it's nearer.'

I told her to leave a note for Pat, telling her to enter him for the Bath race. 'And there's a one and a half mile maiden there the same day; we'll put Polo Stick in it, for a bit of fun.'

I enjoyed the flight in the Cessna - a four-seater, which felt, to me, just about right for one.

There were no hassles with customs on the other side and a rented Citroen was waiting for me; within ten minutes of landing, I was driving through dense oak forest towards Pont l'Eveque.

The Haras du Mesnil was a few miles further into the small, bosomy hills of Calvados. The Haras consisted of a group of steeply gabled, timber-framed buildings clustered beside a beautiful, big old stone manor house.

I drove up the long drive between wrought-iron railings and an avenue of limes, surrounded by parkland of ancient pasture. I parked behind a stable block of brick and timber and walked round to enter by an arched gate.

The yard, half shaded from the afternoon sun by a pair of magnificent copper beeches, was a place of almost incomparable charm and tranquillity. I stood in the covered gateway for a moment, savouring the quality of the place.

All of the boxes were empty. The yearlings I had sent over from Luton and the handful of old, barren mares who were the only permanent residents now would be out grazing somewhere on the fifty acres of ancient pasture that surrounded the house.

I found Henri, the stud groom, a small Gascon with bad skin and shifty eyes, dozing in the tack-room. He blinked and shuffled to attention when he recognised me.

'B'jour, milord.'

'Have you seen Harding?' I asked in French.

'He's up with his precious invalids,' the groom leered scornfully.

I couldn't blame Harding. He wouldn't want to sit around playing whatever evil card game this dodgy little man tried to make him play. I made a mental note to take a closer look at Henri, and walked back to the car to drive to the isolation unit.

The buildings we had commandeered for this were half a mile away in a sylvan clearing on the far edge of a thick belt of trees, well out of sight of the house and any nosy visitors. When I'd reported to

Madame what we were doing, I had told her that we were including facilities to keep any quarantined horses ticking over, so they didn't get completely out of condition. But although I was prepared to justify them, if necessary, I hadn't specifically mentioned that we'd installed a horse-walker and a lunging ring, which she would have considered odd in an isolation yard.

I parked behind the timber clad barn that held the boxes and got out of the car. Here, surrounded by tall conifers, no sound from the outside world intruded. The odd chirrup of goldcrests among the thistled margins and, faintly, the clump of an unshod hoof on the cobbled floor of the barn.

I walked round to the front of the building and peered through the high double doors into a dark interior.

'Cor blimey, Sir. You give me quite a fright. I didn't know you was coming so soon.'

I turned to find Harding standing in the door way of his little bed-sit, tucked in a corner of the barn, with a television flickering silently in the gloom.

'Hello, Corporal, what's to report on the colt?'

'He's in very good shape, Sir H. I've had him on the walker and in the lunging ring every day. He'll definitely look racing fit by D-Day.'

'Let's have a look at him then.'

Corporal Harding turned on the lights and led me across the barn to the furthest box. He kicked up the latch and let me in.

There in the far corner of the twenty by twenty stable stood a handsome, bright-eyed colt, dark bay with a pair of long white socks on his hind legs. He was gleaming with condition and, apart from the slightly thinner mane and tail, utterly indistinguishable from the animal we'd been preparing for the Derby at Square Barrow.

I left twenty minutes later, confident that Harding was doing his job as well as it could have been done, and drove to the house. I parked the Citroen outside the front door and Madame's butler, a solemn Milanese called Mario appeared, like a genie. He carried my case from the car up to the room that had been assigned to me by Madame.

The sun was shining more obliquely now, gilding the leaves of the parkland oaks, which were beginning to throw long shadows across the dark green pasture.

I thought how wonderful it would be to spend most of one's days in surroundings like these, and I sympathised with Madame's frustration that the French tax authorities allowed her to live here only ninety days a year.

Madame al Hassan arrived as I stepped out of the shower. My room overlooked the large gravel forecourt of the house, and I watched her Phantom VI sweep up to the front door. I guessed she'd been driven in it straight from Orly.

It was a little before seven. I'd been told that dinner would be served at nine, and two more guests were expected. I wondered what Madame had up her sleeve. She didn't like to waste an opportunity to create new liaisons, or introduce fresh blood into her already vast circle of acquaintance.

I stayed watching as the chauffeur climbed from his seat and smartly swept open the back door of the Rolls Royce. Madame stepped down, accepting a slight support to her elbow from the driver. But when she was out, she stood straight and walked with careful, unhurried steps towards the front door, which, I guessed, had already been opened by the butler.

I walked away from the window and carried on dressing. Although Madame was notoriously formal, she was too European in her attitudes to insist on black ties for dinner. I got into a plain, double-breasted suit of dark grey flannel, with a vibrant and frankly unsuitable Dior tie which Madame had given me last time she'd seen me.

As I brushed my hair, I checked in the mirror for grey flecks above the temples and was startled to see signs of imminent invasion. I made a mental note to check out some subtle masking agent; discretion, I felt, was the better part of vanity.

I thought it unlikely that Madame would put in an appearance much before dinner, so when I had dressed, I went downstairs to find myself a glass or two of champagne before the other guests arrived.

Madame's salon was one of the most beautiful rooms in which I had ever taken my preprandial drink. It was furnished in the less showy, more elegant style of the French mid-nineteenth century, enhanced by some eighteenth century English furniture, and heightened by a collection of fine sporting paintings from all over Europe.

Three full-length windows offered a wondrous view of half a dozen yearlings grazing the lush parkland and moving with naturally languid strides through the lowering rays of the summer sun. It was a sight that could not have been improved upon and I stood and drank it up like a glass of fine old claret, admiring it with ungrudging acceptance of its perfection.

I had rung the bell-pull by the fireplace when I'd first arrived in the room. After a few minutes, Mario appeared.

'*Qu'est-ce-que vous voulez, Sieur 'Ugo?*' he rolled the 'r' of 'Sieur' with a pleasing haughtiness.

I asked him for some champagne. When he'd gone to get it, I sat down to leaf my way through the current Racing Review, which I'd found lying on a Pembroke table behind one of the sofas.

Before the champagne arrived, I heard the front door-bell - an agreeably archaic contraption - tinkling in the distance, and shortly afterwards, the salon's double doors were flung open and the butler ushered in two women.

As I stood up, my first reaction was to wonder what on earth Madame was up to, arranging a dinner party with three females and myself. I concluded that, from her, this should have been considered flattering. She obviously thought I was up to the challenge. But when I took a closer look at her other guests, it crossed my mind for a moment that she might have overfaced me.

Bet Your Rocks Off

Before either had spoken a word, I knew they were both French. They both projected that almost imperceptible, certainly indefinable air of superiority which was more than mere affirmation of their obvious attractiveness.

And almost at the same moment, I found myself wondering if, out of sheer mischief, Madame had decided to pitch me against a pair of lesbians.

I refused to admit this as a stumbling block to my instant fascination. I held out a hand and greeted them in particularly bad French, which experience had told me was usually considered attractive. I was intrigued to know if it would work in these unfamiliar circumstances.

But above all, I avoided any suggestion, or hint of body language that might imply that I found them interesting sexually.

When they asked with weary politeness why I was there, I explained that I looked after Madame's racehorses. They claimed to have no knowledge of or interest in racing.

In reply to my reciprocal question, they said they were both in the movie business. I asked them if they would be in Cannes the following week for the Film Festival. Lisette, the darker, more lustrous of the two, was appearing in one of the French entries. Mikie, lighter and more ethereal, had an unspecified involvement in a screenplay.

After that, by restricting my conversation to them, and their interests and listening carefully to what they said, I made some headway, at least on a purely social level.

But at the back of my mind, I kept wondering why Madame had selected this mix for her dinner party. I soon gathered that Lisette was the daughter of the Vicomte de Beaumont who owned a neighbouring stud, so there was an obvious connection there. But it would be most unusual for Madame, who was on the whole a traditionalist, to be entertaining two lesbians.

I thought, perhaps, I'd read the signs wrong, and they weren't, though everything about their manner with each other suggested it, along with the apparently total lack of interest in myself.

Nevertheless, they were both good-looking, with that combative assertiveness which I now expected and had learned to enjoy in intelligent women, though this was obviously preferably when there was a chance it could be followed up with some old-fashioned and discriminatory activity.

By the time Madame al Hassan came into the room, we were getting on fine, discussing the state of English films, about which I knew little but could bluff convincingly. As it happened, I'd once been on intimate terms with an English actress who had gone on to become quite big in Hollywood; I still saw her now and again so I was familiar with the jargon and terms of reference.

As soon as Madame came in, I leaned down and kissed her on each cheek and, as always, her particular scent reminded me of the first time I'd met her in Abdel's room at Harrow.

She reached up and stroked my jaw with a slender hand. 'Hugo, darling. Thank you for coming.'

Bet Your Rocks Off

She smiled charmingly at us all. I offered her champagne, but she declined. This, with her appearance, made me aware that she had aged worryingly fast over the few months since I had seen her last.

Mario appeared with a jug of lime flower cordial for Madame, and another bottle of champagne. Despite the evidence of her greater age, though, Madame was in sparkling form. If she was aware of anything odd about her two female guests, or disapproved, she gave no sign whatsoever.

'Lisette, darling, I'm so glad you've met my favourite young man at last.' She turned to me. 'I've already warned her what a wicked man you are, though I'm sure she can look after herself,' she added. 'Did you know, Hugo, Lisette used to ride my best ponies for me when she was just a little girl? She was one of the finest young riders in all Calvados.'

I was frankly amazed by this piece of information. It was almost impossible to reconcile with the cool, sophisticated Parisienne actress that Lisette now was. And she had made absolutely no mention of a childhood fondness or talent for riding when the subject of horses had come up earlier.

Lisette saw my surprise, and for the first time I caught a flicker of humour in her dark eyes and a tantalising upturn of her lips. She had given me no hint, either, that Madame had told her anything about me.

Madame was addressing Lisette now. 'Hugo has a weakness for equestrian ladies,' she said. 'He persuaded Abdel and myself to employ Lady Tenbury to train our horses. Lady Tenbury used to ride horses for you, didn't she Hugo?'

'Of course,' I said with a grin. Madame could certainly not have forgotten the wonderful party she had thrown in this very house after Annapurna won at Deauville, eighteen years before. 'She was a brilliant jockey. Still is, as a matter of fact.'

Both younger women raised their eyebrows just enough to let me notice. With the hint of a yawn, Lisette asked Madame, 'Jeanne, does Hugo have some star horses to run for you?'

'He tells me so,' Madame said with a gracious smile in my direction. 'We have Private Mountain entered in the English Derby. The colt ran well as a two year old, but we never saw him run at three.'

Her slightly confusing use of tenses had me instantly on edge. Ever since the scam had started, I had been worried that her natural shrewdness would lead her to deduce what we were doing on her behalf.

But she gave the words no particular significance, and glanced at me. 'Abdel tells me you are planning to have a public gallop with him in two weeks. Do you think I should come and watch?'

'Madame, I should conserve all your enthusiasm for the race itself. The way we do these things can appear a little discouraging.'

Madame raised an eyebrow. 'This is very *en*couraging.' A faint smile played on her thin, lightly made-up lips. 'It sounds to me, Hugo, as if you are planning to have a large bet on my horse.'

I smiled back with a small bow. 'I think he has a chance of winning, madame.'

CHAPTER TEN

Dinner, as always when Madame was hostess, was a gastronomic *tour de force*. Conversationally, it was less exceptional. I did my best to sparkle in a way that would be acceptable to the two strange young women, but I was getting a response that was unfamiliar - not necessarily aggressive, but aloof in a way I found disconcerting. There were moments when I felt that, for all her straightforward combativeness, I would much rather have been with Annie than these self-absorbed beauties.

Madame seemed not to notice anything amiss, though, and held forth on several political and arts-related topics with her usual grasp of events, and a good smattering of inside knowledge of the personalities involved.

During the course of dinner, I had mentioned that the only exercise I took besides riding, was playing tennis, but it was only as the girls were climbing into a convertible Alfa to drive home, that Lisette reacted to the comment.

'Sieur 'Ugo,' she said, with a trace of sarcasm on the 'Sieur', 'If you would like to come and play tennis with us tomorrow morning, we would give you a delicious lunch.'

'Mam'selle,' I said, 'I would play tennis with you in return for a cheese sandwich.'

Next morning, I woke dead on eight o'clock - seven in England - and ready to get up. I went down to a breakfast as comprehensive as anyone could have wished. But there was no sign of Madame. She usually took coffee and toast in her room and would appear, fully prepared for the day, around mid-morning.

After I'd had more than enough to eat, I walked down to the stables where I found Madame's Gascon stud groom sitting in the tack room, surrounded by leather head-collars, saddle soap and Brasso, doing nothing.

'B'jour, milord. I trust you had a pleasant dinner last night.' There was an insubordinate sparkle in his eyes. He had obviously spotted Madame's other guests.

I had no intention of explaining, though I'd have enjoyed disappointing him by telling him I thought they were a couple of lesbians. 'Dinner was fine, thank you.'

He obviously wanted to hear more, but I wasn't offering.

'Will Madame al Hassan be coming down today?' he asked.

'Without a doubt, Henri, so get on with your spitting and polishing.'

I left him to it and, feeling a little pressure on the waistband after last night's dinner, briskly walked the half mile to the isolation yard. I had another look at Private Mountain and expressed my satisfaction to Corporal Harding.

'I'm glad you're pleased with him, sir. He's looking first rate, isn't he? And it wouldn't take nothing to get him fit and running again.'

'Well, all he has to do is *look* as though he's fit and ready to run - even though he is beautifully bred and, I admit, it's rather a shame not to be racing him. I must say, when he ran as a two year old last year, I did think he might have been good enough to go out and win the Derby anyway.'

'Why didn't you choose to run him then, sir, and save all this hassle, if you thought he'd probably win.'

'I didn't say "probably", and anyway, "probably" isn't good enough. We want the odds stacked much more heavily than that. Even if I did think we could win with a three year old of his class, by using the four year old, we shorten the odds immeasurably in our favour, and we can be pretty well certain of being placed if we've got him at least ninety-five percent fit.'

'And how's he been getting on?'

'Very well over the last couple of weeks. Another advantage of his being a four year old is that he can take a lot more work than his younger twin would stand.'

I was perfectly relaxed discussing Mountain's performance with Harding as I'd decided right at the start that it would be sensible to tell the ex-corporal exactly what was going on. The more he knew, the better he was aware of what he was preparing his charge for. And I didn't think, if it ever came to it, that he would crack under questioning by Jockey Club security or the CID any more than I would.

I stayed and chatted with him for a while about the other horses in the yard at home and their likely prospects, but the conversation always seemed to revert to Mountain and his preparation for our coup.

I left him cheerfully committed to a few more weeks solitary sojourn with the younger Mountain, dreaming, no doubt, of what he was going to do with his share of the proceeds.

I arrived back at the house to find Madame somewhat creakily descending the front steps, helped by Mario.

'Hugo, cheri,' she said. 'I thought I would like to look at my young horses. Will you show them to me?'

'Of course, Madame.' I took over from Mario, who disappeared like a ghost back into the house, and led Madame to the nearest of the paddocks where a group of yearlings grazed.

She leaned against me and the fence, and gazed happily at the young horses. She knew the pedigree of each of them, back through three or four generations, and proudly recognised distinct family characteristics in some of them, which was more than most bloodstock agents could have done.

We crossed the broad velvet-soft lawn in front of the house to a point where we could see half a dozen more horses, and once again she expressed her delight with them.

When she felt she had seen enough, she turned to me. 'Hugo, shall we go up to your quarantine stables to see the animals there?'

'Of course we can, Madame,' I said leading her towards my car, 'but it may be a little unwise as they have ring-worm; it's one of the few diseases that can be passed from horses to humans.'

'Is that so?' Madame stopped walking and looked concerned.

'It certainly is. I caught it from one of my ponies when I was just sixteen and went back to Harrow with it. It was rather nasty and I was sent to the san. Mind you, there were compensations. A lovely young matron looked after me very well.'

Madame interrupted with an arched eyebrow. 'I don't think I want to hear any more about that, Hugo.'

'I was only going to say that she introduced me to the delights of fellatio.'

'Hugo!' Madame almost stamped her foot. 'You are so bad to tell these things to an old lady.'

I grinned at her. I knew she didn't really mind. I didn't doubt there'd been a time when she'd been a dab hand at the act herself.

'Anyway, do you want to risk it?'

'No, I think at the moment that would be a bad idea. Please take me back to the house. Are you going to Beaumont later to play games with my neighbour's daughter?'

'A little tennis, madame.'

'And you will take lunch there?'

'If you have no other plans for me.'

'No. I have no other plans, and I like Lisette very much.'

'What about her friend?' I probed.

Madame didn't answer directly. 'Those two young women make quite a formidable pair,' she said.

The Chateau de Beaumont was six miles from the Haras du Mesnil. In the full bloom of a Norman May, I enjoyed the drive through the small, rounded hills and orchards that reminded me of the English countryside of Herefordshire. I was also relishing the uncertain reception that awaited me.

The Vicomte de Beaumont's chateau was considered one of the most elegant chateaux in Normandy. It sat on a perfect site, south-facing with its back to a slight, wooded rise. There was still a small formal parterre kept up in front, between the house and a lake, where half a dozen fountains played.

The vicomte had the advantage, unlike many surviving French aristos, of having had pragmatic ancestors who'd seen no shame in marrying into a bourgeois family of substantial Lille industrialists, hence his daughter's practical approach to her career, and the fine condition of his chateau.

The sight of the grand house basking in the early summer sunshine was in itself a supreme joy, and as I made my way slowly up the long drive, I could almost forget that I was there to play tennis with a pair of lesbians who had made it fairly obvious that they considered me an irrelevant and old-fashioned chauvinist. I hadn't worked out why they had asked me, unless it was because they got a kick out of teasing me, but they had been quite right in thinking I wouldn't resist the challenge.

Bet Your Rocks Off

I parked the Citroen on a large, empty sweep of immaculate gravel in front of the house. I walked up six wide, shallow steps to an open front door, carrying a sports bag Mario had produced for me and tugged an old brass bell-pull beside it.

After a while, a small dark maid appeared. I told her who I was and she ushered me into a small salon at the front of the house. It was full of ancient, unrestored furniture, a few gloomy landscapes and the wonderful, musky smell of old pot-pourri.

Lisette looked completely out of place a few minutes later when she walked into the room in a tennis skirt that made no attempt to cover her frilly white pants, and a skimpy ribbed top.

'Hello, Hugo. You came?' she asked as if she weren't expecting me.

'I always come, in the end.'

Her eyes met mine with a tantalising flicker of reaction.

'You can change by the pool, if you want. It's beside the court.'

'Thanks.' I picked up my bag and followed her through the house to the back and, by less formal gardens, to where the tennis court and a swimming pool had been cut into the shelter of the bank, entirely screened from the house by a tall evergreen hedge.

The pavilion between them looked like a recent addition - a small, circular Doric temple flanked by a cluster of burgeoning cypresses.

Lisette waved me into it and I selected one of a series of spacious changing rooms. Once I had stripped off, I found that Lisette's lovely legs, combined with the heat of the sun which had been roasting me as I walked across the garden, had produced a hefty erection which made it difficult to do up my tennis shorts.

When I came out, there was still a tell-tale bulge, but I thought it would be just too bad if the sight of it alarmed the women.

As it turned out, there was still no sign of Lisette's companion. But Lisette gave me a faint smile and I saw her glance at my legs and groin as I walked from the temple onto the elegant terrace in front.

'Where's Mikie?' I asked. 'I thought she was coming too.'

'She always does...' Lisette said, grinning now. '...in the end.'

I couldn't pretend, though I knew she was playing with me, that the thought of Mikie coming, in the end, heated me up and I instantly stiffened again.

Lisette was standing with her long brown legs slightly apart, toting her racket. 'You and I can play a few games first, okay?'

'Sure,' I said.

We walked onto the court and knocked up for a while with two dozen brand new balls. It was a fine clay surface and played very slow. Lisette was hitting the balls with a lot of power, and I soon realised that she was very fit and well-muscled.

As I made a reasonable account of myself, bantering with her in the normal way, although avoiding any obvious sexual innuendo, I reflected on how playing hard, fast tennis was just what you might expect from a pair of lesbians. There were enough of them in the professional game - Billie-Jean and Martina, for a start.

Bet Your Rocks Off

We started to play a set, and still Mikie didn't show up. After three quarters of an hour's hard tennis, I finally broke my athletic opponent's service and scraped a six-four victory.

'Good playing, Hugo,' Lisette said, in English. 'Maybe you deserve a rest. Take a sauna when I go to find Mikie, okay.'

That suited me. Frankly if the other girl had turned up now wanting a game, I'd have had to disappoint her. Besides, the sauna in the temple was up and running and just what I needed.

After ten steaming minutes, I came out, found a pair of trunks in the changing room and plunged into the pool for a quick cooling off. I emerged to find that others had been busy.

Mikie and Lisette were sitting side by side under a parasol at a table which had been laid in front of the changing temple. A summer lunch of exquisite salads, charcuterie and seafood was waiting on a side table, and two bottles of Chablis nestled in a tub of ice.

The food and wine were every bit as good as they promised, but I was disappointed and faintly alarmed to find that I had lost all interest in trying to impress these enigmatic women. And suddenly, of course, their little smiles became broader and more frequent, though I didn't doubt that they would have dried up the moment I showed real signs of responding. The whole game was becoming a bore, and I longed for Annie's dry, challenging but comprehensible parries.

After lunch, when I stood up and announced that I was going, I was gratified to see a flicker of disappointment cross their faces, but I knew they wouldn't acknowledge it openly.

I changed in the temple and came back out to find them both lying naked on sunbeds with their eyes tight shut against the hot afternoon sun. I looked, but I didn't stop.

'Come again,' Lisette called as I walked through the gap in the high hedge.

I crossed the gardens to the house, which seemed to be fast asleep in the hot afternoon sun. It was deliciously cool in the dark and grandly silent interior as I strolled through to the front door and let myself out onto the open square of gravel where I'd left my car.

I drove into the park at Le Mesnil, admitting to myself that I was a little anxious about Madame's reaction. I wasn't even sure that, guessing the predilections of her neighbours' beautiful daughter, she hadn't set the whole thing up just to tease me. Or perhaps she had despatched me as her champion, to see if I could succeed where others had failed.

There was no doubt that there was a mischievous side to Madame's character, as well as a propensity for control. I was well aware and didn't even resent the fact that she liked to bring her influence to bear on anything that went on in the lives of her proteges - of which I was undeniably one. Besides, I also guessed from her attitude towards Annie she really didn't like her trainer at all – perhaps because, despite being both American and working-class, Annie had coped so naturally with the higher echelons of European society. And although she had undoubted respect for Annie's skill with horses, Madame would have been appalled if she thought her favourite little Hugo was still having it off with her.

I walked into Madame's house just after four and was told by Mario that she was having tea on the terrace outside the salon and she would like me to join her.

As I approached, she looked up and smiled with all her usual charm, but when she spoke her voice was thinner and reedier than usual. 'Ah, Hugo. You look as though you have had an energetic game of tennis.'

'Yes,' I said. 'I had a splendid set with Lisette. She's a very good player.'

'But you won?'

I shrugged humbly. 'As a matter of fact I did, Madame.'

She looked at me for a moment through her crystal blue eyes, as if she were about to ask more but changed her mind. 'Sit and have some tea,' she said, fingering an English silver pot.

'I hope you're pleased with the yearlings, Madame,' I said, sitting opposite her.

'I'm very happy with them, thank you. And do you have anything new to report about our horses in England?'

'Well, Madame, several of them are working well. Two are running at Bath next Tuesday.'

'Oh, good. I wish I would be there to see our first runners of the season. But to tell you the truth, I'm not feeling absolutely one hundred percent.'

'I'm sorry to hear it. Is there anything I can do for you?'

'No, no,' she said quickly, loathing the idea of sympathy.

'I think, anyway, that I should fly back to England this evening. There's so much to do at Square Barrow.'

'Can't your Lady Tenbury cope without you?'

'Of course she can, Madame, but it would be unfair to leave everything to her; we're both being paid to do the job, after all.'

Madame smiled. 'All right. I won't fuss. But you do know how I like to see you.'

CHAPTER ELEVEN

I woke at Square Barrow the next morning feeling ambiguous about being back in the routine of a racing yard after my French sortie.

After lunch, I slipped down to Beckhampton to collect Jimmy Collins who had phoned at breakfast time to say he was coming over from Hungerford by bus to look at our yard.

I found him outside the Waggon and Horses. On the way back, we passed an immense Victorian redbrick house and stables, which interested him.

'Is that the Beckhampton Yard, then?'

'That's right.'

'Who's there now - Mr Charlton?'

'Yes. Before him it was Jeremy Tree, and before that Noel Murless for a year or two, though he didn't like it and moved to Newmarket. And for years before Murless, Fred Darling was there.'

'Looks a nice place.'

'Lovely, wonderful gallops, but wait till you see our place; in some ways it's just as good - even better.'

When we reached the yard, with Jimmy muttering guarded approval of his first impressions, I made him a mug of tea and we sat outside, talking and watching the lads do the horses.

Annie saw us and came over.

'You must be the Scotsman,' she said with a warm smile and a charm she didn't often show when she was working.

'I was just telling Jimmy how lovely it is having only fourteen horses. You see, Jimmy, my job is just to oversee things, which means I can sit here drinking tea during evening stables and watch Annie and the lads doing all the work.'

Annie turned to Jimmy. 'Was he always an idle, arrogant little shit?'

'Yes, m'lady. But he's not as bad as he makes out. I remember when we got him from that posh school for his summer holidays and he was still a kid, we used to work him to the bone.'

'I see,' Annie said, pretending to be unconvinced. 'Well, it was nice to meet you, Jimmy, but I've got to go and see what the lads are up to.'

She gave a flirty little wave which evoked an appreciative smile from the Scotsman, who turned to me. 'Ah,' he sighed. 'I do remember her. So, how are things going, Sir H?'

'We've got our first runners next week at Bath - nothing great but we seem to have three useful two year olds. They should all win something before the Derby.'

'And Private Mountain?'

'He worked brilliantly today; he galloped all over a very decent animal called Rocky Spa who was getting twenty-one pounds and a year.'

'I've told you before, you canna handicap classic horses with normal handicappers. He should have given him three or four stone and beaten him rigid.'

'Well, I was pleased.' I caught Annie's eye in the yard and called over to her. 'When will Private Mountain be coming in from his pen?'

'He's had enough already; I'm just going to fetch him.'

'Don't you do any work round here?' Jimmy growled.

'Yes. I think. At least, I try not to interfere with the horses while Annie trains them and tells the lads what to do.'

A few minutes later, Annie walked into the yard with Mountain following her on a lead like a well schooled dog. She walked over and stood with him in front of us. A knowledgeable onlooker would have found it hard to believe that a horse standing so relaxed, looking soulfully at his trainer, was meant to win the Derby three weeks later. The colt was behaving more like an old hunter.

'There he is, completely at ease and nearly a hundred percent fit. But we've got three weeks yet.'

Jimmy was eyeing the horse closely. 'That's never the horse you won with at Newmarket last autumn!'

I tried to cover up an instant panic attack. 'What on earth do you mean?' I asked.

'He can't be - he's far bigger; he's a four year old, or more.'

Fuck - I thought to myself - is it so obvious?

'Of course he isn't,' I said quickly. 'Half our two year olds look three and the three year olds look four. That's why we keep horses in the sun during the winter, like the Arabs. They always mature much faster than horses left here in England, especially in a cold winter.'

'I tell you what - you could have fooled me. To me, he certainly looks like a four year old.'

'Look here, Jimmy, feeding and diets have changed a bit since you were first a lad a hundred years ago. Go to Epsom on the 5th and half the horses there will look like four year olds, and a lot bigger than him.'

Annie had listened to all this with no sign of disquiet. 'I'll show you what a good four year old looks like,' she said. She called a lad to come and hold Green Mountain, while she went over to another box. She came back out a minute later leading High Sierra.

'Now, Jimmy, *this* is what a quality four year old looks like! He'll win a few good races before the end of the season.'

High Sierra was a large horse; he certainly made the four year old Green Mountain look younger by comparison. Jimmy nodded. He watched him closely, and was satisfied that he meant it.

Later, at six o'clock, I drove him back to Hungerford in the Bentley and dropped him at the bottom of the High Street by the Bear Hotel and told him that I had to push on to a seven o'clock meeting in Lambourn.

Bet Your Rocks Off

The truth was, I'd had enough frights for one day and I was going to slip up to the Hare and Hounds for some soothing pints of hoppy ale.

But I was careful not to have too much. Annie had asked me to drop in for a drink at Dairyman's Cottage later as she'd invited her friend Calista and her husband for dinner.

Jackson Carter-Rice took my hand like a member of a tug-o'-war team grasping the rope as he looked me long, hard and straight in the eye. But I couldn't tell if he was looking for signs of pain or guilt for philandering with his spouse, who was, I judged, younger than him by about twenty years.

He was, nevertheless, a chunky, handsome man, six feet tall, with the skin of a well-polished crocodile. Still strong, too, I thought, as my knuckles buckled and I gazed back at him blandly. But I couldn't blame him. If I'd been his age and married to Calista, I'd have been anxious to keep her to myself, too.

I tried to avoid too much eye contact with Calista, but every time it happened, I had the clear impression she wanted to lead me on. I resisted, though, and managed to talk quite civilly to her husband about Abdel al Hassan. It turned out that they had come across one another at Harvard fraternity gatherings, and Abdel had even made use of Jackson's bank a few times, though in what capacity, the banker did not say.

But Annie made a point of shooing me out fairly promptly before they ate dinner, and I wandered home gloomily, regretting that she obviously considered me too risky to entertain for long with her American friends.

But I had to admit, I didn't think I could have kept up the pretence of innocence in front of Calista for very much longer. Usefully, though, I had enrolled the Carter-Rices as additional guests for lunch on Derby Day. For purposes of window-dressing, we needed a few more people in the box besides Abdel, me, Annie and Madame.

When I woke on Sunday morning, I found that Annie, with unexpected compassion, had left a note in my kitchen suggesting that I take a lie in for a change.

She was going to school some two year olds through the starting gates - a job she liked to do without second opinions being offered in the background. She still seemed a little uptight when she came up to the house and I was brewing my first pot of coffee at half past nine.

'In three weeks we'll all be at Epsom,' she said, flopping herself into a chair. 'Are we ready for this? I gotta tell you, Hugo, I'm worried about what Jimmy said yesterday. Does Mountain really look too big for a three year old?'

'You can't tell 'em apart these days. Jimmy's an old boy and out of touch. Like I told him, these days two year olds look three, and three year olds look four and so on.'

'I hope too many people don't think the same as him, though.'

'Don't worry. Our boy isn't that tall - only just over sixteen hands - and I promise you he won't look out of place at Epsom. The favourite's a Godolphin horse and he'll look just as mature, and there are bound to be a few horses an inch or two taller. Our priority now is getting some winners on the board from this yard. We need to have had five or six wins from the stable before the big day; it'll look dodgy as hell if the Derby is our first of the season.'

'So? What are you going to do about it?'

'Don't you mean, what are *you* going to do about it?' All this negativity was annoying me. 'You're the fucking trainer!'

'Now, now, Hugo. Just because it's all getting a bit tense, doesn't mean you can start in with the language. And we mustn't fight.'

'All right.' I forced myself to calm down. 'I'll tell you what I'm going to do about it. I think all the two year olds are capable of winning if we keep them to poor races on little courses. Their class should pull them through.'

'They really need another month or so.'

'Yes, I know, but they'll have to take their chances, and I'm pretty confident the two sprinters'll win - or at least get placed. And then we've got that couple at Bath on Tuesday. In the meantime,' I said getting up and walking over to the oven, 'we have a tender limb of little lamb for lunch, roasted to perfection, though I say it myself.'

With great self-control, I restricted the Burgundy with lunch to a couple of glasses; I had reasons for wanting to stay sober for the rest of the afternoon.

At three, I drove over to see Alfie and Birgitta Templeton, where I played two hard sets of tennis without the distraction of Lisette's frilly panties.

I had earmarked Alfie as a potential ally when it came to placing the rest of my money on Derby Day, and I wanted to keep in regular touch with him and Birgitta so that it looked natural when the time came. I also sounded them out as potential lunch guests in our box. I thought that, with the Johnsons and the Carter-Rices, they would make a typical and unsuspicious party for our box.

I showered afterwards, declined a drink, and headed for Nethercote.

Toby Allerthorpe was away on a dreary golfing binge on some windswept Scottish coast. Laura had rung after lunch to say the house was empty, and she needed filling.

Nevertheless, I couldn't help thinking of Annie as I drove over to Nethercote, and this brought on a murmur of guilt. I tried to dismiss it; after all, I'd done nothing carnal with her for nearly eighteen years. I owed no allegiance to any woman; nor had I, since Emma had walked out. But sometimes, after sessions with Laura, I had felt absurdly disloyal to my beautiful colleague. There was no logic to it, and it irked me. I wished sometimes that Annie had made liaisons of her own. But she hadn't, and I knew that deep within me, I was glad.

Sometimes - like today - I caught a glimpse of something like jealousy in her when the subject of Laura had cropped up; but only a glimpse - nothing conclusive. And as I approached the grand old house that Tom Buckton had left to his daughter, and where she had chosen to live with the ludicrous old poop she'd married, I found it easy to rationalise my misgivings out of existence. I associated this place so strongly with Laura and utterly unrestrained sex that my balls started to ache as soon as I turned into the drive.

On my way back to Square Barrow a couple of hours later, I stopped to ring ex-Sgt-Major Rawlings from a call box near Swindon. Since I'd gone into business with Abdel, I'd been very careful to keep my distance from Rawlings and his Merry Men. I hadn't met him on a racecourse, or in public, or telephoned him from any of my known phones since then.

'Hello, Sergeant-major. We need to meet. Can you make the regular rendezvous, next Sunday, midday?'

This meant the car park of the Reading Service area on the west-bound side.

'No problem; I'll see you then.'

On Monday morning, Kevin Prendergast drove over from Sussex. As he was having his first ride for us at Bath the next day, I'd suggested that it might be useful.

In the last lot, Kevin rode High Sierra, and Annie, as usual, rode Mountain. Before they went, Annie turned to the jockey. 'Right, Kevin. This is where we work. What we're going to do is basically a trial gallop over ten furlongs. Go off at a good three-quarter speed and just let High Sierra gallop.'

I knew that Annie planned to sit in behind High Sierra, two or three lengths down and at the eight furlong marker, go up to him.

They waited to give me time to drive up to the eight furlong marker. I parked and got my bins out, but I couldn't see the first four furlongs of the gallop as it was on a slightly curving gradient. When they came into sight, High Sierra was swinging along very actively, with Green Mountain five lengths behind and not going with any fire.

At the six furlong pole Annie started to scrub along on her horse, while Kevin was sitting quiet as a mouse on High Sierra who seemed really to relish being in the lead. As they passed me, Kevin punched on and within a couple of strides had High Sierra flat out. Annie kicked on too and sat down to ride Mountain as hard as she could.

My stomach dropped. Instead of closing, High Sierra pulled away and was soon five lengths up. By the end of the gallop she'd clawed those lengths back, but only managed to drive her horse up to High Sierra's girth.

To say the gallop was disappointing would be an understatement; it was a total disaster. To do what was expected of him in under three weeks, he'd need to be more than ten percent better.

'Shit!' Annie gasped as I pulled up beside her. 'I'm just not fit enough to drive horses like that.'

She was wringing with sweat.

Kevin wasn't too disappointed, but then he didn't know what we'd been trying to do. By mutual tacit consent, Annie and I put on a brave face for him.

'That gallop was just about good enough to win the Derby,' I said to the jockey. His mount had carried eight seven and Mountain eight ten, as Annie had used our three pound racing saddle like Ulrike the week before on Rocky Spa. 'At level weights, Private Mountain would certainly have won by a length or two, and as he's only a three year old he would get ten pounds at this time of year - so,' I said with a levity I did not feel, 'it looks as though we're in with a bit of chance.'

It wasn't until lunch, when Kevin had gone that I could speak to Annie in private.

'What the fuck went wrong?'

'He was just sluggish,' she said. 'He's not galloping with any fire. I think it's in the mind. You can't expect a four year old who's never run in public to behave like an experienced racehorse. Frankly, right now, I very much doubt he's experienced enough to be placed in the Derby, let alone win it.'

I had to dose myself with three large armagnacs before I could sleep that night.

Never by nature a worrier, tonight I was. Of course, I was over-reacting, but so far, our plans had gone so well that a set back like our star's performance that day took on a disproportionate significance.

CHAPTER TWELVE

As I helped to load Dome Climb and Polo Stick before taking them to Bath next day, I wasn't too sanguine about their chances.

I drove the lorry myself and brought Ulrike and Liam to lead up the horses. We arrived at the hill-top course an hour before the first race, in good time. Dome Climb was entered for the second race, and Polo Stick for the fourth. The sun had been gaining strength all morning; it was beaming down almost aggressively now, and for once, there wasn't too much of a wind across the top of the hill.

I opened up the side door of the box to let some air in for the horses; I didn't want to use the stables and thereby run even the slender risk of taking a virus back to Square Barrow.

I went and declared my horses and found Kevin in the weighing room. He didn't have a ride in the first, so I was able to get him weighed out early. I went back and saddled Dome Climb in the box - always a tricky operation, but he was calm enough by the time I'd finished.

Trusting that Ulrike's natural Teutonic superiority wouldn't allow her to foul things up completely, I strolled up to the parade ring.

The first person I saw whom I knew was my cousin, the pompous and crafty old Brigadier Henry Mills.

I summoned up some warmth to greet him as cordially as I could; two years ago he had retired as the head of Jockey Club security.

'Hello, Brigadier. Are you here on business or pleasure?'

The brigadier twitched a pair of pink jowls that drooped like a bulldog's from his deep jaw. He gave the impression that at any moment he might start to drool like the dog he resembled. 'Business today. I still do a few days a week, keeping an eye on my old villains and generally helping out; of course, when I see a cousin, it becomes a pleasure.' He added with a knowing smile. 'I hear you've come here to land a double today.'

'You're joking, of course! They're very moderate horses; they couldn't keep up with Private Mountain at a canter. The fact is, Annie and I are only in England to train Private Mountain for the Derby; the al Hassans are dead keen to have a serious crack at Epsom.'

'But you've got a yard full of horses at Square Barrow, I gather.'

'Apart from the sprinters and the two year olds, the other horses in the yard are just gallop fodder for a our Derby horse - even High Sierra and he's a bloody good horse.'

'The word is that you've already had plenty on Private Mountain.'

'A little, of course,' I murmured.

'And I hear you've piled onto this one you're running here.'

'What do you mean - piled on? I haven't put a penny on him yet. What price is he?'

'Two to one - he's been backed all over the country, all day.'

'What!? He was only tens in the morning papers!' My indignation was real enough. I hadn't expected the horse to be fancied at all. I'd brought along a couple of hundred quid of Annie's and eight hundred of my own to place a monkey each way; Annie had convinced me he was at least good for a place. 'What's been going on, Brigadier?'

Henry adopted an official, serious voice. 'Even if I accept it's not your money going on, we'd like to know what's happening in your stables. We were told that Lady Tenbury said she was going to have 'a proper bet' on Dome Climb.'

'She did say that,' I said, not giving vent to my fury that this had been reported. 'But a hundred pounds would be an enormous bet for her. A tenner each way on the Tote is her usual mark.'

Brigadier Mills glanced around to make sure we weren't being overheard and gave me a chilly, no-nonsense stare. 'I have to tell you - the dogs are certainly barking that you've come here to land a gamble and a lot of them have put their money down.'

Our conversation was curtailed by the arrival of the jockeys - an explosion of colour into the centre of the ring as the group of seven small, wiry men, decked in a kaleidoscope of colours came in together and dispersed among the sober, beige and grey figures of their owners and trainers.

I had to deal with Dome Climb and his jockey on my own. I tightened the girth and legged Kevin up, telling him he should go very close. Once I'd seen him led from the ring, I went to look at the bookies below the stands. I hadn't expected Henry to be wrong, but I could hardly believe that Dome Climb was now being offered and taken as far as I could see, at seven to four.

I kept my money in my pocket and decided to stand Annie's bet myself at that price. I went up to the stands to watch the race on my own with a growing sense of uneasiness.

Kevin Prendergast did as he'd been told and calmly held up Dome Climb for the early part of the race. When the leaders started to run out of steam with a furlong and a half to run, he moved into the lead. A hundred yards from the post, Kevin must have heard the second and third favourites coming at him; he pulled his whip through from his left hand and, following Jockey Club guidelines, showed the whip to the horse - to no visible effect.

With fifty yards to go, the other two were at his knees and travelling better. He gave Dome Climb a sharp, back-handed crack across his quarters.

Up popped the little bastard's head; his stride shortened, and at the line the other horses were a neck and a half a length in front. In a seven horse race, place bets would be paid only on the first two.

'Sorry, Sir H,' Kevin mumbled as he unsaddled.

'You rode a perfect race,' I said. 'This horse is a chicken-hearted little shit; I've never liked him; he'll always let you down when the chips are down, like today.'

I felt a tap on my shoulder; I turned to find the stewards' Secretary hovering behind me. 'The stewards want to see you and your jockey as soon as he's weighed in.'

Being up in front of the stewards still made my knees tremble, like being hauled up by the head at my prep school. And even when I was innocent, which wasn't often, I was usually found guilty anyway.

While a I was waiting to pick up Kevin from the weighing-room, I glanced at my race-card to remind myself who was officiating that day. By great good fortune, the chairman was an old general of the Third Scottish Dragoon Guards, George Wilkinson.

I'd pulled him out of a mess nearly thirty years before when he'd been a major at the Royal Armoured Corps Training Centre at Bovington. I'd had to perjure myself that he'd been playing backgammon with me one night when in fact he'd been tucked up in bed with another officer's wife.

When Kevin and I found ourselves standing in front of him, I was fairly sure from the very faintest glint of guilt in his eyes, that, even now, he remembered the incident and the debt due to me.

'Good afternoon, Sir Hugo. Two simple questions,' he announced, impressively subduing his conscience. 'Can you explain the betting pattern in the last race; and were you satisfied with your jockey's performance?'

'If I may, General, I'll deal with your second question first. I thought Kevin Prendergast rode a copy-book race. I told him to lie third or fourth, take up the running after six or seven furlongs and make the best of his way home - all of which he did. When the eventual winner and second came at him, he showed Done Climb the whip - as approved by the Jockey Club - and when the horse didn't respond, he gave him a slap, when the chicken-hearted little shit put his head up and shirked the job.'

General Wilkinson nodded, and turned to Kevin. 'Mr Prendergast, what have you got to say?'

'I've got no more than what Sir Hugo said - when the other horses come at me, he didn't try no more and sorta chucked his hand in, sir.'

The general looked at his fellow stewards. 'Well gentlemen, we all saw the race. I propose that we accept the explanation of Sir Hugo and his jockey that Dome Climb is ungenuine in a tight finish.'

The other stewards nodded, and he turned to Kevin. 'All right, Mr Prendergast. You can go now.'

When he'd left, looking relieved, the general turned back to me with a silent invitation to carry on.

I took my cue. 'The betting was more of a puzzle. Dome Climb wasn't much as a two year old and had all of last year off after an injury. Frankly, we've only kept him in training because Lady Tenbury has always liked him - he's a nice horse to have around, well mannered in the stable and a pleasure to ride out; but I've always thought he was a bit soft and probably gutless, which is why I had him gelded at the end of his two year old season. And today was his first run for over five hundred and fifty days.'

'We're discussing the betting, Sir Hugo,' the general prodded me.

'All I can say about that is that he did do a couple of remarkably good gallops, and Lady Tenbury wanted a hundred pounds each way on him today, which for her is a very big bet. I came here thinking he'd be eight or ten to one, and I was going to have a bit on him myself, but he looked no value at the price they were offering on the rails and I didn't have a bet.'

'Are you seriously telling me there was no stable money on him?'

'Yes,' I nodded. 'I am.'

'What about the owners - Madame al Hassan and her son?'

'Mr al Hassan is a Muslim, he never bets; nor does Madame al Hassan.'

One of the younger stewards, keen to show his perspicacity, looked at me keenly. 'Would you mind telling us how long you've known the al Hassans?'

'I've known Abdel al Hassan since I became his fag at Harrow when I was thirteen. I met his mother then, too, and six years ago, I started working as their blood-stock manager.'

General Wilkinson turned to his younger colleague. 'I think we can accept that the al Hassans are beyond reproach,' he said testily. 'Madame al Hassan has been running horses of the highest class since even I was a boy.' He looked at me. 'But it's disturbing that there's been all this money for the horse - according to our betting intelligence officer, there was a very heavy gamble on him.'

'Of course, I was alarmed too, General. I was talking to Brigadier Mills about it in the paddock before the race. I realise that he's semi-retired, but I'd be very glad if he were to come and see me before the fourth race when our second runner goes today.'

'So I see,' Wilkinson referred to his own race-card. 'Yes, Sir Hugo; I'll arrange that for you. If you and Lady Tenbury have a horse fancied for the Derby, you've every right to be worried about the possibility of a leak from your yard.'

After a little more inconsequential talk, I thanked the stewards and exited swiftly to get back to the lorry.

Henry Mills found me in the paddock just as Ulrike was bringing Polo Stick into the ring. With him was Major Peter Coombs, the stewards' Secretary.

'I hear you're worried about what happened in the betting with your first horse today.'

'I am, Brigadier. I'm glad you found me. I was going to ask if you could bring one of your security chaps over to Square Barrow one day so that we can sort out what's going on?'

'I'm sure we can,' the brigadier said quickly, evidently glad to feel needed. 'I'll come as soon as I can. Thursday might be all right, if that would suit you?'

I couldn't think of any reason why Thursday should be a problem and said so.

'Jolly good,' the brigadier said. 'I'll ring and confirm, but could you get your office to fax me a list of all the people who have access to your stables?'

I agreed, and carried on chatting to the brigadier and Peter Coombs until Kevin arrived, touching the peak of his silk cap to them.

In the race that followed, he rode Polo Stick in a performance that was just worth noting, and scraped in third behind a couple of hottish horses from big Newmarket stables.

When we arrived back at the yard, Annie was already waiting to greet her charges with hugs and kisses.

'Well done darling' she said with her arms around Dome Climb's neck, as if he'd just won an Oscar. 'You tried very hard, didn't you, and you were only beaten by such a little bit. I hope Kevin didn't hurt you too much.'

I didn't say what I thought as she repeated this performance with Polo Stick, as if he'd won a race at Royal Ascot, not just come third in some poxy maiden at Bath.

I didn't tell her, either, about the trouble with the stewards, or that a bunch of lunatics or criminals were punting our horses like there was no tomorrow; or that we'd soon be crawling with Jockey Club security, which was why I'd pre-empted them with an invitation.

Mick O'Grady must have been suffering from his usual hangover as he cycled down from the lads' quarters at six thirty the following dawn. He'd hit a stone on the track and sailed over his handlebars - like a shag diving for mackerel in Cobh harbour, one of his colleagues told me.

His mate, Des Hughes came in screaming. 'Mick's had a terrible accident! I think he's dead!'

Bet Your Rocks Off

I ran out after him and quickly established that although Mick wasn't dead, he was unconscious and in a serious mess. He certainly needed a lot of stitches, and twenty minutes later an ambulance arrived to take him to the A&E unit in Swindon.

Dealing with the crisis wasted an hour, and it was as well that Polo Stick and Dome Climb didn't need riding out after their less than scintillating performances at Bath the previous day.

When the two year olds had been exercised, Annie got up on Mountain, with Ray on High Sierra. They did a sensible seven furlong canter up the all-weather, when they jumped down and swapped horses.

Bertie and I put them in the stalls and watched them go a really good three-quarter speed gallop up the short five furlong grass gallop. After two furlongs Annie on High Sierra was leading by three lengths, with Ray whipping in on our Derby horse.

Mountain was manifestly not setting about his work the way he should have been by now, and it took him nearly to the end of the gallop to catch High Sierra and Annie.

I shook my head in pain. If he dilly-dallied like that in the Derby, we'd do our money for sure. I wasn't quite panicking, but I came to the abrupt conclusion that if we took him with the two sprinters to Chepstow on Friday and really set them alight over five or six furlongs with jockeys up, it might just wake him up.

Before I discussed it with my trainer, though, I thought I'd better get her au fait with other intrusive elements in our lives.

After Mountain was back in his stable, and she was satisfied that everything else was under control, I made coffee for her in my kitchen.

'I didn't tell you last night, but I'm afraid we must have someone with a few dodgy connections in the yard.'

'What!?'

I nodded. 'For some reason, a bunch of heavy punters got it into their heads that we were expecting to win yesterday, and they punted Dome Climb very heavily. When the little bastard you love so much didn't finish properly, I was hauled up in front of the stewards as your representative.'

'What didn't he do?'

'I tried to tell you last night. When Kevin asked him the question a hundred yards out, he just stuck his nose in the air and refused to try any more.'

'How hard did Kevin hit him?'

'A single, short back-hander. Hardly disturbed his coat.'

Annie was too much of a professional to let her own prejudices cloud her judgement. She sighed. 'Okay. What did the stewards want?'

'They were happy with my explanation that Kevin was trying and the horse is inclined to be ungenuine. Fortunately, I had the sympathetic ear of an ex-general I once helped out of the shit a few years ago.'

'My God! The insidious old-boy network strikes again.'

'In our favour,' I reminded her. 'And fortunately they believed me when I told them that you, me and the al Hassans hadn't had any money on the race ourselves - on our own horse or any other.'

'Didn't you put mine on then?'

Reluctantly, I pulled her two hundred from my pocket and handed it over. 'The price was so bad, I thought I'd take it myself.'

'Then have it,' she said shoving the money back at me. 'If he'd won, I'd still have wanted SP.'

I took it back; I'd made my gesture. 'I told them how worried I was about these people punting our horses, and the fact that they'd specifically heard you were going to have a bet on Dome Climb yourself, and so I've invited Jockey Club security to come here tomorrow to help track down the problem.'

'You've done what?!' Annie gaped. 'With what we're trying to do here?'

'They'd have come anyway. It made sense to pre-empt them, as if we had nothing to hide. Besides, there's nothing for them to see that won't be on public display on Derby day.'

Annie nodded slowly. 'I guess so. And it'll give us a chance to practise our acting.'

When she'd gone, I rang Chepstow race-course. The Secretary there was only too glad to let our Derby prospect have a proper gallop out of the stalls next Friday.

Meanwhile Annie had insisted on going into Swindon with Des to see the injured Mick. When she got there, Mick had just come out of theatre and was unconscious, so she hung about waiting for him to come round. I ended up doing evening stables with only two helpers. I didn't mind feeding the horses in the evening but I was absolutely sure that I was too old and too grand to be mucking out on a hot sweaty May afternoon.

'You look glum,' Annie said when finally she arrived back at Square Barrow.

'Are you surprised?' I answered as we walked into my house. 'I've worked six years to produce a horse to win the Derby, and today he looked just about capable of winning a seller at Pontefract with the wind up his arse; we've got a lad smashed up through no fault of ours; someone's leaking false information about the yard, and tomorrow, we'll have Jockey Club security crawling all over the place. Now give me one good reason to look happy?'

'You haven't caught an anti-social disease from Lady Allerthorpe yet?'

It was a feature of Jockey Club security advantageous to us that the senior officers were normally drawn from infantry regiments and the juniors from the police force. They were nearly all frightened of horses and I'd never seen a security man lay a finger on one. So I was confident that they wouldn't dash into Green Mountain's box and start gazing down his throat or looking up his backside.

The day they were due at Square Barrow started overcast and uninspiring, but horses had to be worked and everything carried out as normal, as much to convince the lads and work riders we had nothing to worry about as to convince Brigadier Mills and his cohorts.

I was able to take my mind off the impending visitation for long enough to watch a pair of two year olds, Mont Blanc and Hillary's Steps do a three-quarter speed gallop over two furlongs and another two furlongs at racing pace. They both went like horses that had cost at least a quarter of a million quid - which they had. I decided to find races for the two of them the following week when I'd be surprised if one or other of them didn't win.

After that, I put into action an idea I'd had to sharpen up Mountain before his trial gallop the next day. I wanted him to show more enthusiasm early on in his work.

Ulrike was on the four year old miler, Rocky Spa. Annie jumped off Mountain in front, to run seven furlongs at three-quarter speed. Ulrike took off as soon as she could after them. Within two hundred yards she had driven Rocky Spa up to Green Mountain, and the two horses completed the rest of the gallop locked together.

Annie came back looking a shade happier. 'He was kinda sluggish when we jumped off, but as soon as he heard Spa coming up to join him he leaped onto his bridle and really started to pull.' She nodded. 'He felt a lot sharper.'

'Good,' I said, glad of any sign of improvement after yesterday's disaster. 'Perhaps he's beginning to get the idea.'

But I wasn't given the opportunity to dwell on these signs. Henry Mills and his gang were due at the yard at any moment, and I still wasn't sure how I was going to play my part. As long as they didn't start looking too closely at our ringer's teeth, I didn't mind much what they did, but the disastrous day at Bath had made me uneasy. I wished I knew for sure if my cousin had been there purely by chance or if some rumour about our set up, however nebulous was already doing the rounds.

CHAPTER THIRTEEN

It occurred to me that, in my current state of mild paranoia, I was giving too much weight to the idea that ever since the stockbroker Tony Collins and a few of his chums had pulled a stroke with Gay Future at Cartmel back in the '70s, the chippier characters in racecourse security had been keeping an extra eye on the more raffish members of the racing world, and perhaps I was on their hit list.

At five minutes to twelve - the regulation army five minutes early - my cousin Brigadier Mills strode into the yard. With him was a man in his early forties, with short stiff hair and a long, grey pointed face. From the way he held himself, he could only have been an ex-copper or Customs and Excise officer.

The Brigadier held out a hand. 'Hello, Hugo. What a super yard you have here. Meet Terry Brownley, one of our top men.'

I shook Henry's hand, then Terry's.

'Pleased to meet you, Sir Hugo,' he said. He had an odd, twangy voice that seemed to be strangled at the back of his throat. 'I've heard a lot about you from Corporal Harding.'

'How do you know Corporal Harding?' I asked with a large frog in my larynx.

'Before this job, I had six years on the Royal Protection Unit and as you know Corporal Harding works for Her Majesty on and off at the Royal Mews and down at Windsor for Royal Ascot with the coach horses. I met him in the canteens and around the NCO's mess. He's some character, isn't he - he told some amusing stories about you, sir.'

'Were you ever in the Brigade?'

'Yes, sir. Five years in the Welsh Guards, but my wife didn't like it, so I joined the Met, did my sixteen and got my pension; now I'm four years into my Jockey Club pension!'

I tried to smile, to conceal my frenzied thoughts.

Jesus! A friend of Corporal Harding's was all I needed!

God alone knew what Harding had told him about my colourful past. He'd probably search my house for 'sending on medicine' and expect to find a Siamese tart under every bed.

'Well gentlemen, what can I do?' I offered with as much urbanity as I could muster. 'Lady Tenbury's out with the third lot but she'll be back within the next half hour.'

Despite the Brigadier's obvious superiority, Brownley assumed control. 'First I'd like to ask a few general questions,' he said crisply.

I led them into my house, and quite naturally to the hub of activity in my kitchen, overlooking the yard.

Henry Mills made himself comfortable in the large elm chair to which I'd waved him. 'I'll let Terry ask the questions,' he said with an avuncular nod. 'I'm just a retired old buffer along for the ride, really.'

Retired old buffer, my left bollock - I thought. He might have been retired but he was still a ruthless old bugger who wouldn't hesitate to put his dear Cousin Hugo inside if he discovered what I was up to.

The Brigadier had got an MC with the Glorious Gloucesters in Korea. He would have had a VC if there had been a few senior officers to see his actions in the face of the enemy - which I considered to have been the behaviour of a lunatic, but by the standards of British military etiquette was considered outstandingly brave!

He had retired unexpectedly young and allegedly spent the next sixteen years as a spook in MI6 - definitely not the type of person one wanted investigating nefarious deeds. He was made even more dangerous by his deceptive charming and mild manners - the sort of bastard who could stroll round to the Army and Navy Club in St James's Square and spend his time sipping his third pink gin while contemplating whether to use a red hot poker or an electric probe up some poor bastard's anus before dispatching him, wrapped in garden netting with weights, to the bottom of the sea.

Now he sat back, with his eyelids flickering down as Terry droned on. 'I read the transcript of the Stewards' enquiry into Dome Climb's race on Tuesday at Bath. There are just one or two things I'd like to clear up.'

I nodded and tried to look helpful.

'Were the al Hassans the owners of Adare when there was that trouble about him being disqualified at Royal Ascot?'

'Yes,' I answered, sounding puzzled by the apparent irrelevance of his question. 'That must have been six or seven years ago.'

'What effect did it have on them, Sir Hugo?'

'I think poor Madame al Hassan was absolutely shattered; she aged overnight, I remember. It's very hard to tell what effect it had on Abdel. He's something of an enigma, even to me, and I've known him for over thirty-five years.'

'I see,' Terry said, scribbling laboriously in his little note book. 'Can you tell us exactly what your job is and who trains the horses?'

'As you know, Lady Tenbury holds the training licence and is responsible for all the horses that are actually in training. I'm the al Hassan's bloodstock manager and in overall charge of all their racing and breeding. I report to Abdel al Hassan, and get my orders from him. '

'How many horses have you got?'

'Here we've got fourteen including a hack and a couple of lead horses. There are another fourteen or fifteen in France and about thirty back at base in Florida.'

'So you would regard Florida as your headquarters, as it were?'

'Of course. We've got quite a sizeable set-up there. A stud farm of just over two hundred acres which I run, and next to it, a private training set-up of sixty acres or so which Lady Tenbury runs under my general control.'

'What happens here?'

'We come over every summer as the al Hassan horses are bred principally to run on turf in Europe and we race here from May through to September. We've been fairly successful, as you probably know. In our first season we won fourteen races and last year we won seventeen, including a Group One at York and two Group Threes, as well as a Group Two and a couple of listed races with Private Mountain, whom we strongly fancy for the Derby. And that, I believe, is why you're here.'

Terry nodded vaguely. 'What staff do you have here?'

'We run the American system - with three work riders and four stable lads, though one was messing about on his bike yesterday and smashed himself up. He's in hospital so we're down to three. Their job is solely to look after the horses - four lads can easily look after eighteen or twenty horses.'

The Brigadier blinked open his eyes and herrumphed mildly. 'Isn't there a Jockey Club rule that no one lad should care for more than four?'

'Not that I've heard of,' I replied. 'but anyway it wouldn't apply to us because ours don't ride out. In the States we often have lads looking after six or seven horses each.'

Terry noisily flipped over a page of his note-book. 'So you've got four stable staff - where do they live?'

'There was a redundant barn up at the farm which we've done up for the lads - about six hundred yards up that track.' I pointed up the hill.

Terry screwed up his face like a dog with a bone. 'What precisely is the set up here?'

'What do you mean?'

'Who owns this place, and how big is it?'

'The estate was bought by the al Hassans four years ago and it is around six hundred acres.'

'All right, but who actually owns it, and how is it financed?'

'I've no idea exactly who owns it - whether it's Madame al Hassan or her son or a partnership or a family trust. I'm not privy to their finances and I'm disinclined to ask impertinent questions of my employers or go snooping behind their backs.'

Henry Mills evidently also felt that his man wasn't taking the right line. 'Terry, you read the report from Tuesday; the al Hassans are a very well known Franco-Saudi racing family and like General Wilkinson said, beyond reproach. They've got huge business interests around the world and I think you can assume that if the al Hassans wanted ten set-ups like this they could afford it.' He looked at me. 'Isn't that so, Hugo?'

'Yes indeed, Brigadier. Money's never been a problem although everything is very correctly run by lawyers and accountants. In fact, the accountants come down every Friday when we're here to pay the staff and sort out the bills with Pat, our Secretary.'

Bet Your Rocks Off

As I spoke, I'd watched Annie arrive; now she pushed open the kitchen door, came in and beamed at the two visitors.

We all stood up. 'This,' I said, with some pride, 'is my colleague, Lady Tenbury. Brigadier Mills; Mr Brownley.'

'Welcome to Square Barrow,' she said. 'Is there anything I can do to help you now? Unfortunately I've got to go into Swindon soon to visit one of our lads who was badly hurt yesterday.'

'No, thank you,' the brigadier said. 'I think we can manage without you.'

Once Annie had gone, leaving a trace of Madame Rochas in the air, Terry Brownley sat down again, grim-faced. 'Sir Hugo,' he said, 'do you bring any of your staff over from America?'

'No, not any more.'

'Why is that?'

'Firstly, all the American stable lads are Hispanics and they don't settle very well. And besides, all the best ones are family men and we don't have the accommodation here for families, so we decided last year to recruit short-term European staff.'

'Doesn't that pose something of a security risk?'

'Just because they're temporary doesn't mean they're casual labour. We pay top rates and give them four weeks paid holiday at the end of the contract. They come via a good friend of mine who's a Master of Harriers in Cork and knows the horse scene there very well. He recommends local lads who've had some experience in stables and who like the idea of six months in England.'

The Brigadier leaned forward. 'Do you always have only men in the stables?'

'Yes, mostly. Annie and I both prefer them. Apart from one work-rider, we've no girls working here or in America, so all our horses are used to men, although, of course, Lady Tenbury rides work herself on several of them.'

'How does Lady Tenbury get on with the men who work for you?'

'No problem. All the staff are very respectful to her.'

'Do you ever employ anyone here for more than one season?' Terry asked.

'Generally not. If they're any good, when they move on from here they find a permanent billet.'

'So, you have home addresses, and next of kin for all these staff and your exercise staff?'

'Of course.' I handed him a list Pat had prepared earlier for me, with details of the work-riders, the four lads, our regular vets, Pat herself, and even Mrs Brockett.

Henry Mills took it and read through it while Terry Brownley droned on until I sensed that even Henry was becoming restive. At one o'clock, after sixty minutes of cross examination I decided that was enough and stood up.

'Right, gentlemen. It's time for lunch. Would you like some beer and cheese?'

Bet Your Rocks Off

'That would be fine, Hugo; thank you,' Henry said. 'I think we've asked enough questions for the time being. After lunch we'll take a look around the stables.'

I led them into the dining room where the excellent Mrs Brockett had left out some good cheese, French bread and salad, and made a mental note not to be lulled into a feeling of false security.

I'd chosen Chepstow for Mountain's first race-course gallop because it wasn't often used for this purpose by horses of note, and was therefore, uninfested by gallop watchers and other nosy, racecourse low-lifes.

I had arranged, though, for a few special friends and colleagues to attend - people who could be relied on to disseminate any reports in a way which would be constructive for our purposes.

And Laura Allerthorpe had invited herself while we'd been enjoying one of our brief post-coital chats the afternoon before.

That was one of the reasons for my tetchiness. Since I'd started 'seeing' Laura again, I'd promised myself not to tell her too much. I had an odd feeling that the more we saw each other, and the more accomplished her performances became, the less she could really be trusted.

It was in her perverse nature that if she found herself getting fond of me, in a way which would have been very unfamiliar to her, she'd work out her resentment by feeling she could gain some kind of hold over me. But as I trundled across the broad span of the Severn bridge, above the coffee brown waters of the river's estuary, I reminded myself that perhaps my harsh analysis of Laura's motives was due partly to paranoia and partly to my own defence systems kicking in.

As it happened, on the security front, I had been partially reassured by Brigadier Mills' promise that his people would keep their ears open especially for rumours emanating from Square Barrow. He and Terry Brownley had looked long and hard at all our horses the day before, and hadn't batted an eyelid at the appearance of Green, aka Private Mountain, and they had left sounding as if they hadn't a worry in the world as far as we were concerned. At the same time, I knew it would be unwise to underestimate my cousin in his official role.

As racing was due to start on the undulating Welsh course at half-past two, we'd been asked to have our gallop at two, which meant we had to have the horses in the paddock and jockeys up by one forty-five.

We unloaded the horses and took them into the paddock to give them half an hour to stretch their legs. At twenty to two I went across to the weighing room to collect the saddles. I'd told Kevin to weigh out at 8st 7lbs for Mountain. After a lot of ringing around, I'd managed to get a couple of good pilots to ride alongside Kevin on Mountain. Peter Deere, a veteran who occasionally rode for us, was to weigh out at 8st 3lbs for Iceland Hawk and I had a good apprentice who still claimed 5lbs by the name of Michael Goring to ride Spanish Partridge at 7st 10lbs.

Bet Your Rocks Off

Annie and I saddled the horses up and the jockeys came out soon after in colours. All of them had been given their instructions on the phone when we booked them.

Annie went down with the starter's assistant in a Land Rover and waited by the stalls in case the sprinters arrived at the far end in a spin. I sent Spanish Partridge down first as I was worried that the kid wouldn't be able to hold him. When he'd gone a couple of furlongs, I let Iceland Hawk go, followed two furlongs later by Mountain, telling Kevin to go half sharp and try and gee him up a bit.

I watched them go from the gate in the rails. When I turned back, I found to my consternation that I'd been joined by three pressmen, a couple of tipsters and a few punters, as well as my invited friends, Alfie and Bob. Both being keen punters, they were naturally excited about trying to get some inside information. At the last minute, most eyes suddenly swivelled back towards the stands, and I saw that Laura had kept her promise. I greeted her as platonically as I could, given all the reporters who had turned up; I knew they'd be only too glad to weave another thread of gossip into their pre-Derby coverage. But I couldn't really get rid of them, so we all walked down to the furlong pole together.

Annie and I had decided to finish the six furlong gallop there as I didn't want the horses flying into the downhill turn after the winning post, all out of control.

Once I'd reached the marker, I waved my handkerchief to Annie who organised the loading into stalls. As soon as they were in they let go and the two sprinters came out like scalded cats.

After a hundred yards, Mountain was still two lengths down, but Kevin was niggling hard at him and the other two couldn't get clean away from him.

With a furlong to run, Kevin pulled Mountain to the outside and chased after him with hands and heels. By the time he reached us he was level with the sprinters and going much better with his longer stride.

I managed to stifle the sigh of relief that tried to escape my lips. Besides, though it had looked good - more than good given the quality of the company our Derby horse was running with over that distance - I'd have to know the times before I knew just how good.

Amongst the punters watching with me was Geoffrey Scott, the professional gambler who regularly put my money on for me when it suited. I'd rung him a couple of days before and told him our plans for Private Mountain, and asked him to come over and put a clock on the gallop, which he had done.

But I didn't discuss the gallop with him then or even acknowledge his presence, on the grounds that it was safer if the bookies didn't know on whose behalf a professional was gambling.

In the evening, just after seven, he rang me at home to tell me that the time had been very fast. I asked him what that meant for the Derby.

'It's very handy Sir Hugo. If he stays, I'd say you were in with a real chance of winning. Private Mountain did the six furlongs today in sixty-two seconds dead. In the Derby they normally take sixty seven to cover the first six furlongs, admittedly uphill, where it's nearly flat at Chepstow. But if you wanted to, he could lead the field the whole way, certainly the first mile or so.'

'That's nice to know,' I said, trying to remind myself that this was only one man's opinion. 'If he's all right we gallop him over ten furlongs at Newbury next Thursday. You'll put a clock on him then for us, please?'

'Of course. Will it be before or after racing?

'Before.'

Geoff had put five grand each way on Private Mountain for me before the colt had run at York the previous year, at 66-1. He would be drawing on my behalf from the bookmakers some £400,000 if all went well, so I thought it wise to keep him sweet. 'By the way, we run Private Mountain's two year old half sister at Salisbury next Tuesday, and she must have half a chance if it's no more than an average race. You can put something on for me please if she looks good value.'

'Fine. I'll come down.'

'If you do, come and have a quick word with me as I leave the paddock and tell me what her price is. I'll let you know what I want you to put on then.'

'Do you mind if I have a bit on for myself before I see you; I won't move the market.'

'No, fine, but if I were you, I'd wait and see what I'm doing. I should have been able to find out the strength of the opposition by then. Andes Pavlova is fairly useful by the look of her, but she wouldn't beat a real hot pot from Richard Hannon or Mick Channon's yard.'

'Okay. Thanks a lot, Sir H. Nice to do business with you.'

As soon as I put the phone down, it rang again. It was Alfie Templeton.

'I thought the gallop went jolly well, didn't you Hugo?'

'Yeah, they say it was a good time, but it was only six furlongs you know.'

'Still looked good to me. I'm certainly backing him. But now, what about a few monster bookie crushers before the Derby?'

'We're running Private Mountain's half sister, Andes Pavlova at Salisbury on Tuesday. She might just about win. Do you want a lift down in the box? I'll be driving.'

'I suppose you look where you're going when you've got a few hundred grand's worth of horse flesh on board. I'll risk it - and I'll buy you lunch.'

'Not this time you won't,' I said. 'I'll be having a session with our bloodstock agent before the first race, but do bring a sandwich for yourself, and the lad if you're feeling kind.'

Saturday morning tried to depress me with a sky the colour and texture of soggy porridge. Determined to beat it, I went out soon after seven and found Annie.

'Did they all eat up?' I asked.

'Mountain and Partridge haven't quite licked out their mangers.'

'All three we galloped yesterday left quite a bit when I went round last night at ten, so I cleaned their mangers and gave them only half their usual late feed.'

'Nothing to worry about yet,' Annie said. 'It was a good gallop. Will it dry up, do you think?'

'Looks like it'll rain some more soon.'

'My God! The weather in this place stinks. Are you going to come out with me first lot to make up for it?'

When we got back with the first lot, the rain and the papers had arrived.

I went in and found a nasty little piece in *The Sporting Post* under the headline:

DERBY PROSPECT DOESN'T IMPRESS IN UNORTHODOX GALLOP.

Lady Tenbury galloped Private Mountain, her 25-1 shot for the Derby over six furlongs yesterday with two sprinters at Chepstow. Asked why she was working her horse over such a short distance she said, "I have very limited calibre horses with which to work him therefore he had to take his chance with a couple of sprinters today. Next week he'll work on a racecourse over ten furlongs with his lead horse, High Sierra.

CHAPTER FOURTEEN

Just when I was beginning to tire of our Sunday routine - gentle stables, roast lamb for lunch, a crummy old movie on the telly - Annie reminded me on Saturday evening that it was my birthday next day and invited me to celebrate it with Sunday lunch at her house.

'There's fuck all to celebrate,' I said - rather ungraciously, it occurred to me afterwards.

But before lunch, I had to keep my date with Sergeant-Major Rawlings at the Reading Motorway service area. I got there in good time and parked the hired Mercedes with its back to one of the outer fences. I didn't have long to wait before Sergeant Rawlings drove in. He saw me at once but carried on another fifty yards. He parked among a group of cars and made his way briskly into the main building. After a couple of minutes, he came out, sauntered over to my car and got in beside me.

'How's it all going, Major?'

'Not bad, thanks. Not bad at all, but time's marching on and I want you to give the boys a ring and tell them that over the next two weeks I've got three two year olds running and they ought to win. I don't want this touted to their friends, but tell them to have a few quid on.'

'That's very good of you to tip us the wink. Do you need us to come and have a crack at the books for you?'

'No, now it's so close, I don't want there to be any chance that your connection with me is even remotely suspected.'

'Why's that, Major?'

'Because if all goes well on the 5th, you'll be collecting nearly seven hundred grand for me. If anyone connects that money with me, a lot of people might start thinking they should have some of it, especially the IRS in the States.'

'So you told me, sir, and I can assure you, no-one will ever know the money we collect is for you. I never could stand the tax authorities - the sort of little shits who couldn't do National Service because they had flat feet or flatulence. What are your chances looking like now, Sir H?'

'If we can get him there spot on, he'll   be very good value.' I reached behind my seat and lifted up a bulky Tesco carrier bag and handed it to Sergeant Rawlings. 'There's ten grand in fifties in there. All being well, I want the lot to go on, half each way, on the day. If for some reason I've changed my mind, I'll ring you. You'd better jot this down; I'll say, "Just a call to let you know *I won't be able to have a drink with you at Epsom*." If I don't ring, you and the boys get along to Epsom on the big day.'

'Have you got the tickets yet, Major?'

'I've ordered five for the grandstand for you and the other boys which I'll post to you.'

'What's the exact procedure when we get there, sir? We don't want any cock-ups do we?'

'Okay. The entrance to the paddock is in the Queen's Stand, so from two o'clock, wait by the big bronze statue of Generous just behind he stand until you see me come out with the saddle, and if I don't want you to bet any more, I'll come over. This time I'll say, "Nice to see you, Sergeant-major, we must have a drink, *but I can't make it today.*" If I ignore you, which I hope I will, you know what to do. Go to war as soon as you hear the announcement that the horses are about to leave the paddock. You'll have plenty of time as they parade and then canter the whole way round to the start, which is a mile and a half.'

'I thought they walked across the centre to the start.'

'No, they haven't done that for a long time, certainly not for the last three years. Have you got everyone sorted out if everything goes well to collect the ante-post bets on Sunday and Monday?

'Yessir. Everyone's booked a holiday so they'll be available to fly about and rake in the cash. I've taken the whole of the following week off.'

I nodded. 'Good. I hope I won't have to talk to you until after the Derby, then.'

'Much though I appreciate your dulcet tones, sir, I'll be glad not to hear them, too.'

'Then best of luck, Sergeant-major.' I held out my hand, which he shook firmly, with a grim, dependable smile on his lips.

'And to you, sir.'

I was back in my house at one, but feeling hot and sticky so I ran upstairs to have a quick shower and put on a clean shirt. On my way out, I even snatched up Mrs Brockett's efforts at flower arranging in my drawing-room and wrapped a Racing Post around the soggy stalks to take with me to Dairyman's Cottage.

The front door was on the latch. I pushed it open. 'Hello,' I fluted. 'I'm here.'

'Hi, Hugo,' Annie trilled back. 'I'm in the kitchen.'

I went on in to the Mediterranean parlour she called a kitchen where, I noticed, there was now a vast and incongruous white wardrobe of a fridge - essential to the pursuit of happiness for any American.

She turned round, flushed from her efforts. I thought she looked as radiant as I'd ever seen her, especially when she stretched her neck and gave me a soft kiss on the lips. 'Flowers, Hugo? Whatever next?' She took them and arranged them in a vase of her own. ' Would you like a drink?'

'I certainly would.'

'There's a bottle of bubbly in the fridge.' She nodded at the wardrobe.

I opened one side of it and extracted a well-chilled bottle. 'Heavens, how lovely! Cristal Brut '79.'

'Yes, birthday boy, and Chateau Talbot '78 with our lunch.'

'There's no need to go over the top just for my birthday!'

'The big fifty?'

'No, no,' I protested, easing the cork off with my thumbs. 'The medium sized forty-eight, if you don't mind. Glasses, please.'

I filled the two glasses she held out. Inevitably the bubbles spilt over the tops. I took mine and watched, entranced, as Annie sucked the froth from her fingers.

'Mmm...' she murmured. 'This champagne's much better than your six pound stuff from Madame A's butler.'

'It fucking well should be, it probably cost sixty quid a bottle.'

'I hope I'll be able to afford it more often after the Derby. Mountain gave me a real good feel second time up today. But I made sure I didn't mention it to Ray, after all the hassle at Bath.'

'Maybe, though I think Ray's sound. But you're right, walls have ears, as they say.' I waved an arm meaningfully at the walls of her kitchen.

'Okay, Hugo, but don't overreact like you always do. Anyway Mountain felt great,' she nodded. 'He really should peak on the 5th if all goes well. I've been thinking....'

'Careful!'

'Listen, don't give me any of your chauvinist bullshit! There's no one to show off to here.' She wagged a finger at me. 'If we do a couple more pieces of seven furlong work on the all-weather tomorrow, a fast eight or nine on Tuesday and the final winding up gallop at Newbury on Thursday, and that goes well, the following week we'll give him another eight furlongs on the Tuesday, a sharp five on the Friday, and he should be spot on.'

'Sounds about right,' I nodded. 'But you'll have to play it by ear.'

'Yessir!' She gave me a US style salute, which I ignored. 'Now you can do something useful yourself. Could you open the port and decant it. It's a Taylor's '47 and it won't live long.'

'Christ you must have spent some money. All this smart wine!'

'I didn't have to spend much on food, though.'

She led me through to her small but undeniably stylish dining-room. 'There, you see - food fit for any product of an upper class English nursery. Smoked cod's roe, cold pheasant breast, tomato and watercress salad and baked potatoes. I thought it would make a change from lamb!'

'How right you are; I'd no idea you understood my needs so well.'

'Yah, but that doesn't mean I'm gonna cater for all of them, even if it is your birthday; so hands off!'

Next morning, I assumed I was still forty-eight, but I felt like sixty-eight.

My system simply no longer had the resources to pay easily for the pleasure of large quantities of champagne, claret and port.

But we'd had only one work rider the day before, and there was a lot of catching up to do. I stumbled to my bathroom, splashed water on my face, then looked at it in the glass and was grateful, on the whole, that Annie wasn't there to see it.

I was grateful, too, in a way I couldn't quite reconcile, that Annie hadn't allowed me to spoil things by becoming 'intimate', as they say.

The weather, at least, was a little better, and the porridge clouds had been blown off the tops of the downs, to be replaced by higher, friendlier cotton wool numbers.

Somehow, I managed to stay on Barnaby River and lead a couple of gallops, but I wasn't sorry when they were over. On the way in, I rode along with Annie fifty yards behind the other horses. My hangover seemed to have intensified my paranoia. 'Be careful what you say in my house or your own house,' I said. 'If Mills and his henchmen thought they were on to anything, they've probably bugged our homes.'

'No!' Annie gasped. 'That sweet old pussycat?'

'Sweet old mountain lion, you mean. Believe me, if they thought we were having a go at the Derby, there's nothing legal or illegal they wouldn't do and remember, if it comes unstuck, I'll be in the firing line, not you.'

'I don't mind being in the firing line. I can take my medicine like a man.'

'I don't doubt it, but there'll be no need. We've agreed what'll happen if it gets nasty. Ideally you get the first plane back to America. But if you think they're after you, are you clear about what to do?'

'I take a car to a port in Wales and go to Ireland?'

'Right - and the port's called Fishguard. Leave the car in a pub car-park and take a taxi down to the boat and then go over to Rosslare as a foot passenger. Remember to take your passport and credit cards.'

'But won't they find me easily enough in Ireland?'

'It may have escaped your notice, being an American, but Ireland is an independent state and won't worry even if Scotland Yard do know where you've gone.'

'Why do you want me out of the country if it goes wrong?'

'There's no point in your going to prison if it can be avoided, and if I'm in the dock, I get a better chance by myself.

'What do you suppose the chances are that it will go wrong?'

'Not great; basically they've got to get hold of both horses to prove anything.'

'What if they're certain the horse we've run at Epsom is a four year old?'

'Then the shit could really hit the fan, but as we'll have the three year old's papers with us, it'll be interesting. It's a million to one they will look at his mouth before the Derby - unless Mills and Co get very suspicious.

'What happens if they notice he's got a four year old mouth after the race?'

'As long as he's weighed in and the all right's been given, they'll pay out the cash bets that day. In fact I think they'd pay out all the bets, and there would be a technical objection.'

'What happens then?'

'They'd get their vets to state that it was a four year old but we'd be able to produce its papers proving it's three and it must be a miracle of nature!'

'Then what?'

'There's not much point in speculating about it now, but we'd probably be in with a chance.'

'What about Abdel? Would he be okay in the States?'

'Sure; there's absolutely no extradition from the US for US citizens, so you and Abdel would be fine.'

'But he couldn't go to France?'

'There's a chance he would be extradited from there.'

'Or Switzerland?'

'No problem. The Swiss aren't going to extradite an American citizen with large amounts of money on deposit with Swiss banks. Very fine people the Swiss - interested only in making money, not world opinion.'

'But Hugo,' she put a hand on my arm. 'I'm not sure I like the idea of leaving you to carry the can, if it goes wrong.'

'Well, it's my scam, and if it goes pear-shaped, I reckon I've got a better chance of getting off if I'm in the dock by myself. Do you understand, you must get out, the minute we know it's bombed.'

We were back at the gates to the yard now, and stopped the conversation. Somewhat sobered by all this dwelling on the downside, I watched Annie take a group of odds and sods out for the third lot. She didn't need any help from me, and besides, I thought I had better ring my solicitors and deal with a few loose ends.

Bet Your Rocks Off

I got through to Marcus Parkinson with gratifying swiftness, given his comparative eminence these days, but then, he had acted for me for over twenty years.

'Hello, Hugo. Congratulations!

'What are you talking about? The fire's next week,' I laughed.

'Don't say things like that. I saw your horse in *The Post* today.'

'I thought solicitors were meant to read *The London Gazette*, not *The Sporting Post*.'

'As many of our clients have an interest in the Turf, I find *The Post* more useful. How's Private Mountain?'

'Not bad at all.'

'I read that he did a gallop on Chepstow race-course last week.'

'Yes and we give him a real trial on Thursday at Newbury.'

'Isn't that a bit close to the big day?'

'No, nine days. That means we only have to give him one more bit of serious work between then and the Derby.'

'I'm going to the Derby with a client who's got a box; shall I tell them to back him?'

'Ring me nearer the day. If he stays sound and fit, he should still be good value with the bookies. You could borrow ten grand from your clients' account over the weekend and have a punt! But enough of spending my phone bill giving you inside information - how's the sale of the cottages going?'

'It all seems okay. We should complete tomorrow.'

'When will you pay off my ex-wife?'

'Tomorrow, as long as the other side come up with the cash. In fact Pilthers and Co put a caution on the property after we agreed terms, so I've arranged for the buyer's solicitors to bring three drafts; one for £225,000 to pay Pilthers and Co, one for £2,300 for the agents and the balance of £2,700 for us.'

'Two things, Marcus. First, will the £2,700 cover your expenses? And what about the £15,000 for fixtures and fitting?'

'I'm afraid our bill will be a bit more than £2,700 and the £15,000 for fixtures and fittings will come in a separate cheque, rather than a draft, from the buyer's solicitors.'

'Could you ring them and tell them to make it payable to your firm. Keep it in your client account, you never know when I might need you suddenly!'

'I don't like the sound of that.'

'Just joking; I mean vis-a-vis Emma.'

'Ah, fine. I'll ring you tomorrow and let you know when everything's completed.'

I put the phone down feeling satisfied: Emma dealt with in a full and final settlement, and a useful cache of money lodged with my lawyers for contingencies, and final bets.

When Liam Brennan started asking me questions as we hacked back from the gallops on a sublime May morning, I immediately became suspicious.

'Well, boss,' he asked with the familiar cockiness of a hardened work-rider. 'How do you think the filly will run this afternoon?'

My first thoughts were - is he gambling himself? Is there any record of it? Or is he simply selling information?

'Hard to tell,' I said as nonchalantly as I could. 'Our first two year old of the season. We'll just have to wait and see, won't we?'

Besides, I added to myself, I'd already tipped this bloody Andes Pavlova far too widely in my efforts to demonstrate how unsecretive we were.

Back in the yard, I got everything organised to go to Salisbury. Alfie arrived just as Annie and the second lot came in and we left the yard at half-past ten, with me driving the box and Des Hughes to lead up.

Andes Pavlova was in the third race and I had arranged to meet Mungo Castle, our bloodstock agent outside the weighing room an hour before the first race for a drink and something to eat.

Mungo was in the rumpled linen suit and shapeless Panama he always seemed to wear from May to Glorious Goodwood at the end of July.

'Hi,' he drawled, laid back as ever. 'Let's go to the Owners' and Trainers' bar and get a bottle and some smoked salmon.'

'Fine by me,' I agreed.

After we'd settled ourselves in a corner, we got down to business.

'I saw you galloped Private Mountain at Chepstow on Friday,' Mungo said. 'How did he go - really?'

'Well enough. I think it woke him up a bit.'

'I'll be down to have a look at Newbury on Thursday. Do you gallop him before or after racing?'

'Before.'

'What about the filly today? Has she got a chance?'

'What have you heard about the opposition?'

'It looks like a very ordinary race to me; I haven't heard anything much.'

I nodded. 'There don't seem to be any hot pots from what I can gather. I'll get more from Kevin in the parade ring. Come out and see what he's got to say, if you want. But the reason I needed to see you today, Mungo is to tell you I do think we've got a bloody good chance in the Derby and,' I paused, 'the al Hassans will want to cash him if we win.'

Mungo made a lop-sided, disbelieving face. 'Will they indeed?'

'What would he be worth?'

'But surely, if he wins well, wouldn't they want to keep him and run him in the Irish Derby or the Arc?'

'No. This is very confidential, Mungo. We're training him just for the Derby and if he wins, Abdel doesn't want him to run again. So, what will he be worth?'

'That would depend on the winning distance.'

'Okay,' I said impatiently. 'Say he wins by a length.'

226

'I suppose he'd be worth seven or eight million quid, but if he won well, by four or five lengths, anything up to ten million. But why does al Hassan want to sell him?'

'That's simple. First, Abdel's desperate to win the Derby for his mother, and once they've done it, he'll be content. Secondly, although they've got limitless funds by our standards, an extra eight or ten million would offset a lot of the money they've spent over the past six years. Besides, don't forget, we've got Private Mountain's dam, Mont Nijinsky and two of her half sisters, and the best part of a dozen of their offspring. Abdel's convinced that if Private Mountain retires unbeaten having won the Derby, these will be worth much more, and there's nothing to gain in letting him run again, and risk getting beaten.'

Mungo nodded. 'That's all true enough.'

'Okay,' I said. 'Don't tell anybody until after the Derby, but if we win and want to sell him quickly, who do you think the most likely buyers would be?'

'Maybe one of the big studs in Ireland. I don't think there are any Private State stallions standing there at the moment. Perhaps the Aussies, or more likely, the Japs. They'd always be interested in a Derby winner.'

'If you can subtly line them up, we'd be happy to do a deal the week after the Derby. Abdel insists that he doesn't want him to run again if he wins and the horse is definitely for sale.'

'What if he doesn't win?'

I grunted and heaved a shoulder. 'We'll give him a good rest and get him ready for an autumn campaign.'

Later, while I was saddling Andes Pavlova for her race, Brigadier Mills turned up.

'Hello, Hugo. Filly looks nice.'

'Thanks, Brigadier. Any news?'

'No, but I'd like a quick word with you, if I may, as soon as you've got the saddle on.'

When I'd checked that the filly's tack was all in order and she was walking calmly round the parade ring with Des, I walked to where the Brigadier stood with one of the local stewards. He moved away, so that we could talk without being overheard.

'We can't work out where all that money came from for your horse at Bath,' he said. 'But you must watch your security.'

'We have been, but I haven't identified a leak yet. It's very weird.'

'Weird isn't the word I'd have used; I'd say rather sinister. What about your runner in this race?'

'Unless there's a hot pot we haven't spotted, she should win it.'

The Brigadier nodded. 'Best of luck, then. Let me know if you have any problems; I'll be watching over you, don't worry.'

That was all I needed - I thought bitterly - I was going for the biggest scam in British racing for over a hundred years and I'd already got a former head of Jockey Club security for a self-elected guardian angel.

When the jockeys came into the paddock, Kevin walked over and we were soon joined by Mungo and Alfie. I asked the jockey who he thought the dangers might be.

'None of 'em have run before, as you know Sir Hugo. The two Newmarket 'orses think they're in with a chance, but they're both a long way behind the best of their stables, and Tom Jenkin's 'orse, Bournemouth Pearl is half fancied by his connections, but he doesn't have many winners.'

'Good. You should just about win this, then. She's half fast away from the stalls, so jump out, have her handy, third or fourth, and go for home a furlong out. We want to win this race, so if you've got to, give her a couple of good smacks.'

'I'll do my best, Sir Hugo.'

I gave Kevin a leg up and the horses left the paddock. As I walked from the entrance, Geoffrey Scott sidled up to me. 'Did your jockey say anything useful?'

'He seems to think the other fillies are pretty ordinary, so we should win. What price is she?'

'Three-to-one, joint favourite with the two Newmarket fillies.'

'Kevin says they're nothing special. I'll have a grand to win.'

Geoffrey nodded. 'Okay.'

Andes Pavlova, a very visible grey, jumped from the stalls like a coursing hound and shared the lead with one of the outsiders for the first two hundred yards until Kevin managed to anchor her in third place.

At the furlong marker he let her take up the running, quickly going three lengths clear and, although one of the Newmarket fillies showed some last minute speed, Pavlova coasted home an easy winner by a length.

Thank God! Something had gone right.

On the way back, Alfie was jubilant over Square Barrow's first win of the season. He'd had a very large bet - what he called one of his bookie-crushers - and was burning with enthusiasm for Private Mountain's gallop at Newbury in two days' time.

When we arrived at Square Barrow just after five, I went into the office to find I'd another result. A fax from Marcus Parkinson informed me that he had received the money from the sale of the cottages, and my ex-wife could now be paid off, once and for all!

CHAPTER FIFTEEN

Midday on Thursday, nine days before the running of the Derby, I arrived at Newbury feeling unusually nervous. What was going to happen in the next ninety minutes or so would be among the most critical of my crisis-packed life.

I'd brought Mountain and both our lead horses, High Sierra and Rocky Spa. Annie arrived soon after me with Ray, who was going on Rocky Spa. Kevin was due to turn up and ride High Sierra. We left the lads unloading and made our way to the box which Abdel had taken for the day. He had phoned the previous week to say he would be coming especially to watch. It would be the first time either Annie or I had seen him for over a month, and now that the culmination of six years of planning was so close, I couldn't pretend that I wasn't feeling the pressure.

I ordered coffee and we carried it out to the balcony to look down over the green expanse of the course where a handful of people were busy with final arrangements for the afternoon's racing. As we watched, a spot and a buzz in the east turned into a Bell JetRanger, which came in fast, circled and dropped into the centre of the course.

231

I lifted my binoculars and watched Abdel hop neatly from the aircraft and walk unaccompanied across the turf towards the stands.

A few minutes later, one of the Leatherby and Chistopher waiters ushered him through the door of the box. He was wearing an immaculate Savile Row suit in Prince of Wales check with a thread of blue in it, a pale canary shirt and plain navy tie.

He stood for a moment and looked at both of us with a faint smile on his narrow, brown lips. 'Good morning, my dears,' he said, with a sudden twinkle. 'Annie, you manage somehow to look thoroughly professional, and thoroughly beautiful at the same time; there aren't many women in the world who can achieve that.'

I was impressed; it was a fine compliment, well delivered.

'You look pretty dapper yourself, Abdel,' Annie replied.

He put his head on one side. 'Hugo,' he nodded at me.

'Morning, boss,' I greeted him. 'Glad you could be here.'

'I'm only sorry that mother couldn't come.' He made a regretful face. 'She said you were over at Le Mesnil the week before last?'

'Yes, she rang and asked me to come over and show her the yearlings.'

'Did that cause any problems?'

'Nothing we couldn't handle.'

He nodded. 'Did you notice that she seemed a little less... firm than usual?'

'Yes. I did. I hope it wasn't a sign of anything serious.'

232

'The fact is, she's getting old. She never thought she would, and previously, she'd have loved to come and watch what we are doing today.' He gave a slight lift of one immaculately tailored shoulder. 'All the more reason for our carefully nurtured plans to yield a perfect fruit.'

'Of course,' I said, understanding very well his priorities.

'So,' he said, turning to Annie. 'What is your plan for Private Mountain today?'

'I'll ride Mountain, of course. Ray'll be on Rocky Spa and Kevin on High Sierra.'

'I look forward to seeing how our expensively retained jockey rides. I was impressed with his riding on the filly that won for us.'

Despite the fact that for most of his life, Abdel had taken no interest whatever in horses and racing, since he'd become involved, he had shown a remarkable understanding of what was required from his horses and the people who handled them.

Annie nodded. 'They'll go ten furlongs from the mile and a half start which means Rocky Spa can lead them along the back straight for four furlongs. It's a long turn and Kevin on High Sierra should go on then for the next five or six furlongs. When they turn into the straight, they'll have another two furlongs to run, to where you and Hugo will be standing.'

Abdel walked across the box and gazed down at the course. 'So they'll finish two furlongs from the winning post?'

'Yes,' I put in. 'We want a really good fast gallop down the back straight before they get to the left hand turn. That's why we're using Newbury - it's left-handed like Epsom. Of course, the contours are different, but it'll show us if he can really go on the left rein.'

By one o'clock in the pre-parade paddock, a fair-sized crowd had gathered. Hugo Lewis, one of the more persistent of the tabloid racing hacks and half a dozen others, Alfie and his wife, Birgitta, chatting with Mungo and a gaggle of bookies' representatives and punters, including, of course, Geoffrey Scott, had all clustered round to watch.

Abdel had barely spoken since leaving the box. Now he was standing close beside me.

'So, Hugo, the moment of truth?'

'That happens in nine days' time, at Epsom, though I suppose you might say there'll be a minor moment of truth today.'

Abdel looked at the three horses walking round. 'They look fine, all very well, especially Private Mountain.'

I thought Abdel, like us, had decided simply to convince himself that Green Mountain really was Private Mountain, and thereby avoid any embarrassing slips.

'It may all seem okay, but we need to see our Derby horse quicken up to High Sierra. I told you on the phone - he's been frankly unimpressive when asked to go on in a couple of gallops, though I'm hoping the fast work at Chepstow last week will have put him right.'

'Inshallah,' Abdel said quietly.

'Amen to that,' I said. 'You must excuse me for a few minutes Abdel. I have to get the jockeys' saddles. Why don't you have a quick word with our agent?'

I waved at Mungo to come and join us in the centre of the ring, and left him talking to Abdel.

As Annie and I walked out, I was accosted by Henry Mills and his shadow, Terry Brownley.

The Brigadier unconsciously echoed Abdel. 'The moment of truth soon, eh Hugo?'

'I'm busy praying.'

'I shouldn't imagine the almighty listens to you all that much.'

'The Lord loves a sinner; I remember someone telling me in bible classes when I was a child, and I've never forgotten it.'

'Well, we'll be deputising as your guardian angels,' Henry said, reiterating the very thought I'd had the other day at Bath and I wondered how the old bastard kept pitching up at the right moment - now you see him, now you don't.

I shook him off and went back to the pre-parade paddock to find the three horses being put into saddling boxes. It took Annie and me a few minutes to get the saddles on. Abdel came over and watched us closely.

I was just looking at my watch, hoping that it might induce Kevin to turn up, when the jockey appeared, nonchalant as ever. He listened keenly, though, to Annie's instructions to him and Ray.

When she'd finished, before I legged her up on to Mountain, I spoke to her alone.

'Happy?'

'Tell you later. How do you think I should do this?' she added with sudden uncertainty.

'Keep within a couple lengths of Kevin until you get into the straight, then balance him and at the furlong marker, pull out to the right and go up to finish level, but for God's sake, try not to win the gallop by more than half a length. That's why you mustn't make a move until the last furlong or so. Okay?'

'But what happens if he doesn't quicken, like that gallop we did over ten furlongs?'

'I hope to hell we cured that with the gallop at Chepstow.'

'Well, if he doesn't quicken..?'

'Yell at him - you're good at that. Slap him down the shoulder and if he still doesn't go on, pick up your stick and give him a couple of hard cracks - but I don't think you'll need to.' I gave her what I hoped was an encouraging grin, unused to seeing her nervous.

Once Annie was up and taking a few turns around the ring with the others, I went over to the gang of press that had gathered to give them a few details of the weights and to invite them to come down and watch from the track, if they wished.

We were all moving off towards the gate onto the course when I felt a presence at my elbow. Looking down I saw that we had been joined by Jimmy Collins.

'God!' I laughed. 'Where on earth did you pitch up from?'

'I wasna goin' to miss this, Sir H. No if I'm gonna put the house on 'im.'

'Bollocks! You'd never put that much on.'

'Maybe not,' Jimmy agreed. 'But enough to keep me interested.'

'Well, it's great to see you.'

'You too, Sir H, but tell me, why don't you start them at the ten furlong marker and finish at the winning post, same as anyone else?'

'I should have thought that was pretty obvious to you, Jimmy. I want Rocky Spa to give the other two a good lead down the back straight before they hit the turn; it'll be more like Epsom.'

'I see you're asking Private Mountain to give three pounds and a year to High Sierra.'

'No, I'm not,' I answered more sharply than I meant. 'He's giving him three pounds and <u>two</u> years. Don't forget High Sierra's a five year old.'

'Are you sure you haven't got another Running Rein horse and he's only giving one year?' Jimmy chuckled.

'Chance would be a fine thing!' I guffawed blandly for the benefit of any ear-wigging press men.

Around twenty or thirty people set off down the course, led by Abdel, Mungo and me. The journalists, bookies' scouts and punters followed a few yards behind.

When we reached the two furlong marker, everyone turned to look across the course at the point from which the gallop would start. There was a sudden shuffling and a groan. From this elevation, we wouldn't see the start or anything of the first eight furlongs of the gallop until the horses had just turned into the straight.

I glanced around, worried especially about Abdel's reaction, and feeling a pillock for not foreseeing this problem. My eyes lighted on two pairs of compact aluminium step-ladders carted down by a couple of the photographers. Using the bribe of an exclusive session at Square Barrow, I commandeered one of them and put Abdel up on it. He didn't look entirely happy about the arrangement, but it lightened the atmosphere. The other photographer's ladder was grabbed by one of the race-course commentators, who gave us a sample of his work.....

'They're off to a level break. Rocky Spa has gone up a length on the outside..... They're going a cracking gallop ... they've covered a furlong and Rocky Spa is clear of High Sierra on the rails and Private Mountain half a length down in the middle. They're at the two furlong marker - no change in the order - and still going a good gallop. The three furlong marker - Rocky Spa is having to be ridden now to keep his lead. Now they're coming into the long sweeping turn - High Sierra has gone on with Private Mountain about a length down - they've passed Rocky Spa, who's being pulled up. They've done six furlongs.....'

Fifteen seconds later the two horses swung into view on the straight. As soon as Kevin had High Sierra balanced, he started to ask for more. Mountain, a length down and to his right, was galloping well within himself.

Bet Your Rocks Off

When Annie saw Kevin kick on, she asked her horse to extend and quicken too. But as in the previous gallop, it was High Sierra who produced the greater reaction, and within a matter of strides he was two lengths up.

Annie gave Mountain a couple of slaps down the shoulder. There was still no obvious response from him, though he must have quickened as High Sierra didn't increase his lead.

But with a furlong to run, the gallop was looking like a wash-out. High Sierra was ridden out by Kevin with hands and heels only and still two lengths up; Private Mountain, hard ridden with the occasional slap down the shoulder was making no more impression.

As they entered the final two hundred yards, Annie upped her whip and gave Private Mountain a good fore-hand smack as hard as she could behind the saddle. There was still no noticeable reaction. Three strides later, the horse got another reminder, and as they flashed past us, I saw Annie had managed to drive him up so that he was just about on High Sierra's shoulder.

But there was no question - High Sierra had won the gallop and Kevin had never picked up his whip.

Everyone started to talk at once, except Abdel, who climbed down from the step ladder displaying no reaction at all. The whole crowd started to walk briskly up the course to the point where the horses had pulled up near the winning post.

By the time we reached them, they were being led round by our lads; Kevin and Ray had taken off their saddles and gone back to the changing room.

Annie was sitting on the grass with her saddle, her cap off and her face glowing with exertion. When we joined her, she didn't get up at once. She shook her head with a grin. 'I'm too darned unfit for gallops like that. I don't know why I haven't thrown up.'

The photographers laughed, without a pause in their picture-taking.

Abdel held out a hand and helped her to her feet. Once she was up, she gave us both a nod. 'I'm getting back to the stables to check the horses.'

When she had gone, I held an impromptu, low-key press conference, remaining non-committal in my own reactions.

When the press and the other watchers had decided there wasn't any more to hear, they wandered off, and I was left alone with Abdel.

He didn't speak, but gave me a quizzical, open-minded look.

I made sure nothing in my expression would give away what I was saying to anyone watching me through binoculars.

'Well,' I sighed with a slight heave of my shoulders. 'That went not too badly.'

'Oh?' Abdel said, unimpressed.

'Annie's wearing a smuggler's waistcoat under that silk, with eleven pounds of lead in the pockets. I told the press that Mountain was carrying eight stone ten, but actually, he's got nine seven.'

Abdel, disguising his feelings like me, nodded thoughtfully. 'Ah, I wish you had told me before. It makes more sense now, but the horse still wouldn't come through when he got up to the leader.'

'Yes. That hadn't escaped me. But I know what to do, and we'll work on it.'

Abdel gave me a slight bow. 'I have every confidence you will. Goodbye, Hugo.' Without waiting for a response, he peeled off to the waiting helicopter, and a few moments later, the pilot had turned on the engines.

I walked back to the race-course buildings where Annie would be divesting herself of eleven pounds of dead weight in the privacy of the otherwise unoccupied ladies' changing room. I had wanted a few words with Kevin, but he was nowhere to be found. Looking at the card, I saw that he didn't have a ride until the fourth race, so there was no point in hanging around for him.

I went along to the stables where I dealt with the mundanities of washing down the horses and by the time the second race was off, they were loaded and I'd started the thirty mile trip back to Square Barrow.

It was a long haul from Square Barrow to Haydock Park next morning, and whatever I did, whichever radio station I found, and however much I tried to chat to the recovering but monosyllabic Mick O'Grady who'd come with me, I couldn't stop my mind circling ceaselessly round the question of what I was going to do to be absolutely certain that our Derby horse performed on the day.

I'd had the sense to start soon after six, and we rolled in to the race-course just before ten. Despite its proximity to the unlovely conurbations of Wigan, Warrington and St Helens, Haydock Park was as pretty a course as any in England and better run than most. As soon as I'd got our runners, Spanish Partridge and the two year old, Hillary's Steps safely stabled, I went to the canteen and ordered a big cooked breakfast.

I found a table to myself and was trying to concentrate on *The Sporting Post* when a girl, already dressed in her Tote Investors uniform, excused herself in unabashed Scouse and plonked her tray of grapefruit juice and muesli on the other side of my table.

She was a bright-eyed girl, Barbie in a black wig with short legs - a cracker, probably, by local standards - and ignoring her was not an option. Besides, I always liked talking about betting.

As it turned out, she knew a lot about her product and did an excellent selling job on the recently introduced Trifecta.

This bet, in which one had to name the first three horses in the correct order of some of the more unreadable handicaps, could pay monster odds. And it was very hard to get right.

Despite that, after the girl had gone, I spent half an hour sorting out the top four horses in Spanish Partridge's race, assumed he'd win, and selected three others to perm every way for second and third places in the Trifecta.

I was coming out of the canteen when I bumped, quite literally, into cousin Henry, Brigadier Mills.

'Hello, Hugo.' There was a disquieting, sardonic smile on his face. 'You're here early.'

'I've already been here an hour, actually.'

'Why's that?'

Bet Your Rocks Off

'We've got two runners here today and I drove them up myself.' I glanced at my watch. 'Look, Brigadier, I'm sorry; I've got to run. I've arranged to meet my jockey.'

'Best of luck today, and we'll be watching out to see if there are any more funny movements in the market for your runners.'

He carried on, joined by Brownley, his officious little sidekick who had just appeared out of nowhere.

I watched them go, knowing that any sudden movement in the price of our horses was very unlikely. Since the last leak, Annie and I had been scrupulously discreet in all discussions about our own betting intentions. As it happened, I'd decided on the strength of Partridge's last gallop and provided he travelled well to the track, to have a large bet on him. The racing papers were quoting him at longish odds that morning, and there was no reason why his price should come in significantly.

Nevertheless, I felt impelled to take another look at the horse, and walked to the stables.

Satisfied, I came out and flipped open my mobile to call my bookies. I asked what they were quoting on Partridge. They offered me six grand to a monkey. I took it.

Pleased with myself, I made my way to the weighing-room where I hoped to find Kevin Prendergast who was riding Hillary's Steps in the opening maiden race. I wanted to catch him before the race, but not just to give him his riding instructions.

As usual, he turned up at the last minute, but I button-holed him and led him away from the doors.

'I'm late, guv,' he protested.

'I just want a very quick reaction to yesterday's gallop,' I said quietly.

Kevin gave his shoulders a negative shrug. 'My horse won, easy, like, and I never touched him.'

'How did the other horse look to you, though?'

'If you want to know,' Kevin said in the voice of someone who is aware they aren't going to give the desired answer, 'he seemed to be running bloody green. He didn't look like he won a couple last year. Even when Lady Tenbury picks up her whip, he hasn't really done much.' Realising that he might be generating too much disappointment, he tried to downplay his opinion. 'But don't forget, Sir H, I was in front; I never had a real good look.'

'Yes, Kevin, I understand that. He got up to your shoulder, then he just stayed there. I'll need you to come and do some more work on him at home next week to teach him to come through.' I looked at the time. 'Okay, you'd better get on now.'

He nodded curtly and rushed off, while I wished he possessed a little more charm.

Kevin may have lacked charm, but he had ambition and determination in abundance. He rode Hillary's Steps superbly and won by an easy two lengths. The colt had earned us our second blood that season and looked certain to win next time out, even with a penalty.

Bet Your Rocks Off

I noticed on the screens that the odds against Spanish Partridge were starting to come in a little, and I was glad I'd already got my main bet on.

Abruptly, I remembered the trifecta I'd so laboriously worked out. Of course, the eventual price would be computed only once all the bets were in at the off, but I thought I'd better get it on now in case I forgot later.

I walked briskly to the Tote betting shop and saw my breakfast companion's gleaming black mop behind on of the tills.

I handed her my card. 'On my account, please.'

'That'll be fine, Sir Hugo,' she grinned, filling in the form for me. 'How much a line?'

'Oh, fifty, I should think.'

'Fine,' she gave me a friendly nod and handed me back a copy of my bet. I stuffed it straight into a pocket and hurried off to check my next runner.

CHAPTER SIXTEEN

Spanish Partridge was a handsome brute, short-coupled and pugnacious as a boxer. He couldn't get an inch more than seven furlongs, but he excelled at six.

I'd seldom felt so confident about a horse as I saddled him then watched Mick, still hobbling a little, lead him round the pre-parade ring.

I dug my mobile out of an inside pocket and dialled Square Barrow.

Annie answered.

'Hi,' I said.

'Having a good time?'

'What do you think? You saw Hillary romping home?'

'He'd go faster with better horses behind him,' Annie observed.

'I wished you'd told me; I didn't have a bet.'

'I had no idea how he'd react to a real race track. Back him next time. And how's Spanish Partridge?'

'Disgustingly well. Travelled like a lamb. Should be a fat wallet day today. But much more important, how's our boy?'

'I didn't want to do too much on him after that gallop yesterday; but he made a serious impression on High Sierra at even weights until he got up to him. Then he just seemed to want to hang about with his nose on the other's girth.'

I could hear a frustrated, plaintive note in Annie's voice.

'Look, darling,' I tried to mollify. 'Don't worry too much. I believe I've thought of a way to deal with it.'

'How? Tell *me* for God's sake; I'm supposed to be the trainer.'

'Not now; not over the phone. We'll talk tomorrow; there's no rush.'

'What are you talking about - no rush? The Derby's in a week, for God's sake!'

'Relax, Annie, and if I were you, I'd get a good lump on Partridge; it could be the last time you get a price.'

In my life so far, I was conscious that I had a history of making infallible prophecies that went adrift and, though I was very used to putting chunky wagers down, I couldn't stem a stiff adrenaline rush as I watched Spanish Partridge stride into the ring.

Kevin came in with the other jockeys and sidled up to me where I stood, on my own and ownerless. I suppose I must have been off somewhere on another plain when I heard him ask, rather desperately, 'So, what's the story, Guv'nor?'

'Just go like hell. You're well drawn on the rails, so use them, even if you're tempted to move over with the bunch to the other side.'

'He's going well, isn't he?' he asked with an anxious note that made me look at him.

'Have you had a bet on him?'

Kevin looked at me with wide eyes that failed to disguise the lie. 'Come on, Sir H; you know I don't bet.'

'Well, if you don't fuck it up, you should win. And you're lucky I'm not a steward!'

'So are you, Sir H,' Kevin returned sharply as I legged him up.

I watched him move off on Spanish Partridge, and tried to convince myself that it was absurd to assume he was referring to our Derby coup.

Sometimes, though, with only eight days to go after six years planning, it seemed incredible that the whole world didn't know.

I took a deep breath and grinned at a few of the competing trainers and owners standing in the centre of the ring. A lot of them had been asking after Annie, still fascinated by her appearance on the English turf a couple of years before. Of course, Hillary's Steps' win had focused people's attention on our second runner that day, and shortened his odds to eight-to-one.

Once Mick had led Partridge out of the ring, I walked thoughtfully and alone from the paddock.

''Ullo, Sir Hugo. Planning what to do with the money?'

I glanced to my left. Lurking at my elbow was Chris Lewis; short, wiry, red haired and ferret-faced. He was wearing a nasty little curly brimmed trilby and carrying, as he always did, a dog-eared, spiral-back pad.

'What money?' I asked coldly.

'What you're going to win on this next horse, of course.'

'I haven't had a bet.'

'Yes, you have. A little bird heard you when you were using your mobile outside the stables this morning.'

I was shocked by own indiscretion. Not that this particular piece of information mattered a damn, but it was so easy with mobile phones somehow to assume that you were making your calls in private. I supposed that was why most people, including me, it seemed, talked so loudly when they used them.

'Ah.' I conceded defeat with a grin. 'I admit that I am confident; still, at least it's too late for you to nap the horse in your tipping line.'

'What about your Derby horse then; should I nap that?'

'You watched him at Newbury yesterday. Make your own mind up.'

'I would normally, Sir H, but you do have a bit of a reputation for stage direction.'

'Well, you'll just have to decide whether you were watching a tragedy, a mystery or a farce, won't you?' I gave him a farewell grin before striding off so fast he'd have to have run to keep up on his little legs.

He didn't. He knew he would have plenty more chances to badger me before the big race.

Whatever I may have thought about Kevin Prendergast's manners, morals and general demeanour, that day he seemed determined to justify the generous retainer we were paying him. He followed my instructions to the letter and brought Spanish Partridge home a good length clear.

When I also registered that the second and third were both in my trifecta, my cup, for a few moments, ranneth over.

The late afternoon sun was splashing obliquely through the trees as I walked with Kevin from the changing-room to his car. I congratulated him on producing a splendid double for us, but I really wanted to talk to him about Mountain.

'What did you think when you rode him at Chepstow?'

'I told you then, Guv'nor. He's certainly pretty sharp over the short distances, but we never really asked him the question over twelve furlongs. I tell you what, if he don't win the Derby, he'd be a shit hot seven furlong horse.'

'For God's sake, Kevin!' I exploded. 'The horse has been bred to win the fucking Derby; of course he'll get the trip; we're not interested in winning poxy little sprints with him.'

Kevin, slightly taken aback, shrugged. 'I'm just saying, I've never ridden him or seen him run the distance, that's all. But don't worry, Sir H, I'll be pushing him all the way.'

'Yes, of course,' I said, trying to calm down. 'I know you will. By the way, the press are beginning to pester me and they'll be around you like flies this next week; just tell them something meaningless like you've got a good horse and every chance on the day.'

'That's what I always say,' Kevin grinned. 'They know it means "Mind your own fucking business" - and no-one's feelings are hurt.'

As I was walking back to the stables to oversee the loading of our two victorious runners, Brigadier Mills materialised from thin air once more.

'What a super double.' He wasn't the first to say so that afternoon, but I smiled my acknowledgement. 'What I can't understand,' he went on, 'is why there wasn't more money on that second horse of yours.'

'I agree,' I agreed. 'He won some good races last year, and he looked fantastic in the paddock. I can only assume that most punters are blind and suffer from acute amnesia.'

Brigadier Mills had the good grace to laugh. 'Yes, that must be it. Anyway, at least there didn't seem to be any particular shenanigans over either of your horses today, so have a good journey back, Hugo, and I'll see you next week.'

I nodded. 'No doubt.'

It was just after ten on Saturday morning when I nearly ran into the postman's van, late as usual and careering up the track to our yard as I drove the lorry out. On board, entered for a six furlong handicap at Kempton, was Iceland Hawk, the small four year old sprinter that we'd paced against Mountain.

I couldn't face another journey with a deaf mute, so this time I'd brought Des Hughes with me. By the time we'd reached the M4, I was regretting it; in contrast to Mick, Des never stopped talking, and I was the monosyllabic one.

As it happened, I wasn't feeling too perky, having broken my rule and stayed in the pub until after midnight.

The trouble had been that when I got back from Haydock, exhausted but full of fizz, I naturally wanted to talk over the days' successes with Annie, only to find that she had gone out, and no one knew where.

Then she'd phoned me at six thirty in the morning to tell me she wasn't back at the yard and I must do the early stables.

I don't know which had pissed me off most - the early start, or Annie staying out all night.

I was stunned by my own reaction, because up until then she'd shown no particular interest in any men - including myself, I had to admit. But suddenly to find her playing away from home came as an unexpected blow.

On top of this, I'd come to the conclusion that our tactic for today's runner was wrong.

Because we were anxious to look like a serious yard while we went about our coup, it was important that we were seen to be trying to win and sometimes succeeding.

So far this year, our hit rate had been absurdly high, but given that we had run very few horses and Annie was effectively an entirely private trainer to the al Hassans, with access to their vast buying power, this wasn't so odd.

However, Annie and I both enjoyed competing with the bookies as much as with the other horses, and when we thought we could crank up the odds with some creative race management, we did.

Our runner that day had won three out of five races the year before, but he hadn't been seen on an English track for nine months; and it was only the truly outstanding horses that tended to linger in people's minds that long. But in order to defray any residual interest, we had engaged Darren Ford, a promising young apprentice. We were meaning to give the impression that we didn't think the horse had much of a chance, but the boy's five pound claim would come in very useful.

Now I thought maybe we were leaving a little too much to the horse.

I soon discovered that Chris Lewis thought the same. I was making my way to the weighing-room when he tapped me on the elbow.

'I realise you're wanting to put the punters off the scent,' he said in his nasal Streatham accent, 'but I think you'll find you've overdone it.'

'Oh, and why is that?' I asked as if I didn't give a damn what he thought.

'That boy's had a few results, but mostly on horses that have had a dozen runs or more - not on anything at all green.'

That was exactly what was worrying me. 'Bollocks,' I said. 'Iceland Mountain's run five times; she knows what to do.'

'I didn't tip her,' Hugo said unequivocally.

'Am I meant to be grateful?'

'Would you be grateful if I didn't tip Private Mountain next week?'

'Frankly, Hugo, I couldn't give a toss what horse you tip. I don't suppose all the punters who use your line could put on enough together to move the price half a point.'

He looked at me for a moment without speaking; I was struck by an unforeseen bitter resentment behind his eyes.

'You fucking toffs think you know it all, don't you,' he snarled. Before I could answer, he'd stomped off towards the main stand.

I thought how wrong he was. If I'd let him, he'd have seen that this fucking toff was currently undergoing a serious crisis of confidence.

Later, even while I looked hard at Darren Ford as I gave him instructions, I knew the boy was only half listening. I repeated the instructions and made him confirm that he'd understood them. I still thought he hadn't taken them on board, though.

Once the race was being run, and the first three furlongs covered, I could see that he had no real idea of what to do. He must simply have been very lucky to get his few wins.

Completely ignoring my directions, he let himself get carried over to the stands side on the straight six furlong course and even without a corner to negotiate, he managed to get boxed in by four

254

other runners, all ridden by streetwise, hard-nosed older jockeys who didn't let him out until they were fifty yards form the post and the gelding had too much to do to catch the leaders.

And there was no doubt, given the right break, he'd have got there.

I started to tear up the Tote ticket I'd bought at the last minute and noticed a few people looking at me with interest. I gave them a never-say-die grin and strode off to greet my returning horse.

I couldn't even be bothered to bollock the jockey; from his face, I guessed he'd learned the lesson well enough.

Listening to Des droning on the whole way home didn't do anything to improve my mood. I didn't feel like ringing Annie; she knew my number if she wanted to talk to me, and I hadn't heard a squeak from her since she'd phoned in the morning.

As soon as the box was parked in the yard, I jumped down, watched them take the filly off, and walked to my house.

There was a note from Annie on my kitchen table.

"I'll be round at seven thirty for a large Pimms."

Nothing else.

No - "How did you get on?" or - "Bad Luck," or - "Sorry for waking you at sparrow fart while I was getting laid."

I took a deep breath and reminded myself what a ridiculous hypocrite I was being. After all, I'd made it clear to her that it was none of her business what I did with Lady Allerthorpe, or anyone else.

Calmly and deliberately, I got together all the ingredients for a large jug of gin Pimms, mixed it and carried it outside to my small but flower-filled terrace. I went back in and gathered up glasses and the pile of letters that the postman had brought as I'd left that morning.

I was good at identifying items of post, and prided myself on knowing more or less what was inside an envelope from what was on the outside.

But the fourth envelope foxed me.

It was a small, cheap blue one, of the sort that I sometimes received from members of the public who felt they had to express their appreciation or, occasionally, disgust at something I'd said or done. But it was addressed with a computer printed sticky label, and post-marked 'Bristol'.

I inserted my Spanish letter knife - a miniature sword with "Toledo" inscribed on the blade - and slit it open.

I pulled out an untidily folded sheet of plain white A4, on which three sentences were laser printed near the top of the page.

I know about your derby horse. I want £10,000 or I tell Mills. I will ring monday.

I read the words five or six times, without moving, as if frozen in a trance, while questions and visions of catastrophe swirled around my head.

Bet Your Rocks Off

It was unbearable even to consider that all the money and years of preparation for this spectacular scam might be jeopardised by some greedy little bum who thought he'd sussed what we were doing.

I took a few deep breaths and gulped down a mouthful of Pimms. Annie would be around in a few minutes, and I needed to get my thoughts in order.

I knew I couldn't share my panic with her. There wasn't anything she could do to help, and she was already under enough pressure with Private Mountain's unresolved training problems.

There was no point in telling Abdel, either; I could use my own money. At Haydock, Spanish Partridge had won me six grand from the bookies, and my fifty pound trifecta, paying seventy-six pounds to a pound would produce just under four thousand from the Tote.

Much though I hated to yield up that kind of money, I guessed paying it was the only option.

However little this blackmailing bastard knew, it only needed Mills to have a serious poke around and take a look inside our Derby horse's mouth for him to see at once that we were planning to run a four year old Mountain, whatever his passport said.

The simple fact was that until a horse was eight years old, its age could be accurately judged from the growth of its teeth.

Ten grand to be certain that cousin Henry didn't come down with a search warrant at this stage in the game was well worth paying; if anything, the blackmailer had seriously underbid his hand.

But then, I didn't know how much he - or she - knew.

I wondered who the hell it could be. Through my mind trooped a parade of lads, work riders, farriers, vets, vets' assistants and feed merchants who regularly turned up at the yard.

I thought that there probably wasn't one of them who wouldn't have liked an easy, tax-free ten grand, if they reckoned they could rattle me enough.

But I managed to convince myself that it wasn't the end of the world. If this person really knew what we were doing, he would have asked for a great deal more than he had. Nevertheless, if someone, somehow had a vague suspicion, and was just trying it on, I simply couldn't risk the chance that Mills would be prompted. I was still sure that the Brigadier's blood relationship with me would count for nothing once he was within smelling distance of a good pull. And then he'd be extra keen if he foresaw any serious family escutcheon-blotting on my part.

I made up my mind. I would tell no one, wait for the phone call, and deliver the ten grand wherever I was told. As I came to this conclusion, Annie arrived.

'Hi, Hugo,' she called with an airy wave as she walked through the yard towards my little flag-stoned terrace. She was wearing a diaphanous silky frock which allowed beams of evening sun to shaft between her legs, and she carried a floppy, shapeless straw hat with which she fanned her face. 'Oh great!' she said gleefully. 'A lovely big jug of Pimms.'

Bet Your Rocks Off

I said nothing, and pushed the blackmail note back in among the stack of post I'd brought out with me. She let herself in through the wicket gate to join me. Silently, I drew up a chair for her and filled a tall glass with amber fluid, lumps of ice and assorted fruit and veg.

She looked at me with wide, innocent eyes which - we both knew - didn't suit her. 'Who's in a sulk, then?' she cooed.

'I'm not sulking,' I grunted. 'I'm just bloody knackered. I had a late night, an early start, no help, and a drive to Kempton and back to watch a dimwit throw a race.'

She nodded. 'We got one thing right, though; at least he went off at nice long odds.'

'I don't suppose the bookies took a penny on him besides ours. I knew once I got the little bastard in the paddock, I was fucked.'

Annie nodded. 'We can't always get it right. So, what else is eating you?'

'Nothing,' I said. 'It would have been helpful if you'd given me a bit of notice before going off for a twenty-four hour sex session.'

Annie smiled tolerantly. 'Why? Are you jealous, Hugo? Anyway, it wasn't twenty-four hours, and there was absolutely no sex involved. I've been visiting with a fag and an eighty year old lady.'

'Oh, well, why the hell didn't you tell me?' I hadn't wanted my relief to show, but she saw it.

'Every time I go out, tell you I'm not going to have sex?'

'All right, all right,' I dismissed the idea. 'Who were you with?'

'Abdel and his mum.'

'Is Madame over here?' I asked with surprise.

259

'Yes, she's on her way to Spekeworth to stay with the Duke and Duchess of Dorset for a few days.'

'She didn't tell me she was coming over early,' I said.

'She wants to see you next Thursday; she'll be back at Claridges.'

'Okay. So tell me when they asked you up, and why?'

'Abdel phoned Friday evening when you were on your way back from Haydock. He said his mother wanted to talk to me, and he'd send a car to get me. I tried to call you later but you were obviously in the pub without your mobile.'

'Yes,' I sighed. 'But did they want to see me too?'

'Not then, no. They just wanted to talk about training, and Mountain. I told them the truth...'

'But Madame doesn't know about the switch.'

'No, no, I don't mean that; I mean I told them we're still concerned that he's running so green and not coming through.'

I nodded. 'As well to tell them, but I've been having some ideas about that; I'd rather talk about it tomorrow, though. What else did Madame have to say?'

'How do you know she had anything else?'

'Because I know you; and I know Madame.'

'Okay, Hugo, she did, and I'm not such a dumb cluck I didn't see at once that she was trying to warn me off you.'

I looked at her sharply. 'But why would she think you're - as it were - *on* me?'

'She seems to think that any woman around you can't leave you alone; or perhaps she just thinks you can't leave them alone - I don't know - but as examples she cited two French girls, sometime dinner guests of hers called Lisette and Mikie.' Annie saw my brief grimace. 'Ah,' she said. 'So you remember them?'

'Yes, but I can't think why Madame thought they were interested in me. They were a pair of dykes.'

I stood up. I was tired, I was still very jittery from the nasty little note I'd been sent, and I didn't feel like justifying Lisette and Mikie just then; I didn't feel like it, and I didn't know how.

'Okay, I've had it, Annie. If you don't mind, I'm going to bed.'

'But it's only nine o'clock.'

'So, you've got a good book to read, I expect, or you can always find some nice mindless crap on the box on a Saturday night.'

Annie stood up, too. 'Oh come on, Hugo. Don't take it like that. It's none of my business who you get off on - French dykes, English nymphomaniacs; why should I care?'

She leaned up and gave me a quick kiss on the lips and as I reached to catch her round the waist, she'd flitted through the gate and was away across the yard.

CHAPTER SEVENTEEN

I had no sleep to speak of that night. My mood lurched between despair and optimism as different versions of events were dragged through my restless head.

But by the morning, I was at least fairly certain about what I was going to do.

I got up at seven. Annie was already at her post, organising the morning feeds. I watched for a while, trying to kill some time until I thought it was late enough to ring the man I'd been wanting to speak to since before dawn.

I guessed that eight o'clock was about the earliest I could call on a Sunday morning. At half past seven, I went back to my house and managed to occupy half an hour making a bowl of porridge and eating it with a spoonful of downland honey.

As I ate, I thought about Piers Bowring, the only person I knew who could help me.

He was a strange, cussed man - at best, distant and ungiving in his manner.

He wasn't rude, but employed only the bare minimum of politeness in his dealings with people.

Bet Your Rocks Off

He had a reputation for operating on his own terms, or not at all, which he could justify with his track record.

He was <u>the</u> specialist in kidnap, ransom and blackmail. When insurers at Lloyds had made the best use of their own people or the smaller firms, and had still got nowhere, they called in Bowring.

Although he had spent eighteen years in the Guards, including two tours with the legal assassins at 22SAS in Hereford, I didn't come across him until I'd started working at Lloyds, not long after he'd come out of the army - with a faint question mark over the circumstances of his going - and set up his hostage release company.

I didn't like him much and didn't expect him to do me any favours, like offering a discount for old times' sake, but I was sure he was the right man to talk to. One advantage of his formidable taciturnity was that he was impeccably discreet.

As soon as the clock struck eight, I dialled Bowring's number in Surrey.

I was answered by a man with a voice that was a caricature of a Guards NCO's, asked to give my name and telephone number and told that Major Bowring would ring me back within fifteen minutes.

I sat and waited like a jittering school girl, pouncing on the phone every time some imitative warbler outside trilled, and I was conscious that even in these circumstances, the strength of Bowring's personality was formidable.

I'd got through a fresh mug of coffee when, finally, he rang.

'Hello, Hugo. What can I do for you?'

'Can we meet, as soon as possible?'

'You want my professional advice?'

'Yes.'

'I'm afraid I can't see anyone today. Where will you be tomorrow?'

'I'm supposed to be racing at Leicester.'

'Good. I'll see you there, before the first race, if that's convenient?'

'Yes, of course.'

'Fine. Until tomorrow.'

He rang off before I'd fixed a rendezvous or said goodbye. That was the Bowring I remembered. And simply talking to him, confident that I could get him on my side, seemed to ease the pressure. In the meantime, there was nothing else I could do, and Annie was due in for breakfast any moment.

'How can you eat those stinking things?' Annie's nose wrinkled at my kippers.

'They're very good for the brain.'

'Oh, you'd better keep it up, then.'

'That's no way to talk to a Master of Arts of Trinity College, Dublin,' I said, pouring a cup of coffee for each of us. 'But we have more serious problems to contend with.' I took a long swig from cup as I rallied my thoughts. 'Mountain can win the Derby - I'm sure of it after seeing him run with all that extra weight at Newbury - but only if he learns once and for all to take the lead.'

Annie nodded. 'So, how do you think we're going to get him to do that?'

'What do *you* think? Blinkers?'

'No, not blinkers; I think he'd just panic. I'll get Kevin down on Tuesday. I'm afraid it's time to get tough.'

Rocky Gold was entered for the second race on Monday's card at Leicester. As far as I was concerned, the only reason for running the filly was to sustain the pretence that we were operating a real yard at Square Barrow.

Annie, out of habit and vanity, didn't like to send out no-hopers, but she knew we had to look as though we were operating a conventional yard. Rocky Gold was a three year old mare who'd shown a little form last season but didn't seem to have taken to the job this year. She certainly wasn't going to win today and in any other circumstances, I'd have found someone else to take her to the Monday meeting at Leicester. But I made sure that we arrived in plenty of time so that I was free to roam around the course for half an hour before the first race.

I didn't doubt that Piers Bowring would show up, but I wished he'd made a more specific arrangement. After few minutes, I decided the best place to wait for him was in the members' bar and made my way there through the swelling crowd. I ordered a bottle of champagne and two glasses and took them to a small round table in a corner by a window.

Bowring came into the bar, still fairly empty, and glanced around. I saw him a second or two before he spotted me. He was dressed in a quiet fawn suit, his dark, wavy hair was conventionally cut, beneath a flawless Lock's Panama. Around his neck, against a pale blue shirt, was knotted a black and light blue Old Etonian tie.

He saw me, nodded briefly and made his way to my table.

He looked, I thought, like an adman's dream of a thorough English gentleman until, closer, one could see his eyes - pale grey, almost motionless with an opaque curtain just behind the pupils, that permitted one way vision only.

I waved him at a chair, and picked up the bottle of champagne to pour a glass for him. He put a hand out. 'No thanks. Vodka, and a little ice.'

I didn't resent his off-hand behaviour; I'd seen it before. I knew it was his way of establishing the bases of negotiation. I bought his vodka and took it back to our table. He ignored it.

'Is it all right to talk here?' I asked.

He looked around and nodded. 'Yes, but keep it quiet, and if I put my hand up, just stop.'

I nodded. 'Okay. Thanks for coming.'

He lifted a shoulder as acknowledgement. 'So, what's the problem?'

'I received a letter on Saturday telling me that if I don't hand over ten grand, the writer will pass on some very sensitive information about our yard.'

'How much is the suppression of that information worth to you?'

'With luck, millions.'

'If that's so, your man clearly doesn't know the whole story, does he?'

No,' I agreed, 'but even if he's just guessing, and puts certain people on their guard, it would have the same effect.'

'I see. And what do you want to do about it?'

'I was going to pay him.'

'Why?'

'Well, it's not very much, and I think he'll just go away if I do.'

'That's most unlikely. Once you've paid up; he'll know that he's definitely found a seam, even if he doesn't know the value of it, and he'll certainly come back for more.'

'What would you suggest?'

'First of all, I should make clear my company's terms of business. Our "call out" charge is fifteen thousand pounds or ten percent of the sum demanded, whichever is the higher, half of that payable up front. After that, we charge our time and expenses.'

'Sounds a lot.'

Bowring shrugged. 'It's what you might call a niche market, and there's no real competition.'

'Okay. I think I'll go it alone,' I said. 'Pay up and see what happens.'

Bowring looked as if he couldn't care less. 'That's up to you, of course, but he will be back,' he said quietly, 'you can be sure of that;

call me then, if you want, and in the meantime, as part of our pre-sales service, if you give me a list of everyone who works for you, or who is in regular contact, I'll have them all checked out; it'll save time when you do call.'

'Can I have it faxed somewhere?'

'Yes.' He took a wallet from his inside pocket and pulled out a card which he handed to me. It was printed with the words, 'Piers Bowring and Co Ltd. Fine Art Shippers' with a London address and phone numbers.

When he had left, with a barely perceptible goodbye, I noticed that he hadn't even touched the drink I had gone to the trouble of getting for him.

'Who was that then?'

I looked up and saw Chris Lewis grinning at me, all the animosity he'd shown two days earlier apparently evaporated.

'Good God,' I said. 'Do they let people like you in here?'

'Yes,' he answered, 'for nothing, like you.'

I looked at the bottle, two thirds full, and the untouched vodka.

'Do you drink vodka?' I asked.

'Of course,' Hugo said.

'You can have this one, then. My last guest didn't even pick it up.'

Hugo nodded gratefully, sat down and took a swig. 'He looked like a proper toff. Who was he?'

'Chap I used to know in the army, asking me if we'll have a horse of his in the yard.'

'Will you?' he looked interested now.

'Possibly,' I said launching into a quick flight of fantasy for Hugo's benefit. 'We could take another five or six, over and above the al Hassans', and they won't mind. And of course our strike rate's been pretty good, so people are asking.'

'You didn't get it right Saturday, did you? That horse would have won with a proper jockey on board.'

'But we feel it's our duty to encourage the youngsters, too. After all, even flat jockeys don't live for ever.' I started getting up. 'Now, if you'll excuse me, I've got to go. You can have the rest of the champagne too, if you want.'

'Well, thank you, Sir Hugo.' Hugo tugged an imaginary forelock, and I left him with his notebook out, filling a glass with a smile on his face.

We hadn't expected the filly to win, and she finished like a donkey. Her lad, the gentle, flame-haired Bertie was the only person on the course taking any notice of her as she came back in. Kevin Prendergast couldn't jump off quick enough. 'She'd make a nice lady's hack,' he said. 'but please don't ask me to ride her again.'

'You'll ride what you're told if you want to keep your nice fat retainer.'

'All right, Sir H. I'm sorry, but this filly's a poodle. Did you have a bet on her?'

'No, Kevin.'

'There you are then.'

'There are no yards that go out and win every time, you know that. Anyway, I can tell you now, we need you at Square Barrow to work on Private Mountain tomorrow morning.'

'I know, Lady Tenbury phoned and told me. What are we going to do?'

'What do you think? We're going to teach him to come through.'

'How?'

'Lady Tenbury will tell you. Eight o'clock will do; you can come for a bit of breakfast before we go out.'

Driving home with Bertie dozing beside me, I was given the opportunity to reflect on how quickly one's acts of kindness can be repaid by an appreciative God. If I hadn't bequeathed the second half of my bottle of champagne to Chris Lewis, I would have set all the lights flashing and bells ringing on the breathalyser into which I was asked to blow by a policeman fifty miles down the MI.

He had stopped me for a routine check, he said, and hearing my rather lazy voice had made the common mistake of thinking that I was drunk.

When the device didn't register, he inspected my licence and apologised with some embarrassment, and a little awkward diffidence. 'I'm very sorry to have inconvenienced you, Sir Tarrington,' he mumbled.

'Oh, that's all right,' I boomed cheerfully. 'Most of my relations think I'm pissed half the time.'

After that, as we trundled homewards, and I was asking myself, not for the first time, if it really was necessary for me to be a truck-driver for Abdel, simply in order to oversee the security of our horses and plans, when my thoughts were interrupted by the phone.

For once I'd remembered to bring my mobile and Annie was taking advantage. We talked for a few minutes about the race, and confirmed that Polo Stick would run on Wednesday at Warwick. I told her Kevin was coming next day, and rang off. A few minutes later it trilled again.

'Hello?' I answered it.

'Did you get my letter?' The question was asked in a bizarre, squawking sort of cartoon voice, like one of Donald Duck's nephews, and I realised at once that someone was disguising their voice with helium. It had to be my blackmailer.

I glanced at Bertie. His ginger head was flopped against the passenger door; his eyes were closed, his mouth open.

'What letter?' I asked.

'About your Derby horse.'

'Go on,' I said calmly.

'Well,' the voice squawked. 'Did you?'

'Yes.'

'I've got Mills' number here in front of me. He gets the next call if you don't answer right.'

'Carry on, then.'

'I want the money tomorrow night. Get it and drive to Tescos in Newbury. Get there at seven-thirty, stop in the car-park, take your mobile and stay there until I call you again. If you're not there, or anyone follows you, the deal's off and I ring Mills. D'you understand?'

'Yes,' I said calmly. 'If I'm not there you'll ring Mills.'

'Well, will you be there?'

I detected a hint of desperation through the squawk. 'You'll know that tomorrow at seven-thirty, won't you?' I said.

I took some satisfaction in terminating the conversation then, on my own initiative. It might make the little bastard sweat a bit, maybe panic him into making a stupid move.

In any event, at least I felt confident now that, with Piers Bowring's help, I could gain some control over events.

I woke early, escaping from dreams about faceless men with Donald Duck voices, piles of cash, and Piers Bowring telling me not to give it to him.

There was nothing I could do about the blackmailer for a few hours, until the banks were open, but I wasn't going to get any more sleep so I climbed out of bed and a few minutes later I was on my way down to the yard to help Annie.

It was a dull, gun-metal grey sort of a morning; the kind of morning in May that leaves you feeling cheated. Even the larks seemed reluctant to get up and deliver their morning trill.

Bet Your Rocks Off

I found Annie and as I watched her handling the feeds and pulling out the horses for first lot, I noticed a new, distinct tenseness about her.

It shouldn't have surprised me, but ever since she'd come to work with me, three years before, I'd had the impression that the scam wasn't quite real to her, and she'd come along for the sheer hell of it.

But seeing her jaw firm and a more than usually determined look in her eyes, I found myself wondering how important the whole thing was to her.

Even now, I still had no real idea of what her circumstances were when I'd found her again and persuaded her to join me; and she'd never given any indication of whether she was doing it for the money or the craic, although I'd concluded from some pretty ineffectual probing that she wasn't sitting on the kind of cash that a woman of her tastes needed to maintain standards; it was impossible, though, to confirm it from anything outward.

She had been just as mysterious about her love life, and as far as I was concerned there was a ten year gap in her personal history that she had no intention of filling in for me.

She'd lightened up a little after she'd been out with the first lot; the three year old grey, Polo Stick, entered to run at Warwick the following day, had produced a spectacular gallop.

I made appreciative noises, but the truth was that by this stage, I couldn't get excited about any horse besides our bogus Derby horse.

Kevin turned up with a co-operative air and in good time for a hearty breakfast of dry toast and black coffee before our next outing to the gallops.

Mountain came out of his box looking very good, lean and muscled, carrying no surplus flesh. Kevin said so without prompting, visibly impressed.

A lad legged him up, while Ray got on Iceland Hawk, currently our quickest horse over seven furlongs.

I drove Annie in the Land Rover and we met the two horses and riders at the bottom of the grass gallop.

Annie got out and walked through the long dewy grass towards them, and I followed.

'Okay, you guys,' she said as soon as she was near enough for them to hear. 'Start together; Ray, you get Iceland going right off the mark. Let him off the bridle as soon as you can and make him give all he's got.' She walked up to Kevin on Mountain and handed him a long, flexible cutting cane. 'Now listen, Kevin. Iceland will jump off faster than you, but he doesn't stay a yard over seven furlongs. You get up to him by the six furlong marker; when you do, I want you to use this stick in your left hand and give the horse two real hard cracks that he'll never forget. If he doesn't go through in the next few strides, do it again; either way, as soon as he's passed Hawk, drop the stick; I don't want him getting totally whip shy. As soon as you get to the top of the gallop, pull up and jump off. There'll be a lad waiting to lead the horse right away from you; I'm afraid he won't like you for laying into him, but if you do it right, he won't forget it either.'

Kevin nodded. 'All right, Lady M. I know what you want: he has to learn when the whip comes out, he's got to go to work.'

I listened and almost felt sorry for Mountain, although I knew that even if it hurt like hell, it wouldn't have any long term effect, beyond giving him a healthy respect for the stick.

We watched from the top, near the mile marker. When Kevin was lying half a length back and coming to Iceland after seven furlongs, he lifted the whip in his left hand and brought it down with a powerful crack across the horse's quarters. Instantly, Mountain lengthened his stride and powered past his opponent. Kevin dropped the stick, as he'd been told, and rode him out the next two hundred yards to the marker where we stood.

I turned to Annie. 'Well done! That was the right thing to do.'

She gave me a guarded nod. 'It's almost there; he came through, but he still so green; I mean - he's never raced, for Christ's sake; he doesn't know what it's like to be really fighting his way home. He just wasn't galloping on as hard as he could for the last hundred yards or so. I'm going to have to give him a real chance to go on in front before the race...'

'Annie, he's just performed.....'

'Against a good sprinter,' she finished my sentence for me. 'I must see him finish much more aggressively than that to feel comfortable.'

'All right,' I said. 'I know what else you could do if you wanted to give him a taste of finishing really hard and willing. We'll try it on Friday.'

Despite Annie's reservations, I thought Mountain had performed well and I left the gallops feeling optimistic, but as we neared the yard, I had to start focusing on negotiations with my blackmailer.

When I'd told Bowring that I thought my anonymous extortionist would quietly bugger off once I'd paid up, I hadn't been entirely honest; but at Bowring's prices, it seemed worth taking a chance on handling it without using his expensive services.

I didn't like the idea of pulling ten grand of my own from the bank, but at least my winning bets on Partridge were providing all the cash.

Once I was back in my house, I phoned my bookie and confirmed that my account was a little over six thousand pounds in credit, which would appear as a cheque at the end of the month. The Tote's cheque would arrive that morning, and I could pay it in when I went to Marlborough to get the cash.

While I was waiting for it to arrive, I put together a list of all the lads, work riders and people who were in regular contact with the yard and faxed it to Piers Bowring's Art Shipping company's office. I didn't think he would do anything about it until I'd shown him some money, but if I had to call him in, it was as well to have everything ready. Personally, I was doubtful about the relevance of this list. I'd mentally checked off every person on it, and there wasn't one of them

Bet Your Rocks Off

I would have judged as being disposed to turn on us, especially for such a comparatively small sum.

The postman arrived late, as usual. I had to check myself from sharing my thoughts with him as he ambled up to the house with a stack of dreary circulars.

I quickly spotted the Tote envelope and tore it open to extract my cheque for £3,750. It took me a couple of unwilling seconds to see that some error had occurred. The cheque was for £37.50.

With a sinking heart, I looked at the details of the transaction and saw that the blasted Scouser Barbie girl had marked down my Trifecta at fifty pence a line, instead of fifty quid!

Pulsating with frustration, knowing it was my own bloody fault for not checking the ticket, I bounded upstairs and dug around for it in my stud tray, where I'd left it on Friday night.

The ghastly tidings were right. I must have just said "fifty", and she'd taken it that, like ninety nine percent of punters on these multiple bets, I was playing for pin money and meant fifty pence.

Dopey, air-headed, Liverpudlian tart! I bellowed at myself, knowing that the mistake was at least as much my fault. But I still had to find the money for my blackmailer.

The trouble was - getting all my ante-post Derby bets on and making sure I didn't get behind on payments to my ex-wife, especially while I'd been in the very final stages of settling up for good, had left me running on a very tight track.

CHAPTER EIGHTEEN

I nearly lost my temper when the spotty, dandruff-shouldered, ghastly-suited individual who was supposed to do the job that my bank manager had once done, started asking me for cash-flow forecasts and likely prospects of imminent funds to reduce the borrowing that I was trying to arrange.

'I've just told you, Mr Gwatkin,' - which was the miserable little turd's name - 'my bookmaker only settles up once a month; there are no exceptions, and they let us do the same to them. They currently owe me six thousand pounds; I can get a print out of my latest statement for you.'

'You are aware, I suppose, Mr Tarrington, that gambling debts are not recoverable under the law?'

'Are you suggesting that a well-respected public company would welsh on its debts?'

'Well, they might....'

'Don't be ridiculous! Even if they are run by grey little men who wouldn't know a game of cards from a Brasilian rumba, they do know if they started welshing, no-one would ever bet with them again, and believe me, they make a hefty enough profit from gambling without needing to resort to welshing.'

I wasn't going to grovel to the tin-pot computer operator, but I was determined not to break into the small cache of funds sitting in my solicitors' clients' account which I was preserving for my final raid against the bookies on Derby day and half an hour later, I left the bank clutching a bag full of brand new fifties, cling wrapped in ten small bundles of a thousand pounds.

I was stuffing the cash into the undersized safe in my office when the phone rang.

I picked it up.

'This is Piers Bowring.'

'Morning Piers.'

'I want to send you a confidential fax. Are you there to receive it yourself, in private?'

'Sure.'

'It's on its way.'

With his customary brusqueness, he cut off. I put the phone down as the fax line started ringing.

A minute later I was looking a sheet of paper which told me that Mick O'Grady's great grandfather had been shot by the Black and Tans in 1921. His father had been a member of an active IRA cell in Cork in the '80s, with a history of extortion. Mick's mother's family were from 'Derry, where his uncle was suspected of being a member of the INLA.

I read the shattering document twice before stuffing it in the shredder.

Mick O'Grady, the quiet, gentle one, who didn't need much booze to take him over the top - the other lads teased - was the last of them I would have thought would be practising extortion.

Though, it was often said that it was the silent ones to watch.

But then I thought of Annie going into Swindon hospital for the few days he'd spent there nursing the crack on his head, and his obvious gratitude and adulation of her afterwards, and he seemed an even more unlikely candidate.

I went out and walked down to the yard where the lads were putting some of the horses out in the pens for a few hours fresh air and green grass.

Mick was leading out High Sierra, to whom he was particularly attached. I tried to read something into his demeanour, but failed to spot anything even vaguely suspicious.

I was thinking about Mick, too, as I drove to Newbury in the Mercedes for my tryst in the Tesco car-park.

I arrived at seven twenty-five, parked, opened *The Sporting Post* and waited.

I couldn't read a word on the page in front of me. My heart was pounding and a clammy sweat had broken out under my shirt, prompted by the knowledge that someone, somewhere among the steady stream of punters using the supermarket or, perhaps, in the riverside public gardens, was watching me.

Bet Your Rocks Off

And despite all my instincts to the contrary, I couldn't dispel a picture of a desperate and very different Mick O'Grady.

At seven thirty, my mobile bleeped.

I flicked it on.

'Go into the supermarket and get one of their bags.' Once again the voice was disguised by the application of helium to the larynx. The change in the density of the gas surrounding the vocal chords made them vibrate faster and so at a higher pitch. There was no way I could detect Mick O'Grady's voice behind the distorted squawking vowels. 'Then come back to the car. And keep this line open. I don't want you to call anyone else.'

I didn't say anything, but climbed out of the car, locked it, and did as I'd been told.

When I was back in the car, I put the phone to my ear and found that my instructor was still breathing gently over the air.

'I've got the bag,' I said.

'Good. Do you know where the Co-op is?'

'Is this a kind of shopping trip or what?' I asked.

'Shut up! Do you know?'

'Yes.'

'Drive there now. There's people watching; if you're followed, Mills gets the call. And keep this line open.'

It was a circuitous route through the old town to the rival supermarket. I guessed the blackmailer had devised a simple way of checking that I wasn't being backed up by anyone, or able to contact them ahead.

When I reached the Co-op car park, the phone came alive again, and I guessed that my instructor had me in eye contact now, if he hadn't before.

'Put the money in the Tesco bag and put your paper on top of the money. Do it now...... Have you done it? Then walk over to the newspaper recycling container. Try to put the bag in; you'll find it's full, so just leave it propped up against the side. Then go straight into the store, and don't cut off this call. Stay in there for no less than ten minutes before you come out. If you disobey any of these orders, or we see any one who's followed you here, Mills gets the call, and we get the money. Do you understand what I'm saying?'

'Yes, thank you.'

In fifteen minutes I was back at the car. I could see that my Tesco bag had gone from where I'd dumped it. I lifted my mobile to my ear but the caller had disconnected.

I had to concede that he'd done a good job.

There was, for instance, a steady trickle of eco-friendly punters dumping their papers, as I had, in piles beside the replete container. It was ideal for the blackmailer's purposes.

And it seemed to me that he'd very effectively made sure I wasn't accompanied.

I set off from Newbury to Square Barrow in a state of emotional limbo. I'd spent ten thousand quid to lift a burden from my mind, but it still didn't feel lifted. Before I got back to the yard, I stopped off at the Waggon and Horses, the lads' favourite pub in Beckhampton.

Bertie and Des Hughes were there, and greeted me cheerfully. 'What are you havin', Sir H?' Des asked, never slow to stand me a drink.

'A pint'll go down well,' I said, and sat down in a way to suggest that I'd dropped in for one of my occasional chats.

I was burning with impatience to ask them if they knew where Mick was, but I couldn't look as if I'd come in to check up on him.

A minute or so later, I didn't need to ask. Mick walked in from the gents and picked up a half-empty pint glass of Guinness which I hadn't noticed on the bar beside Des.

He acknowledged me with a brief, self-conscious smile, and carried on a conversation that he'd obviously been having with Bertie before he went to the lavatory.

Now, it was imperative to know how long he'd been there. If he'd been in Newbury collecting my cash, he'd had a good ten minutes' start on me, but that was all.

Des was still in a buying mood. 'Who's having another one, then?' he asked his mates. 'Jesus, Micky, have you already done your first pint?'

'It's okay,' Mick said apologetically. 'I'd a hell of a thirst on; I'll get these.'

He pulled a wallet from his pocket with, as far as I could see, a couple of notes in it, and paid for two more drinks.

I was finding it very hard to sustain anything like a normal conversation. I was battling with the fact that several circumstantial factors bore out the possibility that Mick O'Grady, product of a line of committed terrorists, had carried out the simple piece of extortion of which I'd just been victim.

But when I looked at his face, and heard him stammer his views in reply to the raucous opinions of the other lads, I simply couldn't believe it.

A soon as I'd finished my pint, I made up some busy reason for going and left.

It was nearly nine by the time I drove into the yard; an hour to kill before late feed. I thought, given the closeness of our D-Day, I could be excused for breaking our code and going to see Annie. I walked down to Dairyman's Cottage, but there wasn't a light to be seen; she was either out, or sleeping early in anticipation of a five-thirty start.

Twelve hours after handing over my ten grand, I'd hardly slept a minute. I'd convinced myself that whoever it was, it wasn't Mick and nor, I guessed, could it have been Bertie or Des.

Besides, I'd started to think it must be someone at arm's length from our yard, who had somehow sussed what we were doing.

Taking a line, quite irrationally, through Mick's dodgy connections in Cork, I started thinking of a young Irish veterinary assistant attached to the practice who looked after most of our problems.

Bet Your Rocks Off

I'd noticed that he always took what seemed to me to be an excessive interest in all our horses, and was constantly badgering Annie or me for information.

I'd assumed he was just an enthusiastic punter; God knows, there were enough of them around - the bane of a trainer's life - but there was a sort of bogus bonhomie about him that I distrusted instinctively. And it occurred to me that he may have been made suspicious by the very fact that we never let anyone near our Derby horse.

As doubts, confusion and premonition crowded in on me, I was beginning seriously to regret that I hadn't taken on Bowring from the start to help me deal with my blackmailer.

Later, the postman turned up, on time for once.

His arrival turned the previous night's horrific fantasies into reality.

Posted the night before with a Reading post-mark, was another letter produced in the same way as the first blackmail threat.

This time it contained a demand for a hundred thousand pounds, by Friday.

When I'd read it, the paper literally dropped from my hands while I gazed across the room through a quivering blur.

'Hugo?' Annie asked sharply. I hadn't even heard her come in.

I tried to focus and turned to her.

'Oh, hello.'

'Good God! What's happened to you? Why are sitting there like a fish with a hook up its butt?'

'It's nothing really,' I said, collecting myself, and casually picking up the blackmail demand at my feet. 'An old schoolfriend I used to sit next to at Harrow has died; I was rather fond of him.'

'You are a sentimental old teddy bear, aren't you,' Annie cooed.

'If you say so.' I stood up and tried to concentrate on the normal functions of the day until Annie had gone.

I knew that it would do nothing but harm to share my fear with her, and was determined to keep any hint of the threat from her, but I could hardly contain myself while she sat around drinking coffee and discussing Polo Stick's prospects at Warwick, where, I remembered with horror, I was supposed to be taking the horse to race that day.

But I put on a performance that would have got me accepted for the RSC, and Annie left without an inkling of what was going on in my head. As soon as she was out of the door, I phoned Bowring's number in Surrey.

Once again, the NCO type answered and asked how he could help.

'I spoke to Mr Bowring on Monday about a contract; I'd like to confirm that I want him to go ahead.'

'I'll get the major for you, sir.'

A moment later, Bowring's calm, *sotto voce* tones came soothingly down the line.

'Good morning Hugo. Had the next demand, have you?'

'Yes. A hundred K,' I blurted.

'Not over the phone,' Bowring came back quickly. 'Where can we meet?'

'Warwick, this afternoon?' I offered, tentatively.

'Excellent. One o'clock, on the lawn in front of the weighing-room.'

I thought fast. I'd only just make it. 'I may be a little late,' I said.

'I'll wait.'

He put the phone down, and I did the same, with great relief.

When I told Annie I had to be at the races by one, even though Polo Stick didn't go until four twenty, she didn't ask why, and obliged by getting her runner ready to load in record time.

The day had started, like the previous one, under a sky like a sheet of corrugated iron. Now this had been stirred a little by a sharp westerly which was rousting up the clouds over the tops of the downs and letting the sun in through burgeoning chinks. By the time I drove into Warwick races with Polo Stick, the sun was shining strongly.

I parked just after one, and left Des Hughes to look after our apprehensive young gelding. I spotted Bowring from behind, dressed more or less as he had been two days before at Leicester. Uncannily, he turned to me just before I reached him.

'Hugo,' he nodded, and gestured that we should walk away to a quiet corner in the shade behind the stands.

'So,' he said. 'You gave them the money yesterday?'

I nodded, and told him exactly how it had happened.

'Not professionals,' he commented with a disparaging shake of his head.

'It seemed like a good operation to me.'

'Not at all, not if they'd had a serious surveillance team on them. And they would have insisted on used notes.'

'It may not be 'they', of course,' I said.

'Agreed. But if you want me to handle this job, you're going to have to tell me about this 'sensitive' information your man has threatened to broadcast. To do the job, I need all the facts.'

I made a face. I'd guessed this would be coming, but, in some ways, I was almost glad to unburden myself on Bowring. If anyone could understand and handle the idea, he could, and I had no doubts about his discretion.

He listened while I spelled out how our coup had been conceived and planned. He gave no visible reaction, approving or otherwise. When I'd finished, he simply nodded.

'I'm glad I'm in the picture now. So, let's talk business. My fee won't cause you any problems, I'm sure, given the funding behind your yard.'

'No, it won't, as long as you can send an invoice for security services, guarding Private Mountain.'

'Fine. You'll get a bill for the first half by fax today. Please pay it by return. Here's my personal mobile number.' He handed me a card with eleven digits printed on it. 'Don't divulge it to anyone and if you can't remember it, disguise it somewhere and destroy this card. Let me know as soon as you hear anything, every time they contact you. Any instructions I give you, please follow to the letter.' He looked at me expressionlessly with his silver blue eyes. 'And don't worry. We'll have this wrapped up by Friday night.'

He turned and walked off towards the stands, leaving me staring after him with relief and a little shame at my utter dependence on him.

I had no idea if Bowring stayed at the races, but I didn't see him again that day. Our horse came in a creditable third, and I set off for home feeling that events were under control.

I was just turning onto the new Cirencester by-pass when my blackmailer rang, speaking with this now familiar squawk.

'Did you get my letter?'

I glanced at Des to see if he'd heard anything odd from where he sat, but he was nodding away to The Corrs in his head set.

'Yes,' I answered.

'Make sure you get the money.'

'I don't think I can.'

'Then I'll talk to Mills. Do you want that?'

'But I can't do it by Friday.'

'Then you won't have a runner in the Derby. And I know you can get it. There's plenty of money. I'll ring you, Friday. Make sure you answer.'

He cut off, and I did the same. I pulled Bowring's number from my pocket.

He answered at once.

'He's rung,' I said.

'What did he say?'

'To wait for a call on Friday.'

'Fine. We've got other things we can get on with until then. If there's any change, tell me at once.'

I switched off, feeling a fool for having even this cryptic conversation with Des in the cab; but the Irish lad was still nodding away, wrapped, I guessed, in fantasies about the Irish girls he was listening to.

When I drove into the yard at Square Barrow, Annie was waiting for me.

'I didn't bother you because there was nothing you could have done, but we had a visit from your charming old cousin, Henry Mills.'

'Shit! What did he want?'

'Relax,' Annie sighed, with what looked almost like a tender smile on the flawless symmetry of her face. 'You worry too much. He was thinking of us. He said he'd had reports of some large amounts being laid on Private Mountain, and they treat any sudden movement in the price of an outsider as significant.'

'Outsider!?' I expostulated. 'Private Mountain's not an outsider. Henry's got a nerve. The horse won well last season; he was highly rated, and that gallop at Newbury proved nothing either way to Jo Public. He's just been too cheap until now, thank God, and I still think he'll go away at twenties.'

'Don't get so uptight, Hugo. He said it was just a routine call, so I took him down and showed him the horse...'

'You did what!?' I exploded his time.

'For God's sake relax. What's wrong with you? I knew it would be much safer to offer to show him the colt before he asked, and he didn't go anywhere near his mouth. I very much doubt that he or his side-kick could read a set of teeth anyway. The point is, he went away happy.'

'All right,' I accepted grudgingly.

'But there is a nasty little surprise for you in your office.' Annie nodded at a muddied, middle-aged Jaguar which I'd already noticed, parked beyond my house.

'Oh, God. What?'

'Go and see for yourself. I'm afraid I couldn't get rid of him, at least, not without a gun.'

'Hello, Sir Hugo.'

'Hugo! What the hell are you doing here?'

The rhino-hide of Chris Lewis's face contorted into what I guessed was a smile. 'Just dropped in to thank you for your hospitality on Monday.'

'What do you want?'

'I thought you might be expecting trouble.'

'Trouble? Why should I be expecting trouble?'

'A visit from a former head of Jockey Club security made me think you might be.'

'How the hell did you know he was coming here?'

'I didn't; I followed him. Just lucky, really. I was up at Lambourn, watching horses work and called in for a quick one at the

Hare and Hounds. Soon as I drove in the car park, I saw old Brigadier Mills leaving. I know what he does, so I thought it'd be interesting to see what he was up to. And surprise, surprise! He led me here!'

'Good God! Did he see you?'

'No, don't worry. He never knew he was followed and I waited till he left before I came into to see Lady Tenbury.'

'I'm not worried,' I denied hastily. 'But do you often do that sort of thing?'

'It can be very rewarding. And I see you've made provision for your horse's safety,' he added, nodding at the fax by the desk, where Bowring's bill protruded, completely legible.

'There's nothing odd about that. I should think half the field have made some kind of provision.'

'A couple of lads with a dung fork, maybe, but seven and a half grand's worth?'

I lightly shrugged one shoulder. 'My owners are naturally rather paranoid; and it's their money.'

'You won't mind if I tell my readers, will you?'

I did mind, but he was going to do it anyway.

'No,' I said. 'Why should I?'

'Well, if people hear that you're spending all this money protecting him, they might conclude that maybe you reckon he's got a better chance than the bookies think.'

'It can't be helped. Of course, it'll bring the price in, but I've already had a bit on.'

Hugo's eyes lit up. 'You have, have you? How much?'

Bet Your Rocks Off

'As if I'd tell you.' I tried to give him a matey grin. I didn't think I'd pulled it off, but he seemed to accept that I wasn't going to tell him anything else that evening.

'Ah, well, I like to see an outsider's connections confident a few days before a big race.'

'Good, then you'll leave here a happy man.'

I walked to the door and held it open for him. He shambled out with a grunt of goodbye, and eased himself into his much-abused car.

He had just lurched out of sight when the phone rang. It was Madame, reminding me that I was due to meet her for lunch next day at Claridges. I couldn't say no, but I knew it would be hard to keep up a convincing front under her shrewd gaze for a few hours, and it would be complicated by our having a runner the next day. Annie's pet, Dome Climb was entered in another maiden race at Chepstow.

CHAPTER NINETEEN

'Hugo, my dear boy,' Madame greeted me with a squeeze and a waft of Chanel. I'd been shown into her suite overlooking Brook Street and she was standing, just, supporting herself on the back of a gilt French chair. When I leaned to kiss her on each cheek, she was trembling.

'Madame, you must sit,' I said, and helped her into the chair where she settled gratefully.

I began to get her up to date with a little social gossip, which I knew she liked, but I was worried by the alarming deterioration in her appearance. Her skin, despite a lot of skilfully applied make-up, seemed to have developed more wrinkles and a sickly yellow glaze since I'd last seen her.

A few moments later, after a brief knock, the door was opened and a waiter came in bearing a tray, obviously in answer to an earlier summons. He placed it on a table where he mixed a brace of king-sized dry Martinis and gave them to us.

'To your good health, Hugo, and every good luck for our Derby horse,' Madame proposed in uncharacteristically bad English. 'How does he look?'

'I've brought you some photographs, Madame,' I said, and pulled an envelope from my jacket.

She took them, and I saw them quiver in her hands.

'He looks wonderful, Hugo. I'm very proud of you. You've done a beautiful job.'

'And Annie,' I added. There was only the slightest tensing of her upper lip, but I spotted it. 'I hear she came and saw you last week,' I went on, more casually than I felt.

'Oh, Hugo,' - she spoke my name in French - 'I'm so sorry to have been indiscreet. Naturally, I assumed that your relationship with Lady Tenbury would tolerate no secrets; after all, you were very close, weren't you, since a long, long time ago.'

'Madame, our relationship since we started working together for you and Abdel had been strictly professional.'

'A-ha,' she laughed. 'Then it doesn't matter if she hears of your little tennis parties?'

I couldn't see anything to be gained from swimming against the current. I smiled. 'No, of course not, Madame.

All right,' she said crisply. 'That will do about your sex life, as long as you are happy, my dear boy?'

'Thank you, yes,' I said, though happy didn't at all describe my current state of mind.

'So, sit down and tell me about each of my horses. I'm so glad we have won some races already. Abdel told me he thought we wouldn't.'

'Unlike most normal horse-owners, Abdel isn't a crazy optimist.'

'No,' she agreed. 'But I am sure he thinks we will win the Derby.'

I smiled again, encouragingly, while I wondered if our horse would even run in the race.

Despite the knot tightening around my guts, I managed to spend the next hour or so over a lunch of supremely and traditionally cooked tournedos, telling Madame in minute detail how we were dealing with each of her horses.

When she seemed satisfied that I'd told her everything there was to know about the animals in training, I asked nonchalantly, 'How is Corporal Harding getting on?'

'I think, very well. I am very pleased with them.'

I detected no hint of subtext in her words, and by the time I left at three to drive back to Square Barrow, I was confident that she still had no inkling of what we were doing for her.

Although I knew there was no point, I had to ring Bowring on the way home.

'What's happened?' he asked.

'I haven't heard from him yet.'

'I see.' There was a pause. 'Why are you ringing?'

'I just thought he might have been in touch.'

'He said he'd ring on Friday, didn't he? I expect he'll ring then, unless he decides he doesn't want the money after all. Let me know when he has.'

He'd buggered off as usual before I could answer. Not that I had a satisfactory reply to offer. I felt a fool for contacting Bowring in these circumstances; victim counselling was not one of the services he offered.

To take my mind off a threat about which I could do nothing, I checked in with Annie to find out what had happened to our horse at Chepstow.

'Hi,' she answered sounding chirpy. 'We had another winner.'

'Oh hell!"

'What? Aren't you pleased?'

'Of course, I'm pleased but I forgot to back the bastard, that's all.'

'He is not a bastard; he ran like a real star.'

'I find that very hard to believe after his performance at Bath, but well done. Did you have any trouble with hacks or hustlers?'

'No. I took lots of a body-guards; Alfie and Birgitta came with me; and Calista.'

'Good God, I should think you'd need a squad of body guards with you two on the loose.'

'It was great to have her with me; Jackson's in Hamburg tonight, so she's coming back to stay with me at the cottage.'

'Oh good,' I said instinctively.

'Just you keep away. She won't want you sniffing around.'

That's what you think, I said to myself with an sharp twinge of guilt over my last encounter with Calista. I put the phone down with Annie's husky laugh echoing in my head.

Then Laura rang.

'Where have you been?' she asked in an oddly plaintive voice; I was conscious that I hadn't seen her or spoken to her since the Chepstow gallop, nearly two weeks before. And a hell of a lot had happened since then.

I deliberately misunderstood her. 'I've been having lunch with Madame al Hassan at Claridges.'

'Well, where are you now?'

'Readingish.'

'Come on down to Nethercote.'

I was puzzled that there wasn't the upheaval in my groin which just the thought of being with Laura usually provoked. Then, with alarm, I realised that it simply made me want to yawn.

But I still had business to discuss with her before Saturday, and now seemed as good a time as any. 'Okay,' I said. 'I'll be with you in forty minutes.'

'I'll be waiting and ready,' she gurgled, and put the phone down.

I shook my head, confused.

Nothing. There wasn't a whimper of reaction in my genitals. I guessed it must have been a reaction to the tension produced by the blackmail, but I'd never experienced this sudden absence of libido and it shocked me.

Bet Your Rocks Off

Later, as I drove in through the gates at Nerthercote, I guessed that the sight of Laura would put things back to normal. I parked the car on the thick bed of gravel Toby Allerthorpe had piled in front of the house, and walked across to the tall, stone portico.

The front door was just ajar. I pushed it, stepped into the dark hall and sniffed in the familiar manorial aromas of wood smoke, Madeira and oak floor-boards.

'Hi, Hugo.'

I looked up. Laura was standing at the top of the broad flight of stairs. She looked at me from beneath lowered lashes; her short, dark brown hair was in alluring disarray, and she was completely naked.

I slowly walked up the stairs towards her, half-conscious that other forces were taking me in hand.

I couldn't take my eyes off her. Her skin was an all-over light tan, with not a ripple of cellulite detectable beneath it. Her breasts were big and self-supporting, tipped with nipples like small pink pebbles. Her bush had been trimmed to a neat narrow, inverted isosceles triangle. Her bodywork, I thought, was a triumph of will over mileage, though I didn't need to remind myself that Laura took the care of her body, which was her principal asset, very seriously.

When I had arrived at the top of the stairs, she reached out and put a hand on my right buttock; she kneaded it gently as she turned her mouth to mine for a long, damp kiss.

'Where's Toby?' I asked between mouthfuls.

'Who gives a shit?'

'I don't - as long as he's not here.'

'Of course he's not here. He told me he was going to play golf. He went off without his clubs so I expect he's gone to see his whipper in Bath.'

'Toby has a spanker?' I asked, not surprised.

'Yes,' she hissed angrily. 'Since I told him I wasn't going to flagellate his great fat backside.'

'Gosh, you sound cross,' I teased.

'No I'm not; I'm bored stiff with the old bastard. Come on, let's get in the shower and fuck.'

'In a minute,' I said, leading her into a spare room which we sometimes used. I picked up a bed-cover to wrap round her. 'Before we do anything, I want to tell you about the arrangements for Saturday.'

'Tell me afterwards.'

'No; I'll tell you now, while I can still think.'

She pouted and reached out to grasp my balls and twisted them gently. I pushed her off.

'Listen, you want to help; you've got to know what to do.'

'Go on then,' she sighed and flopped back sulkily.

'What are your plans on Derby day?'

'We're having lunch in Peter Vickers' box.'

I nodded. 'He won't want you there much before twelve thirty, I shouldn't think, so you can meet me at Barry Cope's seafood bar at the far end of the parade ring at eleven thirty. Do you know where I mean?'

'Yes, Hugo,' Laura yawned.

'Listen! The security around the race-course slows things up, so aim to be there by eleven. Have you got a car pass?'

'Yes, Vickers sent me one because Toby's coming from London separately.' Her fingers started marching up my thigh towards my genitals again.

'For God's sake, pay attention Laura; we're talking big bucks here.'

'Sorry.' She chewed her lower lip in bogus contrition.

'I don't want you to put my money on until I'm absolutely certain the horse is going off right, so when we meet, you must do as I tell you for once in your fucking life, because I won't give you the final okay until after lunch. I want you to put five grand each way on with the Tote, but so you don't draw too much attention to yourself, you'll have to go to five different windows. I'll give you the money in bundles of two grand, okay?'

'How much are you putting down altogether?'

'I'm not telling you that.'

She shrugged. 'What do I do with the tickets if the horse wins?'

'Go straight to five different windows again as soon as they're weighed in and collect cash. I can't do it myself; too many people know who I am, but I want the bets paid right away in case there's any bother.'

Her antennae immediately picked up my slip, and I cursed my carelessness. 'What sort of bother?' she asked sharply.

301

'Oh I don't know - if there's an enquiry or something, whatever. It's easier if you collect, then bring the money along to me later.'

'All right, but what's my cut?'

'Five percent of the win - eight or ten grand.'

She made a face. 'That's not much.'

'Then put down some of your own, and get some on with the bookies too.'

'Are you going to?'

'Of course I am; that's all arranged.'

'How much will you win in all?'

'Plenty. Well over a mill, anyway.'

Laura was impressed. 'And don't you get a share of the horse if it wins?'

'Yes; two nominations a year.'

'That could be worth another million.'

'Not quite,' I grinned.

The thought of all this easy money acted on her like an aphrodisiac. She flung off the cover and lay back on the bed, pulling me down with her and tugging my hand to her hot, hungry vagina.

Then my mobile trilled.

'Shit,' she snapped as I withdrew my hand and dragged the phone from my pocket.

'Hi, Hugo; you sound out of breath. Are you running or...' Annie hesitated a moment. 'Where are you?'

'Just stopped at the service area.'

'Oh?'

'Yah. I should be back in half an hour.'

'See you, then.'

I punched off the phone, wondering why I'd said I was coming back right away. Annie hadn't asked me to. Normally I'd have spent an hour or two with Laura.

But I didn't want to.

'I've got to go.'

Laura gazed with bewildered panic at my flaccid cock. 'What do you mean, you've got to go? You haven't even come yet!'

'Crisis back at the yard - a real turn-off, you know, I can't perform as you deserve if I can't concentrate.'

'I don't mind Hugo; even your worst is good.' Uttering this flattery was too much for her. She became abruptly morose and petulant. She grasped my dwindling penis and manipulated vigorously with her skinny fingers. 'At least you can have the good manners to remain standing until you've squirted,' she insisted.

I didn't know what the etiquette books had to say about this aspect of social encounter, but I could see her point and, noblesse obliging, stayed where I was for the distressingly short time required for honour to be satisfied.

I left Laura looking mutinous, but damned if she was going to make a scene or behave hurt.

As I drove away, past the ragged topiary of which old Tom Buckton had once been so proud, I had a sudden premonition that I wouldn't be going back to that particular fount of pleasure again.

I hoped Laura hadn't felt it, though; I didn't want to be dealing with any trouble of that sort at such a critical moment.

It had always been one of Annie's attractions for me that I never knew what she was thinking. But when I saw her half an hour later, standing in my kitchen with her hands wrapped around a large cup of green tea, I sensed a hint of wounded ego.

'My God, Hugo, such guilt!'

'Guilt? What guilt?'

'You look shifty as a riverboat card-sharp, and I know why.'

'Oh? Why?' I looked at her with bland innocence.

'I don't want to talk about it.'

'But you just did,' I protested.

'Not any more.'

I gave up, but I was sure she knew exactly where I'd been.

'Fine,' I said with a shrug. 'Anything to report here?'

'Not a lot. Ulrike looks sick and when she rode Mont Blanc, he made a hell of a fuss and got all coltish; she must be having her period.'

'These things happen,' I said tolerantly.

'Yeah, well,' she went on scratchily. 'I hope she's in tomorrow, we've got a lot to do.'

She was well wound up; I didn't blame her. She was responsible for a Derby runner who'd never run a race in its life; and though we both knew the animal had it in him to outperform every other contender, there was still, even now, less than forty-eight hours from the race, a question mark over his will to win.

'You know I told you at the beginning of the week that there was one last stratagem we could try...' I started to say.

'Yes; I'm still waiting to hear it.'

'I wanted to leave it until tomorrow so the experience will be fresh in his mind, along with the memory of what Kevin can do with a whip.'

'So? Let's have it.'

'We're going to try an old trick of Fred Darling's. I once saw Sir Gordon Richards talking about it on telly and I'm certain it'll suit our boy's temperament.'

Annie nodded impatiently for me to get on.

'Fred Darling had a filly who was outstanding in most ways,' I said, 'but a bit iffy in a finish. So, in her last gallop before the Oaks, instead of taking her away from home as he normally did, he reversed the gallop and aimed her back at the stables. She ran like a dream, really sweetened up and two days later she won the Oaks. Old Sir Gordon said it was one of the most inspired pieces of training he'd ever seen.'

'You're right,' Annie nodded, eagerly this time. 'It's so simple, but it could just suit our boy.'

I was in my kitchen, just after nine, making myself a quick supper, when the phone rang. It needed only the first strangled words to get my nerve ends quivering.

'Take the money to Epsom with your horse tomorrow.'

This change in venue completely wrong-footed me. Naively, I supposed, I'd been assuming since I'd had the second letter that I'd have to go back and do the circuit of the supermarkets in Newbury to make the drop, as I had with the first.

I'd been gearing myself up to telling Bowring that was where it would happen. Suddenly to be told it was to be in the middle of the hurly-burly of an Epsom Oaks Day race crowd fazed me for a few seconds. But I recovered enough to try and talk my persecutor out of it.

'I'm not going anywhere near Epsom tomorrow.'

'You've got a runner declared, and if you don't show up, you'll have Mills all over your place before you know what's hit you.'

I stifled a resigned sigh. 'Okay, where?'

'Take your mobile. I'll call you as soon as you reach the course.'

'How will you know when that is?' I wanted to keep him chatting. I knew that the effect of the helium would quickly wear off, and though he could always top it up with another squirt, there was a chance he might let his own voice slip out before he realised it.

'I'll know. Just make sure you get there two hours before your race.' There was a pause. 'And don't forget the money. A hundred grand in used fifties.'

'I've already got it,' I said, as Bowring had instructed. 'What do you want it in?'

'Wrap it in newspaper, and put it in a plastic bag.'

Bet Your Rocks Off

'At Epsom, tomorrow?' Bowring said, betraying a moment's disbelief.

'Yes. I've got to get there two hours before our race.'

'He must be mad.' Bowring's contempt was audible even over the phone. 'How will you be going?'

'I drive the lorry.'

'The blue three-horse box?'

'That's right.' I noted that he knew our vehicle as a matter of course. 'What about the money?'

'Just take a parcel of newspaper.'

'Anything else I should do?'

'No. Do exactly as your man says. Leave everything else to us. We'll keep Mills' phone busy, in case your man gets touchy; we'll be with you all the way. I'll be in touch with you tomorrow evening.'

He put the phone down.

I did the same, trying to credit his supreme confidence. Not that I wanted to disbelieve. I had nowhere to find a hundred thousand in used fifties. My last fifteen grand, which had been transferred from my solicitors' account that day, was already earmarked for a few last bets and Laura's part in my operation on Derby day.

I spent some of the next night dreaming of a horse who went off like a rocket, but as fast as he ran, there was a man who looked like Donald Duck hanging on to his tail and dragging him back.

The rest of the night, I lay awake sweating.

At six thirty, I gave up and went downstairs.

The two telephone conversations I'd had the night before suddenly seemed utterly unreal, or at least unconnected with the reality of our horse's chances in the world's premier flat race next day. It was as if Piers Bowring had burst on the scene in a flash of blinding light, like some soldierly archangel and simply banished the blackmail threat with the sweep of a celestial swagger stick.

I was very glad I'd had the will not to tell Annie about the blackmailer now that, for once, she was displaying some tension herself.

Although when I'd suggested it, I'd been confident that our mutual enthusiasm for Fred Darling's ploy was justified, I now thought it was far too little, too late - if the blackmailer hadn't already told Mills to go and look at Mountain's teeth.

Annie hadn't asked Kevin to come and ride Mountain for this last piece of work. When the colt came out of his stable, alert and uttering little snorts of excitement, she put Ray on him, and Ulrike, notably surlier than normal, on Andes Pavlova.

I didn't question her decision in the yard, but as Annie and I hacked out behind them I asked her why she didn't ride Mountain herself.

'I mean,' I said, 'It's a bit risky putting a man up after Kevin gave him such a caning on Tuesday, and we decided from the word go we'd be safer if you always rode him.'

'Stop fussing Hugo. I want to see for myself how this goes, and Ray's a much gentler rider than Kevin. Besides for Christsake, I really don't think there's any chance he's going to suss anything he doesn't know already. And quite frankly, the staff are beginning to wonder why I always ride him myself.'

I still wanted to disagree, but I supposed she had a point, and today was not a day for squabbling.

It was only when the horses reached the point at the stable end of the gallops, where they usually started their work, that Annie told the riders to carry on at a walk up the gentle slope of the grass gallop to the five furlong marker.

Ray made a face. 'Why did you need Ulrike if we're only walking them?'

'Just do as you're told!' Annie snapped in a way I'd never heard and the two work riders slouched on up the grassy slope.

I looked at her. 'Relax, darling.'

'Don't "darling" me.'

'Look, I know you're worried. And I'm not saying there's nothing to worry about, but the tenser you get, the more you'll communicate it to the riders, and their arses will tell the horses.'

'I don't need a lecture in human-equine relations right now. But it was you who got me into do this job and winning this effing Derby has been the one single purpose of the last three years' work.'

'For God's sake, d'you think I don't know that?' I said. 'But you've done you're best; even if he doesn't win, at least you've earned a good wage for a few years.'

309

She stopped her horse, and I pulled up automatically beside her. Her turquoise eyes glinted at me. 'Do you seriously think I've done all this for wages? Don't you think I've put every goddam cent I could find on this horse? I *need* proper money Hugo. I should have thought you knew me well enough. When you told me what you were planning, I knew right away it was my best shot at collecting a serious pile of dough.'

'I never realised you were that hard up or that obsessive; I thought you were doing it for me.'

'There are lots of things you don't know about me. For fifteen years you and I never communicated. You have no idea where I've been or what's happened to me.'

'I heard things.'

'U-hu,' she shook her head. 'Calista wouldn't ever tell you, whatever else she may have done. Listen, if I'd wanted you to know my life story, only I could have told you. But Hugo, I am sort of doing all this for you, too,' she said more gently, then added, 'because I thought it would work.'

'"Thought"?' I queried.

'Okay - think.'

'But what do you need the money for so badly?'

'That's my business.' She tossed her head, as if telling me her personal priorities had somehow eased the tension, and started trotting up towards the horses who had nearly reached the marker. 'Okay you guys,' she called to Ray and Ulrike. 'Turn around.'

Bet Your Rocks Off

The two riders wheeled their horses. Private Mountain was up on his toes, tugging at his bridle, showing signs of wanting to get on with something more energetic than a quiet walk.

Ray scowled. 'What now?'

Annie ignored him. 'Okay, Ulrike, lead Pavlova off at a three-quarter gallop until you hit the three marker, then really let her have her head, right down to the bottom of the gallop. Ray, hold yours up as much as you can, so you're a length or two off at the halfway mark, then let him go; he'll know darn well he's going home. I want him to have a real good blow out; I'm expecting him to lead Pavlova by six or seven lengths at the bottom. Okay?'

Ray and Ulrike nodded, seeing what we were trying to do.

'Just give me and Sir Hugo time to get back down there.' Annie wheeled her hack and cantered towards the lower end of the gallop.

'Twelve, thirteen lengths!' I bellowed exuberantly at Annie as Private Mountain charged across the line. Since he'd caught up with the filly three furlongs out, he'd galloped all over her; left her standing.

There was a corresponding gleam in Annie's face. 'Okay.' She nodded her head in admiration and, less obviously, relief. 'That was the best piece of work I ever saw him do.'

'What do you think?' I blustered, not controlling my own excitement.

'Calm down Hugo. You can start wetting your pants tomorrow, around three forty-five. But I'll give you this - if he remembers and runs like that tomorrow, it'll take a hell of a good horse to beat him.'

Ray and his moody girlfriend had pulled up their horses and were walking back towards us.

'Was that okay?' he asked with sour cheekiness.

'You didn't have a lot to do,' Annie said. 'But it was fine.'

'He'll win tomorrow, won't he?'

This unequivocal confidence was rare in Ray. I was impressed by the hint of a smirk in his eyes. Like most of the lads, he must have already helped himself to a large helping of ante-post. I didn't object to that at all; it was when lads started betting against the yard that one had to start worrying.

Back at the stables, there was a palpable buzz as word of how Mountain had worked quickly spread. But Ulrike flopped off the filly with a mushroom coloured face. As soon as Ray had seen that his mount was being looked after by his lad, he sauntered over to me where I stood talking to Annie.

'Sir H, Ulrike's sick as a dog - you know, women's stuff. She didn't ought to have come out at all this morning, but Lady Tenbury insisted.

'She didn't insist,' I said. 'I heard her tell you on the phone last night not to bring her in if she felt lousy, so it's your fault.'

Ulrike had sidled up to hear the conversation. Though obviously queasy, she shot a sharp resentful glance at Ray. 'You didn't say ziss.'

'She only meant if you was at death's door,' Ray said without apology, and I wondered why women put up with that sort of treatment, especially from chippy losers like Ray.

'Take her home,' Annie said quietly, choosing wisely as ever not to become embroiled in a trivial squabble mostly about the flexing of egos.

'I'll have to stay there, if I do.'

'I don't see....' I started to challenge.

'You go, Ray,' Annie said. 'Take the rest of the day off. We can manage very well without you. But I'll need you in tomorrow - seven sharp.'

Ray nodded, grasped his girlfriend by the elbow and led her round to the back of the stables where his tired and dusty Cavalier was parked.

'Come on.' I tried to dispel the nasty smell the incident had left, coming after such a spectacularly good piece of work on our Derby horse. 'Sod the miserable little bastards. A bottle of Bolly for breakfast.'

'No way,' Annie shook her head. 'If you start on the champagne now, you'll never stop.'

I heard the horses clatter back into the yard and through the window saw Annie jump down and talk animatedly for a few moments to the other work riders.

I watched her oversee the horses being swabbed down and led back to their stables before she walked across the yard towards my house with a jaunty swing of her hips.

She came into the kitchen. 'Coffee, please Hugo.' She dropped onto a chair and leaned forward to peel off her chaps. 'I really think Hawk will win this afternoon.'

'Worth a bet?' I murmured automatically.

'Yeah,' she nodded, 'though there hardly seems any point, with tomorrow and all.'

'Everything else okay?'

'Sure, but do you know what's happened to Mick? He wasn't here to do his horse'

'Mick O'Grady?' I blurted, not quick enough to disguise my re-awakened suspicions.

'Yes. Why so agitated?'

'Nothing; it's just that he's usually so reliable.'

'Oh, I expect he'll turn up.'

I tried to dismiss from my head the thought that the evening before, Mick O'Grady had gone off somewhere, squirted helium down his throat and rung to tell me where to take the money.

Although Bowring had so effectively put me at my ease after that, I now found myself staring at the reality again.

'Hugo? What the hell's the matter with you?'

'Nothing. Kipper bone in my throat, that's all,' I extemporised.

Annie laughed. 'That'll teach you to eat the filthy things.'

Bet Your Rocks Off

Iceland Hawk was entered to run in a good six furlong event, part of the day's prestigious card and the race just before The Oaks. It would be a good race to win under any circumstances, worth over thirty thousand to the winner, but I couldn't work up much enthusiasm as I watched Mick and Bertie load the horse.

Mick turned up twenty minutes after Annie had told me he was missing. He said he'd been to the doctor, who lived in the village and had always told our lads to call on him at home in an emergency, in return, presumably, for a little sporting inside information.

Before I went to get up in the lorry with Bertie, I nipped back into the house and rang the doctor's home. An answering machine referred me to the surgery. The surgery told me he was out on a call, and they had no idea if any patient had paid a visit directly to the doctor's house early that morning.

I climbed into the lorry, telling myself over and again that Piers Bowring was in control of events; that the identity of the blackmailer was irrelevant; whoever it was would be apprehended and kept out of the way until I gave Bowring the all clear - once Corporal Harding arrived in his lorry from France with the real, three year old Private Mountain, and removed Green Mountain to France.

I glanced at the plastic carrier bag on the passenger seat and thought how small it seemed, to hold such a large amount of money. But I had carefully worked out exactly how big a bundle of two thousand fifty pound notes would be, and reproduced it with folded copies of *The Sporting Post*.

As I drove, I glanced in my mirror from time to time, but I saw no signs of anyone following me. I reached the race-course with less trouble than I thought; the crowds at Epsom weren't what they'd once been on Oaks Day, now that so many people preferred to watch the race on television; I was a quarter of an hour early for my first contact with the blackmailer.

I left Bertie in the lorry, and I walked down to the stable entrance to wait. While I was there, dead on time, my mobile vibrated in my trouser pocket.

I clicked it on. 'Hello?'

'Get the papers, and walk with them from the stables, past the Winning Post pub and along Downs Road to Car-park B. Walk through the first entrance. A car will drive up to you, and a guy in a Bill Clinton mask will lower the window and say, "Have you got the papers?". Don't say nothing. Just hand over the parcel, and walk away. The car number's false; don't try and follow. We'll check the money, and if it's right, we won't phone Mills. Any bit of bother, and he'll be down at your yard looking in your horse's mouth.'

At the end of this long instruction, the man's voice had returned tantalisingly close to normal; tantalising close to a voice I thought I could recognise. But not close enough, and I heard the hiss of an aerosol as he topped up the helium lingering in the back of his throat.

'You get that?' he squawked.

'Yes.'

'Start now. We'll be waiting.'

Bet Your Rocks Off

He was gone, and left me wondering about "we". I didn't suppose it made much odds to Bowring if he was dealing with one or more people; he certainly hadn't displayed any anxiety over that. But I felt hopelessly vulnerable as I set off back to my car to collect my bag of *Sporting Posts.* It probably wasn't more than six hundred yards from the stables to Car Park 'B'. It took five or six minutes to walk, but it could have been an hour's march as I thought of my blackmailer losing patience with his finger poised to dial Mills. I was sweating like a pig in a sauna by the time I reached the exit where I'd been told to wait. The driver of the innocuous pale blue Ford Escort was wearing a complete rubber mask of a caricature of the American President's head.

As the car drew up beside me, the driver's window came down.

'Got the papers?' The indistinct growl was undisguised by helium, but muffled by the mask. I couldn't identify it as the squawker, or anyone else.

I handed over the bag, reassured to see that there was only one man in the car. Though I didn't doubt that Bowring's men were very close; it would take barely a few seconds to establish that there was no money and then ring Mills.

Despite Bowring's assertion that they would keep Brigadier Mills' mobile number fully occupied until the threat had been removed, I'd have been happier if I'd been able to see some evidence of Bowring's men.

All these thoughts raced through my head in the second or two the transaction took, and before I knew it, the car had skidded off, indicated right, hesitated few moments at the exit, before turning left out of the car-park, and down the hill against the arriving traffic.

I looked around vainly for something that looked like my rescue team. There were a few cars travelling behind the Escort in the same direction, but nothing suggested any of them were Bowring's.

I turned and walked back towards the race-course. I was presenting myself at the main gate, when the phone in my pocket vibrated again.

'Hugo?'

'Yes.'

'I can report a positive result in carrying out your instructions.' It was a simple, matter-of-fact statement. Bowring's voice displayed no sense of triumph or pride in a job well done.

'Thanks,' I replied as impassively as I could while desperate for more detail, which I knew he wouldn't offer.

'We'll keep the position under control until your cut-off point of midday Sunday, plus twelve hours. I'll make contact with you then on Monday.'

He was gone before I had a chance to respond.

But I reminded myself firmly of the paramount fact that Brigadier Mills was not going to be alerted twenty-four hours either side of the Derby. And even if our blackmailer thought he could cause trouble after that and there was a nasty smell for a day or two, nothing would get out to the public, as there would be no evidence anywhere to substantiate a claim that our Derby horse wasn't exactly what we'd said he was.

It was a measure of the power of Piers Bowring's ego that doubting his assertion wasn't even a remote option, and I walked on to the race-course stable compound completely confident that the blackmail threat was now entirely neutralised.

The optimism I felt was confirmed an hour later, when Spanish Partridge, after his sterling performance at Haydock, put up an even better show and won by half a length, earning Square Barrow Stables another thirty thousand pounds in the process.

CHAPTER TWENTY

The songbirds in the beech copse outside my window were still clearing their throats when I rose on Derby dawn. I'd gone to bed sober at eleven and slept like a child until my alarm woke me at four.

It had been a clear night; the last stars were fading in the west and the sky over the Marlborough Downs was already showing early streaks of pink and turquoise.

As I shaved and listened to the first of the larks getting up over the long grass at the top of our gallops, I was supremely conscious of the day - that events in a dozen hours' time would change my life completely, for better or for worse.

I thought about my partners - Abdel, quietly, relentlessly determined to see his mother appeased, and Annie, more desperate than I'd realised to acquire a large sum of money, which she could easily have done ten times over if she'd been prepared to marry one of the several billionaires whom rumour had cast as eager suitors.

I walked to Dairyman's Cottage and tapped on her front door.

She opened it a moment later wearing a bathrobe with her hair wrapped up in a towel. She looked fresh and healthy and smelled of some subtle floral essence. Without a drop of make-up, she looked to me as fresh and beautiful as she had ever done.

'Good morning,' I said. 'You look wonderful.'

For once, she seemed grateful for the compliment. 'Do I? Thanks Hugo. I thought I'd take my time and go for it today; I've got four outfits to wear - could take a long time choosing,' she laughed. 'I don't want all those women bitching when I go up to get my trophy.'

'Confident, too?' I laughed.

She smiled and nodded. 'Since yesterday, I'm confident. I don't know why I didn't think of the reverse gallop before, but it put Mountain in such good spirits at the same time as the whole yard's hit form.'

'We've hit form okay; that was a cracking race Hawk won yesterday.' I scented a pleasing aroma in the air. 'Do I smell bubbling Java?'

'You do.' She beckoned me into her hall and her kitchen, where she poured coffee. We drank it almost in silence, both deeply preoccupied and probably reflecting each other's thoughts - a peaceful prelude to the serious business of the biggest day of our lives.

'Okay,' I said. 'Time to get going. Des should already have given Mountain his handful of oats. I'll go and get the lorry started.'

'Are you sure you really want to drive him yourself, Hugo? I mean - to the Derby?'

'Since when have you cared about that sort of thing? And of course I'm going to drive him. You don't think I've spent all these years looking after him just to ease up on the final day when it matters most?'

'All right. I understand, but people will think it's a little bizarre, you turning up in your Derby clothes, driving a box.'

'I won't get into my morning suit until it's time to go over to the race-course; I can change in the lorry.'

Alfie Templeton had told me he was going to order a vulgarly capacious chauffeured limousine to convey him and his wife, the Johnsons and Annie to Epsom, but it wouldn't be leaving Square Barrow until after nine. Appreciative that she'd wanted to get out of bed and have breakfast with me before the sun was up, I left Annie to carry on sorting out her wardrobe. Despite our separate private lives, I felt she and I were as close now as we'd ever been, more so in some ways than in the first throes of hungry love twenty years before.

I'd been moved in a way that was utterly unfamiliar by her recent, last minute revelation that she had a motive for our scam above and beyond the glory and the craic. I was sure it wasn't the money itself that she wanted, either, but some other vital personal objective that required it.

I felt guilt, or at least some regret, that I hadn't troubled to delve into her reasons over the three years we'd been working together. But she was fiercely private, and she'd been right that I knew nothing about her life of the previous fifteen years. I had, I supposed, been mildly curious, but I'd never been much interested in the past - at least, not from a personal point of view - only the now, and the next week. I'd always prided myself on suffering from neither nostalgia nor regret. Besides, I'd deliberately not looked closely at Annie's recent private life.

I didn't doubt that a lot had happened, and frankly I didn't think some of it would please me much, so I'd been happy to concur with her policy of a total news blackout. But it did mean that I may have been dealing with someone who was an entirely different creature to the one I'd known so well as a twenty year old. Of course, in some people's eyes, I may have changed too, though that had never seriously occurred to me.

It must have been the gentle, untrammelled silence of the early morning that had me wandering down these woolly paths of philosophy, and it didn't last long. Mountain was boxed up and ready to go by five o'clock. Des and Bertie were coming with me, but all the lads, Dick Hill and some of the farm staff had come in early to see our hero off for his day of glory; only Ray and Ulrike hadn't turned up, which didn't surprise me after her performance the morning before.

I took Dick to one side, and gave him a thousand quid - fifty quid each way for himself and every lad in the yard. I reckoned he'd still get twenty or twenty-five to one if he got in to the bookies in Swindon as soon as the doors opened at ten o'clock.

'Spread it around as much as you can and make sure they'll pay in you in cash this afternoon if we win.' Nobody knew that Dick was anything to do with the yard, so, with luck, news of stable money going onto Mountain wouldn't filter back to the on-course bookies with whom I'd be having my final fling.

But I wanted Dick to come back with plenty of cash that night, to be certain that everyone was as drunk as hell by the time I returned with the horse.

I had exhausted the full gamut of available conversation with Des and Bertie by the time we reached the M4, and we trundled on with only the ghastly local radio station they'd chosen for company. I tried to ignore the hiss and thump of the music as I reviewed all our arrangements for the day.

Taking a horse to run in the Derby, a superior animal and at peak fitness, with an inbuilt twelve pound advantage due to his age, was a unique experience, even for me, and I was trying to cope with it as calmly as I could.

Now that the threat of Brigadier Mills being alerted to this discrepancy by our blackmailer had been defused by Bowring, our chances seemed a lot better than evens and, as if I were going into military action, it was hard to keep my excitement under control; I found I was driving the lorry in a sort of daze, barely conscious of the fidgety little lads on the seat beside me, and very conscious of the bundles of fifties tucked inside my jacket.

But I knew instinctively what I was doing and, as I'd planned, we avoided the snarl up of Saturday cars which would infest the roads around Epsom later that morning. The sun was already growing warm and drying the dew on the flawless turf as we rolled into the purlieus of the historic race-course at half past seven.

Bet Your Rocks Off

The entrance to the lorry park was seething with uniformed security men. The sight of a dozen or more policemen had me gulping, but I slapped a steely grin on my face and nodded my way through them.

We unloaded the horse, and Bertie led him, with me by his side, through the gates and security posts to the stables.

No one seemed particularly surprised to see me in jeans and a buckskin jacket at that time of the morning. They were far too busy, anyway, going about their own business. The air was full of expectation and excited bonhomie. Although we were all competing against each other, there was a strong sense that we were also sharing the experience, and there was good deal of warm-hearted, mutual good wishing.

Once we'd got Mountain into his box, I sent Bertie off to find a blacksmith. He came back fifteen minutes later with the race-course farrier who tidied up the horse's feet and tapped a set of racing plates onto his hooves.

Satisfied that everything was looking as good as it could, I stepped outside the box to be greeted by a sight that freeze-dried my corpuscles.

Cousin Henry and his officious little side-kick were making straight for me. In their wake was third man I didn't know, dressed in a rumpled grey suit. Brownley had a fawn folder tucked under his arms, which he started to take out as he got nearer.

'Morning, Hugo,' the brigadier said with a grim smile. 'Just to show there's no nepotism round here, I'm starting with you.'

'Starting what with me, Brigadier?'

'We're spot-checking runners against their passports.'

My jaw dropped. I'd never known this to happen. 'Good God, Brigadier, this is the Derby, not a seller at Hereford.'

'A lot more at stake, then,' he answered crisply. 'This is Mr Allardice, a Jockey Club vet. Can you let him have your horse's passport, please.'

I fished the document from my jacket pocket and handed it over mutely to the vet, who seemed somewhat overawed by the whole procedure. He took it and opened it at the centre page which contained the diagrammatic representation of the external characteristics which Private Mountain shared, down to the last whorl, with his elder twin brother who was standing patiently in the middle of the stable.

I lifted a disdainful shoulder, and stood aside to let them enter the box.

Inside, I was quaking.

It needed only a competent vet to make a thorough examination of Mountain's teeth for the whole scam to go up in smoke, taking me with it.

I put a hand on the stable door; it was trembling like an aspen leaf in a summer breeze.

The vet walked slowly round the uninterested horse, nodding confirmation of each feature shown on the chart. My pulse stopped - on hold for a few seconds - as he cursorily lifted Mountain's front lip to bare the colt's large incisors, and let it down. He stood back and glanced at Brigadier Mills. 'That's him all right,' he nodded.

I realised that once he'd seen that everything matched perfectly, it simply hadn't occurred to him that the horse might be the wrong age. The gasp of breath expelled from my pent up lungs seemed to echo right around the stable, but if Cousin Henry noticed, he didn't show it.

He took the passport from the vet and handed it back to me before leading the trio out of the box. 'Best of luck, then, Hugo,' he said, rather unenthusiastically I thought, and strode across to the box opposite.

A few indignant exclamations confirmed to me that he was, at least to some extent, carrying through the charade that ours had been a random spot-check.

I winked at Bertie and Des as we closed and padlocked the stable door.

'Breakfast time,' I said, and we walked over to the canteen - a squat, ugly building of the fifties, which the public never saw, and which had thus avoided the relentless upgrading of the main buildings.

The place was already packed, but I felt a little conspicuous among the diminutive breed that seemed to dominate the working end of racing. There was a palpable buzz around the main players in the Derby, and I heard more than a few cheerful calls of 'Good Luck, Hugo', 'All the best, Sir H.' I felt like a school house Captain about to lead his team out to play.

Among the tables full of ticket girls, Tote clerks, waiters, barmen, security men - all the people responsible for making Epsom work for the few hundred thousand people that would turn up - I sat down with a trio of well-known upper-class tinkers who sold a variety of goods - hats, books, fudge, binoculars - at the major race meetings around the country.

The book-seller, whom I'd known at Harrow, tried to tap me for information. Was my horse going to win and, if so, would I write a book about it? He obviously thought both were no more than remote possibilities. We laughed a lot, and it was good to forget the tension for a short while, but as I went back to check on Mountain, the deliciously unwholesome fried breakfast I'd eaten failed utterly to settle in my churning guts.

The colt was standing still, calm enough but alert and expectant in his box. Although he'd had his gallops at Chepstow and Newbury, he'd never been to a track to race for real, and he was probably puzzled by all the excitement among the other horses who were fast filling the boxes around him.

Still feeling slightly limp with relief that the vet hadn't considered checking his teeth properly, I went into his stable and routinely felt his legs and feet. He seemed fine, and I went off to the lorry to change, trying to keep my hopes in proportion.

Emerging from the horse-box in my black tails, canary waistcoat and checked trousers, though, my immediate priorities had altered.

Bet Your Rocks Off

One way and another over the last ten months, I'd already bet over twenty-two grand on Mountain to win the Derby. Sergeant Rawlings and his team were placing another ten thousand for me on the course that afternoon, once I'd given him the nod; and I'd brought with me a spare five grand for Alfie to put on, if I was feeling bullish enough. Nevertheless, although the odds would probably not be so long, the last ten grand which Laura was putting on the Tote for me would comprise a significant part of my gamble.

Nervously, I wondered what time she would turn up, and hoped to God she didn't decide to indulge in one of her contrary moods that day. Sanguinely, I thought that unlikely, given her taste for easy money.

For the next hour, though, there was not a lot for me to do. After I'd dropped off a small leather bag containing the al Hassan colours - pink with gold chevrons, sleeves and cap - at the weighing-room for Kevin's valet, I wandered through a security check and metal detector into the Queen's Stand, the static ocean liner that housed members and their friends. I took the lift up to the top of the stand, from where I was able to survey the whole colourful panoply of Derby Day.

I couldn't help feeling strangely detached from it all - an observer, rather than a participant in the great event. I swung round and put up my glasses, just able to pick out the spot - the exit from Car-park B, where, unbelievably, less than twenty-four hours earlier, I'd handed over my parcel of newspapers to the blackmailer in the Bill Clinton mask.

I wondered, without wishing to know too many details, how Bowring had dealt with him - at least, where he was keeping him until the potential for damage was passed.

With still half an hour to go before I was due to meet Laura, I was finding it hard to relax. I walked downstairs and out through the stands, taking care to avoid a TV producer and an old-Harrovian presenter prowling for victims - anyone to interview to fill up the hours of coverage allocated to the big race.

It wasn't modesty that deterred me from the cameras; I didn't like the overweight, overwhiskered public tipster, and I simply didn't trust myself not to appear rude or suspiciously over-confident.

Outside, I went back to the weighing-room to declare our runner before buying the day's papers and making my way round the parade ring to Barry Cope's seafood bar. As I didn't feel like drinking so soon after my heavy breakfast, I sat at a small table in a corner and tried to read the racing pages in the daily papers I'd bought. I was looking for suggestions that any of the hacks had an inkling of Mountain's secret.

Of all the regular tipsters, only Chris Lewis had made Private Mountain his major selection, with the comment that in his public gallop the colt had appeared outstandingly mature for his age.

I winced. I recalled that I had seen Hugo talking to Jimmy Collins at Newbury when we'd taken Mountain there.

At that moment, glancing for a second over the top of *The Sporting Post*, I caught sight of Terry Brownley lurking in the entrance. I didn't let him see that I'd spotted him; I pointedly relaxed and leaned back extravagantly in my chair to demonstrate my pristine conscience. Of course, I didn't know for sure that he was up there to snoop on me, but he didn't strike me as a natural lobster and champagne punter, and I wouldn't have put it past Henry Mills to carry on harbouring suspicions about his colourful cousin.

I refused to be shaken.

Fuck him - I thought, and returned my attention to the paper.

The *Telegraph's* principal correspondent took the view that the Godolphin favourite would stay only ten furlongs. He was complimentary about Private Mountain, as well as Lady Tenbury's spectacular record that season - five winners from just ten runners

'Hello, Hugo.' The voice behind my shoulder was sugary and accommodating.

I was so relieved to see Laura that I realised only then how uneasy I'd been about her showing up.

'Luscious Laura!' I burbled. 'You're nice and early.'

The hurt she'd affected to feel a couple of days before didn't seem to be troubling her now. 'Just going to do my home-work and plan a route to get round five Tote windows in the shortest possible time.'

'Good, but don't forget there'll be ten times more people here in two or three hours and before the race, half of them will be at the windows trying to get a last minute bet on.'

'Don't worry about a thing, Hugo. I'll get it all on. Have you got the money?'

I glanced at my watch. Annie wasn't due for another twenty minutes. I thought I would be wise to consolidate my regained ground, at least for today. 'How about a quick gargle first?'

Laura's eyes sparkled. 'Great. I need some breakfast.'

I knew Laura could take as much liquor as I and confidently ordered a bottle of the house champagne.

I regretted it as soon as the bubbles in the over-priced pop began to stir up the bacon and eggs in my stomach, encouraging them to surface with an aggressive stab of acid indignation. I hoped the champagne wasn't trying to tell me something.

Laura, though, looked relaxed as she leaned across the table conspiratorially. 'If our horse wins today, how much do you think I'll be collecting from the Tote?'

I lifted a shoulder. 'A hundred and fifty grand, maybe two hundred if we're lucky.'

'Goodie! What about the stake?'

I thought about it for a moment. 'I'll meet you by the statue of Generous and give it to you then, just before you need it,' I answered. I glanced at my watch and stood up. 'Annie'll be here any minute.'

Laura got up, too, swigged the last drops of champagne from her glass and stretched up to give me a big, warm wet tongue between the lips. 'There you are, Hugo. Sorry we can't lunch together, but I couldn't really share a table with you and your Lady Tight-arse.'

'I know perfectly well you're lunching with Toby and the ghastly Vickers, so don't give me that.'

Bet Your Rocks Off

She laughed. 'I'll be round for my little purse at two-thirty.' She flicked a wrist at me and strode off with just the faintest wobble in her pert behind visible through a cling-film, silver-grey satin dress.

I was still watching, though thinking of other things, when I heard my name again.

'Oh, Hugo!' There was less tolerance and more admonishment than in Laura's utterance of the word, but I was glad to hear it.

I turned to find Annie eyeing me as if I were a boy with my hands in a jar of sweets. I resisted the temptation to quail, but what really made me catch my breath was her spectacular beauty.

She was wearing make-up now, but so subtly as to be almost undetectable. She had chosen a simple classic Chanel suit in a pale turquoise that emphasised the lapis lazuli of her eyes. Around her smooth, long neck she wore a simple diamond pendant. Her golden hair, usually gathered up in a practical bun, fell in sumptuous waves to her shoulders.

'Hello Lady Tenbury, or Lady Tight-arse, as my last guest referred to you,' I greeted her with deliberate bathos.

'Not so applicable to her these days, I observe,' Annie said dryly.

I couldn't help laying a gentle hand on her own shapely behind. 'But she got you right.'

Annie didn't immediately shake me off, as I half expected. She gave me a quizzical, though not disapproving glance. 'Okay, Hugo; you've made your point. Alfie and Birgitta and the Johnsons are having a look around with Calista and Jackson. I said we'd meet them all in the box in twenty minutes. I've been to see Mountain; he looks fine; we won't touch him now until we need to get him out an hour before the race.'

'Did you see Bertie?' I asked cautiously.

'Yeah, sure; he was in the box with Mountain.'

'Did he tell you about Mills' visit?'

She was instantly alert. 'No. What?'

'Oh nothing, just bumbling about checking everybody had the right horse; they waved ours straight through of course.' I down played the event. The last thing Annie needed now was more cause for tension.

'Oh, fine,' she said, relieved. 'But there's been a minor crisis down at the yard.'

'What?' I asked sharply. No crisis was minor on a day like this.

'Ulrike turned up in floods of tears; she was still feeling lousy but she was upset because Ray didn't come home last night and there was no sign of him this morning.'

'Oh,' I said, relieved that it really was a minor problem. 'Tell him if he doesn't show up again, you'll sack him.'

'Hugo, that's beside the point. I'm talking about Ulrike, poor thing; she's been a really good work rider for us, and Ray's a selfish, chippy bastard to treat her like that, especially when she's feeling lousy.'

'That's probably why he slipped off to see someone else.'

'Of course, she doesn't think he's done that; she thinks something terrible's happened to him so I told her to go and tell the police.'

'They won't take any notice,' I said. 'A man going AWOL for one night doesn't constitute a missing person in their book, I'm afraid. Anyway, there's nothing you can do about it now, so stop worrying.'

'Sure,' she agreed. 'When are our esteemed owners arriving?'

'In about half an hour. I'll make sure the box and lunch and everything's in order. You know how fussy Madame can be.'

'Okay. By the way what did Lady Saggy-arse want? I see she's still all over you.'

'Not for much longer, I can tell you; I arranged for her to run an errand for me today and once she's done that, I'm going to hand in my resignation.'

'Oh, really? Why?'

'To tell you the truth, I don't really know; but naturally, I'll let you know when I do.'

'I hope you haven't given her an important errand. She's not really the brightest and I should think she's totally unreliable.'

I chuckled. 'She won't let me down on this one, I can assure you.' I knew that Laura was far too keen on money to muck up the simple task I'd set her.

We went up to the box to check on the catering arrangements and to welcome our guests properly. We'd invited them specifically to make the event look less of a private conclave between us and the al Hassans. Fortunately, when they all trooped into the box, they seemed to be getting on well and I felt we looked like a typical Derby gathering.

I asked our waiter to make a jug of Bloody Mary for them, and a cup of tea for me. 'Not a good day for me to get pissed,' I explained to a puzzled Alfie as I took him to one side and slipped him an envelope with five grand in it. 'Could you get two and half on each way for me - in two or three hits at the best price you can find in Tatts?'

'Sure,' he nodded. 'But is that all you're having?'

'No,' I said quietly. 'Other arrangements have been made. But wait till they've cantered down before you start betting, just in case there's some last minute hitch. I mean, if you see Private Mountain galloping hard the wrong way up the five furlong chute without a fucking jockey - don't have a bet!'

'It's all right,' Alfie laughed. 'I'm not that bloody stupid.'

'Okay, and if all goes well, collect the cash today but don't bother about getting it to me till Monday.'

He nodded. 'So provided he comes under orders, you think...?'

'Yes, Alfie. I think I can confidently advise that the time has come for a serious, ball-crunching bookie-crusher.'

CHAPTER TWENTY-ONE

Satisfied that everything complied with Madame's fastidious standards, I left the box to go and meet the al Hassan's.

There was a great deal of coming and going in the stand and I squeezed into a lift that smelled of Dior, Chanel and expensive new clothes. I was amused to find myself crushed up against the elegantly suited, lightly scented sixty year old frame of Sir Toby Allerthorpe. He saw me, and I knew at once from a nervous embarrassed shiftiness in his eyes that Laura must have told him something of our liaison.

'Morning, Hugo,' he boomed, as if there weren't five other people in the lift. 'Best of luck with that horse of yours. I hear you're planning some kind of coup in the Derby.'

My heart stood still for a moment; I couldn't believe I was hearing this. What the hell had Laura told him? And why the hell was he talking about it in front of a gang of strangers?

I was pulling myself together with what I hoped was a humorous twinkle, when suddenly the big duffer started guffawing in a loud, oafish bray, and I realised he thought he'd cracked a hell of a good joke.

I smiled indulgently and thought about throttling him with the beastly, bad taste tie he was wearing with his morning suit.

The other people in the lift grinned knowingly, pleased to have witnessed an inside joke. To show how relaxed I was, I waited for everyone else to leave the lift before I took a deep breath and carried on.

Crossing the lawns in front of the stand, a nudge on my elbow stopped me.

It was Geoffrey Scott, our professional punter.

I thought you ought to know, Sir H,' he said without moving his lips. 'I've just had a funny pull from one of the betting intelligence officers. He says they've heard rumours that I've backed your horse heavily abroad, and wants to know if was I going to lay off or who was my principle. I blanked him and told him to fuck off. I said obviously I wasn't going to tell them if I was going to lay off and I certainly wasn't going to tell them whose money it is. But there's definitely a bit of a smell over what we stand to win from our off-shore ante-post hits.'

I listened to him, and thought about it for a moment. I shrugged, reminding myself that Scott would never tell anyone I had anything to do with it and there was no way they could trace the bet to me; I'd given him the cash and he'd used his own debit card to place it.

'Thanks for telling me, Geoff. But I can't see any real problem. I'll see you next week.'

He looked relieved at my confidence; I didn't doubt he'd piled a lot of his own money on the horse too.

Bet Your Rocks Off

I certainly didn't want him to know how nervous he'd made me; I wasn't going to tell him about Mills, but I'd have been surprised if the Brigadier's hand wasn't somewhere behind the betting intelligence officer's line of enquiry.

Trying to keep calm, and convince myself that there really wasn't a problem, I made my way across the track, past the enclosure where the open-topped buses housed rowdy, unsophisticated parties.

With a another nasty jolt, I saw a Bill Clinton, identical to the one who'd taken my packet the day before, on top of one of the buses. I relaxed when I saw several others, and a few Monica Lewinskys to go with them. I wondered what they'd be doing all day, and carried on across the down towards the helipad to greet the al Hassans when they arrived.

I stood and watched the arrival of a steady stream of choppers from which spilled racing luminaries, pop stars, footballers and droves of manifestly mega-rich men with their trophy women in tow.

At last, I saw Abdel descend from a newly landed machine. I waited for him to turn and hand his mother down, but he walked away from it alone. I approached him and offered him a hand in greeting.

'Good morning, Hugo,' he said. 'How is our horse?'

'Couldn't be better.' We set off at a crisp pace. 'I told you how well he worked yesterday,' I said. 'He came through and romped home in fantastic style, no trouble at all with the downhill, either, and that's reassuring for this course.'

'He travelled well today?'

'No problem. I drove him here myself.'

Abdel nodded his approval. 'Your conscientiousness is commendable.'

'Thanks, Abdel, but where's Madame?'

His light coffee features showed a flash of regret. 'Sadly, when I went to fetch her this morning, she said she just wasn't feeling well enough to enjoy a day like this. She hates people to go to a lot of trouble when she can't appreciate it fully.'

I knew that was so; I'd often heard her say it.

'I'm terribly sorry,' I said sincerely. 'I really think we might win.'

'I had wanted very much to see her receive the trophy and go to the royal box to have tea with the Queen, but there it is; she'll derive great pleasure from watching it on TV and seeing me receive the trophy on her behalf. For me, it will more than make up for all the pain she has felt over the years for suffering that public fiasco in front of Her Majesty at Ascot.'

I'd always had the impression that Madame was as tough as she was chic, and I'd sometimes wondered if perhaps Abdel wasn't overstating his mother's sensitivity, but watching his face now, I didn't doubt that he believed it himself.

As we walked across the down towards the flower-decked stand on the other side of the course, Abdel didn't show any appreciation of the traditional working-class razzmatazz of Derby Day, diluted as it was compared with the days when people only saw the great race if they came to it. His nose wrinkled fastidiously as he passed each burger stand, and he gazed, perplexed, at the perambulating pearly kings and their consorts.

He looked very relieved when we finally arrived at his box. There was no one else there; I guessed the women had dragged the party off to have a look around at the people and all the activity going on everywhere.

'This all looks very good,' Abdel said, gazing at the table laid for lunch, the flowers we'd specially ordered for Madame's benefit, the ostentatiously dated champagne in ice-buckets. 'I see we're expecting six extra guests.'

'Yes,' I nodded. 'Though quite frankly, Abdel, I won't really feel much like a party until the whole thing's over.'

'I understand, Hugo, but I made it clear that we must appear to be treating this race just like any other reasonably optimistic owner.'

'I appreciate that of course. That's why Annie's asked the Carter-Rices. They look like a party on their own.'

Abdel looked impressed. 'The Jackson Carter-Rice's?'

'Yes. He's running the European end of the bank.'

'Yes, I know him. We were both at Harvard. Well that's fine; I hear that Mrs Carter-Rice is very decorative.'

'You could say so,' I nodded with a grin. 'I know he's looking forward to meeting you again.'

'Well, there it is. Tell me, what do you think of them?' This was a most unusual request from Abdel, who generally showed very little interest in the personalities or even general characteristics of the people with whom he came into contact.

'They're good company. Jack's an exceptionally erudite man - for an American. I expect you know, after Harvard he was a Rhodes scholar at Oxford. While he was there, I think he must have caught a fondness for all things British which he still hasn't lost. In fact, it's odd he didn't marry an English woman. Mind you,' I smiled, thinking of my own experience with her, 'what Calista lacks in Englishness, she makes up for with an enormous knowledge of anything European - especially if she can buy it in Bond Street or the Via Condotti.'

Abdel nodded slowly. 'It will be a pleasure to see them, no doubt. And what about our other guests?'

'Alfie Templeton we thought would be ideal for our purposes. He's a big, loud self-made man - good-natured and intelligent; his wife Birgitta is Swedish, beautiful, and not so bright. Joe Johnson was in the army with me; he and Helen are a pair of typical English Sloane Rangers - very reliable, rather solid.'

'And quite dull?' Abdel added. But he seemed pleased with what we'd arranged, and called in our waitress to serve me some champagne.

Annie appeared in the box a few moments later. I couldn't help thinking again how wonderful she was looking. Abdel faintly raised an appreciative eyebrow.

'Good morning Abdel,' she said brightly. 'Your horse is looking fantastic; he's perfectly relaxed and very happy.'

Bet Your Rocks Off

Abdel bowed slightly. 'I'm delighted by your confidence. And I look forward to seeing him. Ah, here are our guests.'

The Carter-Rices came in and immediately filled the box with their personalities. Although Jackson was twenty years older than his wife, they were, it seemed to me, well-matched. Alfie and Birgitta and the Johnsons followed and the air soon resounded to a satisfying buzz of excited conversation.

Calista treated me to a subtle display of warmth and sparkle that showed no regrets over our one illicit liaison. At the same time, she was careful not to let Annie see a hint of it - or Jackson, for that matter.

Over lunch, I wondered how I'd let myself end up in bed with her - not because she wasn't perfectly desirable, but because she really was close to Annie - a significant force in Annie's recent history, it seemed, and for some unaccountable reason, our single epic liaison made me feel very disloyal.

As it turned out, the Americans and the Templeton's played an important role at the lunch-party. Without them, I guessed it would have been a very subdued affair. Abdel never said a lot, and I certainly wasn't at my most talkative. Everything was as good as it should have been; the food the best to be found on an English race-course. But at first it seemed that for Abdel the occasion would not effervesce without Madame, for whose benefit, ultimately, the whole plan had been conceived.

At the same time, Annie and I couldn't deny our optimism. The rest of the party picked it up, and so, after a while, did Abdel. It was the first time I'd ever seen him anything like excited at the prospect of a race, and by the end of the meal, everyone was quite exuberant.

I wasn't drunk, though; I'd restricted myself to a glass of champagne and one of Chablis, with a lot of fizzy water. But I was wallowing in a kind if surreal dream-world, where the race was already won; and once lunch was over, I almost had to force myself to get on with my next task.

I left Annie talking earnestly to Abdel, and proceeded like a sleep-walker to the lorry. From under the passenger seat, I extracted a smart Italian lizard skin bag containing ten thousand quid and carried on to the stables while the first race was still being run.

Mountain was quite cool, calm but alert and expectant in his box. Des was all ready and waiting, with every strip of leather bridle and brass buckle gleaming. He had groomed Mountain until the coat on his hard-muscled quarters gleamed like a newly shelled conker.

Once the winner of the first race was being led into the enclosure, Bertie and Des proudly led our horse from his box and walked him down to the pre-parade ring at the end of the straight, just below the stables. A light, helpful breeze had sprung up over lunch, and he didn't sweat up at all.

The Godolphin horse was already out and looked stunning. He'd won his last four races including the Thousand Guineas and seemed an indisputable favourite. Most of the other runners, as they appeared, looked impressive too, especially the French second favourite, who'd won both his races on the Paris circuit that year by not less than five lengths. I was beginning to feel that perhaps, after all, Mountain was really going to need the advantage of his extra year.

Annie appeared at last. She'd been talking to Kevin in the weighing-room in the Queen's Stand, and said she didn't want Mountain saddled up until the last minute. I thought she was probably right; there was no point getting him on his toes too early. I left her with the horse and went off to watch the next race.

After it had been run, I went to pick up Kevin's saddle. On the way, I saw Chris Lewis; he'd seen me first, though, and I couldn't side-step him.

'Feeling happy, Sir H?'

'I see you've done your best to shorten the price on my horse.'

'I've got a duty to my readers, Sir H, and when your old mate Jimmy Collins told me what he thought of the horse when I saw him at Newbury, I couldn't overlook it, could I?'

'Why, what did he tell you?'

'He said he thought a hell of a lot of him - said he looked and acted like an older animal, which would give him a definite advantage. And I agree with him.'

I nodded. 'Yes, he does seem quite forward,' I said as if it had never occurred to me before. 'We've certainly been able to get a lot of training into him.'

'Well, best of luck, Sir H.'

'Thank you,' I said stiffly, and carried on to fetch our saddle.

On my way back from the weighing-room, by the big bronze of Generous, I spotted Sergeant-Major Rawlings and pointedly ignored him. But I slowed my pace, looking around for Laura. I was just beginning to feel my blood pressure rise when she appeared from behind the statue.

Laura seemed to me as alert as ever, and the faint doubts Annie had sown earlier were quelled.

'Hi, Hugo. Reporting for duty.'

I handed her the lizard skin bag on a long strap, which contained ten bundles of forty fifties wrapped in rubber bands. 'Here's your bag,' I said loudly. 'You left it in the bar earlier.'

'Great!' she answered, with convincing surprise. 'I'll be able to have a bet now.'

'You certainly will,' I agreed.

She casually hung the bag over her shoulder without examining the contents.

'How was lunch?' I asked, as if I cared.

'Dull as shit,' she said.

'But you're all ready for your job?'

'Of course.'

'Okay,' I said, more quietly now, 'as soon as you see Mountain in the parade ring - he's number three - get betting. And call me on Sunday night so we can fix our meet for Monday.'

'I hope to God you're right about this horse Hugo. I've put a pile of my own on it.'

'Very wise,' I said.

Bet Your Rocks Off

She turned and strode off with my last ten grand dangling from her shoulder.

As the runners in the preceding race left for the course, we were called up as a group and led the horses to the parade ring behind the stand.

The saddling stalls were in a temporary canvas structure set inside the ring, facing the back of the stand and on the edge of the horses' walkway. Mercifully it wasn't flapping too wildly in the breeze.

Annie and I claimed a few square metres of the flawless turf in the centre, from where we could survey all the runners striding round, now obviously excited, each with two lads at their head.

Although the previous race was still going on, the area around the ring was fairly full, and as soon as the race was over, Abdel arrived with the Carter-Rices. I spotted Alfie, Birgitta and the Johnsons leaning over the rails, grinning with excitement at their vicarious involvement. Annie and I went off to saddle the horse without any problem, and Kevin strutted into the paddock on his short legs, still cock-a-hoop from his win the day before.

He nodded approval at his mount, while Annie described to him how well the horse had finished at home the previous morning.

Abdel listened carefully, from where he stood gazing with well-disguised pride at his creation. I knew that as a result of the intense study he had made of the anatomy of the racehorse, he was well able to make a valid comparison with the rest of the field.

'The favourite looks well,' he said,

'He does,' I concurred, 'but I agree with the Telegraph; I don't think he'll stay beyond ten furlongs, especially here.' I nodded at the French horse. 'And he's looking fractious; see how sweaty he is already.'

'Ours is by no means the largest horse in the field,' he observed quietly to me.

'Not quite,' I nodded.

'He's the most developed, though, but not excessively,' Abdel went on. 'Is everything else all ready to go?'

'I spoke to Corporal Harding last night. He'll be on his way by now.'

'And there have been no other problems?'

I thought of the week long nightmare of the blackmail and Henry Mills' suspicious intrusions. I shook my head. 'No. Nothing else to worry about.'

'Good. You've done well; and Lady Tenbury.'

'Tell us that after the race, Abdel.'

We turned back towards Annie who was still giving instructions to Kevin.

'We know he has the speed - okay?' she was saying.

Kevin nodded vigorously.

'So with your low draw, use the rails and lie up in the first three or four.' Annie's voice was quiet but authoritative. 'When you come around Tattenham Corner, stay on the rails two or three lengths off the pace, but don't get boxed in. Do nothing yet, just keep out of trouble. You'll get the trip, don't worry about that; the al Hassans have

348

owned horses from this line for generations and we know exactly what we're doing with them. When you're two furlongs out, you still want to be a length down on the leaders, but don't move yet; you can't come too late on this horse. Two hundred yards out, pull over to the right. Whatever you do, never pull to the left, understand?' Annie fixed him with an unwavering eye. 'Never to the left or on the inside in this race. So move out until you've plenty of daylight in front of you. Get yourself ready to pounce then go for it in the last hundred yards. But remember, it's a long hill, so for God's sake, whatever you do, don't start too early.'

Kevin nodded. I knew he was listening and I knew he would do exactly as he was told. A more independent-minded jockey might have worked out that he was going to win a few furlongs from home, and gone on then to win the race by twenty lengths, and arouse the instant suspicions of everyone who knew anything about the running of racehorses.

The bell rang. The thirteen runners stopped and their lads turned them inwards; there was a scurry and some running around as trainers and jockeys sorted out their horses and mounted. The bright sun gleamed off a riot of colours as the little harlequins were legged up and were suddenly the dominant figures in the circle.

We all walked across to the far end of the parade ring where Des and Bertie had pulled our horse in. I put Kevin up. Mountain began to jog, aware that at last something big was about to happen.

Abruptly, beside us, one of the rank outsiders in the race started to play up, rearing and bucking so furiously that he came close to dropping his jockey. Mountain instantly picked up the vibes and started dancing himself. I swore at the other plunging horse, and grabbed Mountain's bridle from Bertie. With brisk strides and a firm hold, I led him round in a large circle for a few minutes to calm him for one of the trickier moments before the race, when the runners would be organised to go down for the parade in their race-card order.

To my relief, it took Kevin and me only a few turns and plenty of verbal reassurance to calm our nervous colt. I glared angrily at the northern trainer of the useless, harum-scarum animal beside us - now wearing a ladder of white foam on its neck - and handed the reins back to Bertie.

Annie, Abdel and our guests left the ring, but I waited until the boys had got Mountain safely into the chute which took the horses down to the course and the parade. I rushed up through the Queen's Stand, but by the time I reached Abdel's box, all the horses had been let loose from the parade, and Mountain was cantering up round Tattenham Corner with the others on their way to the start.

I could see through my binoculars that he'd taken a hold and Kevin was having to fight him; I felt the blood drain from my face; I was so tense that even the slightest sign of a set-back was making me feel physically sick.

Bet Your Rocks Off

But Kevin got him to the top of the hill in one piece and managed to settle him and bring him down to the start without any more problems.

I turned to Annie. She was chewing her lip and gazing at the television screen in the corner of the room, which showed a close-up of the runners milling around in front of the starting stalls. The northern colt was still playing up, but sensibly, a long way from the other runners.

The five minutes that followed dragged painfully; at three minutes before the 'off', the starter gave the signal for the horses to go behind.

They carried on circling behind the stalls, waiting their turn to be urged in to their allotted, narrow slot by the bobble-hatted handlers. As far as I could see, Kevin now had Mountain completely settled, but I still found myself praying to a much neglected God, first that Laura had successfully put all my money on with the Tote, and then that nothing else would happen to upset Mountain's running.

Certainly, if I'd been asked to make a snap judgement of the horses in the paddock on the strength of looks alone, I was sure I'd have picked ours. And having seen the truly scintillating turn of foot he could produce....

I mentioned all these things in my monologue with the Almighty, and wondered if Abdel was doing the same with his Allah.

The pre-race tension was reflected in a marked drop in the noise made by the hundred and fifty thousand punters on the course. By the time the starter was climbing up to his rostrum, barely a murmur filled the air, and the voices of individual bookies could be heard urging any last minute waverers to give their money to them.

When the smooth voice of the commentator announced "They're off!", there was a noticeable cheer before the hubbub subsided once more as the horses covered the first few furlongs of the Derby.

We stood side by side - Abdel, Annie and I - with binoculars glued to our eyes. I watched Madame's hideous pink and gold colours slide along above the rail on the far side, as far as I could see, in fourth place. The commentary confirmed this view until just before the left-handed swing at the top of the back straight when two runners pulled past on the outside.

But Kevin kept Mountain on the rails without losing any more ground all the way round the gentle curve, looking beautifully balanced as the ground dropped away towards Tattenham Corner.

The noise had swelled into the traditional incoherent roar as the horses began to swap places more often, and punters saw their chances wax or wane. As they turned into the straight for the last three and a half furlongs, still dropping slightly, the field was tight bunched, with Mountain in the middle by the rails, looking in serious danger of getting trapped.

I suddenly wished Annie had told Kevin to pull across coming down the hill, before he got to Tattenham Corner, even though that would have used up a few lengths around the long bend.

As they came into the straight, the leader and the second horse, a hundred to one no-hoper, began to come back to the field, but by the time they hit the rising ground, Kevin and Mountain still hadn't found a way out.

They'd past the two furlong marker before Kevin could move out and find a way past the two runners stuck to the rails in front of him, as the leaders started to draw clear and open up the field.

I rammed the soft rubber rims of my glasses harder into my eyes, and wondered what Abdel was thinking. I didn't dare look or ask but I sensed him beside me, motionless, not uttering a sound, jubilant or despairing.

Down on the track, Mountain still had three horses in front of him. As far as I could see from my angle, he had the chance of a clear run.

But a hundred and fifty yards out, he still hadn't moved up to go through.

I took my glasses down for a moment. 'For God's sake, Kevin!' I shouted involuntarily, 'get your fucking whip out!'

A woman in the box beside us, wearing a sort of eagle's nest on her head, turned and pursed her mean little lips in disapproval.

I ignored her and put up my binoculars again. I took one deep breath and didn't draw another for the last nine seconds of the race as, at last, Kevin raised his whip in his left hand.

Gritting my teeth, I wondered if Mountain would remember.

A moment later it was obvious that he had not forgotten the caning he'd received on our gallops five days before. He shied violently away from the whip, flattened, accelerated and lurched sharply to the right.

Annie gasped and clutched my arm with a clenched, quivering fist. 'My God, he's ducking! He's running all over the place.' Abruptly, her voice changed to a scream she hadn't used since she was a kid by the railtrack in Mingo Junction. 'Kevin, put your fucking whip down!'

The eagle's nest in the next box spun round again, aghast, perhaps, at the flagrant inconsistency of our instructions. In the second or so Annie took to say it, I saw five years of hopes, plans and dedication fall apart, and I was gazing at a future bleak and corrupted irredeemably by failure in a coup in which everything had been more generously stacked in our favour than any I'd ever staged.

But even as Annie was screaming, Kevin did as she wanted and dropped his whip. He hunched himself over the horse's withers and drove him back on course with his hands and heels.

The French horse, having galloped with a near perfect rhythm the whole way round, was beginning to tie up, while Mountain scudded on relentlessly up the sharp slope of the last fifty yards as if he had wings. Beside him, the favourite seemed to melt into the background, and three strides later, he was in front, just ten yards from the post.

As he crossed the line, a thousand trumpets blasted in my head with an explosive, brilliant white vision of triumph.

It was the most delicious sensation imaginable; better in its way than any sexual experience I'd ever known, though - I admitted afterwards - a lot harder to organise.

Bet Your Rocks Off

I managed somehow to focus my blurred vision on Mountain, and Kevin pulling him up, still standing in his stirrups, alternately raising his fist in an unseemly gesture of triumph, and crouching to thump the horse's neck in recognition of the part it had played.

As he wheeled Mountain back to leave the track, even through the fog of my euphoria, I hadn't forgotten that I had still to be wary of the few pitfalls that remained before an incontestable triumph had been achieved.

I took down my glasses and turned to Annie. I'd never seen tears in her eyes, but now they glistened like a pair of sparkling aquamarines. I took her in my arms and hugged her and felt hers wrap around my neck as her chest heaved.

'Well done, my angel,' I whispered. 'I never doubted you'd do it.'

'Bullshit!' she whispered back. 'But thanks.'

We clung together in complete unity for a few sublime moments before we released each other and I turned to Abdel.

Abdel had already, at his most expressive, patted me once on the shoulder as Mountain had flashed past the post. Now at last, there was a light of definite, though unsurprised glory in his eyes.

I was aware, of course, that I'd rather oversold the chances of our pulling off the coup, and my positive noises had always been so unequivocal and consistent that what he'd just witnessed was simply what I'd told him to expect.

Over Abdel's shoulder, I noticed that the eagle's nest had turned around again to look at us in an entirely altered state of awe, having worked out that we were the winner's connections.

'Let's go and bring him in,' I bellowed, leading our party on a cavalry charge out of the box, thundering down the stairs, and out on to the lawns in front of the stand, running with everyone around us in a blur, and out onto the course, towards the point where the horses had pulled up and were turning to come back in.

Beside us, puffing to keep up, with cameras and lenses bouncing around them, the photographers tried to take pictures of Lady Tenbury, the first woman in Britain to train a classic winner, and the elusive Sheikh Abdel al Hassan, who owned it.

Bertie and Des, nimbler and quicker off the mark, had already got to Mountain and were leading him towards us with tears in their Paddy eyes. Kevin was beaming as if his face had been slashed from side to side, acknowledging ecstatically all the congratulations that were being shouted from every side.

We got up to them and Abdel took the bridle with a rare, shy smile on his face and led Mountain through the rails to the winner's enclosure in front of the stands.

Kevin jumped down, and Annie helped him take the saddle off. There was a continual flurry of people around us as we stood talking, smiling, beaming like a gang of cats with a bucket of cream, and acknowledging the congratulations that flew around.

Bet Your Rocks Off

When Kevin got back from weighing-in, he followed Abdel and Annie up to the temporary dais that had been erected to receive their trophies from the wife of the sponsor's chief executive.

It was hard to tell who of Abdel and Annie was the more excited. Abdel turned to me with a momentary nervous smile before they hurried off together, out onto the thick sward opposite the Royal Box, where the presentation was taking place.

Abdel carried back his trophy to our group, positively beaming for the first time in his life, and I felt it was a special achievement simply to have made him look that pleased.

'That was excellent,' he said now, shaking my hand almost heartily. 'My mother will be so overjoyed.'

On the televisions that proliferated around the public places on the course, the commentators were happily justifying their failure to predict a win by Private Mountain, skilfully taking credit for pointing out the reasons why they should have done   .

But there was no serious resentment of Private Mountain's win, the first to have been achieved by a woman. The favourite, the Godolphin horse had finished two lengths second, and people were already talking about a re-match in the Irish Derby, or the King George and Queen Elizabeth Stakes.

Mountain himself looked well pleased with his achievement - his first taste of race-course victory. I was almost sorry he wouldn't ever get the chance to prove himself again.

When the formalities were over, and Abdel had been photographed with Annie and the Derby winner, Des proudly led him away. He and I, acting head lad, had to take the horse back to be swabbed and smeared for dope tests, while the owner and trainer were ushered away for the presentation and to be interviewed by a BBC racing presenter before joining The Queen for tea in her box.

When we took Mountain back to the stables after he'd given samples of every bodily fluid the Jockey Club vet could think of, we found Brigadier Mills hovering around again. I had an anxious moment as he walked towards us with a face like stone.

When he reached me, though, he held out a hand and almost gave me a glad eye. 'Well done! Lady Tenbury has done a magnificent piece of training. And I see there were no leaks this time,' he added with a chuckle.

'That was partly because we didn't really have any idea he would win,' I lied. 'We knew he was good, but he hadn't had a race this season and we had nothing really to judge him against.'

'That's funny,' Henry said with a faint twitch in his left eye. 'I got the impression you were cocky as hell about him.'

'Just to keep up stable spirits,' I laughed, wondering when on earth I'd shown him any sign of complacency.

'You had a bit on, I take it?'

'Of course,' I grinned. 'A couple of grand.' A plausible sum, I thought.

He looked at me closely for a moment without speaking, then nodded. 'Well done - a tidy win at those odds. Well, I'd best be going about my duties,' he said, and marched off to look for trouble elsewhere.

A few minutes after he'd gone, when I was thinking about getting back to the stands, Annie appeared.

'Hi, Hugo. How is he? I didn't get a chance to have a proper look at him with everything going on.'

I shrugged. 'He's fine. Not that it matters much,' I added more quietly.

Annie shook her head. 'Don't remind me.'

I raised a hand. 'Okay, I'm sorry.'

She went into the box and, out of habit, felt Mountain's legs and looked up his nose. She came out looking wistful but said nothing about the colt's future.

'Shall we get back to the box?' I asked.

She nodded. We left Des on guard and made our way back to the Queen's Stand.

'How was it?' I asked.

'Couldn't have been better. The guy from the BBC was charming. Abdel was quiet but dignified, and after the presentation The Queen asked us back for tea in her box, just like you said she would. Abdel was over the moon, like a little boy, and when she said, "I'm so sorry your mother wasn't here to receive the trophy herself," I've never seen him smile so much; it was very touching.'

All of our party except Abdel were in the box. We drank some more champagne while we re-watched the race on video, each time reliving the horror when Kevin's whip had driven Mountain almost diagonally across the track, before he'd dropped it, gathered up the horse and taken him on to win.

'My mother sends her warmest thanks and congratulations,' Abdel said, coming into the box. 'I have just been speaking to her and she wants you both very much to meet with us for dinner at Claridges.'

Reluctantly, I shook my head. 'I'm sorry Abdel, we can't. I have to see this horse back and get things ready for Corporal Harding.' I didn't want to be more specific in the enclosed surroundings of the box.

Abdel nodded. 'I understand. But there's no reason why Lady Tenbury shouldn't come back with me in the helicopter.' He turned to her. 'Is there?'

'None at all.'

'Of course, you can stay the night at Claridges, if you wish, and I'll have a car take you home tomorrow morning.'

I wondered how Annie would react. I knew she found Madame tricky, at least, was aware that Madame didn't like her much. But she nodded her acceptance. 'That would be really nice.'

CHAPTER TWENTY-TWO

It was half past six, and I was almost completely sober as I drove the lorry out of the stable compound at Epsom. I'd changed from my old black tails into a more suitable pair of Levis for the journey back.

In the inner pockets of my buckskin jacket nestled eighty grand, two monster wedges of fifty pound notes which Alfie had collected from the on-course bookies for me.

Once we were on our way, I peeled off four notes and handed two each to the happily dozing Des and Bertie.

The lads thanked me profusely, and promptly went to sleep, which suited me. The first ecstasy of winning was tempered now by my preoccupation with the next phase. Although the horse had won, the win would not be incontrovertibly logged in the records for another two weeks, when Madame would finally receive the prize money.

But unless a major upset occurred within the next couple of days, the off-course bookies with whom the sergeants had placed some of my money would pay out on Sunday or Monday; the bets they'd placed on course, they would have cashed already. Laura should have collected my Tote winnings by now and Geoffrey Scott would have his Switch account credited by the Gibraltar bookies by midnight that night; he had arranged to give me the whole amount in cash on Wednesday. And, apart from the people who'd placed them, no-one would ever know that the bets had any connection with me.

I wondered how much money Annie had put on herself, and how she'd done it. I was still very curious about her reasons for needing the readies so badly. Certainly, I hadn't seen her so relaxed in a long, long time as she was once Mountain had crossed the line.

And there had been, as we had hugged in the first few minutes, a new, inescapable closeness between us, and I was aware that even as we had hugged, our bodies were pressed tight together in a way that wasn't just physically exciting - one would have expected that - but had also left me almost aching with a need for her.

I was conscious, too, how disappointed I'd been when she'd accepted Abdel's invitation to dinner without me; though I'd made sure it hadn't shown.

We rolled into Square Barrow soon after half past eight to a rapturous reception from all the lads and farm staff. The only absentees, I noted, were Ulrike and Ray.

While Des put Mountain away, I heaved a case of my cheap champagne from the house and opened every bottle. Once everyone had a full glass in his hand, Dick Hill and I went back into the kitchen where he produced the money he'd already collected from the betting shops in Swindon.

Bet Your Rocks Off

We divided it up into piles of six hundred quid each for the lads. Dick took it out to them, and after half an hour or so, when the champagne was finished, I sent them all up to the Waggon & Horses where they would get seriously drunk - as they believed they deserved.

I simply wanted them all out of the way at midnight.

I sat on my own in the kitchen, calculating the day's final haul. The Tote had closed at twenty-eight pounds to a one pound stake for the win; eight pounds for the place - better than I'd hoped and returning a profit of a hundred and seventy thousand pounds. Alfie's bet had earned me seventy-five grand, and the sergeant's on-course bets just under a hundred and fifty.

I already knew by heart the returns on all my ante-post bets - one million, one hundred thousand, making over a million and a half in total!

While I was gleefully mulling over my vast profits, and the joyous fact that I wouldn't have to share them either with the Taxman or my ex-wife, the phone rang a dozen times with people offering congratulations, the extent of their pleasure dependent, no doubt, on the size of any bet they'd had on Mountain.

It was about ten o'clock when Madame rang.

She sounded fainter and reedier than last time, but still very much in control.

'Hugo, Hugo, my sweet boy, I am so proud of you!' she wheezed. 'I always kept faith in you, when others would not have done.' I had no idea who she was referring to, if anyone specific. 'And you have vindicated my trust supremely. I am very, very grateful for the honour I have received today with your great help.'

I was almost overwhelmed by the unusual fulsomeness of Madame's praise and gratitude, and I revised my earlier view that Abdel had been overstating her vulnerability at the time of the Adare incident. I told her truthfully that there was no one else I would rather have done it for.

When she'd rung off, I didn't bolster my nervous euphoria with any more drink. To fill in the dragging hours until midnight when Corporal Harding was due, I watched the various TV channels which were still reviewing the day's race, and studied the video a few more times.

At five to midnight, I went outside to listen for sounds of the approaching lorry. It was a warm still night in which the only man-made sound was the sporadic roar of a motorbike burning down the old Bath road a few miles to the south.

The owls were tooting and shrieking around the beech copses and hedgerows, and the occasional stamp of a hoof on concrete through scattered straw reached me from the stables.

I saw the lights wavering off the road before I heard Harding's small, three-horse Ford Cargo. A minute later, it lurched into view and pulled up in the middle of the yard between my house and the first of the boxes.

'Good evening, corporal. Everything okay?'

Bet Your Rocks Off

The little man jumped down from the cab like an eager terrier and all but saluted in lieu of wagging his tail. 'All present and correct, Sir H,' he uttered with crisp satisfaction.

'Right. Let's get on with it. Take your Mountain off the lorry and put him in that box.' I waved at the Derby winner's. 'I'll just take mine out and put him in a spare box at the end of the row.'

I wasn't being paranoid, but I was sure that the sooner I had a three year old colt in Private Mountain's box, the better. I went into Mountain's stable and switched on a torch to check where he was. The Derby winner looked up from his empty manger quite content after his exertions and a clear testimony to Annie's skills in horse husbandry.

I slipped off his brass-tagged leather head-collar and replaced it with a cheap nylon one and a slightly grubby rope.

I led him out and three doors down to an empty box. I tied his rope to a ring beside the hay rack and put my lamp down in a corner to throw the minimum of light through the stable door, which I also closed. Once Mountain was settled, I switched on the electric clippers I'd left in the stable earlier and as deftly as I knew how, I hogged the splendid colt's already skimpy mane.

When I'd finished, I stood back and shone the torch at him. Although he still looked a good horse, the hogging effectively disguised him as a high quality polo pony.

I switched off the torch and let myself out. The Derby winner's box was now occupied by the genuine three year old Private Mountain. I went in and shut both doors behind me again. Slightly holding my breath, I flicked on my light. Corporal Harding was still holding the animal's head. He had just strapped on the well-polished , brass-named head-collar, and to my great relief, I saw a mane on the horse that wasn't far off the length and thickness the older clone's had been until a few minutes before.

'You've got the four year old as well?' I asked the corporal.

'Of course, Sir H. In very good order. Not a sign of ringworm on him now,' he chuckled.

'Good. There's an empty box round the back, already watered, with a full manger. Put him there while I tidy up this mane,' I said, 'then get a set of racing plates, rasp this chap's hooves, tap on the plates, then hook them of again, so his feet will look as though he's been racing today.'

Corporal Harding bustled off, and I was grateful that as a young trooper he'd been keen enough to take an army course in farriery.

Once I'd teased the younger Mountain's mane into something as close as I remembered the Derby winner's had been that morning, I stood back to allow the corporal to do his stuff.

He did a fine job, rubbing dirt well into the fresh clench holes he'd made. 'Good,' I nodded, confident that the identities of the two horses had been satisfactorily reinvented.

We loaded the Derby winner onto the lorry, along with Barnaby River, the stable hack, also hogged and, to an amateur eye, not dissimilar to the four year old colt - a pair of unregistered polo ponies destined for Deauville.

Bet Your Rocks Off

As far as the lads and anyone else who was interested were concerned, as a result of the corporal's visit, a four year old had come from quarantine in France, and the old hack had gone.

'Well done, corporal. How are you feeling?'

'Fine, sir.'

'Still up to another four hour drive?'

'If I drive like the clappers, I'll just make the seven o'clock ferry from Folkestone. I'll be back in France by ten o'clock local.'

'Good. And you've sorted out a destination for Mountain?'

'I have indeed, sir.'

'Once you've got the hack safely in the yard, you'll be free to go. One month, okay?'

'Thank you very much sir.'

I handed him five grand in a bundle of wrinkly fifties. 'Well you have a good time, and there'll be another bonus waiting for you when you get back.'

'Indeed, sir.'

The little man leaped nimbly back into the cab and started up the lorry. It seemed to my hyper-sensitive ears to be making a hell of a racket. He turned it and crawled back down the long drive to the road, and as the sound dwindled, the quiet of the midsummer night returned and quelled my thumping pulse.

I took a few deep breaths of the crisp, hay scented air and wished him Godspeed.

There was something unfamiliar about the sound of the car skidding to a halt outside in the yard, and I woke resenting it. I guessed, as I blinked my eyes open, that it was responsible for rousing me from my deep and pleasing sleep of triumphant dreams.

I wondered who the hell it was. A glance at my bedside clock told me it was eight o'clock. I'd ordered the lads who were due to do the morning feed not to appear until nine; the horses, I felt, would understand.

I couldn't see the yard from my bedroom window, but I could hear the horses now, eager for their overdue breakfast, banging their hooves on the stable doors and whickering at the first sign of human life that morning.

I heaved myself out of bed and went down to the kitchen whose window faced the first run of stables.

Standing in front of Private Mountain's box, beside a white Volvo with a broad blue and orange stripe, was a tall young policeman; he was putting on his cap and gazing up at the curtained windows of my house.

There was a convulsion in my guts; a nasty taste in my mouth told me that their contents had been involuntarily and shamefully projected there.

All the dreams, all the growing certainty of the last few hours instantly collapsed inside me - my muscles with them. I was suddenly aware of a tingling flabbiness in my limbs and for some time, it seemed, I couldn't persuade them to move.

Bet Your Rocks Off

But even in this catatonic state, my mind was reversing crazily back over the last few dozen hours to see what had gone wrong - so wrong that it had brought the police here already.

Even the sight of the unchallengeable three year old colt, looking out over the lower door of his box did nothing to reassure me.

It was only when the policeman had walked through the small picket gate and up the short path to my front door that I was able to shift myself into action.

I walked in a daze through the small hall and opened the door.

'Good morning, sir,' he asked in a local accent. 'Are you in charge of these stables?'

It seemed an odd query. I looked back at the guileless brown eyes beneath the peak of the cap. 'Well, sort of,' I mumbled. 'I'm the racing manager for the owners.'

'I see. And who would they be?'

'Don't you know?' I asked, not disguising my surprise.

'No, sir. We only know that a man called Ray Manning worked here.'

'He still does, as far as I know.'

'I'm afraid not sir.'

I stared at him. I didn't need him to spell it out. I wondered if all policemen were trained to convey news of death without using the words "dead" or "killed".

'What's happened?' I croaked.

'He was found in the old harbour in Bristol.'

'Drowned?'

'That was the ultimate cause, but he was full of pure heroin.'

'Heroin?' I whispered, astonished. 'How?'

'I'm afraid I haven't seen the pathologist's report, but I imagine he injected it sir. That's what they mostly do. But we need to ask you a few questions. May I come in?'

'Yes, yes, of course,' I muttered as realisation that this visit had nothing to do with Mountain sank in. I opened the front door wide, and showed him through to the kitchen. 'Coffee? I offered, needing it badly myself.

'No thanks, sir. You know - sitting in the car all day.' He gave me a man to man smile as he pulled a small notebook from his top pocket.

'So, what can I tell you?'

'When did you last see Manning?'

I thought back across the abyss of time that seemed to have elapsed since then. 'Friday morning, I think. Yes, that's it, Friday morning. His girl friend works here too. They'd both come in and we'd already done some work but she complained that she felt lousy and he asked if he could take her home. Then she came in yesterday - didn't see her myself, I was already at Epsom...'

'Oh? It's race-horses here is it?' the policeman asked with slight interest.

'Yes; it's race-horses,' I nodded. 'Anyway, Lady Tenbury, who's the trainer here, told me that Ulrike - that's Ray's girlfriend, came in very upset because he'd gone off and not come back the night before.'

'Yes. One of my colleagues - a WPC - has seen the young lady; it was she who reported the missing person and supplied the description.'

'Has she been told yet?'

'Oh yes. It was her who told us where he worked.'

'Did she have to identify him?'

'Not yet. But she was able to describe a rather intimate tattoo.'

'I see. Well the fact of the matter is that she's more up to date with his last movements than we are. I can categorically state that we haven't seen him in the yard since Friday - about half past nine in the morning.'

'Were you aware that Manning was a regular user if heroin?'

'Not at all. He was a good work-rider. He wasn't a bad jockey before that in Germany; of course, there's not so much competition there.'

'He also had a record for drug use in Germany. Weren't you aware of that, sir? As well as a record for personal use in the UK, dating back six years.'

'Nope,' I said truthfully. 'I'd no idea. He was a surly bastard sometimes, if you know what I mean, but we kept him on because he was perfectly competent, and his girlfriend is a very good work rider.'

'I understand.' The constable nodded. 'What about other people who work here. I suppose there are quite a few?'

'There are, but I've allowed them to come in late today as we won the Derby yesterday.'

The policeman opened his eyes wide in sudden realisation. 'Oh, yes! I'd heard it was a local trainer - and a woman for the first time. I hadn't put two and two together. I'm sure some of our lads had a bet on the horse, but I'm not a racing man myself. Never had a bet in my life.'

I can believe it - I thought, looking at his self-righteous face. 'As you can imagine, things were pretty chaotic here yesterday,' I said. 'I'm afraid the lads all went off for a bit of a celebration.'

'I'll have to call back another time then sir. And perhaps you can tell me where I can find lady..' he glanced at his notebook - '... Lady Tenbury.?'

'She's in London, but I expect she'll be back here some time today. That's her cottage there.' I nodded at Dairyman's through the window.

'I think the young German lady would like to see Lady Tenbury.'

'Where's Ulrike now?'

'She was very shocked when we told her we'd found her boyfriend, so she's resting up at the station in Marlborough, but she'll need to stay somewhere for a few days; she's got no relations here in England, but she doesn't want to back to Germany yet.'

'That's fine. I've got a friend, Mrs Templeton who's Swedish but speaks very good German. I'll get her to phone the station to arrange to pick up Ulrike as soon as possible and look after her until she's able to cope.'

'Right, well,' the policeman symbolically snapped shut his notebook and tucked it back in his pocket, 'that'll do for now, but if you give me a phone number, I'll let you know before we come again. And I'm sorry to bring such bad news at a time like this.'

I shrugged. 'There's no good time for bad news is there, but thank you for letting us know. I'm sorry I couldn't tell you more. Presumably it's all fairly straight-forward from now on? I mean, he took an overdose and fell in the harbour?'

'Where drugs are concerned, things are never straightforward, sir. There's a lot of money involved, and we've had one report that he had a pile of cash on him just a few days ago. But there was no sign of any on him, or at his flat.'

'You searched his flat?'

'Oh yes, sir, in case there were more drugs.'

'Well, of course, anything else I can do....'

'Thank you sir. No need to get up. I can let myself out.'

I took him at his word, and saw him emerge a few moments later and walk back to the police car.

Private Mountain, all unaware of what I'd just been through because of him, looked up with interest as the policeman emerged; he gave his stable door a hopeful kick.

I sat down at my kitchen table and tried to cope with my relief, and my alarm at what the policeman had told me.

In front of me, the Derby winner's racing plates were still on the table where I'd put them the night before, and I thought that I should get them sent up to Madame as soon as possible; she would appreciate it greatly if they arrived that day.

I picked them up, found paper and made a parcel of them before ringing Boris, our local taxi, to ask if he wanted to make a quick hundred quid before lunch.

After that, I phoned Birgitta. Alfie answered, still effervescing over his monstrous bookie-crusher. I quietened him down and told him I wanted to speak to his wife.

When she came to the phone, I gave her a very diluted version of what had happened to Ulrike, and asked her if she would be prepared to pick her up and take her home for a few days. As I'd hoped, Birgitta said she would go straight round to the police station.

I was just putting the phone down when the first two lads arrived.

Sean and Mick looked as if they been shoved through a meat-mincer.

Their complexions were blotchy, and their eyes bloodshot. They walked into the yard in a ponderous trance, like the living dead in a black-&-white horror movie.

They shambled to a halt outside the feed store.

'Go home!' I bellowed from the kitchen window. 'You'd be about as much use as a condom in a convent.'

They looked up slowly, gazed vaguely towards me before turning round and silently shuffling back up to the hostel. I watched them go without regret. I could mix and deliver fourteen feeds perfectly well on my own.

As I performed the tedious but undemanding task, my mind swirled like a fairground ride. The visit from the young copper had startled me and left me jittery; and I still couldn't come to terms with the shock of Ray's death from heroin at such a critical moment.

But by the time I'd finished, two rather more alert members of staff had arrived, and focusing on the task of trying to maintain the illusion of a working yard, I gave them the task of organising some imminent runners on the horse walker.

I went back to the house, feeling steadfast in the face of turmoil, and decided not to ring Annie yet; she deserved, I generously conceded, her own time and space after what we'd been through.

And if she couldn't enjoy a lie in at Claridges, where could she?

I got into the Merc and drove down to Devizes to find a newsagent. The Sunday papers, especially the tabloids, were full of photographs of Annie and the horse, some of Abdel, one or two of me, beneath headlines proclaiming the alarming news that the Derby winner had been trained by a woman, and an American woman, to boot. I bought a copy of all of them, planning to go straight home and peruse them over a bottle of Bollinger, but, unwisely, I let myself be tempted by the prospect of a glorious reception to stop off at the pub.

This had - I justified - the benefit of looking like very normal behaviour. But I was supremely careful to disguise my intake and hardly drank at all. I left with the promise that I'd be back in the evening, with the trainer, standing drinks all round.

I drove into the yard and didn't notice the noise of an approaching chopper until I'd switched off my motor. I got out and looked up to see something similar to the machine in which Abdel had arrived at Epsom the day before. It circled while the pilot identified an empty paddock where he could land.

When it had come down, and the blades were gently swooshing round, riffling the sward and scaring the horses in the nearest boxes, Annie stepped down and walked without any elaborate crouching under the rotor, away from the helicopter.

Even I couldn't help noticing that she was wearing an entirely new and painfully expensive outfit, with a thousand pound bag hanging from her shoulder. I sauntered over to meet her as she reached the gate and turned to wave at the pilot.

The noise and draught from the chopper abruptly swelled and it lifted off. I leaned down and gave Annie a heartfelt kiss on the cheek, but waited until the helicopter was a couple of hundred yards away, disappearing over a clump of beeches, before I spoke.

'Welcome back. I've been waiting to look at the papers with you.'

'No you haven't. You've been drinking beer; I can smell it in your breath.'

'Only a pint,' I protested.

'Anyway, how did it all go last night?'

'Fine. Come and meet Private Mountain.'

'Shh,' she said instinctively, putting a finger to her lips and nodding towards the stable block.

'Okay, okay,' I said, 'no one can hear me from here; and anyway, there's only Bertie and Des in. Sean and Mick came in earlier but they looked so rough I had to send them home and do the feeds myself.'

'How does he look?'

We were rounding the end of the stables now, and I led her to the box.

Annie let herself in and walked around the horse, gazing at it and giving it a few congratulatory pats. She glanced at me with a grin. 'You're sure the corporal came?'

It was my turn to put a finger to my lips.

'Perfect,' she shrugged. Once more she patted the colt, who looked as if he wondered who the hell she was.

We walked over to the house. She didn't speak until we were inside.

'So far, so good, Hugo. D'you know, I never really deep down thought we'd pull it off, but you never doubted it, did you?'

'Of course I did,' I grinned. 'Every fucking day.'

'No rude words Hugo - just because we won,' she admonished, as she always did. 'But I am rather proud of you.'

'So's Madame; she phoned me last night to tell me.'

'I know, she said she was going to.'

'And about fifty other people; most of whom I'd never heard of, as well as a string of hacks. But how was dinner?'

'Nobody really ate much. I didn't feel like it, Abdel never eats anything and Madame has the appetite of a sparrow.'

'How was she?'

'For once, not too hostile toward me. I think she's finally coming round. D'you know - I have the feeling that she never really believed a woman could actually train a Derby winner, but Abdel told her that it was my training, not your advice that had clinched it. Naturally, I told her how much help you'd been. Anyway, she seems to have forgiven me at last for whatever I'm supposed to have done wrong.'

'And how was she otherwise?'

'Frankly, lousy. She wasn't moving around much, but there's still plenty of fight in her eyes. She doesn't have any idea at all of what we pulled off, and she's happy as hell. She made Abdel tell her a dozen times about tea with Her Majesty, and what she'd said.'

I shook my head. 'It's amazing what turns some people on, but there it is, as Abdel would say, and that was the whole point of the exercise as far as he was concerned.'

'His father must have been an awful man, for Abdel to love his mom so much.'

'I don't think he saw anything of him for the few years he was still alive. So the mother takes on the role of father, and loving women as partners becomes harder for the adult child.'

'Okay Hugo; that's enough psycho-crap for a Sunday morning. Let's have a look at the papers.'

I agreed and showed her into my small drawing-room. 'Champagne?'

'No thanks. I'll explode if I have any more. Tomato juice and chilli sauce, please.'

I had the same, with a shot of Stolichnaya.

With a flourish I carried in half a dozen newspapers and dropped them on the low table in the centre of the room.

We opened each in turn, wallowing in the glowing prose and well-chosen shots. The consensus of opinion was overwhelmingly benign:

A well-deserved victory by an impressive individual from a thoroughly businesslike trainer.
The first woman ever to win the Derby.
The new Jenny Pitman!

'Not quite,' Annie said.

'I'll drink to that.'

Somehow, seeing the whole episode recorded in print gave it, for me, the final stamp of reality.

Absurd, when one considered what a lot of balls the newspapers usually printed, but I guessed it was the result of years of conditioning.

'Of course, they've all been on the phone again, wanting to come down today, but I said there's no way I'm organising a photo call until midday tomorrow, and they won't be allowed on the premises if they turn up before then. I hope you agree.'

'I sure do. I just don't need all that hassle right now. I suppose we'll have to get Kevin over, too?'

'Yes, I've rung him. And there are a couple of girls in Marlborough who can do a bit of food at short notice. I'll organise it all, if you like?'

'Thanks, Hugo.'

We agreed a few details for the press call, but I couldn't put off telling her the less savoury news any longer.

'There was a copper on the doorstep at half eight this morning.'

Annie dropped the Sunday Mail in which she was reading a gratifying description of how she'd looked the day before.

'What!? Why the hell didn't you tell me?'

'Calm down. It wasn't anything to do with the race; I thought it was when I saw him, like you, but he came to say that Ray was found last night....'

'Where, for God's sake?'

'Floating in the old harbour in Bristol.'

All the colour drained from Annie's cheeks. 'My God!' she whispered. 'What happened? Why there?'

I gave her an exact account of what the policeman had said. I told her about Ulrike being taken to the police station in Marlborough, and that Birgitta had gone and picked her up to look after her. Before I'd finished, she'd pulled her phone from her bag and was dialling the Templeton's number.

Five minutes later, she was skidding out of the yard in her BMW, intent on seeing for herself how Ulrike was.

I watched her go, and pondered how seldom any plans seemed to run smoothly, even when the impediments weren't in any way connected.

Watching her go, though, I was glad I hadn't told her about the other threat that had hung over the yard all the previous week.

On the face of it there wasn't any point, other than, I supposed, to impress her with my sang-froid, and coolness under fire.

While I was debating this, I thought I'd like to hear from Bowring himself exactly what he'd done, especially now the only evidence to back the blackmailer's claim was safely across the *Manche*, and heading, I shuddered to recall, for a dog food factory or, perhaps, a cheap restaurant.

I dialled Bowring's number. It was answered after two rings by the usual uncompromising NCO's voice.

Major Bowring was unavailable, I was told. He would be informed that I'd called.

I put the phone down wondering why Bowring insisted on running his affairs in this irritating, para-military way, but then, I had to concede, he seemed to get results. I didn't at all begrudge him the fifteen grand he'd earned by picking up my blackmailer for me.

By eight that evening, it seemed that everyone with the faintest of connections to Square Barrow, Annie or me, and quite a few more besides, had heard that we were getting the drinks in at the Waggon & Horses.

The squat thatch-roofed inn was almost bulging with the infectious effervescence caught by most of the people there from the comparatively few who had actually won anything.

The only notable absentees at the start of the evening were the owners of the horse. But even this was put right by the totally unexpected arrival of Abdel in a limo.

Abdel was a rare visitor to the yard, and the area in general. Few people had ever met him, but he received, nonetheless, an overwhelming reception.

Watching him in a crowded room - which I knew he disliked - he appeared to be handling the whole thing with a proper sense of duty. I guessed that his main purpose in coming was not to celebrate on his own account, but to gauge the reactions of the other revellers as he listened to innumerable toasts to the winner.

Of course, he knew, with Annie and I, that the horse who had done the winning was probably no longer with us. I presumed that didn't worry him at all and his own triumph, beyond the vindication of his mother's shame at Ascot, was in seeing the supreme success of a very private, practical experiment in revolutionary genetic engineering.

But in general, for the short hour he was in the pub, he behaved himself and shook hands with anyone who wanted to.

Bet Your Rocks Off

As he left, Abdel turned to me. 'Perhaps, on the twenty-second, when we receive our prize money - a more discreet celebration?'

Later, as Annie drove me the short distance home, I thought of another set of absentees from the party.

'No sign of Sir Toby Allerthorpe.'

'Or his whore of a wife.'

'Now, now. You should be generous in victory.'

She glanced at me oddly, but didn't respond.

'I'm glad Calista came,' she said instead. 'She's been such a good friend.' I hoped she didn't see my guilty wince. 'Oh, it's okay, Hugo,' she went on. 'I know she slept with you.'

I looked at her, amazed. 'She told you?'

'Yes, of course, the day after it happened. We've compared views on lovers before, you know.'

I was appalled to hear it. 'You discussed my...' I huffed, remembering what it had been like, '.. performance?'

Annie smiled but said nothing.

And I found myself considering her swapping opinions with her friend.

It was the first time since she and I had worked together for three years that she had made any kind of admission that she'd had any love life at all since our first liaison eighteen years before.

Of course, I'd assumed she had; everybody had to have some kind of sex in their lives. But I'd never discovered with whom or, for that matter, when. There had been the occasional phone call, short and cryptic, which I'd overheard; nothing more.

But now she had referred to the possibility, however obliquely, I was seized with a gagging jealousy.

'Cat got your tongue?' she asked facetiously as we pulled into the yard.

'Yah,' I answered, and left it at that.

She dropped me without a further word outside my house, and I let myself in, feeling absurdly let down.

I must have sat for an hour or more in my drawing-room, with only the moon outside for light, while I swigged, slowly and without real commitment, a large cognac I'd poured for myself by way of anaesthetic.

After a while, the pressure on my prostate needed relieving, and I went out to the back of the house.

As I peed onto the compost heap, drawing deeply on my last cigar of the evening, I glanced down at Dairyman's Cottage, and saw that the lights were still on, upstairs and down.

Without stopping to think about the wisdom of it, I hopped over the low fence and walked a hundred yards down the crunchy track to Annie's house.

When I reached her front door, I paused.

I took a long drag on my Monte Cristo, held my breath for a few moments, exhaled, and tapped.

I hadn't even heard her come to the door when it opened.

'Hello, Hugo. Are you lost?'

'Yes.'

'Are you sober?'

'More or less.'

She shrugged, then nodded. 'Come in.' She opened the door and beckoned.

It was only now that I saw she was wearing just a short, flimsy nightie which covered the top few inches of her long, slim legs.

'Are you sure you want me to?'

She shrugged her shoulder again. 'No, frankly, I'm not sure. But I can't sleep either. Go into the snug while I put on more clothes,' she added.

'Oh, no,' I said. 'Don't do that.'

She went. I hung about, reading the invitations on her mantelpiece without taking in a single name, while the image of Annie in her nightie continued to trouble me.

She glanced through the door, wearing a terry robe now. 'Drink?'

'Tea.'

If she was surprised - and she ought to have been - she didn't show it, and reappeared a few minutes later with two mugs of Earl Grey and lemon.

'Are you sure this is all you want?' she asked, placing it on a flimsy glass table in front of the sofa where I now sat.

'I didn't mean to appear quite so limp-wristed, but I dare say it won't harm me.' I took a sip.

Annie lowered herself into the chair opposite, contriving somehow not to flash too much upper thigh at me.

'So,' she asked. 'What's on your mind?'

I couldn't tell her. Instead we reminisced, for the next half an hour or so and another mug of tea, about the events of the previous day, and the coups we'd staged in France and Germany, minor rehearsals, it seemed now, for the crowning achievement of the Derby.

But as I talked, laughing and mimicking, I found old memories of our love-making fresh in my mind, and I wanted her more than I ever had.

Abruptly, I stopped mid-sentence, and looked at her, abandoning all pretence of what I was thinking.

'Do you know, I think I'm going to have to go.'

She raised an eyebrow, a few millimetres. 'Oh?'

'If I don't, I might do something very stupid.'

'It wouldn't be the first time.'

'No,' I agreed. 'But I don't want to spoil the mood while it lasts.'

I stood up, utterly sober, I discovered, and leaned to kiss her.

For a moment, our lips touched; the first time they had in years.

CHAPTER TWENTY-THREE

A man from Bowring's office rang next morning.

I was told he would be calling at Square Barrow, in person later in the day. This surprised me. I hadn't expected, now that the deed had been done, to see the Major again until I had another assignment for him.

But I was given no indication of what time to expect him.

I put the phone down, and thought of Annie. Bowring, pathologically discreet, would certainly not reveal to her the nature of our business. But I was even more undecided whether or not to tell her what had happened. Now, the idea of concealment seemed unacceptably dishonest.

On the other hand....

I gave up; these things, like nature's streams, find their own courses.

I turned instead to the matter of the press conference and photo call. Annie and I had talked about it a little the night before - the correct presentation of our triumph and our hero.

The racing hacks would be baying for news of our plans for Private Mountain, and we would have to throw them some juicy bones on which to gnaw - some plausible options, bearing in mind that the animal now in the yard was barely fit and hadn't seen a race-course for nine months.

Not that there would be any problem in finding an excuse not to run the animal when the crunch came. The priority was to let them photograph the horse, with and without the trainer, as much as they liked, before filling them up with rich food and champagne.

I hustled Mrs Brockett into action, and with the weather forecast looking good, made arrangements with the Sloanes from Marlborough for an *al fresco* lunch.

I hadn't spoken to Annie that morning, though I'd seen her earlier, from my bedroom window, leading out a small string of older horses who were due to run over the following week or so. We'd abandoned any plans to race for the next few days, given our shortage of work riders, with Ray dead and Ulrike out of commission, and because, frankly, neither of us could give a toss just then. At the same time, though, we knew that if we were to be sure of quelling any suspicions in the minds of professional cynics like Brigadier Mills, we couldn't afford to drop our guard.

I thought of Mills later, when the hacks started arriving, and with them, Terry Brownley.

I went up to him, making a show of singling him out. 'Morning. Come to bask in the reflected glory like the rest of this lot?'

His long, ferret face twitched as if he'd just smelt a bit of humour and didn't think much of it.

'We always like to check things over after a big race.'

'Would you like a private view of the winner before we parade him to the press?'

'Yes, please, and I've brought our own vet to have a look at him this time.'

'Have you indeed? That's a bit of a liberty,' I bridled instinctively, before I could stop myself.

He noted it with satisfaction, while I assured him hastily that there was no problem. Feeling reasonably confident, I was introduced to the vet who had now walked into the yard from the make-shift car-park in the paddock. I led both men to the three year old's box and let them in.

After a cursory external examination, the vet went straight for the mouth - the first time any knowledgeable official had bothered, I smiled to myself.

Evidently satisfied, he stood back again, before crouching to examine the horse's feet.

'What's the point of all this?' I asked casually, but not without a justifiable trace of indignation.

'I'm simply doing what Brigadier Mills asked me to do,' the vet replied, obviously conscious of the offence he might have been causing.

I kept my views on Brigadier Mills and his nasty, obsessive leeriness to myself. 'Well, I'll leave you to it. I must go and look after the gentlemen of the press.'

'I'm sure you must, sir,' Brownley agreed.

The vet looked around. 'Where do you keep your weighing machine, sir?'

'We don't have one.'

'Don't you? Why not?'

'We put more store by other things than pure body weight,' I said, dismissively.

The vet shook his head.

I let myself out of the stable with a catalogue of all the questionable things he might find scrolling through my head.

As I was emerging, I saw Annie. I hadn't yet spoken to her that morning, and suddenly, I found myself bizarrely embarrassed.

'It's okay, Hugo, you didn't do anything wrong last night. Surprising and totally out of character, maybe, but nothing inappropriate, as our esteemed president would say.'

I thought at once of the man in the Bill Clinton mask, and Bowring on his way here.

'There's a Jockey Club vet here,' I said in a loud voice which the officious little Brownley would hear. 'Carrying out some kind of routine check.'

Annie was about to express her doubts, when I stemmed the words with a look.

'Oh, right,' she said blandly, while she made a worried, quizzical face at me.

I ushered her away to talk to Chris Lewis, who'd just rolled into view, looking for a drink.

Bet Your Rocks Off

Hugo sidled up to me. 'You must be a happy man, and a good bit richer than you were a couple of days ago. I was in there too, you'll be glad to hear, knowing you'd already had a good wedge on.'

'I never told you what I'd put on.'

'Well,' Hugo shrugged his dandruff flecked shoulders, 'I knew you was very confident, but I kept one bit of information to myself.'

Now he mentioned it, I realised that he hadn't shared with his readers the intelligence that he'd threatened, concerning my seven and a half grand bill for 'protection' from Bowring's organisation.

'Very thoughtful of you Hugo, but you still tipped it.'

'Didn't move the price much, though, did it? Anyway,' he wheedled, 'if you've ever got something like that happening again, you'll know you can rely on me...'

He looked at me like an old street mongrel seeking a tit-bit.

'Look, Hugo; I'm glad you won; I'm rather glad the horse won, as a matter of fact, and yes, I was fairly confident, but I'm not a fucking prophet.'

'I didn't think prophets went in for that sort of thing,' Hugo mused.

'Just have a drink Hugo, and let me get on, please?'

I left him looking slyly after me.

He was the sort of man who assumed every result was the product of some human predetermination, and though he may have felt pretty certain we'd pulled off some kind of a coup, I was absolutely certain he hadn't an inkling how we'd done it.

Brownley left with the vet, polite but uncommunicative to the last, though I detected from the slight decrease in his bumptiousness that he knew he'd been chasing a wild goose.

'Give my regards to Brigadier Mills,' I said.

When they'd gone, Des finished grooming Private Mountain, and led him out for the general inspection and admiration of the forty or so journalists, photographers and TV cameramen who had turned up. Kevin had arrived by then, to share in the glory, and had changed into a set of Madame's silks for the posed shots that everyone wanted.

Annie, still in her jodhpurs and a loose white cotton blouse, sat on the stone wall in front of my house, by Private Mountain's head. She looked, frankly, lovely - relaxed, and as pleased as any trainer who'd just won the Derby.

She answered all their questions, remarkably predictable and unoriginal as they were, in an easy, intimate way that they loved. None of them went off message until one, not recognisable as a regular racing writer, asked, 'Who's the man in your life now?'

I was standing discreetly at the back of the crowd, but, absurd as it seemed, I half expected them all to turn and look at me. And for the first time in many years, I felt myself redden.

It was an horrific experience, to be revealing so much of one's inner thoughts so plainly.

But, luckily, and to my surprise, not a single face turned in my direction, and the involuntary indiscretion hadn't been observed - except by Annie, who had glanced at me very swiftly before gesturing towards the handsome, flawless colt at her side. 'He is,' she declared with a laugh.

'Is that so?' a voice said quietly in my right ear.

I spun round to find Bowring.

'Piers,' I jabbered. 'I didn't see you arrive.'

'I can see that you might be preoccupied, but can you spare me a moment?'

'Of course.'

'Somewhere discreet?'

'Yes, certainly.' I led him round to the back of the stables and onto the track that led up to the start of the all-weather gallops.

When we emerged from between the high hedges into the open, he glanced around and nodded. 'This'll do.' He pulled an envelope from his pocket. 'Here's my bill for the rest of the fee.' He handed it to me.

I took it and shoved it into my jacket without opening it. 'You could have posted it, you know.'

He ignored my facetiousness. 'I like to give my clients a full report of any action I've carried out on their behalf. Generally, it's best not committed to paper or other interceptable channels.'

'Yes, of course,' I nodded. 'What's the story?'

'As you'll have gathered, the individual who was blackmailing you was apprehended by my people within minutes of your handover on Friday. As we thought, he had little or no inexperience in extortion. When he took your packet, he wanted to turn out to the right, but he hadn't realised till then that a temporary one-way system had been set

393

up, so he'd never have had a chance to get away cleanly. We kept him in close custody, and during that time made an assessment of the likelihood of attempts at further extortion after the primary event. When we discovered that the man was a heroin addict, we concluded that even after the removal of the evidence, he would be very strongly motivated to pursue further demands, which would at least be damaging to your reputation, and might well prompt more authoritative, far less welcome investigations.'

'A heroin addict?' I croaked, my throat tightening with a horrible suspicion.

'That's right, thoroughly hooked; piece of complete scum. Anyway,' Bowring said lightly, flicking a tiny, foolhardy spider from his sleeve, 'you'll be glad to hear that he's no longer part of the equation.'

'What do you mean?'

'I mean he was going to die of heroin poisoning sooner or later, so we just helped him on his way.'

'Who was he?' I asked huskily, although I already knew.

'One of your staff - chap called Ray Manning. Not, as we first suspected, the Irishman whom I saw just now holding the horse back at your stables.'

I stopped walking and stared at him. 'You killed Ray?'

Bowring gave me a faintly puzzled look. 'As a matter of fact, no. He was a known junkie; that's why he was chucked out of Germany; you should have checked. As to his rather unseemly demise, he was entirely the agent of his own destruction; we simply acquired some totally pure heroin, which he used willingly - that's understating it - positively ravenously. Unfortunately, his body simply wasn't prepared for such quantities of the uncut drug.' Bowring shrugged one linen clad shoulder.

'I didn't ask you to kill the poor bastard,' I said.

Bowring stared back icily. 'I've just told you, we didn't. When he told us what he knew, or, at least, what he'd guessed, we realised he was going to be a continuing threat to you. You had instructed us to remove the threat; we were able to create circumstances by which your blackmailer did it himself. Rather neat, I thought.'

I imagined Ray, grumpy, bonily handsome Ray, always knowing best, and doing second best, floating face down in the oily waters of the empty harbour.

'What did he tell you, then?' I asked.

Bowring started walking again. Reluctantly, I followed, had to walk sharply to keep up, feeling that by doing so, I was condoning what he'd done to Ray.

'He'd guessed there was something very particular about your Derby horse - looked after by the stupidest lad and always ridden by Lady Tenbury. Everyone discouraged from going too near it; you and Lady Tenbury always handling it yourselves. He became sure that something devious was being planned, so he went in when no one was around and examined the horse for himself. He came away aware that somehow, you'd entered a horse for the Derby which was four years old, giving it an enormous advantage. In other words, he knew you were organising a coup. Of course, he didn't know how, so, obviously, he was just testing the water by asking for only ten thousand the first time. As I told you then, if you paid it, he would know that he had, as it were, a sale on his hands, and he knew he could up the ante.'

It was hard to argue with Bowring's cold logic. He had done precisely what I'd asked him to do, just rather more thoroughly, given the permanent nature of his method. I pulled the envelope from my pocket and opened it. Inside was an invoice, as agreed, for a second tranche of seven and half thousand pounds.

'I'll have a cheque sent this week,' I said.

From an outer pocket of his fawn linen jacket, Bowring pulled a second, much bulkier envelope which he handed to me. 'It might help if you were to bank this.'

I opened the packet and found a bundle of brand new fifty pound notes. I looked up at Bowring. 'What's this?'

'Seven thousand eight hundred pounds we found in Manning's flat. If you check with your bank, I think you'll find they're the notes you drew out last Monday.'

'You went to Manning's flat?'

'Not personally, of course.'

'But wasn't his girlfriend there? She went home ill early Friday morning after the first bit of work.'

'Naturally, my man waited until she went out that evening. I should think whatever was wrong with her was Manning's idea, because he needed to take the day off on Friday to collect your second drop.'

Bet Your Rocks Off

Chris Lewis was watching Bowring go.

'That was your new owner wasn't it?'

I stared at the ugly little snoop. 'What on earth are you talking about?'

'You were talking to him the other day at Leicester, weren't you. You said he was thinking of sending some horses to this yard.'

'Yes, of course,' I blustered, remembering. 'I was wondering how the hell you knew who he was. I'd forgotten you'd already seen him. Anyway, there's a good chance he might send us a couple of very decent horses - especially after yesterday.'

'Where will they be coming form?'

'For fuck's sake, Hugo, I'm not likely to tell you that, am I?'

'You'd be surprised how often you can catch people though,' he chortled.

As he wandered back to the makeshift bar, around which most of our guests were now clustered like pigs around a trough, my mobile rang.

'It's Mungo.'

'What news?'

'We have a bid from the Japs, subject to fertility tests.'

'How much?' I held my breath.

'Seven and a half million.'

Not bad; not enough but not bad. 'Tell them we'll consider it. How long will the tests take?'

'If I push, maybe three or four days, especially if we want them confirmed in the States.'

'Push, Mungo, push.'

He laughed. 'Right. Bye.'

'What did he want?' Annie asked, walking up to me.

I glanced around, to be sure no one was within earshot. 'He's had a bid of seven and a half.'

Annie made a not-bad-but-not-great face.

'Quite,' I agreed.

'Let's hope his sperm count's up to scratch.'

Later, we sat at the table in my kitchen. The yard was agreeably empty of journalists and cameramen; it was a quiet moment in the stable routine.

Mrs Brockett had made us some tea and gone home.

'So, how have you done, Hugo?'

'Geoffrey Scott rang at lunchtime; he's already been credited with four hundred and twenty-two thousand from the ante-post bets he placed off-shore.'

'Goodie!'

'He's drawing out the full amount in cash and handing it over Wednesday morning - less his cut. I've also calculated that Sergeant Rawlings and his merry men should collect just under seven hundred thousand from what they placed over the winter, and another hundred and sixty grand from what they put on for me on Saturday. I should be getting the bulk of that tomorrow evening, after they've all been collecting for two days.'

'Did you put anything else on?'

'Sure,' I grinned. 'I gave Alfie five grand on the day; I've already had eighty grand back from that, and Laura put ten grand on with the Tote for me - so there's another hundred and eighty to come from that.'

Annie made a quick, sour face. 'You haven't had it yet?'

'Not yet.'

'Do you know she put it on?'

'Of course I do.'

'Why? Because she told you she had?'

'Oh, come on Annie, now you're just being bitchy. I know she's a bit of a slapper, but she's not a bloody crook.'

Annie sniffed, to indicate that she wasn't prepared to discuss someone like Laura. I couldn't ignore a twinge of excitement at this sign of jealousy.

'I'll ring her now,' I said, picking up the phone.

Toby Allerthorpe answered himself.

'Hello, Hugo. How are you? Very well done, by the way. Sorry not to have made it to your binge at the pub yesterday.'

'And we were very sorry not to see you,' I said, unconvincingly. 'Is Laura around by any chance; I asked her to do me a small favour on Derby Day.'

He didn't seem at all put out by my wanting to speak to his wife, and a moment later, she was on the phone. 'Hi, Hugo. What can I do for you?' The stupid question was dripping with innuendo.

'You know perfectly well. Have you got my money yet?'

399

'Come round tomorrow, about midday, and I'll have it for you.'

I put the phone down and grinned at Annie. 'I'm collecting tomorrow.'

She looked dubious, but said nothing, and I sensed that, as far as she was concerned, the Laura position had finally to be resolved.

'What are you doing for dinner?' I asked.

'Calista's asked me to her place. Jackson's sending a car for me.'

'To take you to Eaton Square?'

'That's right, if you don't mind doing the early feed and looking after the first lot tomorrow?'

How could I object? I nodded glumly as she got up and went back to Dairyman's to prepare herself for the evening's feasting, while all I had in prospect was a few pints in the pub and an early night.

Not long after Annie had gone, my telephone rang again.

'Sir Hugo Tarrington? I have the Sheik Abdel al Hassan on the line.' It was typical of a Claridges telephonist to use a title that the holder himself never used.

'Hugo?' Abdel sounded distant. 'My mother isn't well, I'm afraid. Of course, she has been very gratified by winning the Derby, but if anything, the excitement hasn't helped her condition. She wanted to come and see you at the stables, but I think this is now very unlikely before she goes back to Switzerland. Tonight, I return to Florida for a few weeks. Please continue to send me your reports. And thank you for all you have done.'

Bet Your Rocks Off

'Hang on Abdel, won't you be back for our prize-winning party? And we've had an offer for Mountain that we should discuss.'

'Oh?' He sound completely uninterested.

'Yah,' I said. 'Seven and a half million.'

'Unconditional?'

'No, of course not. They want a fertility test.'

'I see. Then keep me informed, please.'

It sounded as if the possibility of selling our colt for that kind of money was utterly trivial to him. But then, when you counted your wealth in billions - at least hundreds of millions - as I was fairly sure Abdel could, I supposed it wasn't a big deal.

I stood on the doorstep under the old stone portico at Nethercote next morning, and confidently shoved a thumb on the big china bell push.

While I waited for it to be answered, inescapable memories, now relegated to forgoing chapters in my biography, insinuated themselves into my mind. But the most recent encounter with Laura - incredibly, just a week ago - had not yet been burnished by time into one of those gilded fragments of my personal myth. Just then, the whole thing looked frankly tacky and, in a new experience for me, shameful.

I'd always been wary of too penetrative self- analysis, though, and was glad that a possible outbreak was stemmed by the opening of the door and the appearance of a stout, rustic woman I'd seen about the place before. Whoever she was - some kind of domestic, I supposed - she was expecting me.

'Morning, Sir Hugo,' she said in a recognisably Wiltshire burr. 'Lady Allerthorpe give this to me to give to you.'

She thrust towards me a large manila envelope, sealed, and with the word 'Hugo' scrawled across it in her little girl's hand.

Anxious as I was to rip the thing open, I felt I should restrain myself, at least until I was in my car.

'Is Lady Allerthorpe here?' I asked.

'No. She went last night.'

'Went where?'

'She didn't say.'

'Has she gone for long?'

'A month, at least, I should think. She took ever so many clothes with her.'

'Good Lord. Has she left Sir Toby?' I asked, indiscreetly, I knew, but the woman was bound to know.

She looked at me with her lips tight for a moment or so, then nodded. 'You can't hardly blame her, being so young, and probably wanting a family. Mind you, she'll be back. This house is hers.'

I was suddenly struck by the appalling thought that she might decide to descend on me at some point. But then, would she have left the packet with this woman if she planned to see me?

I had to look in it.

I tore it open. Inside were several neat bundles of fifty pound notes which looked familiar. I took them out; five in all, each, I was almost certain, two thousand pounds. And there was a sheet of pale blue writing paper with a Nethercote heading.

Dear Hugo, here's your ten grand. Everything was such a rush I never got a chance to put it on. At least you haven't lost it! See you, Laura XXXXX.

I held it in my quivering hand and read it a few more times through the mist that seemed to have gathered in front of my eyes.

I parked the Merc in front of the house and climbed out with my packet of money.

Annie appeared at the tack room door, saw me and walked over.

'Did you get it then?' she asked with her eyebrows raised.

I couldn't answer; I headed up the path for my front door.

She followed.

Inside, I looked around to make sure Pat or Mrs Brockett weren't on the premises before I ushered Annie into the kitchen.

'I don't know what the fuck Laura's done, but she's just given me back my stake money.'

'No winnings?'

'No.'

'Did she say why?'

'She wasn't there. The old house-keeper had been told to give it to me when I came. Apparently Laura went off last night, taking enough clothes to last a month. There was this note with the money.' I fished it from the envelope and handed it to Annie. While she read it, I poured us both a large gin and found some cold tonic in my fridge.

Annie read the letter and turned it over, expecting more.

'Is this it?'

I nodded.

'She's double-crossed you; I told you she would.'

'She hasn't double-crossed me; she's given me back my money.'

'The horse paid twenty-eight to one on the Tote; she's given you back one twenty-eighth of your money, Hugo.'

'But she didn't get it on. That's the money I gave her; I recognise the bundles. She hasn't touched them.'

'I told you she was a useless, air-head and totally unreliable, and a scheming bitch.'

'Look, Annie, I'm not going to defend her intellectual capabilities, and I don't deny that she's a chronic nymphomaniac, but she's not a bloody thief.'

'The little whore's taken you! She's helped herself to a free bet. Can't you see that? The trouble with you Hugo is sometimes you're just not cynical enough for this world; you're too darn nice.'

'No I'm not,' I snapped back, indignantly. 'I'm a complete shit.'

'You wish!'

'What do you mean "I wish"? You've always said what a bastard I am.'

Bet Your Rocks Off

'That's just what I mean - you believe everything anyone says. You like to think you're such a dispassionate cynic, systematically exploiting the weaknesses of everyone around you, but do you think if you were, I'd have spent the last three years working with you?'

Annie was holding up a mirror to me that didn't make sense, like those wavy, twisty mirrors there used to be in fair grounds. I couldn't reconcile the apparent inconsistency in her attitude.

'Look, of course I'm pissed off that she couldn't get it together to get the money on, but it's not as though she stole it.'

'Yeah,' Annie sighed. 'Maybe she's not quite so dumb as I thought. But the fact is, she's cost you a hundred and seventy grand. Aghh!' she added abruptly, and I followed her gaze out to the yard.

A large Rover had just pulled up. From it, Terry Brownley and Henry Mills were emerging.

Laura's chicanery, whatever it had been, was relegated to matters pending in my mind. I turned back to Annie. 'Take this cash, get upstairs and hide yourself away until I get rid of these guys. It'll be a lot easier if there's only one of us to talk to.'

She nodded, and flitted up the stairs to hide herself in my spare bedroom.

With a deep breath I went out to greet our visitors.

'Morning, Henry. My goodness,' I said heartily. 'They are keeping you busy for a semi-retiree.'

'And very grateful I am too, Hugo. I enjoy my work. For me it's a game I love playing.' He stretched his mouth into a tight ugly smile. 'And I love winning.'

'Me too, Brigadier, but I don't see how coming here can help you with that.'

'Don't you?' he asked dryly.

I spread my hands in a mystified gesture. 'No. Your colleague,' - I was glad to see the brigadier wince at my choice of word - 'was here yesterday with the vet. I think everything was in order, wasn't it Mr Brownley?' Brownley gave a non-committal nod. 'But of course,' I went on, 'if there's any way I can help.....'

'Perhaps you can - with a little query that's cropped up.' He pulled a sheet of computer-printed paper from his pocket. 'Now, my records show that you have two lorries registered at this yard - the one I've seen you driving to the races, and another.' He spelled out a registration, which sounded like Corporal Harding's lorry in France.

I was appalled at this raw evidence of the extent to which quasi-legal bodies like the Jockey Club had access to the central computers of government agencies. 'Do you mind telling me how on earth you knew that?'

'From the DVLC in Cardiff,' he answered blandly.

'Are you telling me that Jockey Club officials are wandering about snooping on every licensed trainer, checking that his vehicle tax is up to date?'

'Certainly not. There are only a few yards where we take that much interest. And Hugo, when you turned up here a couple of years ago in a set up like this, given your previous record, you were naturally a prime target.'

'I think that's outrageous, Brigadier, and you my cousin!'

'Be as outraged as you like, Hugo, but could you also help me with this vehicle, please.'

'Of course I can. It's at our owners' stud in France.'

'The Haras du Mesnil?'

'That's right,' I conceded grudgingly.

'Why?'

'Because we also use the stud as a quarantine yard and as a place for a bit of R and R for our horses.'

'Then what was it doing being photographed by a police camera, speeding on the A4 between Marlborough and Hungerford at OO fifty hours on Sunday morning?'

I gave him the full blast of my outraged glare. I hoped he wouldn't detect the sheer, gibbering panic beneath it.

'Are you seriously telling me that you have access to police computers?'

'I'm not here to tell you anything.'

'You don't have to tell me that half your staff are ex-coppers. I bet there's a nasty tale of corruption lurking there.'

'Hugo, was your lorry, or was it not, speeding east along the A4 on Sunday morning? The police will no doubt be asking you for their own purposes within the next few days, so you might as well establish your story now.'

'I don't have a story to establish. I just think it's utterly appalling that perfectly blameless citizens can't go about their lawful business without being hounded by bloody snoopers from every direction.'

'There are other parties snooping, are there?'

'No, but there's you **and** Brownley.'

'Whoever was driving that vehicle on Sunday night wasn't going about their lawful business anyway. They were breaking the speed limit by fifteen miles an hour - fifty-five through a stretch restricted to forty miles per hour.'

'Obviously I'll reprimand Corporal Harding for that,' I said, thinking that I'd have his testicles off with a pair of blunt shears. 'But he was anxious to get the early ferry back to France.'

Brigadier Mills arranged his face in a nasty leer. 'Was he indeed? Why was that?'

'He was due to go on holiday the next day, and had arranged to pick his wife up in France.'

'Why had he been here, then - with a horse box?'

I sighed with a weary shake of my head. 'Why we should have to submit to this kind of treatment, I just don't know, but come on, Brigadier, and I'll show you the four year old Corporal Harding brought over. He'd been in quarantine in France with suspected ringworm, but he's fine now and I was anxious to get him back into training as soon as possible.'

I began to walk towards the end of the yard where the newly arrived four year old had been housed.

Mills turned to his boot-faced side-kick. 'Brownley, please count every horse in the yard, listing their names with a brief description.'

I made my disapproval clear with a frown as we approached the boxes. 'You'll find we've one horse less than last time you came, apart from this new one.'

'Oh?' Mills asked sharply.

'Yes, as he was here, I asked Corporal Harding to take away my old hack to have it put down. We found he'd been having terrible kidney problems.'

'But you said he was going back to France.'

'Yes,' I nodded. 'He was going to sell him to an abattoir there.'

'But why?' Mills asked, as if I were mad.

'Because, Brigadier, he's always looked after disposing of horses for me; it's one of the little perquisites that's developed in the course of our relationship, and he knows he can get a lot more for a good big horse carcass in France than he can here.'

'Even with the cost of taking it back there?'

'There were no costs,' I answered, smugly. 'He was going back anyway; I just told you.'

For a moment, Mills looked stymied, but he rallied fast. 'I'd like to know where this horse has been destroyed.'

'You'll have to talk to Harding about that, I'm afraid. I'll leave a message for him to that effect which he'll get when he comes back from holiday.'

Brigadier Mills glared at me. 'How long is he going for?'

'A month,' I said looking straight back at him.

'Where's he gone then?'

'Brigadier, that's none of my business, and I didn't ask. I simply told him he could have the time off because he's been looking after horses in France day and night for the last five weeks because none of the other staff would go near the isolation unit while the ring-worm was there.'

'Don't you need him back here, then, as travelling head lad?'

'Well, of course that would be nice, and I look forward to getting him back in time for Goodwood. In the meantime, I've become rather accustomed to doing the job myself. After all, it's not as though I'm the trainer in this establishment.'

'Bloody lucky for you you're not,' Mills murmured.

I ignored any nasty innuendo. 'Well, Brigadier, have you seen all you need to?'

Mills looked at me for a moment like a bulldog that was considering biting a chunk out of my leg, before he turned sharply and walked across the yard for a confab with Brownley. From where I was, I couldn't overhear, though I could tell from Brownley's surly face that his data tallied with what I'd told them. Mills walked back to me. 'There is something else I want to talk to you about - better inside,' he said waving at the house.

I heaved an indifferent shoulder and led him back across the yard.

'By the way, where is Lady Tenbury?'

'In Marlborough, I believe. Why? Did you want to give her the third degree, too?'

'No,' he blustered. 'I have no doubt that Lady Tenbury isn't involved in whatever mischief you're up to. I know an innocent front when it's presented to me. But I'll still need to talk to her.'

I shook my head again with a sigh. 'There is no mischief, Brigadier. You've seen for yourself, and your vet's checked.'

'Hugo, I wouldn't expect you to pull off a coup without making bloody sure everything looked right. But something's going on; I can feel it in my water.'

'Could just be the old prostate playing up.'

'Shut up!' he barked.

I smiled to see this sign of his ebbing patience. He was used to getting results a lot more easily.

'The bookies,' he said through clenched teeth, 'are all whinging because they should have had a good result from such a long priced winner.'

'My heart bleeds for them.'

'We have a duty to the bookmakers, too, you know, to ensure that racing is run fair and straight, just as we do to the punters. The ring inspectors and our betting intelligence officers all say there are signs of a coup. There's a nasty odour of rodent in the air, and you're by far the most likely rat on the scene.' His rufescent, jowly face was almost glowing. 'Don't forget, Hugo, I know you past!'

'So you keep reminding me,' I said lightly.

Brigadier Mills took a breath to steady himself. 'So, Hugo, how much did you win?'

'I seem to remember telling you on the day.' I looked pleased with myself.

'You said you put on two thousand. Would you mind telling me why you drew ten thousand from your bank account on Monday last week?'

I gazed at him for a moment in blank horror. 'I just don't believe this! Are you telling me you're being passed information by the clearing banks as well as the police and the DVLC?'

'I've already told you, I'm not here to tell you anything. But you won't deny that you did draw that large sum in cash?'

'No,' I said. 'I won't deny it. I did draw it.'

Mills gave a slow satisfied nod, wondering, no doubt, what bizarre story I was going to cook up for the disposal of this sum. 'And? Would you mind telling me why?'

'Yes, I would, but in order to encourage you on your way, I will tell you. I was going to have a large bet on Private Mountain, but I changed my mind. I wasn't quite so confident on the day.'

'So what did you do with it?'

'If you'd like to come with me, Brigadier, I'll show you.'

I led him into my study, where I opened my safe and took out the packet that Bowring had given me, containing the money he'd found in Ray Manning's cottage. I handed it to Mills. 'In the end,' I said, 'I only used two thousand of it, and a couple of hundred for expenses - I told you, I was hopeful but by no means totally confident Mountain would win. As you can see, they're all new notes. If you'd like to count it and take down the numbers, I'm sure your mole in the bank can confirm that it's the cash I drew out.'

Grimly, Mills leafed through two or three of the bundles, and, as I'd suggested, scribbled a few of the serial numbers in his notebook.

He handed the money back, and I returned it to the safe, which I locked. 'So, Brigadier, if that's all...'

'Not quite.' He wasn't beaten yet. 'I hear there was a unfortunate loss among the personnel of this yard.'

I adopted a serious, mournful face. 'Yes, sadly. One of our best work riders - I'd absolutely no idea he was a drug addict, died of an overdose on Saturday night. He'd been missing for a day and a half. It's come as quite a blow.'

'Quite a coincidence, too, wouldn't you say?'

I stared at him again. 'Coincidence, Brigadier? What do you mean? The man was a junky, he took an overdose of very pure heroin, the police said, and he died. This is cause and effect, not coincidence.'

'I mean that he should have died on Derby Day.'

'I'm sorry; I can't see any connection myself. But obviously, if you find one, please let me know. 'This time, I started gesturing him resolutely towards the door. I knew I had every apparent justification for seeing him off the premises, and so did he.

But he still hadn't given up. Before we reached the door, he stopped. 'Do you have any horses running this week?'

'I'm sure you've checked the entries, Brigadier.'

'I didn't ask if they were entered; I asked if they were going to run.'

'Well, since you ask, no. With the tragedy of Ray,' I said piously, 'and the fact that our other best rider was his live-in girlfriend, we're a little short of work riders this week, so with our owners' permission, we've pulled out of any races for this week, but we'll be back on target next week at Ascot with some of our two year olds.'

'I shall want to see Lady Tenbury before then; please tell her.' Mills resumed his passage. 'I look forward to seeing your horses perform. As no doubt will your owner.' With his tiresome taste for the theatrical, he paused once more in the doorway. I wondered what was coming next. 'I understand, by the way, that Dr al Hassan's speciality is in the field of genetics - cloning and all that sort of thing. Must be fascinating - so many possibilities.'

CHAPTER TWENTY-FOUR

I watched numbly as Brigadier Mills walked down my garden path and joined Brownley by the Rover. They got in and the car moved off slowly down the drive, past Dairyman's Cottage and out of sight.

'Oh dear.' I felt Annie's breath on the back of my neck.

I sniffed a deep breath, straightened my sagging back and turned to her. I leaned down to kiss her lips.

'Don't worry about a thing,' I said with a certainty I didn't feel. 'Whatever theories he may have, there's absolutely no evidence whatsoever.'

'The only evidence would be our four year old Mountain. Do you know for sure the horse is gone?'

I nodded.

'I mean,' Annie pressed, 'have you spoken to Harding? Has he confirmed that it's been shot.'

'I wish you wouldn't say things like that. Of course he'll have obeyed orders. He was told to get rid of it; he'll have got rid of it.'

'And what do we do?'

'We carry on getting ready for Royal Ascot. I'll even give you a day off to go and buy a new hat.'

It would do no good to let Annie know how truly nervous I was about Brigadier Mills and his relentless determination, but I knew he wasn't boasting when he said he liked to win. With a supreme effort of will, I made a show of getting on with running the yard as if everything were utterly normal. I called the staff together in the tack room that afternoon, aware that they were gossiping about the attention we seemed to be attracting from Jockey Club security.

'Right you guys,' I said in a poor attempt at their vernacular. 'We've won the Derby; everyone's chuffed; we've had a few drinks, we've all made a bit of money, and our owners are very grateful. But now,' I paused like Montgomery at El Alamein, 'it's time to get on, and get ready for Ascot. We've got four runners at the meeting, all with good chances. As you know, we've withdrawn from all engagements this week, out of respect for Ray and Ulrike. Unfortunately, due to the rather messy circumstances of his death, the police and the Jockey Club have been round to talk to me about it. But now that's all behind us.' I looked around, giving each of them a little eye contact, just as we'd been taught at Sandhurst back in the Sixties. 'The funeral will be in Devizes on Friday. For those of you who'd like to go, we'll have a minibus laid on. Any questions?'

'That brigadier bloke, and the other geezer, they was down before the Derby, though,' Bertie said.

'That was just routine stuff,' I waved a dismissive hand.

'And Ray may have died of drugs, but he was up to something, too,' Bertie persisted,

'Like what?'

'I saw him go in and out of Mountain's box quite a few times. Once I caught him, and asked him, but he wouldn't say. Just said he was havin' a look at our Derby horse.'

'So why shouldn't he?'

'Because you told us on no account to go in without asking you or Lady Tenbury.'

'Okay, so he disobeyed that instruction, which he shouldn't have done. But the race is over, the horse won. He obviously didn't do anything to damage the horse, so I'm sure it was all perfectly innocent. Besides,' I went on sternly, 'if you did think he was up to something, why the hell didn't you come and tell me?'

The Irish boy looked sheepish and fell silent. It was unfair to expect one lad to sneak on another, but it shut Bertie up.

At lunch time, Abdel rang from Florida.

'Hugo, I have just spoken to my mother's doctor in London. I've chartered an air ambulance to take her to the Clinique Sainte Veronique in Geneva, where I think she will receive the best treatment. If she gets any worse, I'll come back to Europe, of course, but I want you to go over and see her as soon as possible; for some reason, she is always cheered by your visits.'

I resented Abdel's assumption that I would always drop everything for him, simply because he'd been paying my wages, and if it hadn't been for my loyalty to Madame, I might have rebelled.

'Madame and I are old friends, Abdel,' I said huffily. 'I don't need to be ordered to see her.'

He picked up my tone. 'I realise that, of course, Hugo; forgive me. I know you have a lot on your plate. I trust everything else is going as planned?'

'Pretty much,' I answered, wondering why I'd spared him knowledge of the blackmail. 'No problems that we can't handle.'

'You must forgive me, too, if from now on I seem less concerned with the horses, now that we have won the Derby, but I have no further interest in them, academic or otherwise,. As far as I am concerned they were merely a means to an end which has now been achieved.'

I couldn't object to this. He'd said all along that he had little or no interest, sporting or emotional, in horse-racing. I'd also been aware ever since I'd been at school that I understood neither his attitude to his mother, nor his code of personal morality. But I knew that he'd seen the whole scam as an elaborate, practical experiment in genetics and human behaviour, instigated in the first instance to bring about the revenge he sought and the sporting glory he thought his mother craved.

'I know your views, Abdel. But there's no doubt that your mother would like us to make the most of the season. She's enjoyed it all enormously so far.'

'That's quite true, and for that reason we carry on. Please, keep me informed, and ring me when you've seen my mother to tell me how she is.'

He uttered a cursory valediction and rang off.

Later that afternoon, as I was beginning to recover my confidence and felt that we could take anything that Mills had to throw at us, Terry Brownley walked up to the tack-room where Annie and I were genuinely discussing our approach to the following week's races.

I was sorry that Annie hadn't had the chance to escape, but I didn't consider Brownley such a great threat as his boss.

'Hello again, Sir Hugo,' he said, coming in without waiting for an invitation. 'The Brigadier asked me to call in with some new information we've received.'

'Fire away, then.'

'A friend of yours,' - he glanced at Annie, I guessed to heighten any unpleasantness he might cause, rather than to mitigate it - 'Lady Allerthorpe, was recorded as having a very large credit bet with the Tote on Private Mountain.' He paused and registered my involuntary gasp of horror, as well as a sudden and very obvious stiffening in Annie. 'It was noticeable as being the biggest single bet - five thousand pounds each way, paying....'

'Yes,' I interrupted curtly. 'I know what the Tote paid, thank you.'

'We thought you might.'

'Well, of course, I bloody well do. If you win a race like the Derby, you tend to remember all the details.'

'We were wondering what made Lady Allerthorpe, not habitually a heavy gambler, put such a large sum on a relative outsider.'

'So am I. She never told me she had.'

'Is that so?' Brownley said with an insolent raising of his eyebrows that called my a liar.

'Yes, it bloody well is so. But thank you for telling me. If you must know, I did ask her to put a bet on for me, but she told afterwards that she'd been unable to. I wasn't best pleased.'

From my manner, or whatever signals his type of investigator responded to, Brownley apparently decided that I was telling the truth. He looked disappointed, but he hadn't finished. 'We thought perhaps you and Lady Allerthorpe had discussed a bet when she met you at the Club in Queen Anne's Gate.'

I heard this in blank silence, and refused to respond.

'Will there be anything else, Mr Brownley?' I asked.

'Brigadier Mills also asked me to speak with Lady Tenbury, if she was here, about Ray Manning.' He turned to Annie. 'I wonder if you'd mind - in private?'

Annie stood up. Her face gave nothing away; she may even have smiled slightly. 'Mind? Of course I mind. You can go back and tell your boss that if I talk to anyone, it'll be the organ-grinder, not the monkey.'

Somehow, even wearing jodhpurs and T-shirt, she managed to sweep from the room, and strode down the yard towards her house.

Brownley half rose, as is he were going to follow.

'Forget it,' I said. 'I can tell you from long experience, if Lady Tenbury says she doesn't want to talk to you; she certainly won't. You can report that back to the organ grinder - verbatim,' I grinned.

Brownley rose again. His face, normally an unhealthy taupe, had turned the colour of sour cream. Without a word, he left the tack-room and walked back to his car.

I wondered if we'd pushed it too hard; if, perhaps, Mills' contacts within the force were strong enough to instigate a full-scale police raid. Not, as it happened, that the police would find anything and, as far as I could see, every time they got involved in racing crime, they always succeeded in fouling up the investigation. But I didn't much want the press attention it would attract.

I watched Brownley drive away as I walked down to Annie's cottage.

She must have seen me coming; she opened her front door as I arrived.

'Come in.' She looked very pissed off.

'What's the matter?' I asked.

'Don't treat me like a bimbo. Just tell me what's behind all this.'

I opened my palms in a gesture of openness. 'They think we pulled a coup.'

'There's more. This business of Ray. They think there's a connection. And so do I.'

She was still standing in the doorway.

I nodded a question mark at her small hallway.

'Okay. Come in.'

She led me into the snug where we had almost become intimate two evenings before.

'I didn't want to tell you - not at the time, and when it was all over; there wasn't any point. And I still think the less you know the better, frankly.'

'Tell me Hugo. I've got to go back up to London tonight, but I want to know before I go.'

'Why are you going to London again?' I couldn't suppress a plaintive note in my voice.

'I've got some business to do. It doesn't have a thing to do with you or the horses, okay? Maybe I'll talk about it some time, but right now, you must tell me what's been happening, especially if Ray's death was no coincidence, like Mills and that ass-hole seem to think.'

I nodded. 'You'd better get out the vodka and a couple of glasses.'

It surprised me how long it took to tell the whole story, exactly as it had happened. When I'd finished, Annie said nothing while I poured myself a third vodka.

'I'm impressed,' she said finally. 'I never guessed, and I never thought you had it in you to keep so darn cool. But this Bowring guy, he sounds off the wall.'

'He is, I suppose, but he's ruthlessly efficient and so bloody plausible he's almost impossible to stop.'

'Okay.' Annie stood up. 'Thanks for telling me. I don't know what to think. You should have told me before, but I guess I'm sort of glad you didn't. Now,' she said briskly, as if she were shaking the subject from her hair. 'I've got to change and go.'

'When are you getting back?' I asked pathetically.

'Tonight, very late, so don't wait up.'

'I won't, I've got an early start tomorrow. I want to get to Geneva in time for dinner. I've arranged to see Madame, and I've got a bit of money to bank.'

Annie nodded. 'How long will you be gone?'

'Only a couple of days.'

'Well, don't worry about a thing,' she grinned. 'I'll be back in time to do the early feed, I promise.' She stretched up and gave me a quick kiss on the cheek before she turned and scooted upstairs.

I let myself out and went back to look after the rest of evening stables. I didn't hear Annie go, but when next I looked, her car was gone.

At seven, I climbed into the Merc and headed for Reading and another car-park swap.

Sergeant Rawlings was waiting; I'd never known him to arrive after me at any of the rendezvous' we'd arranged over the years.

He was carrying two bulging Waitrose bags. He glanced around before opening the passenger door of my car, and slipped discreetly into the seat beside me.

'Evening, Sir H.'

'Evening Sergeant-Major. How did it go?'

'On target, sir. A few more pick ups to do. And I haven't had a delivery from Newcastle yet; that's due to morrow, as planned.'

I nodded as he heaved the bags onto my lap.

'I don't think we'll do this here, Rawlings,' I said, as if we were contemplating some mutual act best performed by consenting adults in private.

I drove the car out of the car-park and headed west along the M4, off at the next junction, and south to an empty lay-by on the A33 near Stratfield Saye.

Methodically, and mostly in silence, we counted and recorded the exact amount of money he was handing over. It came to seven hundred and fourteen thousand, five hundred and thirteen pounds.

From this, I extracted thirty-five thousand pounds, five percent of the profit, as agreed, to be shared between him and his colleagues for placing the bets. He took the money with a grim, slightly guilty smile, and shoved it into an inside pocket of his jacket.

With hindsight, the decision to drive the Bentley to Geneva was an obvious mistake. But I'd taken the view that it deserved an outing, it wouldn't take a lot longer than a plane to get to Geneva and I didn't give a damn how much gas it guzzled.

I carefully packed the false bottom of a suitcase with the cash Rawlings had brought me, as well as the eighty grand from Alfie. Over it, I laid enough clothes to last a few weeks. A second similar case I left empty, with more clothes in a brace of carrier bags to pack later on top of Geoff's contribution. The money Bowring had recovered from Ray's flat and Laura's stake money I'd already paid back into the bank.

By seven, I was ready to go. I put both cases in the back of my car before looking in on the feed store to find the trainer at her post, conscientiously doling out nuts and oats for each of her charges, in the ratios she had worked out would suit them best at that point in their training.

Whatever she'd been up to the night before - and I could hardly think about it - she looked happy on it. 'Best of luck, Hugo. Call me tonight and tell me how Madame is, if you ever get there in that ridiculous antique,' she laughed at my Bentley.

I set off confidently and although I hadn't yet come to terms with Laura's appalling treachery, I was feeling that I still had plenty to show for my part in landing the Derby.

There was, after all, my share of the prize money to come, as well as my nominations in Private Mountain - a tenth of the sale value of the horse to stud. There was also a hundred and forty five thousand quid more to come from Rawlings, and Geoffrey Scott was meeting me to hand over four hundred and twenty grand at twelve-thirty in the Maidstone Hotel on the M20. I would have one point one six million to deposit with my discreet Swiss bank next day.

'Why the hell are you driving all this money out of the country?' Geoffrey asked.

'I'm taking it to Switzerland.'
'Why not fly?'

'I don't want any customs men ploughing through my luggage and telling their chums in the Inland Revenue. No one checks you onto the boat, though and the French customs don't give a toss how much foreign currency you take in, if they can be bothered to look at all.'

Geoffrey shrugged. 'Maybe you're right.'

We proceeded to check his delivery. When I was satisfied that it was all there, and he'd confirmed his satisfaction with his twenty grand pay-off, I packed the notes into the bottom of the remaining empty suitcase, piled the rest of the clothes on top and securely fastened them in the capacious boot of the car.

Strolling along the Spartan, iron deck of the P&O ferry, I thought of Corporal Harding making the same crossing with the Derby winner and Barnaby River only three days before. I hadn't spoken to him since; I couldn't have done, even if I'd wanted to, because I'd deliberately told him not to tell me where he was.

But, like Annie, I'd have liked to have heard from his own mouth that the horse had been permanently disposed of.

At the same time, just the thought of the magnificent and likeable animal ending up as some French trucker's breakfast filled me with such guilt that I could hardly bear it, even though I knew that the only way to be certain we were never, ever going to be pulled for running a four year old, genetically identical ringer in Europe's premier three year old race, was to get rid of it for good.

Bet Your Rocks Off

And I was confident that Corporal Harding didn't suffer from my qualms, which was why, traditionally in our dealings, he'd always been responsible for disposing of any superannuated bloodstock; by tacit agreement, I never asked where they went or what he'd got for their carcasses.

I went back down to the bar to check the quickest route to Geneva. As I plotted my course, I ordered half a bottle of champagne. I was just settling down to enjoy it, when a large and irritatingly jovial man plonked himself down opposite me, evidently intent on starting a conversation.

'Excuse me,' he said heartily. 'But aren't you Sir Hugo Tarrington?'

The man didn't look like a copper, or a Jockey Club security officer, and he seemed rather impressed to have recognised me.

I owned up to my identity.

He instantly held out a big red hand, with which he squeezed mine like a lemon.

'Rupert Porter. Glad to meet you. Actually, it's not the first time. We were on the same table at a rather drunken Russian soiree at Ivydene - you know, Peter Vickers' place - last summer.'

I frankly had no recollection of him whatsoever; I'd always had a bad memory for faces and it had been getting worse recently, but I nodded vaguely.

'So having met you,' he went on undeterred, 'I had a very large bet on your splendid horse last week. Somehow, I was sure you'd been keeping something up your sleeve, especially as you didn't run the horse this season until the Derby.'

'You spotted that, did you?' I answered, humouring the man, anyway gratified, after the event, that some of our tactics had been appreciated.

He turned out to be surprisingly good company - certainly very well informed and fascinated by my own past antics on the turf. He even remembered our Deauville stunt from twenty years before.

'I always thought,' he said, 'that was one of the best organised coups I'd ever heard of. I only wish I'd been there to see it, but sadly, I arrived in France the next day.'

So the hour past enjoyably enough and I drove off the ferry feeling mellow and pleased with myself, in the knowledge that snugly in the boot of my car was secured over a million tax-free quid in Bank of England currency.

The old Bentley's performance on the French highways was frankly disappointing. I found that if I sat on the AutoRoute at more than seventy miles an hour for any length of time, the engine began to overheat, however regularly I topped up the cooling system. I had to settle for poodling along at sixty-five, which was both highly antisocial in this land of speed-loonies, and very boring.

I arrived in Geneva after ten, too late to go hospital visiting. I pulled up wearily but gratefully in front of the Hotel Dolder Grand and watched as two porters carted my precious suitcases up to a large, expensive room with a view of the lake. Once I'd got rid of them, each with a tip equivalent to my first week's wages in the army, I phoned the Clinique Sainte Veronique, and left a message for Madame that I would come and see her next morning at eleven - after I'd been to the bank, I thought smugly.

Satisfied that I'd done all I could for her for the time being, I turned to my suitcases. As I intended to go out and find myself the best dinner late night Geneva had to offer, I thought the safest place for a million pounds in notes would be the hotel safe.

I opened the first case, and removed the top layer of clothing. As I was doing it, I was conscious of a faint, but unspecific sense of disquiet that the clothes looked somehow different, at least, differently arranged.

Without giving it more than a passing thought, though, I unsealed and lifted out the false bottom of the case to find that where, that morning, I had placed seven hundred and fifty thousand pounds in fifty pound notes, there was now a black, gaping space.

For the second time in a week, I experienced an eruption in my head; this time, unlike the moment of glory after the Derby, there were no bright lights, only a thundering, overwhelming blackness; and, instead of trumpets, a thousand jeering, screaming devils.

Dreading what I was going to find, I unlocked the second case, noticing how easily the combination lock came free.

This time, I was in no doubt that the clothes had been taken out and repacked. My hands were trembling so much that I could hardly unseal the false panel. When I finally did, the blankness that greeted me only confirmed what I already knew.

I sank down onto the large, squashy bed in a state of catatonia.

I didn't know how long I'd been there when at last I managed to reach out for a decanter of whisky on the well-stocked drinks table provided by a thoughtful management.

I poured myself a long slug and downed it in one. I realised that trying to establish for certain when I had been robbed was an utterly pointless exercise; that there was no way on earth I was ever going to see my money again. Nevertheless, I painstakingly mentally retraced every inch I had travelled that day, and I knew without any doubt at all, that Mr Rupert Porter, or whatever the fuck his name was, had kept me busy talking, while his accomplice had picked the easily pickable locks of the old Bentley, taken my cases off to some quiet spot, removed the money, repacked them and put them back, confident that if I checked the cases at all when I returned to my car, the fact that they were there, with my clothes inside, would almost without any doubt, reassure me that I still had my money.

The ridiculous thing was that Mr Rupert Fucking Porter, in telling me how much he knew about me, had almost made it abundantly clear that he knew I must have had a very large bet. It wouldn't have taken a lot to work out that I was very likely to want to take the proceeds out of the country and that there was very good chance, if I went anywhere within a few days, I would be carrying a very fat wedge.

Bet Your Rocks Off

He'd been right. And I'd been well and truly robbed.

There was, I recognised, a horrible, ironic symmetry to the whole thing which, if it had happened to anyone else, would have made me laugh.

CHAPTER TWENTY-FIVE

My head was thumping and I was still feeling sick when I woke next morning.

I was old enough to know that drinking a bottle of whisky on my own always had this effect. I didn't even regret it much; I would never have slept otherwise.

I crawled out of bed and stood under a shower, vainly trying to wash away the pain and the guilt, wondering how I could face Madame and, worse, Annie.

Letting Laura Allerthorpe rip me off had been horrifyingly stupid; actually having the money from the other bets in my hands, and then losing it could almost be classed as criminally insane.

I left the shower, wrapped a towel round my waist and wandered in a daze back into the bedroom. Through the window, the sun was shining over the mountain tops, and the lake glittered at me in a rich, smug Swiss way.

I gazed at it and ground my teeth.

Fuck you! Fuck you all! I fumed in defiant silence.
I won the Derby!

Bet Your Rocks Off

I own ten percent of a horse which will be worth ten million.

Sergeant Rawlings has still got a hundred and forty grand to give me in England.

I owe my ex-wife nothing.

And there's Annie.

I ordered some breakfast and sat morosely on my balcony, chewing a croissant that tasted of nothing, looking at the lake, and seeing only a waste land of nothingness stretched out in front of me.

I hadn't set foot out of the room, when two hours later, I finally summoned up the strength to go to the Clinique Sainte Veronique to see Madame.

The hospital was set on rising ground on the edge of Geneva, amidst pristine parkland of sward and cedars. The lake was visible in flashes between the trees, and the sound of traffic had diminished to the point where the birds could be heard going about their business in the neatly trimmed shrubberies.

In the cool steel and marble reception area of the hospital, I was treated, as a friend of Madame's, with great deference and shown to a sumptuous room that was half bed-chamber, half private ward, where Madame sat up in bed supported by a plethora of pillows and cushions, filled, no doubt, with down from the underbellies of the softest, rarest water-fowl the world had to offer. On the bed-table beside her, flanked by two massive vases of flowers - one from me - stood the trophy Abdel had accepted on her behalf for winning the Derby.

Peter Burden

My first impression of her was that she'd shrunk, she looked so tiny amidst the clouds of puffy white linen. Her face, habitually a healthy tan - whether natural or applied, I'd never known - was now a beige mushroom hue against the whiteness of her bedclothes.

But when she saw me, she gave a radiant smile that seemed to fill the whole room like the sun and banish the glowering clouds of my own gloom.

'Hugo, you are so sweet to come all this way to visit a frail little old lady.'

'Madame Colette, I'm so glad I have. It's a joy to see you; besides, I had to come to Geneva anyway.'

She smiled again. 'Hugo, you are such a liar! And you do it so well; I don't know why I love to see you, but I do.'

'How are you feeling?'

'Frankly,' she gave a nearly imperceptible shrug of her tiny shoulders, 'lousy.' She added a faint, breathy chuckle. 'But there it is.'

It was clear to me that she had no interest at all in talking about her own ailments, and I drew up a chair beside her bed, so that we could talk about horses and people in the way she'd always loved.

After an hour, a nurse came in and tactfully urged me to leave so that Madame could get the rest she needed.

Outside, the nurse said in perfect English, 'She was so glad to hear you were coming; I'm sure it's done her a lot of good.'

I hoped so; I was grateful to have been able to push all my own troubles to the back of my mind for a while as we'd talked and I'd painted sketches of places and scenes, while she'd listened and laughed. I was as grateful to her as the first day I'd met her at Harrow, when she'd forbidden Abdel to bully or abuse me.

But reality closed in on me as I drove down the curving drive to the lakeside, and back to my hotel, concerned, now, about the horrendous cost of my tortured night between its fragrant linen.

There was a message waiting for me there, from Annie.

I told the desk that I would be checking out shortly, and made my way listlessly up to the room. I took a few deep breaths before I picked up the phone and dialled Annie at Square Barrow.

She answered promptly.

'Hugo, thank God! You'll have to get back here as quick as you can. Come by air, not in that old vintage car.'

'Why? What's the problem?'

'That nasty little bastard Brownley's turned up with two more guys. They're going to hang around the yard all day until your friend Brigadier Mills turns up late this afternoon with a vet to take blood samples of every horse in the yard and check them against their passports.'

This didn't chill me as much as I might have expected. I thought for a moment before I answered. 'Okay, I'll come back,' I said quietly. 'But there's nothing to worry about. Whatever he wants, he's missed the boat.'

'Yah, I know. But, Hugo, he'll be asking questions about Ray, and probing and pushing, and,' she paused reluctant to admit it, 'you're a whole lot better at that kind of thing than me. I'm just good at clamming up.'

'Balls! You're good at several other things,' I tried to reassure her.

She wasn't interested in that sort of talk. 'Just shut up, Hugo and get your ass back here, PDQ. Please?' she added in a smaller voice.

'I'll be on the first plane. I'll call you from the airport. Send a taxi up to meet me.'

When the taxi dropped me at the yard four hours later, Annie was so relieved that I knew I wouldn't be able to tell her what had happened to the money.

She tried, of course, to play down her relief in front of Brownley and the two heavies he'd brought with him, but inside my house, out of their sight, she almost collapsed.

'Oh Hugo, I'm so sorry, but I just don't have the stomach for this any more. Thank God Mills hasn't got here yet.'

'Relax, I understand, but there's not a problem; though frankly, you're looking so twitchy, it may be as well if you're not around when Mills gets here. In fact, I think you ought to take a trip back to Florida, to check over those new horses we have there. I can manage here until the prize money has been paid out.'

'What new horses?' She looked at me blankly for a moment, before giving a self-mocking nod. 'Yah, silly me. Okay, if you're sure you'll be okay?'

'I'm used to the heat,' I said heroically and, as it happened, truthfully. 'You start packing.' I held up a hand. 'Or rather, don't.

Better not to let Brownley see you're intending a long trip. Just disappear and I'll say you've gone shopping.'

Annie nodded with a smile. 'Thanks, Hugo. I have to tell you, it suits me fine; I've some very important business to finish in the States.' She put both her arms around my neck and pulled my head down to kiss me on the mouth, this time with the faintest flicker of a tongue.

Henry Mills' vet had come, done his job and gone. Now the brigadier stood in the middle of our yard, looking at his watch. 'Where the hell's Lady Tenbury?'

I looked at my watch too, and thought - somewhere over Ireland about now. 'She did say she had some private business she might have to follow up, but I'm afraid I can't seem to get her on her mobile. If you've finished everything you need to do here, can I offer you a drink while you wait to see her?' I offered fulsomely.

Mills scowled. 'All right. We'll give her another half an hour.'

'Would you mind, Henry, if I didn't invite Brownley and his two gorillas back to my house?'

'No. I'll send them home.'

Once I'd put a large Glenmorangie in his hands, and settled him in a deep, yielding chair, I innocently asked how he'd got on.

'Did you find what you were looking for?'

He took a slug of whisky. 'What do you think?'

'I've no idea, Brigadier. I don't know what you were expecting to find.'

'Don't you?'

'Of course not. I'm not an expert in racing security.'

'Well, you bloody well ought to be by now.'

I ignored his imputation. 'So, did you find anything?'

'Yes, thank you.'

'What?'

'We'll let you know, in due course.'

'What did it tell you?'

'I can tell you that I'm in absolutely no doubt that you did something to win that Derby.'

'Oh, Brigadier,' I said ingenuously. 'I think most of the credit for training the horse must go to Annie. Of course, I helped, but she was the real skill behind his success.'

'That,' Mills said through tight lips, 'is why I would like to interview her. I'm beginning to feel that she's avoiding me.'

'That's not surprising, is it? You've been so aggressive every time you've been here, simply because you've got - how did you put it? - a feeling in your water that there was something dodgy about the result. From what you told me, the only complaints are from a few tight-fisted bookies who always hate paying out long priced winners because it hurts their pride.'

'In my position, I have every right to interview Lady Tenbury, and I don't want to have to make it a disciplinary issue.'

'She'd probably sue you if you did. Another whisky?'

Mills heaved himself puffing and straining from the depths of the armchair and got to his feet. 'No, thank you, Hugo. I think I've been made a monkey of for long enough. Please ask Lady Tenbury to contact me tomorrow without fail.'

I nodded. 'Sure.' I followed him to the door. 'Sorry you won't stay for another, Brigadier. Perhaps next time?'

Mills herrumphed a reluctant goodbye, and stomped off to his car.

I stayed outside and watched him go until I was summoned back inside by a trilling telephone.

'Hello Hugo. Mungo.'

So finely tuned by events were all my senses, that I knew from the three words that he was not the bearer of good tidings.

My throat dried. 'What's wrong, Mungo?' I croaked.

'Rather bad news, I'm afraid. Our chap doesn't seem to have much by way of sperm. At least, there's plenty of it, but a shortage of tadpoles, I'm afraid.'

'What the hell are you talking about?'

'I mean that to all intents and purposes he's impotent, infertile - firing blanks, you might say.'

I couldn't speak for a moment. 'Shit!' I spat out the word.

'Yes,' Mungo agreed. 'It is rather a bore.'

'It's not rather a bore, Mungo,' I said, quietly at first, then with my voice swelling. 'It's a total, fucking disaster!'

'Oh I don't know. You could always go on running him.'

'But he won't be worth a fucking penny at stud!'

'Now that's true, it's often the way with horses. You think you've got it all, and then....'

'Mungo, is this test that's been carried out totally reliable?'

'Yes, of course, and confirmed by the lab in the States.'

'Couldn't we get someone to produce another result?'

'Frankly, I couldn't go along with that sort of thing even if it were possible. I mean, I've got a reputation to think about, and besides, any purchaser would almost certainly want their own test from their own nominated lab.'

I put the phone down. The whole, horrible truth had now fully penetrated and was starting to overwhelm me.

Since the supreme achievement of winning the Derby, everything that could go wrong had now gone wrong.

Even Mills seemed to think he'd found something to support the feeling in his water. I was in such a demoralised state, that I almost believed him.

I was only glad that Annie, who had so recently and so fervently shown her admiration for my strength in the face of the enemy, couldn't see me now - a shaking, gibbering wreck with the directional skills of a headless chicken.

I sank into one of my kitchen chairs and reached for the whisky again.

I woke with cramp, a headache and my face on the kitchen table. But dreams of torment and revenge were fresh in my mind, with Brigadier Mills, the villainous Rupert Porter and, strangely, Abdel acting as chief protagonists.

One theme had recurred, and I had to speak to Abdel.

I looked at the clock. It was half past six - late in Florida, but not too late to ring Abdel.

I dialled his personal number, which I knew was known by very few people.

He answered, succinctly, but guardedly. It was impossible to tell whether or not I'd woken him.

'Sorry to ring so late Abdel, but I've had some rather bad news.'

'Hugo, are you all right? It must be very early in the morning there and yet, to me, I'm afraid to say, you sound a little drunk.'

'I'm not, just very tired. I've been up all night worrying.'

'Oh dear. Why's that?'

'Mungo's had a report on Mountain's fertility which says he's firing blanks.'

'He's what?'

'He's infertile; completely useless as a stallion.'

For a few moments there was no response. I wondered if somehow our connection had been severed. 'Abdel? Abdel? Are you..'

'Yes. I'm still here. I was taking in what you said. It's a great shame, of course, but I have to tell you, scientifically speaking, I'm not all that surprised. There was always the possibility that cloned males might not reproduce successfully.'

I couldn't believe what I was hearing. 'What are you saying, Abdel? All along the idea was that after Mountain had won the Derby, you'd be able to recoup all your money, at least, a lot of it, by selling him.'

'That may have been your idea, Hugo. But I always told you precisely my motives for the investment of my time and money, and as far as I'm concerned, provided there are no further hitches, that's exactly what we've achieved. Frankly, the money is irrelevant.'

'But for God's sake, Abdel, that was the basis on which we went into this - that Annie and I would have ten percent of the value of the horse.'

'And so you shall.'

'But we assumed it would be worth infinitely more.'

'Assumptions can be dangerous in all fields of human activity.'

'But it'll mean I've done the whole thing for nothing!'

'Come now, Hugo, that's hardly the case. You've been very well paid and feather-bedded for the last five years. And I have no doubt you had a substantial bet on the horse which paid out at long odds. You must have won a million or two.'

I couldn't speak.

I couldn't tell him how all but a hundred and forty grand of what I'd won had already been stolen or had never materialised.

I closed my eyes, gritted my teeth and put the phone down.

I went through the motions of feeding and overseeing the horses' exercise like a zombie.

The lads must have noticed, but thought better of mentioning it. I managed to concentrate enough to give coherent directions, and, using Annie's notes, even to make some kind of judgements about what was needed for our imminent runners.

But several times I nearly stopped and chucked in the whole futile, fruitless operation.

It was only the thought of Madame and the long talk I'd had with her about her horses and their chances that kept me going. I'd promised her a glorious season, and despite the suffocating pressure, I was still determined to deliver it for her.

As I contemplated the string of disasters that had brought me so low, the big, smiling ruddy face of Rupert Porter lurked in the back of my head, fading in an out of focus like the Cheshire cat. Having had no recollection of him whatsoever when he'd first said we'd already met, I was slowly becoming conscious of having seen him several times around the circuit. It was the red-headed Bertie, a keen observer of his fellow men, who was able to pin-point him for me.

'I know the fella you mean,' he said. 'He's been in the Waggon a few times, always askin' about the horses in the yard. He gave Ray his card one time, told him to let him know how the gallops were going.'

'Good God!' I gasped as yet another possible scenario presented itself. 'Do you know if Ray ever told him anything?'

'I doubt it. We none of us ever do; and there's always people asking.'

I understood that; it went on around every yard that regularly sent out winners. I'd have been surprised though, if none of them ever

443

broke their vow of silence - which was precisely why we had never let them near Mountain for too long.

And I wasn't surprised to hear that Porter had been doing his prep-work. I wondered, too, just how unpleasant he would have been in his bid to get the cash if I hadn't made it so bloody easy for him.

I was thinking about this, alone with a pot of lukewarm coffee in my kitchen after the second lot had gone out, when the phone rang. I answered it and heard Madame's voice.

She sounded weaker than ever, but *compos mentis*. 'Hugo, I'm so glad to talk to you and thank you for coming to see me yesterday. I don't like to ask this so soon, but I wanted you to come back here again; there is something I have to tell you.'

The last thing I needed now was another trip to Geneva, and I didn't even have Annie here to look after the yard while I was gone.

'Annie's in Florida, Madame.'

'Oh, why?' she asked, justifiably puzzled.

'There were a few things that needed looking after over there, with the young stock.'

'Well I dare say she can get back quickly enough. In any event, there's nothing to stop you leaving the yard in charge of your head lad for a day or two.'

I simply couldn't start protesting that we didn't have a head lad or that Corporal Harding wasn't available; it didn't seem fair to burden her with intrusive details.

'Yes, of course I can, Madame. I'll organise things and be out as soon as I can, later this afternoon, I expect.'

Bet Your Rocks Off

'Please hurry, Hugo.'

When she'd rung off, I phoned the clinic back, to ask more precisely about her condition.

'Madame al Hassan is very ill, I'm afraid; if you wish to see her, it is probably best not to delay.'

Galvanised by this replacement crisis, I called Dick Hill and asked him to come down from the farm.

Dick had become an ally and, as a result of my urging, had won seven and a half grand to his twenty pound note, doubled on Mountain's last two wins. I knew I had a deep seam of good will to mine.

He arrived as soon as he could have done, evidently eager to please.

'Dick, I hate to ask this, because I know your views about horses..'

'They have changed a little, Sir H, after all the fun we've had.'

I nodded. 'I was hoping you'd say that. The fact is, Madame's in hospital in Geneva and she's bloody ill. I've just phoned the Press Association and told them that as she is so ill, we won't be running any more horses until further notice, and we've withdrawn all our entries for Ascot next week.'

Dick looked crestfallen. 'That's a bit drastic isn't it, Sir H? I mean, even if she's not well, she'd like to know they were running.'

'Frankly, I'm afraid I don't think she'll be aware of what they're doing. I'm sorry, Dick, but that's the decision I've taken. Now I've got to go back to Geneva to see Madame; she's specially asked.

445

Lady Tenbury's in the States and won't be back for a bit, so I'm going to ask you if you wouldn't mind looking after things here while I'm away.'

Dick nodded, compliantly. 'Be glad to help, though I'm dead sorry those horses aren't going next week. I was all geared up, like, ready for a few good bets...'

'That's the way it goes in racing,' I echoed Mungo Castle's simple philosophical approach. 'Anyway, all you need do is make sure they're fed and exercised for half an hour a day on the horse-walker. No riding out or anything like that. Okay?'

'No problem, Sir H.'

In the thirty or so hours that had elapsed since I'd last seen her, Madame had deteriorated.

She still had enough spirit in her, though, to insist that she be transferred to a wheelchair, in which she was wrapped with blankets like an overblown cocoon.

There was little wind outside, the sun was warm, and I was allowed to take her outside and perambulate her around the peaceful grounds.

'Hugo.' Her voice was little more than a whisper now. 'I just want you to know that I am aware that you might feel Abdel has let you down. I know what has happened about the stallion.' I wondered, for a horrible second, if she had either worked out, or been told about the cloning, until she went on. 'But it is often like that with all species, that an outstanding male does not have the ability to pass on his own valuable genes. Look, for instance, at Abdel.'

I was initially shocked by this blunt revelation, but then, I thought perhaps it wasn't so surprising. 'How do you mean, Madame?'

'The poor boy was born with congenital problems,' Madame whispered into the gentle breeze that had sprung up, 'though I think this has been a source of greater sadness to me than to him. All I ask is that you should bear this in mind if you feel he is being difficult or unfair in his dealings with you.'

'I'll find that tricky, Madame,' I admitted honestly. 'I worked hard to do what we did for you, and the success of the horse as a stallion was an important part of the whole operation. Now you've obviously gathered that Abdel doesn't really care.'

'More than gathered; he told me so. But anyway, if it's any consolation to you, I personally am deeply grateful to you. I understand exactly how much work you put into my horse's success.'

'I'm glad of that, at least.' And I supposed I was, but it wouldn't entirely make up for the bitter sense of betrayal I felt over Abdel's attitude.

And I didn't imagine for a moment that it would satisfy Annie.

I pushed the chair for a few more hundred yards in silence, until I thought we had, perhaps, gone far enough, and the wind was growing a little stronger.

'Would you like me to take you back now, Madame?'

When she didn't answer, I leaned down and saw that she was fast asleep. As gently as I could I wheeled her back and delivered her to a pair of nurses who took her back to her room.

I was invited to wait and find out what her condition was before I left for my hotel - a very much less grand place than the Dolder, where I'd stayed two nights before.

I was fast asleep, lolling across one of the elegant sofas in the large visitors' reception room at the Clinique Sainte Veronique when I found myself being shaken by a bright little nurse.

'*Excusez-moi, m'sieur. Madame al Hassan vous demande.*'

I was awake in seconds, and following the girl's trim figure through the padded corridors to Madame's room.

When I went in, Madame did not look as if she were capable of asking for anything, but I walked forward at the nurse's bidding, and leaned over the bed.

'Madame?' I said quietly by her right ear.

She didn't open her eyes. But with what looked like an immense effort, her lips parted and she whispered. 'Hugo.'

Her right hand, lying outside the sheet nestled in a fold of the supersoft duvet, made a small squeezing gesture. I took it and squeezed back, and felt the tiny, manicured hand grow limp within my grasp.

I glanced at her face. Her mouth was still open, but nothing seemed to move. I turned to the nurse, who bustled over and lifted the limp, bony wrist while she studied her watch.

She gave a regretful heave of her shoulders, and lowered the hand to the bed. She reached past me to close Madame's wrinkled lips.

'*Je suis desolee*,' she uttered in a well practised, professional whisper.

I felt tears tingle in my eyes. And, as if observing myself from afar, I found myself thinking that it must have been years since I'd shed a tear of sadness, or regret. I was surprised, and glad that I still could.

I nodded at the nurse, picked up Madame's fast cooling hand, and leaned forward to kiss the small wrinkled forehead, on which I'd so often seen her eyebrows raised in mock surprise, or mock horror at the stories I'd told her over the years.

I spent a horrible night in my cheap hotel, unable to sleep in the small stuffy room, and further discouraged by the thought that on top of all my other tribulations, my ally and support in the al Hassan racing organisation was now gone.

I was glad to get out of bed early and, having recovered my Bentley from the garage where I'd left it two days before, drove back up to the Clinique.

Arrangements for the eventual disposal of Madame's mortal remains were already in hand.

She was lying now in a sort of giant cold store, awaiting the arrival of her only living relative to identify her formally. Abdel was expected on the ten-thirty flight from Orlando.

There wasn't anything else that I could do, but I was allowed to hang around on the grounds that I'd been Madame's last visitor.

When Abdel arrived, at first he barely acknowledged my presence. He was, anyway, swiftly ushered away to look at his mother's body.

Fifteen minutes later, he reappeared, having, I presumed, dealt with whatever formalities the Swiss demand on the death of one of their residents.

Now he spoke to me. 'Hugo, why are you still here? I thought you were in England when we spoke yesterday morning.'

'I was. I got here on Wednesday evening, saw your mother next morning and flew straight back, then she rang me again yesterday and asked me to come back.'

Abdel's head jerked back in surprise. 'She called you yesterday? But when I phoned, they said she couldn't speak.'

'Well,' I said, treading carefully. 'I think she was in and out of consciousness most of the day, When I arrived, I took her for a walk, and she spoke, very weakly, but making total sense. Then she fell asleep and they put her back to bed. She must have died about three hours later; I was with her.'

'Did she speak again?'

'She said my name once, as far as I know, that was all, but a nurse might have heard more.'

'I think it's very strange that she should have asked you back, but I suppose I should be grateful that you came.'

'Yes, Abdel, I suppose you should,' I agreed.

450

He didn't miss the nuance and I could almost see him raise his guard. He looked at his watch. 'My mother's lawyers are on their way here, as I have a limited amount of time to spare in Europe just at this moment.'

'I'd like to talk to you briefly, Abdel, perhaps after you've finished with them?'

'Like I said, I don't have a lot of time.'

'And our discussion will take very little of it. If you like, I can run you back to the airport, and we can talk then.'

He couldn't turn me down, and he knew it. 'Very well,' he said impatiently. 'But I must go now; I see M. Disch, my mother's attorney has just arrived.'

'I'll be here,' I reassured him.

He didn't answer and bustled off with the lawyer and two acolytes.

Of course, I told myself, it was absurd to feel slighted by Abdel. It had been clear from the start that he'd taken me on, heeded my advice and offered me the generous terms he had simply because he'd concluded I was the best man to do the job he wanted done.

I had to admit, that he was probably right, and that the notion of any kind of special relationship based on our school day acquaintanceship had never entered the equation.

Nevertheless, I felt totally betrayed, by his complete lack of concern over my own position in the aftermath of the Derby and his mother's death. Although, I had to admit, he wasn't in possession of the full facts of that position; he still thought, quite reasonably, that I'd cleaned up at the bookies.

I was damned, I decided, if I was going to tell him otherwise. I'd just have to salvage what I could from the wreckage of our coup.

I sat amid the plush surroundings of the clinic and looked out at the spreading blue cedar in the park beyond the huge plate glass window. I nursed my bitter thoughts while a silent Turkish maid brought as many cups of coffee as I could take.

In the midst of this, one of the lawyer's acolytes glided into view.

'Sir 'Ugo Tarrington?' he asked in a music-hall Frenchman's English.

I nodded. 'Yes.'

'Would you please to accompany me?'

I stood and followed him, mystified that I should be required for these final formalities regarding Madame's demise.

M Disch, his other assistant, and Abdel were gathered in a small meeting room the clinic had obviously provided for the purpose.

M Disch was a short, neat man, with unexpectedly cheerful, bright blue eyes. He stood and held out a hand.

'Sir Hugo,' he said in much better English than his gofer. 'It is most fortunate that you are here.'

I glanced at Abdel, wondering why he hadn't spoken. He was looking out of the window at much the same scene on which I'd been gazing for the past half hour.

'Whatever I can do to help.' I offered with a shrug. 'Madame al Hassan was an old and dear friend.'

M. Disch nodded. 'So I understand. It was for that reason, I imagine that she made a substantial change to her will, which she ratified when she arrived here earlier this week.'

Slowly, I was aware of something like a glimmer of light below the clouds, after a long, relentless stormy winter's night. I didn't speak, in order not to spoil the delicate image.

'I will read it to you in an English translation. A codicil to the will of the Sheikha Madame Colette al Hassan, dated Geneva, Tuesday, June 8th. In recognition of his magnificent achievement in winning the Epsom Derby with Private Mountain for me, I leave to Sir Hugo Tarrington, Bart of England, all my French properties and securities, all furniture, works of art, live stock and all other items and property currently contained within my French estates, as well as all bloodstock and related property registered in my own name, world-wide."

CHAPTER TWENTY-FIVE

In retrospect, it seemed absurd that I'd never even considered the possibility that Madame would leave me anything more than a token - a picture, perhaps, or even a mare, but I'd always been so conscious of the fact that everything she owned had come from her late husband that I'd assumed it would automatically pass to Abdel, if he didn't already own it anyway.

But once I'd signed my confirmation that I understood and accepted the terms and conditions, such as they were, of the will, I'd left the clinic for a very long walk along the shores of Lac Leman to try and reconcile myself to this extraordinary *volte face* in my fortunes.

I had made a follow-up appointment with the lawyers for Monday morning, when the precise extent of my massive windfall would be made clear.

Abdel had frostily declined my reiterated offer of a lift to the airport; he just managed to agree that we would see each other the following Thursday, when his mother would be buried with a small, private service in the cemetery of the tiny church at Le Mesnil, as she had stipulated in her will, having reverted to Christianity on her husband's death.

Bet Your Rocks Off

I realised, of course, that it wasn't the loss of the money that had upset Abdel; it was the apparent alienation of his mother's affections. But there was nothing I could do about that, and I occupied myself for the rest of Saturday and most of Sunday by planning the orderly closure of Square Barrow yard, which was not part of my inheritance, and the transfer to France of the horses, which were now all mine.

That, at least, would be one in the eye for Brigadier Mills, as well as solving the problem of how to maintain the pretence that we were a serious, genuine racing yard.

When I telephoned Annie in Florida on Sunday morning, I told her only that Madame had died, and all racing activity would have to cease.

I didn't explain that the executors of Madame's will had expressed themselves perfectly happy for her horses to carry on racing and earn their maximum potential up until probate was finally granted to me, or that I'd advised them that it would almost certainly cost more than it would gain, which they had believed.

I promised Annie that I would handle Dick Hill. And I would deal with all the lads when I got back to England. For the moment, I'd decided to leave them to carry on in tick-over mode.

I suggested to Annie that she flew to Europe on Tuesday, a couple of days before the funeral, and met me at Le Mesnil, where I would be sorting out the futures of the horses which were there.

I told her nothing about the terms of Madame's will.

Peter Burden

After a short formal meeting, I left M Disch's office in the old town, and retrieved the Bentley from the hotel where I'd spent the last two nights.

I was unconcerned about the lack of *vitesse* offered by my sedate old car; for once, there was no need to hurry. I deliberately took the scenic routes across France to Normandy, stopping when I felt like it to eat and drink, only of the best.

Mario, the butler at the *Manoir du Mesnil*, had been told by the lawyers about Madame's death and the subsequent change of ownership of the property. He had, M Disch told me, volunteered to stay on the premises, along with the rest of the staff, until I had decided what I wanted to do.

I phoned ahead half way through the afternoon, from Orleans and said I would be back after dinner, and there was no need to make any special preparations. But when I arrived shortly before midnight, Mario was there to greet me, with gratifying warmth. I'd known him – at least, pleasantly passed the time of day with him – on many visits over the last twenty years, and we'd always enjoyed an amicable relationship. He appeared positively overjoyed that I was now the incumbent, and made it very clear, that, as far as he was concerned, he would happily buttle for me for the rest of his days and, I assumed, his wife would housekeep, as part of a package,

I'd already thought if that was what they wanted, it would suit me, and on the face of it, affording it wasn't going to be a problem, so I was glad to be able to give him the good news before I drank a last whisky and soda and made my way up to the principal guest bedroom.

Bet Your Rocks Off

To open my eyes next morning, slip out of the glorious Empire bed, and walk across soft Persian rugs on the floor of the huge room; to draw back the curtains on a fine June morning and see the sunlight scattered through the leaves of the voluminous beeches across the deep green turf, was as close to paradise as I thought I would ever come; unless, perhaps, to share that moment with someone else would bring me closer.

I took a few deep breaths of the quiet, morning scented air, and told myself not to get too bloody soppy.

Everybody within fifty miles seemed already to have learned that I was the new owner of *L'Haras et Manoir du Mesnil*; I spent most of the morning fielding phone calls and entertaining locals who just happened to have business with the house that day.

I thought it only a matter of time before Lisette de Beaumont showed up, and I couldn't have handled that. So, after lunch, I told Mario I'd be take no more calls, nor see any callers for the rest of the day. He understood, and I spent a happy few hours, excited as a raw teenager with a new computer game, wandering around my three hundred hectares of pasture and woodland.

When I got back to the house about five o'clock, there was a fax - a scrawl in Annie's distinctive hand - waiting for me.

"Arriving at Deauville with Xavier at seventeen twenty. Will you meet us, please?"

Typically of Annie, she hadn't said how she was arriving at Deauville, or, if flying, where from. Or who the hell this Xavier was, which I took to be the name of some Hispanic male.

It was this that perturbed me most. Why the hell was she bringing an entirely unknown male companion, presumably from the States, to the small private funeral in Normandy of someone this person had never met?

I was astonished, given the miraculous change in my status in the last few days, that I was still able to be so anxious about the problem. But I found I just couldn't let go of it as I drove through the narrow Norman lanes towards Deauville Airport, which I thought was Annie's most likely point of arrival.

At the airport, I soon established that a plane from London had landed at twenty past five, and passengers were collecting their baggage.

I stood by the exit, among the chauffeurs waiting with little cards and signs on which the names of their punters were written. So much had happened since I'd last seen Annie, I felt I should put up my own card for her - 'Lady Tenbury' - in case she didn't recognise me.

Then, I saw her, as beautiful as my fevered mind had painted her over the last week, striding along with a small leather rucksack over one shoulder. Then, with a jolt, I remembered Xavier, and started looking for the dark, handsome moustachioed man that my imagination had painted.

But no one appeared to be with her, until I saw her glance down and smile at a small, blonde, brown-eyed boy of five or six, just visible between the other passengers.

Xavier?

Who was this? A brother? A nephew?

I'd never heard her mention any connections like that.

I waved and she saw me. Her face lit up and she took the boy's hand and quickened her pace until she was in front of me and falling into my arms.

I held her, remembering her own special smell, not needing words or gesture to let her know how glad I was to see her again.

'Mom. Who is it?'

I didn't associate us with the words at first, until I looked down and saw the handsome little boy looking up at Annie, still holding onto a dangling strap of her rucksack.

I let go of her, and stepped back with a question mark all over my face. 'Mom??' I asked, incredulous.

She smiled, hunched her shoulders, jutted her chin, and nodded. 'This is my little man, Xavier. Xavier, this is Sir Hugo Tarrington.'

The boy held out a hand as, I was sure, he'd been coached. I took it, and we exchanged a firm shake. 'Pleased to meet you, *Sirr* Hugo,' he said in a voice that fleetingly reminded me of Ray Manning's helium induced squawk.

'You may call me Hugo,' I heard myself boom pompously.

Annie giggled.

459

'Hugo. It's lovely to see you. I'll tell you all about this later, if you don't mind.'

'Don't mind!?' I spluttered. 'I insist you tell me later - *much later*.'

She didn't want me to take her rucksack, so I led them to the Bentley parked outside. Xavier's big brown eyes opened wide with wonder.

'Wow! Cool!' he said.

I ignored him, opened the boot and deposited their sparse luggage there.

We drove slowly back to Le Mesnil, through the small round hills of Calvados in the golden glow of the evening sun. Annie was beside me, and Xavier happily in the back, as we talked rather self-consciously about arrangements for winding down the racing operation, both being cautious and sensible about the inevitability of it and our responsibilities towards the staff.

When we arrived at the house, Mario flung open the front door with a flourish to greet Annie warmly by name. She raised a questioning eyebrow at me and carried on into the hall followed by Xavier.

I turned to the butler. 'Mario, this is Xavier. He is Lady Tenbury's son.' Mario didn't let an eyelid flicker at this sensational morsel of gossip. 'He says he's hungry after his flight, so would you please take him to the cards room and organise a light meal for him - something that he says he likes. Though he comes from the States and you may not approve, I'm afraid.' I turned to the boy. 'What's your favourite film, Xavier?'

'The Rescuers,' he squawked.

'I'm pretty sure Madame didn't have that in her stock of videos, though she had quite a few surprising ones,' I added, to Annie. 'But Mario, show Xavier what there is, and let him chose something. If he falls asleep after he's eaten, take him up to the Chinese room.'

'*Comme vous voulez, Sieur Hugo.*'

I told Xavier in English what I'd said, and his shining eyes signalled his contentment with the arrangement. Once he'd gone with my solicitous butler, I led Annie into the grand salon, and headed for the drinks table and the fridge behind it.

'When Mario comes down, I'll ask him to rustle up a little bite for us. In the meantime, a glass of Bolly, I thought - unless you prefer a Louis Roederer?'

'Just so long as it's cold and wet,' Annie twanged in Texan. 'You're making pretty free with Madame's staff and stuff.'

'Her executors told me to make myself at home as long as I was here sorting out the bloodstock,' I lied. 'Besides, she wouldn't mind, in fact, I think she'd have wanted me to.'

Annie shrugged. 'I guess you're right. In a way she was sort of in love with you, you know. That's why she never really dug me.'

'Never 'dug' you?' I repeated stuffily.

'You know what I mean, Hugo.'

'Well, I suppose I do, but in the end, she appreciated you for your skills and what you did with Private Mountain.'

461

'She wouldn't have done if she'd known we were cheating.'

'Maybe not, but she didn't know.'

'Anyway, Hugo, now I've got you on my own, and before I tell you about Xavier, what's the story on our scam? Where do we stand?'

I took my time opening the bottle of Bollinger I'd selected, and slowly filled two delicious, lightly frothing glasses.

'I think I ought to tell you the truth about the bets first.'

'I already know about Laura Slagpot.'

I winced, and nodded. 'Of course, but it gets worse.'

Annie made a face and took a sip of champagne.

'Last Thursday morning when I drove to France on the ferry, I had all the money Alfie and Rawlings had given me, and the money from my anteposts that Geoff Scott handed over that morning on the way to Dover.'

Annie nodded. 'Must have been a million and a bit.'

'Yes. But,' - the word prompted Annie's mouth to twitch into a tight, apprehensive pout - 'unfortunately, when I got to Geneva and opened the cases....'

'No, Hugo! I can't bear it! Don't tell me, please!'

I told her, in minute detail, of my encounter with Rupert Porter, and Bertie's subsequent report that he'd been seen around the village a couple of times; that I'd seen him on and off over the years at the races; that if I ever attempted to accuse him of robbing me, he would probably sue me for slander, on the grounds that at the time I said I was robbed, he was sitting with me in the bar of the ferry, in full

462

view of at least a dozen witnesses, for over an hour while we drank champagne and swapped racing stories.

Annie gazed at me and shook her head. 'Of all the dumbest dumbos in the world, Hugo, you are the president. To leave all that loot in the back of an old car, on a ferry - one of the most notorious scenes of common larceny! They must be drinking your health by the bucket load!'

'Annie, I've already been down this road. I know all that you say is true, so please, please don't tell me again. Besides, there's more,' I offered with a masochistic flourish.

'How could there be more?' she almost cried.

I took a gulp and a breath. 'When I found my cases empty, I thought, at least we still have our percentage of Mountain's value - ten mill, maybe, a mill to us - a thousand monkeys each.'

'This is what we thought,' Annie agreed.

'Let me tell you about my conversation with Mungo Castle last Thursday night, after you and Brigadier Mills had left.'

'Give me more champagne first,' she said, 'or I may not be able to take it.'

I poured; I told, and she took it.

When I'd finished, she looked at me and, this time, filled my glass as well as her own.

She started to laugh, and laugh. She walked around the room, almost bursting, until she couldn't stand it any longer, and rushed off into the hall.

I heard the loo flush, and she came back in.

She had calmed down now, but carried on simply shaking her head. 'I guess you think I was being hysterical,' she said, 'but I wasn't. I was laughing because I don't see how we managed to pull off one the greatest coups in racing history, and still so totally screw up the proceeds. I wish we could tell our story; it would make a brilliant movie.'

'Look, Annie, I know it must be a horrible shock; I know you were counting on this money - that you needed it very badly for something - and I'm devastated that this has happened. I can't tell you how sorry I am. Frankly, I wouldn't blame you if you turned right round and walked away, and never came near me again. I wouldn't blame you, but I'd hate it.'

'I wouldn't blame me either,' Annie said quietly. 'And I'd hate it too, so there.' She was looking straight at me now, steadily and without accusation. 'And we've still got our share of the prize money; that's something.'

'Not much, when you look at what we should have had.'

'Well, as our old friend and master would say - there it is.' Annie flicked a wrist and walked across the room to look through the window at a pair of fillies that had grazed into view.

'You're incredible to take it so well,' I said with feeling, until I remembered something she'd said the day before the Derby. 'But I'd forgotten - you put some money of your own on, didn't you?'

'Yah,' she nodded.

'Enough to ease the pain?'

'A little.'

I waited for her to tell me more. I really wanted to know that one of us had walked away with something to show for what we'd done. 'Well?'

She sighed. 'I put the money on, Mountain won and I collected. But I don't have much left either.'

'Oh God,' I groaned. 'What happened? '

'I put it on with Geoff Scott, like you, and he swore he wouldn't tell you. I told him to wait until he'd got all yours on - so as not to screw up the odds for you. I put on everything I had, every spare cent I could raise, but I didn't get such a good price - just fifty to one!' She grinned.

'And you must have got twelve and a half for the place, too.'

'I didn't bet for a place; it was shit or bust for me.'

I was impressed with this heroic recklessness. 'How much?'

'Twenty five grand.'

'Sterling?'

'No, dollars. I picked up over a million bucks last week, and with that, I was able to go to LA and negotiate with Xavier's father, away from Xavier's grandmother, who talked him into hi-jacking the kid in the first place.'

'Annie, what the hell is all this?'

'It's pretty darned obvious isn't it?' She began to wander around the room, now in large, irregular circles, inspecting the pictures and artefacts scattered around it as she went. 'Seven years ago, I made a total fool of myself. Xavier's dad, Romey Gonzalez was one of the handsomest jockeys riding at Santa Anita. There wasn't a

465

woman on the racing circuit who wasn't after him. And I'm a competitive woman. Unfortunately, he was also a lousy jockey, but I gave him rides.' She chuckled. 'Plenty of rides.' She shrugged a shoulder. 'He moved on. I knew a good thing when it was over, and I went back to Saratoga and a little normality. Then I found out I was pregnant.' She took another long draft of champagne and walked back to the window, where the late sun was slanting serenely through the trees. 'So did he, somehow, through the racing grapevine, though I'd made darned sure I'd disappeared before it got obvious. Xavier was born. I took him with me to Calista's country place in Connecticut. Then he got snatched.' She drew in a long breath through her slender, shapely nostrils, but I didn't interrupt. I knew she hadn't finished. 'It was horrific, one of the bleakest years of my life. I'd no money, except what Calli kept shelling out, but I couldn't go on living on her charity, and because I'd been out of circulation, friendships had gone stale and anyway, you know I was never a one for huggy-huggy girly-girly relationships.'

'Well,' I said, 'not with other girls.'

'Shut up, Hugo. Then when you turned up out of nowhere with your crazy scheme to win the Derby, I thought, well, it might just work; I might just get my hands on a million bucks, and I was always pretty darned sure that old Romey would part with his son and heir for a million, so long as I promised he could keep in touch with the boy. And I also reckoned by then Xavier would be just about old enough to take it, to handle the change. So last week I collected my money, and gave it to Romey. His mother will be screaming mad and calling down every kind of curse on my head. I don't suppose I'll be able to take Xavier to the States for a few years now, but who the hell wants to grow up in the States anyway?'

I gazed at her, utterly astonished not just by the story, but by what it revealed about her that I'd never taken the trouble to find before.

I put my glass down and took hers gently from her hand so I could wrap my arms right around her again, and hold her close and still.

She didn't resist, but relaxed and let herself melt into me.

We didn't kiss; we didn't squeeze; it was a long and extraordinary interlude, impossible to say how long, but by the time we let each other go, the sun had set and the broad trees in the park had lost their colour in the dusk.

'Do you want to eat?' I asked with a husky awkwardness.

'No,' she shook her head.

I cleared my throat. 'What would you like?'

'I want to go to bed.'

'Of course, I'm sorry,' I mumbled in a belated - about twenty years belated - attempt at chivalry. 'I'll show you to your room and bring up your, er, rucksack.'

I opened the door of the salon and stood back for her.

She glanced at me with puzzled amusement and walked through. I ushered her up the sweeping marble stairs Madame had installed twenty-five years before, absolutely out of keeping with the house, but classically beautiful.

At the top, Annie stopped and turned to face me. 'Hugo, don't show me to my room; show me to yours.'

'You mean...?' I couldn't articulate the idea.

She nodded. I guessed she couldn't either.

I led her to the end of the corridor and the main guest suite where I flung open both doors and ushered her in.

The lights each side of the resplendent bed were on, and the bedclothes had already been turned down. The room was warm, but not oppressive; a gentle breeze fluttered the curtain at one window, and the scents of a summer night mingled with the smell of clean linen and pot-pourri.

Annie looked around. 'You couldn't have picked a better place for it, Hugo.'

We both smiled.

Standing there, in the middle of the room, we wrapped our arms around each other, and our lips came together. For the first time in eighteen years, our tongues writhed and twined around each other in the most deeply passionate, all-absorbing kiss I'd ever experienced.

And while we kissed, my hands hungrily felt the firm flesh of her buttocks, and her fingers squeezed my thighs and the back of my neck.

We undressed each other without a murmur of embarrassment, and with a lingering delight as we savoured, like a delicate hors d'oeuvre, the fall of each garment into a crumpled heap on the floor.

Bet Your Rocks Off

We stood in front of each other, naked and smiling deliriously. I gazed at Annie with frank wonder. Her skin was smooth and flawless, her bottom firm, her waist slim, and the youthful bland pertness of her breasts had been replaced with the more exciting, purposeful shape of a mother's.

'Lady Tenbury, I'd forgotten what a heavenly body you are.'

'You look a little like Orion yourself.'

She grinned a soft compliant smile, laid her hand on my chest and stretched up to kiss my mouth once more. Her downy bush caressed my thigh. My cock, stiff as a baseball bat, pressed into the warm softness of her stomach as we kissed again.

I lifted her onto the bed. She lay back with her eyes closed and nestled her head into the pillows. 'Be careful with me Huggy Bear. I'm a little out of practice.'

'You'll be all right, Annie-Fanny,' I murmured a name I hadn't used since our last affair. 'You don't forget these things; it's like riding a bicycle.'

Her eyes flicked open with a quick flash of the familiar fieriness. 'Don't joke about it, Hugo. I've made some mistakes in the last few years; they hurt me, and I regret them. But I've loved working with you; you're so consistent, so reliable, and you aren't a quarter of the self-centred bastard you pretend to be.'

'But I am Annie,' I insisted. 'And the only consistent thing about me is that I consistently balls everything up.'

'Okay. Make your confession another time. Right now, just get on and pleasure me,' she said in a soft Southern drawl.

For a long time we played with each other and explored each others' bodies to reacquaint ourselves. It seemed incredible, now, that we should have been so close to each other over the past three years, and yet had so little physical contact. But with deliberate eagerness we made up for it.

Her fingers tingled across the surface of my skin, her lips quested over my body, settled briefly, tantalisingly on the gleaming head of my undiminished erection, and moved on while I ran my tongue around her nipples, and gently sucked each big, wholesome breast.

With a careful hand, I sought the slender, bushy gateway between her thighs and the hot moistness within, while a small hand cupped and caressed my balls.

In her, my fingers massaged with gentle vigour until her pelvis rose and fell as she surrendered control of her breathing and her body's response.

It was a long, hot, ecstatic night, when I learned for the first time that it was possible to make love with the soul as well as the body; a night when I learned that I had a soul.

In the morning, the sun spilled through gaps in the curtains and I looked at Annie sleeping, not the tough, efficient racehorse trainer who'd been my colleague for the last three years, but a small, vulnerable, child-like creature, who, miraculously, still trusted me, despite all contrary evidence.

Careful not to make a sound, I slipped into a dressing-gown and crept from the room. I went down to Madame's small study, where her private safe was concealed behind the fire-back.

Later, I carried a tray up to the room. On it were squeezed orange juice, Champagne, coffee, passion fruit, croissants, a slither of local butter and honey.

Annie was sitting up in bed, against a small mountain of pillows. On her face was a happy smile, which turned to a beam of astonished delight when she saw what I was carrying.

'This is something I never thought I'd witness!'

'Well, there it is,' I said, sounding hurt.

She laughed and made room for the tray, and leaned up to kiss me again. She looked around the room, and through the window where I'd drawn the curtains. 'This may just be a moment in time,' she said shaking her head in wonder. 'But it sure is one hell of a moment.' She gave me a look, understandably rueful at the impermanence of these perfect surroundings.

I returned the look. 'I know,' I nodded. 'There's nowhere in the world I'd rather be than here, especially in summer. But tell me Annie angel, even after this, could you still spend your life with an impoverished and totally incompetent baronet?'

Annie pushed the tray to one side of the massive bed and laughed softly, reaching out a hand to me. 'Of course, Hugo. You may be poor, you may sometimes be crass and overbearing, but at least you're never boring.'

'That's very good to hear, but I've got a harder question for you.' I sat down on the bed beside her, and lifted her hand in mine. 'Could you spend your life here...' I waved a hand that encompassed the room, and the rolling parkland outside. '...with a rather magnificently rich sort of a baronet and lord of the *Manoir du Mesnil*?'

Annie looked at me as if I were a simple child. 'Hugo, I'm sure that fantasising on that scale must be very bad for you; in fact, I bet it causes major stress and encourages heart disease.'

'You're probably right, but fortunately, no fantasising is required.'

I stood and, still with her hand in mine, led her from the bed to the window, where the pastures were looking their most succulent in the morning light, and the secret woods on the sky line, their most enchanting. I swept my hand towards the view, then carried the gesture into the room, encompassing the pictures, the bed, the ancient, priceless Persian rugs. 'All this, every stitch of it, every blade of grass, and every precious racehorse munching it, is mine,'

I lowered my hand, and smiled at her.

Her jaw dropped; and I watched her well-practised scepticism gradually turn to credulity as she absorbed the sheer excitement that this beautiful place, all these beautiful things belonged to me.

'Jesus, Hugo!' she gasped at last. 'You are the luckiest son of a bitch in the whole goddam world!'

Bet Your Rocks Off

'It wasn't luck, as a matter of fact,' I said indignantly. 'That was clear from Madame's will. It was my reward for winning the Derby for her. I feel, therefore, in fairness and with a real sense of justice, that I should share it with you.' Her eyes opened wide; she wanted to speak, but I held up a hand. 'And I've thought of a very simple way of doing it.'

She looked back at me steadily now, and nodded. 'Yeah, I know. Auction the lot, and split the money down the middle.'

I produced from my pocket a ring in which was set Madame's largest solitaire diamond, and I held it up towards her. At the same time, I raised an eyebrow. 'And give the auctioneers fifteen percent of the gross? No, Lady Tenbury; I don't think so.'